Pr... nd

"A superb wordsmith."
Charleston Post and Courier

"A triumph . . . a wonderful novel . . .
amusing, admirable, heart-wrenching, painful . . .
totally convincing and deeply affecting . . .
Grant has developed into a major talent whose best
work, I have no doubt, will continue to be read
and admired for years to come."
New York Review of Science Fiction

"Grant's best to date."
Kirkus Reviews

"Grant [has a] glorious sense of humor . . . [and an]
eloquent focus on our own world, on issues which may
be mainstream but cannot be dismissed as mundane."
Locus

"Brilliant . . . [a] thoughtful, entertaining novel . . .
[a] journey through an alternate reality . . . We care
about what happens to Kaspian. We want to keep
reading because we are ourselves lost. We are part of
his odyssey and we want to see where it will take us."
Portland Press-Herald

"Grant [has] considerable imaginative powers . . .
As apolitical philosopher, Grant would be dangerous;
I'm glad he writes novels instead."
Washington Post Book World

Books by Richard Grant

SARABAND OF LOST TIME
RUMORS OF SPRING
VIEWS FROM THE OLDEST HOUSE
THROUGH THE HEART
TEX AND MOLLY IN THE AFTERLIFE
IN THE LAND OF WINTER

KASPIAN

LOST

A NOVEL

•

RICHARD GRANT

HarperTorch
An Imprint of HarperCollins*Publishers*

This is a work of fiction. Names, characters, places, and incidents are products of the author's imagination or are used fictitiously and are not to be construed as real. Any resemblance to actual events, locales, organizations, or persons, living or dead, is entirely coincidental.

HARPERTORCH
An Imprint of HarperCollins*Publishers*
10 East 53rd Street
New York, New York 10022-5299

First HarperTorch paperback printing: July 2001
First Spike hardcover printing: June 1999

HarperCollins®, HarperTorch™, and ◆™ are trademarks of HarperCollins Publishers Inc.

Printed in the United States of America

Visit HarperTorch on the World Wide Web at
www.harpercollins.com

10 9 8 7 6 5 4 3 2 1

part 1
MAINE

Dear Child I also by pleasant Streams
Have wander'd all Night in the Land of Dreams
But tho calm and warm the waters wide
I could not get to the other side

Father O Father what do we here
In this Land of unbelief & fear
The Land of Dreams is better far
Above the light of the Morning Star

—William Blake, *The Land of Dreams*

EARLIER in the evening they had played one of those games meant to foster cooperation. You were blindfolded. Your hand was placed in the hand of one of your fellow campers, who was blindfolded also. The two of you couldn't talk. The only way you were allowed to communicate was through the sense of touch: your partner's mute palm pressed against yours. Now you were given a task to perform. When it was Kaspian's turn, the task was to carry supplies across a bridge. But there were too many supplies to carry in one trip, and some of the boxes were too bulky for one person to handle. He and his partner were going to have to work something out.

The night was warm. Kaspian could hear mosquitoes whining near his head. Farther out, on the black pond, a loon made one of its schizoid warbling sounds. The hand in his began to sweat.

He wondered whose it was. A boy: he was pretty sure of that. The hand was big, bigger than his own. It was slack and fleshy. Mike Pisegna? The fat kid from New Hampshire? Kaspian suppressed an urge to drop the hand, to push it away. He could smell greasy dinner odors and midsummer sweat.

He groped for the bridge railing. His partner's grip held him back. For an instant he became disoriented—the laughter of the other campers, arrayed unseen all around him, swirled as though he were riding a merry-go-round. Behind his eyelids, retinal nerves flashed like brake lights in fog, streaky and dull.

All at once the night fell silent. Kaspian could not feel his partner's hand. He lifted his head and it felt weightless. Instead of faint red lights his eyes swarmed with blips of pure sparkling silver. A thousand stars. The whole universe stretching wide to him. He opened his mouth (to laugh? to scream?) but everything was so quiet and still; he was happening in slow rewind.

> *We're inseparable, you and me*

said a Voice inside his head.

And Kaspian knew that Voice.

From where, though? It was deep, somehow fake-sounding. He strained to hear it again.

Only now instead of the Voice there were shouts and laughter from two dozen campers all around, and Kaspian's blindfold felt painfully tight, squeezing red bands across his retinas. He tore it off. He stood breathing rapidly, almost panting.

Beside him Mike Pisegna toddled, large and stupid, ketchup splashed down his t-shirt, straining outward with one big arm while clinging to Kaspian with the other. A stack of empty cardboard boxes lay beside them at the base of a footbridge. The scene was lit by Coleman lanterns and the final, pinkish haze of twilight.

Kaspian yanked his arm away. Almost panicky, he took half a dozen steps onto the bridge. He could half-remember something that confused him. All he wanted was for time to stop: not long, just a few heartbeats: time enough to think.

"*Hey,* now."

Firm loud voice of a Peer Counselor. Kaspian felt without looking Walter Gilliland coming toward him, parting the crowd.

"What's the matter here? Somebody doesn't want to play by the rules?"

Kaspian hated Walter Gilliland. He was a shrimpy guy about 18 with nothing better to do than spend his summers bossing around the smaller kids in the Indoc Section. His voice had a nasal, penetrating quality, like a mutant blackfly.

Gilliland reached the bridge and stood beside Mike Pisegna, who was still blindfolded, groping idiotically.

"So it's you, Aaby," he said to Kaspian, making a sheep sound out of his name. "I was *hoping* we could make it all the way till rack time without another one of your Incidents."

Kaspian kept his back turned. He stared across the footbridge, into the woods beyond, shadowed and featureless. The bridge crossed a stream that ran cool and fast, twisting between boulders slick with moss. Some days you saw fish down there—darting minnows, slick gray brook trout. Kaspian could smell the water now. He could hear leaves whipping high in the air, green kites in a breeze off the mountains. He felt wrongly situated.

Gilliland's foot came down on a bridge plank. The structure creaked, adjusted.

"Talk to me, Aaby," he said. "Tell me what's going on with you. I'm eager to understand, really and truly. Despite your repeated efforts to provoke me."

Kaspian didn't want to get started with this. He did not want to argue with Walter Gilliland. Anyway, what could he say? *The blindfold was too tight, I started having hallucinations.* All Kaspian wanted was to cross the bridge and be by himself for a while. Into the woods, the deep closet of night.

"Kaspian Aaby," said Gilliland. It was starting anyway. "Excuse *me?* Are you aware that I am speaking to you?"

"Perfectly," murmured Kaspian.

"What? You said what?"

Gilliland took a step closer. The bridge trembled.

"Are you aware," Kaspian said, still quietly, "that I could turn around and beat the living shit out of you?"

This might have been true: Kaspian was as tall as Gilliland, though three years younger. His fists were thicker. And he was getting angry. The only trouble was, he had never been in an honest-to-God fistfight in his life.

"Very *admirable*, Aaby." Gilliland's voice became higher-pitched, as though he were straining to be heard by the whole audience of miserable, bug-eaten, bad-smelling campers, not just Kaspian solo. "Your profanity impresses me, truly it does. I'm sure we're all very *much* impressed by your command of four-letter words, as we are by your tremendous team spirit and cooperative attitude. You know, if you were to give this exercise a chance, it might just teach you a lesson or two."

A lesson or two. The phrase stuck in Kaspian's ear. It sounded like something his stepmother had said, prior to shoving him along with a couple of bags of clean socks and underwear onto the bus for this so-called Accelerated Skills Acquisition Camp, a summer-long indoctrination meant to prepare him (the way you prepare a piece of meat, say, by pounding the tenderizer in) for the new school he'd be attending this fall: American Youth Academy, an exciting private-sector alternative to the failed public school system. And indeed, Kaspian had learned a lesson or two in the 27-days-but-who's-counting since he arrived here. He had learned for example that the Great North Woods consist largely of insect habitat. He had learned that his team-spirited fellow campers were a rich source of jokes of a particularly raunchy variety, enough to sour you on the concept of sex altogether. He had learned what S.O.S. stands for, and that it congeals on your plate to form a substance akin to Elmer's glue. He had learned that Peer Counselors are assholes and C.I.T.'s are junior assistant subassholes, and that Senior Staff might once have been assholes but have since matured into tightened, impenetrable sphincters. Were these "lessons"? Or did lessons have to be specially impressed upon you by higher authority, as for instance during those many hours of Personal Reflection Time in which Kaspian was required (for sins varied both in heinousness and in originality) to sit alone in the rustic wooden chapel raised on stilts over the floodplain like a wannabe tree house, with nothing but the Word of God for entertainment?

Kaspian waited for Walter Gilliland to get tired of playing around with him, to come to the point, which would be, inevitably, another oration in which the phrase "get with the program" would be heard.

"To tell you the honest truth," Gilliland at this moment was saying, "I've just about had it up to here with this attitude of yours. The Staff and I have given you every opportunity, but you don't seem willing to make any effort whatsoever to get—"

"Shut the fuck up," said Kaspian. Without turning around.

Still facing outward, into the woods, away from Gilliland, away from everybody.

From somewhere among the onlookers came a hesitant titter.

"What did you say?" the shrimpy counselor demanded. "What did you say to me?"

Kaspian opened his mouth to say it again, louder this time. But before he could speak, he had a revelation. Everything became clear to him. He understood that Gilliland was nothing, not worth the trouble of cussing at. He realized that the whole scene here—everything about ASA Camp from the latrines to the canoe docks to the chow hall to the chapel on stilts—was nothing but a game, a simulation, a bunch of pieces laid out like a model railroad set. Complicated yet pointless. Like Life Itself.

He was aware, even now, that he was thinking in a strange and somewhat confused manner. It was as if some echo of that singular moment—with the blindfold on, the million stars in his head—still colored his awareness, like half-heard side-channel ambience. Adding a strange, dimensional effect to the scene before him, which was otherwise flat and gray.

"Now you listen to me, Aaby," Walter Gilliland was saying.

But Kaspian didn't listen.

He would never listen again, he decided. He didn't have to anymore.

He started walking across the footbridge and he kept walking when his feet touched the rocks on the other side. He heard them calling his name and he thought he heard footsteps, too— might have even felt the tug on his arm but soon all of that slipped away from him, spun down into the past. Kaspian just kept walking. Away and away.

Into this whole other night.

FOR a long time he walked without wondering what he was doing, without really paying attention. He felt like an animal that's been held in captivity so long he's forgotten his natural proper habitat, then all of a sudden gets turned loose into it. Acclimation was a challenge. Daylight was just about shot, for starters. What was he supposed to do when it got totally dark? Was there going to be a moon? (There wasn't yet.) Why hadn't he thought of this?

The weird thing was that he didn't care. He didn't seem to notice that what he was doing did not have any purpose. Or if he noticed, this fact did not feel remarkable; it didn't feel like something you needed to be governed by. Many things make no sense. This whole American Youth Academy idea being an excellent example. Was Kaspian like, for example, an actual American Youth? (No. He was a changeling of unknown origin who had gotten switched at birth.) And did he really *need* to transfer from a boring but perfectly okay small-town high school to this high-bandwidth Academy at the cutting edge of pedagogy? (No. It was his stepmother who needed, for reasons of her own, to be rid of him. And who desired, in the bargain, that he be taught a lesson or two. To which Kaspian had replied, Then couldn't I just spend a couple of months at the beach with the *Book of Goddamned Virtues?* And got his face popped.

Yeah, but it made a funny story, and therefore had been worth it.)

The path followed the stream, but at some uncertain point— to elude pursuers, though there appeared to be none—Kaspian turned up a crooked little spur that might have been just a channel for spring runoff. Walking got harder; larch claws grabbed at his hair. You could hardly blame them: Kaspian's hair was an inviting target. It poked out. It was tangly. It was an undefined shade of brown. He hated it but was devoted to its care and kept it closely under observation. It went with his nose, which was also on the bulgy side. His eyes were the wrong brown, flecked yellow, and went with nothing. They just stared back at themselves, emptily. And the mouth was undergoing some sort of transformation, to a thing that when he opened it, people wanted to smack, from a thing that moved female types to utter that dreaded phrase, *cute smile*. Same mouth? Same movie? He couldn't decide.

Kaspian was getting nowhere. Or else he was getting deeper and deeper into a major mess, as per lifetime habit. But at least this particular mess had the benefit of being of his own making, as opposed to Accelerated Skills Acquisition Camp. Not that it mattered, probably. Because in the end he was stuck, he was going to be caught and locked back up in the zoo again. There is no longer a place for creatures like Kaspian in the wild.

Suddenly the larches let go of him. He took a couple of steps—practically feeling his way now, it was so dark—and found himself stepping out into a broad open space, a clearing. You could see across the clearing by what faint light was left. The ground floated like a magic carpet of deep sea-green. On all sides the forest was black, but black with contours, with textures. Everything was dimensionless. Shapes were fluid, distances elastic. Kaspian got a shivery feeling, standing there. A thousand stars burned overhead. The night breeze moved arms of darkness above him.

The light was not that big a deal. Not at first: when it appeared—a faint, bodiless glow that now was tinted orange, now yellow, now lavender—Kaspian hardly noticed it. It simply *fit,* and he gave it no more thought than you would give a bough of leaves, pale and fluttering in the moonlight. He walked a bit farther out into the open space, and then he stopped. It was almost as if the light itself had stopped him.

Now he found that all he could do was look at it. It got larger, or came closer—maybe both?—and there was something about it . . . a *presence,* an almost tangible power. As the glowing sphere grew in size and in brightness, the rest of the world, and Kaspian with it, plunged into silence so deep that the night itself seemed to quail, to draw back into its own darkest crevices. The light changed position a couple of times—not so much *moving* as simply being first in one place, then another—and when finally it stopped, Kaspian felt an electric quiver move up his spine, the hairs of his neck pricking up, his scalp itching with energy. He thought

It sees me.

Which he knew was stupid, or possibly insane.

But the light saw him anyway. He knew that for absolute certain.

It's found me. It knows I'm here.

There were a couple of frozen moments. Then time came unstuck and events spilled out all at once, too quickly to follow. The light took on a shape. The shape was something like a carousel, and it began to spin, and there was a kind of high-pitched sound almost like a flute or a piccolo, but really neither of those. Strange music. Dizzying merry-go-round, all lights and no horses, no visible machinery. Kaspian stood there, maybe thirty feet away from this thing, maybe fifty, stone-still, like a person under hypnosis—aware of what was happening but unable to perform simple actions, such as lifting an arm, nodding his head, turning and getting the fuck *away* from there.

He was afraid; but then again he was not. Not in the way you're afraid of somebody pointing a gun at you. The fear was almost unconnected with him; it seemed to come *at* him instead of *from* him. It came from the light, and as with the light itself he could not be quite certain that it was real. Or rather, in what *way* it was real. Like, could the whole thing just be part of some dream? A waking dream, vision, something like that? You would almost think so.

Then this happened: in the middle of the light, riding round and round on the spinning carousel, Kaspian saw his dead father.

It was his father, dead. Not his father as Kaspian remembered him, blurrily, like a video he had watched too many times during the nine years since the funeral. No: his father, Daddy, now, there, in front of him, reachable, shout-at-able, *real*. Kaspian felt drops of liquid on his forearm and realized with shock that he had started to cry.

"Daddy!" he said out loud.

His father smiled and kept spinning. Everything was okay, everything was cool there on the Wheel O' The Dead.

Kaspian knew one thing now. One thing for sure. This was not a dream and it was not some head trip, a thing he was imagining. It was happening, really and truly; and in a way that he could neither understand nor ignore, it was happening *for him*.

He sucked in a breath and realized that he had lost much of

the sensation of his own body. What had felt like hypnosis before now felt like flat-out paralysis.

Between one moment and the next—without moving or changing—the light vanished. It was simply not there any longer. Kaspian stood as stiff as a rock in the darkness. And then out of the darkness, into a sort of twilight that seemed to constellate around him, stepped three . . . three . . .

Say it, Kaspian. To yourself, anyway.

. . . *three leprechauns.*

Or anyway—if you won't buy that—then something that *looked* like leprechauns. Three very short little guys; but not short and blocky like midgets, and yet not proportioned like ordinary people, either. They had a stoutness about them, and their heads were oversized, and they wore strange old clothes that looked like maybe something out of the Depression. Hobo leprechauns. Only in brown instead of green.

They came up around Kaspian and even though they projected an air of bustling, of doing something in an awful big hurry, it was hard to say exactly *what* they were doing, other than looking at him. But that was enough.

Malevolence. Kaspian could sense nothing at all about these three small guys except for a pure, intense malevolence. It reminded him of the creepiest person he had ever, before then, come in contact with: a Glassport police officer who ended up shooting his fiancée after she jilted him, *after* he had bought them a pair of his & hers turquoise Camaros. But this was way worse than that. Kaspian felt as though the fear which had earlier seemed to come straight at him out of the light had now been transferred to these three little dudes. His body quivered like a stick someone was shaking.

"Why don't you come with us," one of the leprechauns suggested.

Kaspian could not make out which of them had spoken. Maybe none of them had; maybe the words just appeared in his mind.

"Okay," he said.

His own voice sounded as always. Kidlike and kind of dumb.

Later it would be unclear to him why he had just said *Okay;* as opposed to like, *No way* or *Fuck you* or even, sensibly, *Go where?* Actually he was wondering this already. Still, that's what he said, and the leprechauns wasted no time in leading him off toward . . .

Toward nothing. At least, Kaspian had no awareness of having traveled anywhere. He went straight from the realization that the leprechauns were taking him somewhere to, suddenly, standing in a kind of hole or tunnel. It was not much brighter than the twilit field, but a little: enough to see that it stretched ahead and slightly downward for a very long distance. Kaspian tried to look back, but he couldn't turn his head around. He was moving forward—the leprechauns were alongside, not so much guiding as guarding him—and he had no sense of his legs stepping along in the usual fashion. For all he knew, he was floating down the tunnel.

The walls and ceiling and floor—there was no clear distinction between them—appeared to have been cut roughly out of stone. The light was evenly distributed and had no apparent source. There was a smell of something earthy, something hot— like two rocks make when you strike them hard together. Kaspian tried to gauge how far he had moved down that strange passageway but it was difficult, partly on account of having no reference points, as every part of the tunnel was exactly like every other. Then—again, all at once—they were through it.

He was standing in a room. The room was about twenty feet across, round or nearly round. All its surfaces were smooth. The three little guys stood with him for a moment or two, then they turned and a door opened and they left. When they were gone, you could not see where the door had been.

Kaspian found that he could move his body again. He flexed and felt somewhat normal and somewhat an alien to himself. For an instant his mind touched on the question *What is happening to me?*—but that was so terrifying even to think about that it made him feel dizzy.

He sat down on a metal sort of table thing. Had it been here a moment ago? (That question had no meaning. Next?)

The metal was cold, then it got warm. It got softer as well, as though it were changing into an organic substance. A membrane of living plastic. Kaspian settled down and tried to relax but he felt as though he had chugged a 12-pack of Coke. Every nerve end rattled.

The door—or maybe a different one, just like it—opened and closed. Before Kaspian now stood a blond girl about his own age. Blond and pale to the point of being nearly an albino. But her eyes were blue and intense. She wore a white dress or robe. Which? Neither, or both. The flowing cloth, light as fog, made it hard to get a sense of her actual body—or rather in a way it seemed *part* of her body, an outward extension of her being.

Then Kaspian noticed her hands, the most beautiful hands in the world. They were slender and seemingly boneless. One of them lifted toward his face, and the girl smiled a radiant smile, and Kaspian instantly got a hard-on. It was embarrassing and it hurt, being squeezed into a knot in his underwear. But he was damned if he was going to reach down there and adjust it.

"Who are you?" he asked the girl.

She said a name. Kaspian would never remember it. But he recognized it as a name by the way she pronounced it, offhand-edly. He wondered why he could tell certain things but not others. He wondered if any of this *ought* to make sense.

It can't be real, was in one part of his mind.

And yet it was the realest thing he had ever experienced. *More* real than real. As though he had been half-asleep for fifteen years and suddenly, finally, woken up.

The girl began speaking. "We have let you come here—"

"We who?" he said, so quickly he surprised himself.

Her smile was like a wall of snow. "You cannot understand," she told him.

Kaspian twisted his mouth sideways, cynically; he had known she would say something like this. *We are more highly evolved than you. Our brains are seven thousand times more advanced.* Such bullshit.

"What do you want with me?" he said. "Are you going to like, perform experiments on me or what?"

"It was you who wished to come," said the girl. Still smiling. Her voice liquid. One hand making gestures that seemed to have no meaning in the air. "We decided to grant your wish."

"That's crazy," said Kaspian. "Who's *we?* And why did *we* think I wanted to come?"

"Crazy," she repeated, opening her eyes wider. Stars swam in them. She did not seem to be disagreeing with him; rather to be intrigued by his use of the term.

That irritated Kaspian. He said, "Look, if you're going to—"

The girl touched a finger to his lips.

It was like being anesthetized. Kaspian tried to operate his mouth but could feel nothing there, nothing at all from the chin up.

He had to admit, it was pretty slick. She had disarmed him: his mouth had been his only defense. Now, even more than with the evil leprechauns, he felt totally helpless. And he still had a hard-on.

"What I need to do will not be painful," the girl told him. She spoke like a doctor snapping the latex gloves on. Yet she did not make any move, except for that hand in the air, the perfect fingers tracing patterns. Kaspian felt an irresistible urge to lie back, but there was no need for this because the table thing came up and sort of *cupped* him, like a bug in a Venus's-flytrap. It did not hurt. But of course it was the freakiest thing that had ever happened, and he supposed things were only going to get worse from here on.

The numbness that had begun around his mouth now spread through most of his body. He managed to twitch a toe, and he found that he could turn his head from side to side—not up or down, though—but everything in between had fuzzed out on him.

The girl busied herself. Kaspian could not quite see what she was doing because his eyes would not point that way. With peripheral vision he watched her bending over him and then straightening out, moving her arms from place to place—*touching me,* he thought, but could not feel—and after an interval that might have been long or short, she came to stare straight down at him and she said:

"Would you like to stand up?"

Kaspian found that he could, that his body was back to normal. He glanced quickly down at himself but saw nothing askew. No evidence of unspeakable molestation. He stood facing the girl, who looked back in a way that made him feel like a dumb punk. "Now what?" he said.

"I'll show you more," she told him.

Kaspian found himself going along with her as though he had no power to resist, or even to form the concept of resisting. They left the room through a door that materialized for their convenience and now they were standing in a large open space that was a sort of greenhouse. Light flooded through it. As with all the light in this place, or series of places, it came from nowhere. The plants appeared to be made of damp, shiny plastic, pendulous with brightly colored fruit. The girl waved her hand: inviting Kaspian to look around until he had had his fill. When she sensed (correctly) that he had done so, she led him to another space, a smaller one, arranged like a sort of conference room with tables and chairs that were *almost* ordinary-looking; yet even here, something was vaguely wrong, the appearance of everything was a little skewed. Were the chairs just a tad too small? Were they shaped in a way that did not seem intended for human backs? Kaspian could not snap his mind on to what was the matter: it was like some obvious clue was lying there in front of him but he somehow failed to see it.

After that it was on to another room, and this one looked like an exotic lounge in an old 60's Screen-O-Rama, maybe *Dr. No.* And then again it did not. The pieces were all in place yet they were put together wrong.

The girl now sat down in one of the movie-set chairs and stared placidly up at him. You would have sworn she was watching him *think,* observing the processes of his mind. Her dress or gown poured around her, still concealing whatever there was of her body. Kaspian tried to glance elsewhere in the room, feigning disinterest, but the only place he found to look was straight into the girl's face. Those penetrating blue eyes, the snow-wafer teeth.

"You are different," said the girl. "You are funny."

"Ha, ha," said Kaspian. Thank God his defense, his mouth, was operable again. He sat down near the girl in something like a chair that did not feel exactly like a chair. He said, "Isn't this where you like, *explain* things to me? Like, tell me why I was *chosen* or whatever?"

"You came to us," the girl said simply.

"Yeah, you said that before. But I mean, how could—"

"You walked away from your camp and you sought us out. So we admitted you. There was no choosing. Not by us. I might ask you, Why did you choose to come? Is there something you wanted?"

Kaspian opened his mouth to say No but the word would not let itself be spoken. Instead he formed the syllables, "Something, I, *wanted* . . ."

And for whatever reason, or perhaps no reason at all, this brought a memory back to him, a shard from the past he had been trying to retrieve. The memory was of a voice, a familiar voice, though a forgotten one. And the Voice was saying

We're inseparable.
You and me.

THE raised ranch on Mountain Street where Kaspian lived, if you could use that term, with his stepmother, Carol Deacon Aaby, was gray on the outside and faded yellow on the inside. It was like someplace that once had been light but after a while had settled into shadow, deeper than the shadows thrown by the overgrown furring of arborvitae along the street-side wall. Kaspian's room was in the back, a narrow slot between the kitchen and the larger room at the corner occupied by his stepsister NoElle before she went off to college last year, empty since. His room had never felt too small to him, but the house itself was a different story. It felt like a box into which things were stuffed that did not belong together, taped up tight so that nothing could slip out. Even Kaspian's father, in death, had failed to make a clean getaway: you were always coming upon some odd possession of his, a golf club maybe, or a zippered bag for storing toiletries in—some object both pointless and heartbreaking, as though the poor guy had not packed carefully for the afterlife. Kaspian halfway expected to hear his father bumping around some night, down in the junky basement, in search of a lost extension cord.

But the house . . . that didn't explain anything. It didn't explain Kaspian's stepmother, what was up with her. Why she was mad all the time at whatever there was to get mad at: stuff on TV or the mess down in Washington; some rumor she had heard about public-school teachers with *hidden agendas*; gay people gallivanting around in red t-shirts at Disney World. Always something. And increasingly often lately, the something was Kaspian.

It had been bad enough even before the Witch Episode.

There had always been NoElle, for starters. NoElle the Good Decent Person, NoElle who always did her homework and participated in extracurricular activities and prepared herself for college. Who consumed major quantities of hair-care products, went uncomplainingly to church, and probably never once let her boyfriend, a feeb named Julian Laite, even get his finger wet.

Compared to NoElle, Kaspian was a good-for-nothing. He did not like sports, vegetables, religion, or haircuts. His best friend was a runty science nerd named Eli whose father was a Green Party agitator and mother was always in the paper with that stringy hair of hers in connection with some *poetry reading*. Kaspian had no favorite subjects in school—except occasionally History, but only insofar as it impacted upon World War II, for which he had a passion that his stepmother found unwholesome. (She once confiscated a paperback book about the Holocaust he had purchased with his grass-mowing money, pronouncing that "Nothing definitely has been proved about that.") He evinced no burning ambition. He barely muttered the Pledge of Allegiance and the Lord's Prayer when called upon to do so. You could just tell (as Carol Deacon Aaby often told him) that unless he straightened up, he was heading for a Bad End.

And *that* was before the Witch Episode. It had been a two-part episode, beginning just before Halloween last year and wrapping up after Christmas. In Part One, Kaspian's stepmother signed up for a workshop where you learned how to detect signs of "Satanic ritual abuse." The workshop was very effective, because soon she was detecting the signs everywhere. At about this time, the town newspaper ran a seasonal-interest piece about a local woman who described herself as a witch. The woman's name was Pippa and she was depicted in a grainy photograph sort of looming over a jumble of candles and other indistinct items described in the caption as her altar.

What really got Mrs. Aaby's attention, though, was a mention in the paper that this woman Pippa had a nine-year-old daughter. "That poor innocent girl!" Kaspian's stepmother declared. And she resolved to rescue that girl right away from the clutches of the dangerous Satanist. That was the end of Part One.

Part Two was when Kaspian made an unexpected guest appearance. He went to the flower store where Pippa, the mom and witch, worked at the checkout counter. Basically he just went to satisfy his curiosity, intending to give her the eyeball and get out of there. But instead he had opened his mouth—this was something he could not, at times, prevent himself from doing, and the results were usually disastrous—and the next thing he knew he was involved in the whole thing, caught between his stepmother's righteous crusade and Pippa's basically clueless and doomed effort to raise her daughter in peace. There followed the usual plot twists and comic interludes, culminating in the triumph of the witch, the decertifying of a family counselor, the near death of a newspaper publisher, and the peculiar affliction of his stepmother with an outbreak of boils that resisted all forms of treatment both medical and ecclesiastic for the better part of the winter.

By spring, Carol Deacon Aaby had come to appreciate fully the role her stepson had played in this horrible adventure—*betraying both his family and his God,* in her wrathful view—and she began to explore alternatives to letting him *continue down this path.* She decided for starters that he needed firmer discipline than a widow on her own can provide. And he needed structure: a more orderly learning environment than the local high school, with closer supervision and stricter rules.

"Kaspian is not a *bad* child," she told people—never checking and perhaps never caring whether Kaspian was out of hearing or not—"but he is a *willful* child, and you know that can sometimes work out to the same thing. Let them go their own way and they head straight for the elevator going *down.*" At this point she would lower her voice—like it mattered—and confide, "I'm afraid he has inherited some of his father's less attractive qualities. Edward was a good, loving husband, but let's not kid ourselves: he did have a certain *heedlessness* about him. In many ways you could say he never grew up."

"None of them ever do," more than one of her listeners had replied, in a tone of rueful tolerance. But Carol Deacon Aaby did not seem to register that. Tolerance, rueful or otherwise, was not part of her emotional repertoire.

So Kaspian found himself, by the end of the school year, facing a sort of full-court press: he would spend his summer at Accelerated Skills Acquisition Camp, then in the fall would go on to the regular AYA campus down in Lewiston.

He wasn't sure how to feel about any of it. On the one hand it would get him away from his stepmother. But on the other, it sort of left him without a home base, didn't it? Kind of floating from one bunk bed to another?

As if he were all alone in the world.
As if he were lost.

BUT everything that happens is just the prelude to something else. Kaspian awoke on his back covered with sweat and mosquito bites. It was midmorning. He lay in an open place that was mostly rock ledge jutting out of the ground: extravagantly contoured layers of granite and quartz, silent record of some ancient tectonic catastrophe. The mid-July sun was hot and the air was humid, with no breeze. Every part of Kaspian's body flashed its own signal of stiffness and pain.

He felt disinclined to sit up. Instead he rolled onto one side—the left one—and tried to figure out where he was. He could smell his own unwashed body. Far overhead, a tiny airplane buzzed. Summer people commuting to Moosehead. Kaspian tried to remember where he was and what he was doing, and became irritated when he could not.

He needed to take a wicked piss. His legs flexed slowly, as though he had been lying still for an awfully long time. Rocks are not good to sleep on. His urine ran down the striated channels of white and gray until it met the pallid, gravelly soil. Several paces beyond that, a wide double track—the kind made by ATV tires—plowed through scruffy grass and black-eyed Susans. The weeds were high and the track got lost in them. You could see tiny bugs flitting just above the flower heads, like animated grains of pollen.

Near the place where Kaspian had lain, the rocks were covered with a yellow-white, powdery substance. It lay in a rough circle, and when Kaspian was done peeing he bent and touched it with a finger. The finger came up coated with something that felt like chalk dust and smelled like moldy bread. He wiped it on his shorts, leaving a streak.

Kaspian felt a strange mood pass through him as he stood there, looking down. His mind groped after for its source. There was something about . . . about the sight of his own legs . . . the way they stretched what seemed a great distance below him . . .

He snapped on to it.

Over the reality of that moment, covering it, another reality briefly fell, hiding the present from view.

Kaspian saw himself standing up in a strange room after having been stretched numbly on a table. He saw his knees and his grubby All-Stars and felt anew the wave of relief at finding himself intact, unmutilated. Then that other reality melted, like a movie dissolve, and he was left trembling on a sunny rock with his stomach knotted up and sweat chilling his face as the memory, in all its weird intensity and its dreamlike impossibility, pounded into him.

He became afraid. He felt too weak to stand up, yet too jerky with anxiety to sit down. The upshot was that he stood as though frozen in place—but not *truly* frozen, the way he had been last night—as one by one, the stages of the bizarre adventure played back through his mind. Repeatedly he thought, as he had thought before, while it was happening, *This can't be real.* But again he came back to the solidity of believing that—whatever this meant—it had been *more real* than real. It had been like waking up, and now, for all his stiff joints and his thirst and his racing thoughts, he felt as though he was dozing off again, losing that sharp edge, that clarity. His awareness felt dulled.

He closed his eyes and opened them and saw that a dragonfly had come to rest on his shoulder: cardinal red, perfect, glowing. Somehow the vision of this tiny, alien-looking being had the effect of drawing him back out, into the world again, the vivid light of day. He let go of a lungful of air that he had not been aware of holding too long. Startled, the dragonfly shot off, zipping straight like a poison dart.

Kaspian stared one last time at the rocks where he had lain.

His memory stopped short of when or how he had gotten here. Now he felt pressingly eager to be someplace else. He scrambled down from the ledge in the direction of the ATV track.

The ground underfoot was beaten, its nutrients leached. In Kaspian's ears, a humming noise seemed to lie just at the low edge of audibility. Tangled among the black-eyed Susans was some kind of electric-purple vetch. Their colors looked implausible together. Unnatural. The humming grew louder as he walked, his legs still a bit shaky, as though this process of lurching forward one foot at a time was unfamiliar to him.

Before him stretched a mangy field that was halfway along toward reverting to woodland. At the far edge of it, the track joined up with a wider service road that followed some utility lines. There were trees on both sides now. The vegetation immediately under the high-tension wires was about two years old, having grown in since the last application of herbicide by the power company. This was the kind of place where you saw moose. But Kaspian did not want to see a moose now; he lowered his head, intent on keeping his footing. He realized that the humming sound came from the wires overhead. Why do they hum sometimes? Probably only a couple of guys know— engineers without many friends, working mostly alone, reading science fiction at night in their raised ranches. The power lines ran on forever and ever, as is their way.

Kaspian gave no thought to where he was going. The memory of what had happened to him last night was lodged in the center of his brain; it made other things hard to focus on. Kaspian only knew that he wanted to get back to, like, *ordinary life*—the details didn't matter.

The sun edged higher and finally the power lines exited the woods, traversing the back end of a high school athletic field. Kaspian stood for a couple of minutes, staring at the baseball diamond, the chain-link safety mesh behind home plate. Ugly. The grass was brown and high, with bare dirt showing through. Back sides of schools pretty much all look the same.

What school was this, though? It was plain brick with a few 80's touches: colorful linear patterns in the masonry and a hipped green metal roof over the gym, with operable skylights. Kaspian had just about decided to head over that way when he heard the sound of a car starting up. For some reason—or probably no reason—he grew cautious. He stepped into the far reaches of left field, approaching the school at an oblique angle, warily. It made him feel like an infantryman, making his way through no-man's-land, and he drew a funny kind of comfort from the thought. (He had been on the WWII trip for two years now.) As the sound of the car got louder, he ducked down a little, positioning himself behind the subtle rise of the pitcher's mound. This made him feel ridiculous, but you can't exactly *unduck*.

A non-dangerous-looking vehicle edged out from behind a wall of the school and slowly cruised over the pavement, passing garbage dumpsters and orange driver's-ed pylons. The car was a dull color, maybe green, several years old, of no discernible make or model: a Nick at Nite car, one of those squarish vehicles you see on old TV shows, where cars actually matter.

It stopped and the driver's door opened. A man stepped out, and if Kaspian had felt like an infantryman before, imagine how he felt *now*. The guy was dressed entirely in green & brown surplus camouflage. He wore an ammo belt with various pieces of equipment attached to it, none of them recognizable from this distance. Around his neck hung a camera with a bulging zoom lens and a small pair of field binoculars. His face was shaded by aviator glasses and a ball cap of the kind you see aged veterans toddling around with, after they've gotten back from their 200th-year reunion.

Kaspian was a little freaked at first, but the ball cap reassured him. This was just some kind of kook. Maine in summer is full of retired military guys who spend their winters down in Florida. You get the feeling that they're looking for something to do.

What this guy had found to do remained mysterious. Bird-watching seemed unlikely on a high school athletic field. Kaspian decided to stay put and maintain his surveillance. The guy paced around a bit and stared here and there at the pavement. He bent over and touched his finger to the asphalt and then brought it back up and looked at it. He shook his head and pulled out a small notebook from one of the many pockets of his camo vest. Naturally he was the kind of guy who kept a pencil tucked behind an ear. Probably a Lucky Strike behind the other one. Smoke 'em if you got 'em. Kaspian loved it.

Suddenly the guy looked up, right in Kaspian's direction. You could not tell what he was seeing or not seeing because of his aviator glasses. He kept staring for half a minute or so. Then he turned sharply and marched back to his car and cranked the engine. As he backed around, maneuvering out of the parking lot, Kaspian could hear the car radio, turned up loud. It was a call-in talk show. Kaspian almost could have guessed which one, because his stepmother listened to them also as she drove around town. Often she talked back to them. He guessed that the guy in camo did not talk back; only listen hard and stomp the gas pedal.

He watched while the car rounded the corner of the school. The inevitable NRA decal was a bright red dot on the rear window. Then the car was gone and the war game was over.

Kaspian walked the rest of the way to the school, quickly now. Just inside one of the rear doors stood a bright red Coke machine: an agonizing sight because he was seriously thirsty but had no coins in his pocket and anyway, when he tried the door, it was locked. Cruel but not unusual.

He could tough it out. If there was a school then there was a town nearby. Probably Florence, the town closest to ASAC. He could imagine how Senior Staff were going to take it when he called in for a ride.

Around front, Kaspian stood beneath the naked flagpole and read

KIM HANSEN HIGH SCHOOL
Sinai Falls, Maine

His mouth twisted sideways, kind of smiling but not exactly. This was worth a t-shirt, at least. *Where the Hell is Sinai Falls, Maine?*

There were yellow stripes down the middle of the road and not much else. No signs, no other buildings nearby. Half a mile in one direction he could see a church steeple. The other way, he made out a low structure that might have been a gas station. Petroleum beat the Father Almighty, in Kaspian's book.

He noticed as he walked a palpable quality of silence that filled the day. It was not just an absence of sound but like an element, a penetrating substance in which everything was soaked: locust trees, saggy gray asphalt, switchgrass, faded highway paint. You sort of slipped viscously through it. The sunlight landed with such hard-edged brilliance that objects seemed to give back a luminosity of their own. Kaspian wondered how much of this was his imagination.

Most, he guessed.

But not all.

The gas station morphed into something a little closer to the edge of the chart, social-spectrum-wise. Projecting from its white cinder blocks was an awning—a swirly teal nylon waveform suspended by ropes—and a signboard still too distant to read. One ancient Volvo and one pickup truck drove past him en route, but these only served to call attention to how otherwise traffic was nil. Sinai Falls clearly didn't add up to much. Kaspian thought of trying to hitch a ride in the Volvo, but it felt like almost too much trouble to stick his thumb out. Besides, he looked and smelled crappy; and *besides,* he was kind of curious now.

The sign said SHARDS, in letters formed by pictures of standing and leaning stone slabs, overgrown with vines. The gas station had been converted to a pottery shop. From outside, he could look through the old thick plate glass window and see the potter herself: a woman about the age of his stepmother but from a whole different society, Birkenstock Nation to the max. She wore a long billowy brightly colored cotton dress like some South American *curandera,* and her hair was full and wild and two-thirds gray. She stood with her back to him, arranging items on a shelf, which Kaspian supposed was the only thing for her to do all day out here, other than make more pottery. You might wonder how somebody could earn a living in such a way, in such a place, but Kaspian had lived in Maine all his life and he recognized that this was simply one of the eternal mysteries.

The woman must have felt him staring. She turned and looked at him. Her eyes were bright and open to possibilities. Still, even *curanderas* get taken by surprise. She smiled without speaking. It was his move, he guessed.

He stepped through the door and said, "Do you have a phone I could use?"

She kept smiling emptily for a second as though she hadn't heard. Then slowly she shook her head. "There's a phone up at the house," she allowed after another couple of moments. Kaspian felt funny now because it was obvious there were a lot of things he hadn't begun to think about.

How to explain himself, for example. How to explain who he was and why he was standing here, late one July morning in a place he had never been. A place he did not—not yet—remember how he had gotten to.

"Would you like something to drink?" the woman said. Her eyes grew gentle, examining him frankly from top to bottom as though he were an errant neighborhood kid, one of her own kid's friends. The irises were the same wild gray as her hair.

Kaspian said, "If you've got a Coke I'll love you to death, I swear."

The woman laughed—a nice spontaneous sound. "I'm afraid I don't. But I think there's some Blue Sky soda. Let me see."

She went behind the counter where she kept a tiny refrigerator. "How about raspberry cream?"

Kaspian inhaled it. He set the empty can down with a certain reverence.

The woman was observing him in a manner that made him inclined to caution. She said, "I don't mean to sound like the Mother of All Things. But are you all right? Are you in any kind of trouble? I don't recognize you from around here."

Here we go. He stared down at the counter: old maroon linoleum, with deep black oil stains.

"I'm from a camp," he said, hoping it was casual. What was

he trying to hide? And from who? Himself? "I guess I kind of got, you know—lost in the woods or something."

"What camp?" said the woman. Not suspiciously, though that's how you couldn't help taking it.

Kaspian shrugged. "Um, ASAC? Part of American Youth Academy? Outside of Florence?"

"Outside of *Florence?*"

The woman looked at him hard. But if she wondered whether he was lying she seemed to decide that he was not.

"How long did you say you were lost?" she said.

He shrugged again. "All night I guess. I woke up lying on some rocks this morning. I guess maybe I sort of . . . fell asleep or something."

The woman frowned. She made a clucking noise and then said, "Here, would you come with me a minute?"

He couldn't see why not to. She led him through a door into a large open space that once had been a repair bay; now it was a pottery studio. Right around the corner on a wall was the standard Delorme road map you see in gas stations all over the state, helpfully tacked up so the attendant can give directions to tourists. The woman got close to it and squinted. Kaspian's eye drifted by habit down the greasy surface of the map toward his old hometown about midway along the coast, a place he simultaneously longed for and wished never, ever to see again. The woman placed the thumb of one hand on a dappled green area way up north where a tiny dot was labeled SINAI FALLS. Then—with a significant thump—she set her opposite index finger down on the dot labeled FLORENCE. The thumb and finger were separated by about two hand-widths of map distance. The two towns were easily 60 or 70 miles apart.

"Now there's no possible way," the woman told him, in a perfectly congenial voice, "you could have made it all the way from Florence to Sinai Falls in a single night. Not on foot. And look, you would have had to cross Wolf River. You couldn't have done *that* without knowing it."

She stepped away from the map, making room for Kaspian. He didn't take more than a glance at the places she had been pointing to. He didn't doubt that she was correct. He just didn't know what to say about it.

She placed one warm hand on his shoulder, the fingers small but strong, touching him in what he imagined was a motherly way. (His own stepmother did not go in for touching.)

"There's a phone up at the house," the woman told him for a second time. "A bathtub, too. Plenty of water this time of year. We don't usually run low till the latter part of August. My son's home on vacation, he's probably got some clothes you could borrow. And I *know* you'd feel better if you had something to eat."

Kaspian was quite sure he had said nothing to imply that he felt bad in any way, nor that he needed or wanted this kind of fussing over.

The woman sighed. Like she was reading him. "You might as well go on up. Here, I'll show you the way. You've got to call your people at camp, at least. They'll be glad to hear they haven't lost a counselor after all."

Kaspian opened his mouth to correct her, but he flashed in time onto the fact that as far as this woman was concerned, *counselor* was not a term of opprobrium. And later, on the winding path up to the house, when she asked how old he was, it was easy and almost natural to say "Eighteen." It was kind of like giving her what she expected. Though also it made him wonder what he *did* look like, to have instantly aged two and a half years in a stranger's eyes.

CLIMBING up the path to the woman's house was a trip back in time. We are setting the Way-Back machine for July 1972: Twilight of the Counterculture. Tin soldiers and Nixon coming. Tens of thousands of battle-weary revolutionaries scattering before them. The hippies are heading back to the land; they have got to get themselves back to the Garden. But where they have ended up is a random scatter of dead-end places like Sinai Falls, Maine—a country of poor soil and failed farms and low real estate prices. Yet here they have come and here they will stay, determined to make a Garden out of it.

Okay: old story. Kaspian knew it inside and out, though it had never been taught in any History class, and though his own father—one of those retreating, beaten revolutionaries—had not lived long enough to tell it in his own words. Despite all that, as he followed the friendly woman in the bright peasant dress up the hill, through scrappy woodland that had been lived on and loved and fought and altered (though never tamed) for many years now—a whole generation—Kaspian felt strangely and completely at home.

The house was just an old house, white clapboards and chimneys and many-paned windows. But it had a look about it. Solar hot-water panels were mounted on the roof, and a greenhouse built onto one side. The whole yard was a garden, vegetables and flowers and fruit trees interspersed, with a pergola at the center overgrown with vines that Kaspian recognized from the sign in front of the pottery shop. He wondered if they were grapes or hops or what. Kiwis maybe. You never know what old hippies will grow. Under the pergola in a reclining aluminum lawn chair lounged a skinny guy with baggy pants and no shirt and seriously snaky black hair. This person faced the other way and might have been asleep. From a boom box nearby rose music suitable for committing suicide by. College radio music, Kaspian guessed.

The woman led him past a fenced kitchen yard in which there were chickens and geese. The rooster had no tail. Beyond in a small field stood a vanilla-colored pony, swishing its tail at invisible flies. From the hilltop you had a view of the countryside, which was quiet and green and empty. A stream twisted through the low ground, curling around the house, and on the stream bank the woman, or somebody, had built a sod-roofed wood-fired sauna, with its own little pier so you could dive into the icy mountain runoff.

Now they stood at the kitchen door. The woman turned to Kaspian and she held a hand out and said, "My name is Inanna. Inanna Rugg."

Yeah, right, thought Kaspian. He took the hand and looked into her eyes. Very kind and gentle. His favorite story about old hippies was when his friend Eli was really little—about four years old—and Eli's mom and a bunch of other peace & love types were standing around the Real Food Co-op, which in those days was just a tiny storefront in the working-class village of Dublin, and Eli had gotten impatient with all the soft-voiced nattering and had picked up a suggestively shaped piece of yellow squash and

BLAM

BLAM

BLAM

BLAM

raked it back and forth, blowing all the gentle hippies away.

What made it so funny was that you could just imagine how his mom had been, like, *mortified*.

"I'm Kaspian," he told the woman, smiling a little as he recalled this.

"Ah!" she said, smiling back at him. "Like the Prince."

"Only with a *K*," he said, for the forty-nine quadrillionth time in his life.

Nonetheless the woman, Inanna, was pleased. She led him through a kitchen that was *exactly* what he expected—a ton of herbs dangling in bunches from the exposed, smoke-darkened beams, and a big enameled wood-burning cookstove in the middle of it all, like some kind of holy altar—then beyond to the living room where the greenhouse had been added on. Which he had to admit was pretty cool. The greenhouse had a gravel floor with stuff just growing out of it, and a little bubbly pool, and lots of pretty birds that got excited when they saw Inanna.

"Hello, sweeties," she sang back to them. "Come on," she told Kaspian, "let me show you where the bathroom is. I'll find you a towel and some clean clothes you can change into, then I'm afraid you're going to be pretty much on your own. I have to get back to the shop. But Malcolm is outside if you need anything. Only good luck waking him up."

Why? wondered Kaspian, idly. Just out of habit, doubting

things. Why did she have to get back to the shop? There couldn't be more than one or two customers in a whole day, from the look of things. And why was she just leaving him alone in her house like this? Why were old hippies so fucking *trusting?* You kind of halfway wanted to rip them off, just to show them.

Just to teach them a lesson or two.

The memory of his stepmother—same age as this woman, but a completely different species—made him cringe. It made him sorry for having entertained mean thoughts. Probably this woman was just genuinely nice and he ought to respect that, or at least cut her some slack. Maybe her name really *was* Inanna.

"Okay, thanks," he told her. An effort to sum all this up.

She nodded, and left with a farewell whistle at the tiny birds. Finches, Kaspian guessed. Many colors. Flitting among crowns of thorns, cattleyas, jasmine, magenta-flowered abutilon.

And so once more he found himself alone.

Only now inside a time machine.

In Birdland.

SUN entered the bathroom through a skylight. There were potted plants on a wide shelf, and paintings by the same person who had done the SHARDS sign. The bathroom once had been something else; you could tell because it contained *much* more space than any crotchety Maine farmer would have invested in the distasteful processes of bodily necessity. Plus who wants another big room to heat through the winter? But hippies, they don't care about things like that. Winter is a *joy* to them. The body with all its needs and promptings is a sacred thing, a source of infinite pleasure.

Between these two extremes—the Puritan farmer and the pagan hippie—Kaspian felt himself in a kind of agnostic trough. He thought as he pulled his t-shirt off (a simple process, yet he took it slowly because his limbs were tight and sore) that the body, his own particular body, was a pain in the butt. Though there were some things it was good for. But on the whole it was too confusing, too alien.

Things would be clearer if his body would decide once and for all what shape it was going to be: tall or short, well formed or blobby. Were his arms ever going to be as muscularly developed as his legs? Would the rest of him catch up with his hands and feet? How much longer was his facial hair going to remain stuck at this fuzz-on-the-lip stage? Are these freckles ever going to fade away, or not? And what exactly (he asked the mirror) is this nose's *problem?*

Kaspian leaned over the bathtub—a claw-foot monster, long enough to float a kayak in—watching the water level rise. Transparent bubbles formed and burst, like quantum thingies emerging and self-annihilating in the foam of space. His reflection wobbled and broke apart and regrouped. Somebody once had taught him the story of Narcissus, but he didn't get it, or he didn't like it, or maybe he just decided (this was a habit of his) he wasn't going to believe it, he wasn't going to pretend that way. Myths are crocks, just like religions. If you believe in anything you are deluded. Reality is a total crapshoot and you can ask any physicist if you have any problems with this idea. It's all about staying alive, gaining experience points, advancing to the next round. Sort of like a strategic military simulation—say like *Close Combat II,* one of Kaspian's old faves—where everything *appears* to be governed by complicated rules, only in the end it all comes down to a roll of the random-number generator. Except in Reality there is no high-level A.I. to keep things fair, to adjust the game parameters to your level of skill. There is no strategic objective. All you can do is keep refining your tactics, keep maneuvering. Stay alive. Because if your character dies, then you're dead and the game is over. *Really* over.

Well . . . but metaphors are a crock, also. The only thing that was not a crock at this particular moment was the tub of hot water. Kaspian slipped the rest of his clothes off and gathered them up in a ball which he tossed, as per habit, across the room.

He raised one leg over the edge of the tub and stuck his foot down, experimentally. The water was exactly as he liked it: barely standable. This way, you could stay in for a while. He brought the other foot over and squatted carefully down, steam rising up into his face and making the smells of his body more intense. Already you could see the skin of his ankles underwater turning pink. Kaspian eased his butt lower until it just grazed the surface of the water. One millimeter at a time he let himself in. The heat was so intense it made his heart pound. Water flowed up into his crotch, and the sensation there made him think—if *think* is the word—about the strange pale girl. He thought of her bending over him, while he lay helpless on that table, unable to look down. He looked down now: studied his tangle of brown pubic hair, his chubby penis bobbing up at him, his scrotum baggily afloat.

What did she *do* to me? he wondered lazily. What was the big secret?

The girl—his memory of her—seemed to counter with questions of her own:

Why did you come to us?

Was there something you wanted?

At which point, Kaspian's memory seemed to bump into a wall of some kind; or into a looking glass, a two-way mirror through which you could very faintly glimpse the hidden room on the other side. He knew that *something* had happened next but he could not remember what. There was very little—a sound, a voice, what else?—between that moment and his waking up on the rock.

The effort of remembering, and the lulling effect of the hot water, made him feel tired. He closed his eyes and sank lower in the tub. Outside the window, he could hear the boom box softly playing its suicide song.

FORGETTING is a drug. Forgetting is a gift from the soul to the brain, a blessing of peace. Forgetting is a boat you climb into, out of the black cold depths; it rocks you safely, though precariously, far from any shore.

Forgetting is waking up: finding yourself in a room with white walls and gentle, even lighting. It is a glass of cool water near the bed.

Reach for the glass. Feel the smoothness of its curve, the apparent solidity that can shatter if you go too far, if you screw things up as usual. Now take the glass in your hand, raise it to your mouth.

Fall into it.

Drown.

Remember.

FOR an instant, Kaspian was gripped by a sensation of falling. He flung his arms out, banged into enameled cast iron, then realized where he was. Safe in a bathtub, with bruised elbows. The water had cooled to slightly higher than room temperature. He must have drifted off.

Feeling dumb, he pulled the stopper and dragged himself out. He dried off perfunctorily and stepped over to where Inanna had left him a stack of clothing, neatly folded, on a stool. The stool had a crudely handmade look about it: hippie woodworker learning her craft. The clothes were aged and mellow cotton—jeans torn and mended, a mold-gray t-shirt bearing the legend

CAT

The *other* white meat

Kaspian laughed and tried the jeans on. They fit, more or less, though he guessed the previous occupant had been taller than him, and a little skinnier in the hips. Inanna's son, he supposed. The t-shirt was large and comfortable.

Gathering his own clothes up—and noting with some embarrassment how awesomely filthy they were, as though he had worn them all summer—he felt a hard, lumpish thing beneath the fabric, maybe something he had left in a pocket. Peculiar: he couldn't remember *putting* anything in a pocket—seeing as how he hadn't been exactly *planning* to leave camp and wind up 70 miles away. He pawed through the dirty clothes until he located the cause of the bulge in a front pocket of his shorts.

Mystified, he dug down in there and felt something a bit larger than thumb-sized, hard and light, like a plastic chess piece. He pulled it out. It was a bear, a molded toy bear, mainly brown, though you could see that the eyes and nose had once been black and the teeth had once been white. It was fairly realistic in detail. Kaspian turned it slowly between his fingers. He could not imagine where it had come from. Its expression was funny, as though it were trying to growl and bare its teeth but instead appeared to be grinning at you. A friendly bear.

Kaspian smiled back at it.

"Hey," he said. "What are *you* doing here?"

The bear watched him through tiny once black eyes, saying nothing. Or anyway, saying nothing you could hear. Something about that grin, though; those discolored rows of teeth.

All at once

Kaspian screamed

louder than he had ever screamed in his life.

He dropped the bear and then, heart exploding, he got down on his knees and grasped frantically after it. He lifted it again, gently now, and closed his eyes and just held it in his fingers for a moment. Then he opened his eyes again and stared at it.

Cautiously, he smiled.

The little bear smiled back.

REMEMBERING is falling back asleep. It is floating down again, into the dream you were having. It's a story that you make up as it goes along, trying to explain things. It is your movie. It is your own private lie.

Remembering is all in your head. It's no different from imagination. It's just so obviously made-up: a cheesy special-effects monster stomping the shit out of Tokyo.

Remembering is a really bad idea. Because true or not, made-up or not, remembering is Real.

Stick to the warm white room, if you can. Stay in bed. Don't reach for the glass of water. Just close your eyes and believe in it, believe in its solid presence beside you.

Float to the surface.

Forget.

THE bathroom door cracked open.

Kaspian quickly closed his hand around the bear and lowered it to his side.

Into the open space of the doorway stuck a head that was connected to a scrawny body with no shirt. The head sported an unnatural, somewhat menacing hairstyle: black oily strands hanging low down both sides, coiled and ropy like snakes. Gold hoops of mixed sizes dangled from two ears and one eyebrow. The eyes themselves were small and black and the nose pointed at Kaspian like a tiny weapon, a paralyzing ray.

"Hey, man," this strange entity said. "Are you okay? I mean, sorry to burst in and all. But I heard somebody, you know— really *yelling.*"

Kaspian felt as though he were standing before some empty space so deep and black that it made you dizzy, just to think about. He thought he might be about to faint. He thought also he might laugh. Can you faint and laugh at the same time? He stared with his eyes way open, in amazement, at the figure in the doorway, though that is not what he was amazed by.

Slowly he grasped that this was the son of the woman who had brought him here. Inanna. Inanna's son.

"I'm Malcolm," said the person in the door. He blinked like somebody just wakened from a nap, still putting the world back together. He frowned. The door opened wider so you could see more of him, his baggy pants held at the top by a rope, the hair on his scrawny white chest. "Who are you?" he asked. He was being very polite, all things considered.

"Kaspian," said Kaspian. His voice was like a gulp. "Um, your mom said it was okay—"

"Ah."

The guy relaxed. His mom. That explained everything. The screaming too, apparently. He seemed to forget about it. "Well, sorry to bother you. I'll be out in the kitchen getting some grub if you need anything."

And just like that—poof—he was gone. The heavy wooden door bumped shut.

Somehow he had given Kaspian a little of his sanity back, though. It was as though he had thrown out a life preserver— casually, a simple toss, no big deal—then disappeared back into the cabin.

A leggy avocado plant stood on a table by the window. Slowly, carefully, Kaspian placed the little bear inside the pot, where moss had spread over the potting soil. He looked more comfortable there.

There was so much Kaspian had forgotten. So much he had lost—or thought he had lost. That was the empty space he was staring into: his whole past life. He wanted to turn away from it, to forget again. But that would be hard now.

A night . . . this would be when Kaspian is four or five . . . the family is hanging out in the living room. The TV is on but only NoElle, his stepsister, three years older, is watching it. Some stupid show, noise and laughter. Kaspian's dad is reading *Uncle Henry's Sell It or Swap It*. This would make it Thursday night, because that's when *Uncle Henry's* comes out. His stepmother must be around but Kaspian cannot see her. In this memory, as in many of his memories, she is invisible. His daddy sits in a large comfortable chair reading funny ads out loud to Kaspian, who does not really get what's funny about them—he is very young—but laughs anyway, and this makes his daddy laugh too. Both of them laughing brightly at some country widow selling off her husband's collection of "prize beer steins, including many from foreign lands." Or a man who has given up on fitting together the pieces of a sailboat from a kit, and now wants only to "recoop a portion of out of pocket costs."

Now they are down on the carpet. His daddy tries to tickle him, but Kaspian is not in a mood for kidding around. He needs help, urgent help, locating a lost treasure. Daddy's face becomes grave when the nature of the quest becomes clear: Kaspian has lost a small plastic friend named Ring Bear, the companion and protector of a miniature action figure from a fantasy-adventure cartoon. The cartoon is called *Ringbearer!* and in his childish mind Kaspian has misconstrued the title and bestowed it upon the plastic beast. The action figure's name is Karl Jaeger. Karl and Ring Bear: an inseparable team.

They look everywhere. Kaspian and his daddy. Crawling on the carpet, reaching blind under chairs with ruffled skirts down to the floor, finding some crayons and valuable coins and a miniature Slinky, but no Ring Bear. Kaspian is getting frantic. What if Ring Bear never comes back?

What if he's gone forever?

Kaspian waits for his daddy to assure him that such a thing will never happen. But his daddy is quiet.

In this memory, time seems to run backwards. First Kaspian has lost the bear, and then he is playing with it, moving it forward across the frontier of empty floor between the living and dining rooms, side by side with Karl Jaeger. Then he is receiving it as part of an otherwise forgotten birthday present, a set of realistically molded animals that also includes some plastic reeds and water lilies and a Plains Indian in a birch-bark canoe. Then the box is covered with wrapping paper, laid on the table with other presents to be opened, after Kaspian has blown out the candles and made his wish.

And *now*—eleven years from that Thursday night in the living room—he was standing in a bathroom in a hippie farmhouse, sliding dirty sneakers onto clean feet.

There were tears in his eyes. The long-lost plastic toy sat under a potted avocado plant. Such things cannot be, of course, and Kaspian was sane enough to understand that. He picked up the bear, which must be imaginary, and studied it for a few moments longer, then plunged it into the pocket of this borrowed pair of jeans. He took a series of slow breaths, readying himself to face the world. "The world" in this case being Inanna's son, home on vacation.

Malcolm.

Kaspian gave himself one parting glance in the bathroom mirror. He did not look like somebody who has been abducted into the Otherworld, transported 70 miles in his sleep, and left high and dry with a vanished childhood possession tucked into his shorts. This was good. The rest was strange, and somewhat scary. But at least there was one thing good.

MALCOLM was sitting at a table on the back deck, off the living room, eating a bowl of Kellogg's Corn Flakes, with the silly trademarked rooster named Corny on the box. His many earrings and one eyebrow ring wagged as his head dipped down and came up again. Each of his upper arms bore a strange tattoo: three blue stripes running in parallel around the biceps. The main house stereo was on, playing something horrible by a woman named Mari Boine, a native Sami from northern Norway. Music to leap into icy water by.

Malcolm, still shirtless, toasting in the noonday sun, glanced up as Kaspian stepped out onto the deck. He raised his spoon in salutation. Kaspian feebly smiled.

"Breakfast of Champions?" Malcolm said, when his mouth was a little emptier.

"That's Wheaties," said Kaspian.

Malcolm's expression turned grave. His features were on the pointy, delicate side. He brooded over his earth-toned bowl—momware, obviously—as though some serious wrong turn had been narrowly avoided. Behind him a sequence of comic-book frames, ready for coloring, lay on a drafting board. From what Kaspian could make out, the story arc concerned an enormously bloated and sociopathic amoeba.

"I don't really live here anymore," Malcolm said after some time of watching Kaspian stand there indecisively. "I go to the Corcoran School of Art down in Washington. I'm just home on vacation."

Kaspian wondered why you would call someplace home if you didn't live there anymore. He supposed this was an advanced, college-level problem. Just now he had his own stuff to deal with.

Malcolm, your friendly-at-all-costs type, pressed on: "So are you um, passing through, basically? Did Inanna take you in off the street, or what? That's a great t-shirt. I think I used to have one like that. Only I think mine was yellow."

Kaspian pulled up a chair. The table was heavy wood, and he figured he could use the solidity. For that matter, he could use the Corn Flakes. There was an extra bowl and he heaped it full. He was willing to bet anything that the matching momware pitcher contained something along the lines of organic goat's milk.

The first spoonful tasted so good, he tried to remember how long it had been since he had eaten. It felt longer ago than dinner last night.

"What's today?" he asked Malcolm.

Malcolm consulted the sun, the cereal box, the tall orange daylilies blooming along the edge of the deck. "Wodan's Day," he finally said.

"Wednesday?" said Kaspian. "No, I think it's supposed to be Sunday."

Malcolm nodded: amenable to this possibility also. But he asked, "What do you mean, *supposed* to be?"

"Well . . . Saturday is when they always do Cooperative Games. Saturday night. That's when I left camp. So today would be Sunday."

Malcolm nodded. He scooped up another mouthful of cereal and mashed it thoughtfully about his mouth. "No, it's Wednesday," he said without swallowing. "I'm pretty sure. Last night was Reggae Reprieve on WURS."

Kaspian gave up. He closed his eyes. The Corn Flakes in his stomach transubstantiated into the Food of the Dead.

"Okay," he quietly said. "So it must be Wednesday, I guess."

Sometime—not now, but eventually—he would get around

to asking himself what had happened to Sunday, Monday, and Tuesday.

When he opened his eyes again, Malcolm had finished eating and was staring at him across the table.

"I saw a dude who looked like you once," Malcolm said. "Looked the *way* you do, I mean. Not looked *like* you. Down in Belize. Doing a little eco-tourist stint, you know? Couple of spring breaks back. Kind of cool. Sad to see the way the people live down there, though. Some of them, anyway—others were doing all right. One old guy, he lived in this tree house, right up in some kind of big gnarly banyan-type thing. The *buzz* was, he was some kind of wise old medicine man from way upriver. Only these days he's retired from active shamanism, right? And he's kind of working the Don Juan trade. Lived with a mestiza chick named Petra, who was like his agent. They'd gotten him set up as a local attraction for tourists doing the *ayahuasa* circuit. Anyway, one of the guys I was traveling with just had to go see him, had to check this wise dude out. Probably he was cruising for *yage,* but who knows? Anyway, we didn't see the guy for a couple of days. Then one morning he's back, sitting there on his sleeping bag. Just sitting. Didn't say anything. Didn't *do* anything. We said to him, Hey, bro, where you been, you okay, stuff like that. And I mean, the dude just *stared* at us. But it wasn't that—it was the *way* he stared at us."

Malcolm paused, as though giving Kaspian a chance to catch up. "You look like that," he finished, softly.

Kaspian just stared at him.

Malcolm shrugged; he turned jerkily away; he appeared slightly embarrassed.

"But I don't *feel* like that," Kaspian said, rather suddenly. "I don't feel all that different."

"Different from what?" said Malcolm.

Kaspian shrugged.

Malcolm said, "How do you feel, then?"

Kaspian said nothing. He felt like someone who has slipped into a waking dream, and even though he's perfectly conscious and aware that he is dreaming, he can't get out of it, can't get back to being fully awake in the way he was before. He is stuck; he can only ride along with it, waiting for his chance, a moment when he can slip back to the other side, to ordinary waking reality.

But how could he convey any of this to Malcolm? Whom anyhow he hardly knew. So he just smiled feebly and went back to his Corn Flakes.

To his astonishment, Malcolm reached over and touched him. Very lightly, on the arm. It was like one of his mom's gestures: it meant something too pure and simple for Kaspian to wrap his mind around.

"That's okay, bro," Malcolm told him. "I've seen some weird shit from time to time. And you look like you've seen some weird shit too. Am I right?"

Kaspian opened his mouth, but nothing came of it. At last he said, "I don't know." He felt as though he were speaking the greatest, deepest truth of which he was capable. "I can't figure it out. The whole thing is like . . . too impossible."

"Ah," said Malcolm. Then, after some deliberation, he added, "Well, that's more common than people think."

"It *is?*" said Kaspian. "*What* is?"

"The impossible. It happens all the time. Around here especially. You can't let it worry you."

Malcolm looked the opposite of worried, that's for sure. He sat there flexing his scrawny shoulders, digging the sun. For some reason Kaspian thought you could imagine this guy in a circus: walking the high wire, swallowing swords, facing down ferocious beasts. Your first impression was not exactly *art student*.

Kaspian stared again, more thoughtfully, at the sketches spread across the drafting board. Big blobs eating little blobs. Little blobs multiplying in the big blobs' guts. He said, "So, are you working on like, a comic book or something?"

"Or something. It's my senior project. Only my advisor doesn't get it, I don't think."

Kaspian kept his mouth shut, except to shovel Corn Flakes in.

Malcolm went on, "I was kind of hoping to get some new ideas over vacation. This is a pretty good place to do research.

But so far I'm kind of stuck. I haven't even picked a title yet. Right now I'm kind of leaning toward *When Eating Was Sex*."

Kaspian nodded. As if this made perfect sense. Which maybe it did, to an art student. He decided that he liked pretending to be 18. People used the word *sex* to you in contexts unrelated to incurable disease and eternal damnation.

"Why is this a good place to do research?" he asked, hoping this was an intelligent follow-up.

Malcolm waved a hand around. "It's just one of those places. You know. Where you see things differently."

Kaspian guessed there was no arguing with that.

"Here," Malcolm said, pushing himself back from the table. "I'll show you some stuff. Okay? I think you might be interested."

Kaspian wasn't sure he wanted to be shown anything else. He felt like he had seen enough to hold him for a while. On the other hand, if he sat still too long he might decide it was time to call the camp and turn himself in. The thought of that filled him with dread—more so since he had been gone four days already—so he stood up and told Malcolm, "Sure."

"Cool." Malcolm lightly propelled himself across the deck, past the giant amoeba on the drafting board. He vaulted over the daylilies, down to the solid Earth.

Kaspian followed more slowly, still fighting the stiffness in his muscles and some other, nonphysical impairment. Wondering where life was taking him, he stepped down from the deck and set off after Malcolm, Malcolm the somewhat too friendly, Malcolm the irrepressible. Malcolm who doesn't live here anymore.

THEY passed through a garden of herbs and vegetables and flopsy, old-fashioned flowers—hollyhock, monkshood, pot marigold—and down a footpath that circled the field with the vanilla-coated pony in it. The pony clomped along with them, just inside the line of dull silver electrified fencing. Pointing this out, Malcolm said:

"I used to bring my friends out here and get them to piss on that. Want to try?"

Kaspian shook his head, but Malcolm wasn't expecting an answer; he just kept walking at a long-legged, twitchy stride. The path led them into a woodland where ostrich ferns grew as tall as Kaspian's chest. A pair of bluejays shrieked in territorial outrage. The sunlight scattered into yellow scraps. Everything seemed intensely alive; even the rocks were furred with exotic outgrowths. Kaspian thought of how different this was from the woods behind his house back in Glassport, where you followed a trail littered with candy wrappers and the occasional condom packet down to the Wabenaki River, with its nice view of the credit card center and the wastewater treatment plant.

Just as the path was fading to a barely discernible indentation in the ground, Malcolm spun about. He raised a hand in a curious gesture, neither pointing nor waving nor warning Kaspian away; just signaling for alertness. The air smelled cool and charged, as it did after rain.

Malcolm turned to the right and led them down an easy slope into a hollow place under a stand of tall trees that opened widely at the tops, like huge green vases.

"Chestnuts," he said, gesturing up at them. "They're dead most places. And look."

He pointed to a spot where a large brown and gray stone appeared to have split in two, the halves parting like an avocado seed beginning to sprout. Kaspian peered into the gap and saw that a slow but constant seepage of water was coming out. He touched a finger to it: cold as newly melted snow. A little farther down the slope, it collected in a small, almost perfectly circular pool. Malcolm walked down there and squatted beside it. Kaspian could see his upper body reflected in the faintly quavering water: slender and nearly white, floating like a ghost over the black depths.

When Kaspian caught up, he saw that someone—Malcolm, almost certainly—had built a sort of shrine nearby, tucked up under the nearest chestnut tree, sheltered by its own small roof of cedar shingling. The shrine held an assortment of stuff—interesting rocks, a wooden elephant, a brass bell, conical chunks of incense, a shallow momware bowl—but the main attraction was a painted statue of somebody in lotus position, white-skinned and naked except for a wrap of tiger hide. The figure had long hair painted black, with a cobra curled around its neck and peeking out from behind one ear. In the center of its forehead was an extra, vertical eye. The detailing was precise and elaborate: earrings, body markings, smallish pointed nose. It did not take Kaspian long to note that the image was practically a clone of Malcolm, cast in glazed clay.

"That's Shiva," said Malcolm. "Shiva Mahadev. He's kind of my primary deity."

"No kidding," said Kaspian. He hoped it didn't sound *too* smart-assed. But really: the whole thing was a little extreme. His stepmother was fanatical, but at least she didn't have her body done over to look like the Blessed Virgin Mary.

Malcolm was smiling, in the same cryptic way the statue was. It was eerie, to look back and forth between the two of them.

"Actually, *most* of this is a coincidence," Malcolm said. "I had practically never heard of Shiva until one day I was looking through this book of Indian art. And like, *there he was*. It's kind of amazing, don't you think?"

Kaspian halfway smirked.

"So what I figured was," Malcolm went on, "I just about had everything covered except the snake and the trisulas. Those are the body markings. I've never been much into snakes, but I figured, as far as the trisulas go, why not? They're not really obvious if you wear a shirt."

"What about the extra eyeball?" said Kaspian.

"Oh, everybody's got one of those."

He reached out and touched Kaspian lightly in the center of his forehead. It was very much like the way that strange pale girl—the angel or alien or ever-what-the-fuck she was—had touched him. Only this time it didn't cause his face to go numb. Malcolm just watched him with that screwy little smile. Then he took his finger away.

"The third eye is the one inside, the one you have visions

with. Yogis train themselves to see with it. But sometimes, you know, it opens by itself."

Malcolm dug into a pocket and pulled out a Snickers bar. He peeled the wrapper back slowly, careful not to break off any chocolate crumbs. Then he laid the bar down in front of Shiva. The statue did not appear to take note of it.

"It helps if you make some kind of offering," he explained to Kaspian. "It doesn't have to be a big thing. Just something with some level of value to you. I mean, this is totally optional, actually."

Kaspian wondered if anybody had ever hinted to Malcolm that he was a wee bit strange; or whether, growing up in a hippie household, this sort of thing passed for normal.

"So . . ." Malcolm ducked down and from underneath the altar he pulled a chair-sized cushion, the indoor/outdoor kind intended for lawn furniture. He plopped this down and told Kaspian:

"There you go. Have a seat. Make yourself totally relaxed and comfortable."

"What for?"

"Just . . . to be comfortable. Because it feels better. I mean, you don't *have* to."

Out of nowhere, Kaspian laughed. He laughed partly at the expression on Malcolm's face—a boyish sort of open-eyed and hopeful look—and partly because all of a sudden, everything struck him as overwhelmingly ridiculous. He had left the sane world behind on Saturday night and there was no telling when, if ever, he was going to get back to it. He flopped down onto Malcolm's cushion. "Okay," he said. "I'm comfortable now."

"Cool."

Malcolm's smile was a private, almost secretive thing. He squatted on the ground, folded his legs into lotus position, and bent forward into a compressed shape that looked exactly like a pretzel. He held this pose for at least twenty seconds, with what seemed perfect ease. Then he sat up, twisted around to face Kaspian, and said, "Don't you feel how *silent* it is around here?"

Kaspian would have said No—because there were birdcalls,

and a trickle of water into the pool, and wind fluttering through the chestnut leaves—except that from the first instant, as soon as he heard the word *silent,* he knew precisely what Malcolm meant. It was the thing he had felt while walking down the road, as though the quietness were a quality of the air; a subtle energy. So he nodded.

"Yeah," said Malcolm. He closed his eyes and let his head fall back. "Most of the time, most places I've been, you don't feel that. Not unless you take the right kind of drugs or learn the right meditation techniques. But here . . . it's just like, part of the scene."

"But what is it?"

Malcolm shrugged. "I figure it's some kind of field of consciousness. Sort of like the way you've got magnetic fields and gravity fields and so forth. I figure there are consciousness fields, too. Some places they're stronger than others. Right around here the field is pretty intense."

Kaspian could not tell whether this made sense or not, so he kept his mouth closed.

Malcolm went on, "See, this is the problem I'm working on for my senior project. It's like, *how do you express an alternate form of consciousness?* How do you convey what it *feels* like to be a totally different life-form?" He frowned in his earnestness, as though struggling to pin down difficult ideas. "The way I look at it—and I've thought about this a lot—this consciousness thing, whatever it is, must be a property of the universe somehow. I mean, it must have the same kind of reality as light, and gravity, and autopoiesis."

"What?"

"Autopoiesis?—the distinguishing property of life, the way it produces and maintains itself. As opposed to ordinary physical processes that just sort of go till they stop. I'm just citing that as an example. What I'm saying is, whether we *understand* these things or not, we can see they're universal. They pervade reality at every level we can think about. In other words, and this is my point, they are *not just human constructs.* It's true that the only way we *know* about light is that we can see it, and measure it with our instruments, and interpret it with our minds. But really, the light is out there, with us or without us. The same with autopoiesis, which applies to all living things no matter how big or small they are, including whole systems and ecosystems and, for all we know, galaxies and the cosmos itself. And the same with consciousness. It's out there. We didn't make it up. It doesn't depend on us. We experience it in certain ways, and interpret it, and make use of it. But it doesn't *belong* to us. It's a property of the universe. See what I'm saying?"

"No," said Kaspian. "I mean, yes. In a way. But really, no."

Malcolm sighed. "Yeah. Maybe it's just fucked up and doesn't mean anything. But I *think* it does. Listen: you *do* feel different down here, right?"

"Sure," said Kaspian. "But I mean . . . it's a nice place. It's calm, it's pretty. Anybody would feel different."

"Maybe. But lots of places are calm and pretty. This is different. But even if it isn't. What *is* it about a place that makes it calm? What do we mean by that? Because calmness, that's a state of consciousness, isn't it? So if a *place* is calm, isn't that a way of saying that this place has, like, a certain *quality of awareness?*"

"I don't know," said Kaspian. "Is it?"

"I don't know either. But that's my theory. That consciousness is not inside our heads. It's like an aspect of the environment. We move from one place to another and we come under the influence of different consciousness fields."

"What does this have to do with your comic book?"

Malcolm bent over and scooped at the ground with a couple of fingers. He brought them up covered with dirt.

"Now here we have the living Earth," he said, staring at the fingers closely, which made him slightly cross-eyed. "That's a phrase you hear a lot, but it's really literally true. This is the Earth, and it's living, and in fact a lot of it is actually shaped by the dynamic processes of life. What dirt is, for instance, is mostly the bodies, living and dead, of various organisms, and also their waste products, along with grains of rock that have been broken down by fungi and minerals that have been pumped around by biological cycles. Oxygen, for instance, is both a valued commodity and a hazardous waste product, depending on what kind of organism you are. So the amount of it in the air is strictly regulated by a sort of biospheric treaty among all organisms. It stays high enough but not too high. And so does the exact ratio of mineral salts in the ocean. Everything around us is part of this giant living system, this one superorganism, even the parts of it that are temporarily dead—that is, not currently part of the body of some living being or other. Actually I think the idea that *anything* is truly dead is a dubious concept. Because the ultimate reality of the Earth is that everything, every molecule, is connected to every other thing. All our fields interpenetrate."

"We're inseparable," said Kaspian. Quietly.

"Exactly," said Malcolm, worked up. "So let's put two and two together. I'm saying that the Earth is alive and everything is connected. *And* I'm saying that consciousness is a fact of the universe, it's not the sole property of human beings. So what does this give us? To me, it gives us this. All *consciousness* is connected, and all beings share it. *Human* consciousness is a flashy thing, but it's not the only kind. Other life-forms have their own forms of awareness, and those can be impressive too. Like say, a single ant is not too smart, but look how intelligent a *colony* of ants is. And look at how trees are able to live for hundreds of years because of, basically, *diplomacy*—they form stable alliances with each other, and with organisms in the soil, and with tiny insects in their canopies. *We* should be so fucking smart. See, I think *everything* has a kind of consciousness, even though it might be totally alien to our own, so that we don't even recognize it for what it is. And I think there are places you can go—this is one of them—where the usual background noise of human consciousness is a lot weaker, and you can start to feel the presence of some of the other kinds. You can feel the awareness of the soil and the trees, and the ants and the fungi."

"Ah," said Kaspian. "The fungi."

"Exactly," said Malcolm. "See, with my comic book, what I'm trying to do is unfold the consciousness of a radically different kind of being. A mysterious kingdom of living things whose evolution diverged from ours 600 million years ago. Truly, an

alien race. You know, fungi used to be considered plants, but they're not anymore. If you look at their genes, they're more different from plants, evolutionarily speaking, than plants are from humans. They're totally their own thing. What they are is rulers of the Underworld. They turn corpses into topsoil. They're the great and original recyclers. They can break down fucking *rock*. Some people think that the only reason there's petroleum is that for a while after plants evolved, fungi hadn't yet figured out how to decompose the cellulose walls. Now I guess they're working on plastic."

Kaspian sighed. He envied Malcolm this: a passionate interest in *something*, even if it was something weird.

"So this is what you do down here?" he said. "You come down here and like, *think* about stuff?"

Malcolm's skinny shoulder blades twitched up and down. "Sometimes I think. Sometimes I sketch. Sometimes I meditate. It's a good place. I wish there was somewhere like it down in Washington."

They sat for a while without speaking. You could do that comfortably with Malcolm. Kaspian let his mind go blank, which was a relief. Then after a while he said:

"What made you think I would find it interesting down here?"

"Oh, that. Well." Malcolm gave a semiembarrassed smile. "When I saw that look on your face, back at the table . . . You know, people tend to have certain, um, *experiences* around Sinai Falls. I guess this is what they call a window. It's actually fairly well known—among people who know about things like that. And I thought maybe you . . . well see, it ties in with my overall theory, the consciousness thing. Because it seems like whatever is warped or jacked-up about the consciousness field around here, it goes from one extreme to another. By the pool here, like you said, it's very calm. Other places, it's kind of *not* so calm. I wonder sometimes even . . . this might sound strange . . ."

"No way," said Kaspian, "I can't believe that."

"Yeah, ha. I hear you. But anyway, let's suppose that the biosphere does have this global field, this superconsciousness.

Then it follows, doesn't it, that other places might also. Other planets, like. Or dimensions, realms of being, whatever. So theoretically, you could wander into one of those alien consciousness fields. Or it could reach out and enfold you. Which would explain a whole lot of world literature, and I mean especially sacred texts, the Bible included. Because when you come down to it, most religious literature, and a lot of literature in general, consists of one peculiar head trip after another. Visions, apparitions, abductions, revelations, travel to unknown lands, encounters with unnatural beings. Almost all of which is, as we were saying a while ago, totally impossible. Yet these things happen, evidently. They *keep* happening. They happen a lot right around here. And even if they *are* impossible, they're apparently pretty convincing to the people concerned."

Kaspian slowly nodded. With one hand, inattentively,

he touched the small lump in his pocket
where Ring Bear snuggled
against his thigh.

INANNA Rugg's telephone hung on an off-white wall where pencil marks charted the progress of Malcolm the Kid, growing up. The scene was so totally caz that certain numbers and other bits of data had been scrawled right onto the old plaster.

Kaspian lifted the handpiece and drew it close to his head; then he moved it away; then he pulled it back harder, stretching the cord out. He could hear the dial tone. He could hear the television in the living room. The History Channel. Weimar Germany, inflation, beer halls, founding of the National Socialist Party. Kaspian murdered half a minute by letting the phone dangle, spinning by its cord, until the kinks were gone. Do all people twist their phone cords in the same direction? Do they twist it the opposite way in the Southern Hemisphere? What unknown laws govern the world we inhabit?

The place where Kaspian stood was a kind of hallway-cum-pantry just off the kitchen, where an upright freezer waited to receive the year's garden surplus. It was unplugged now, and when Kaspian investigated he found that it was being used to store winter clothing. There was lots of Polartec: somewhat surprising in that you would have expected hippies to wear chiefly wool they had sheared from their own free-range sheep, wouldn't you? It was obvious by now that Kaspian was stalling.

Something urged him not to make this call. Something other, that is, than the obvious fact that he hated ASAC and would, as recently as last Saturday afternoon, seriously have considered trading one (1) testicle for a guarantee of safe passage to anywhere else in the world, plus maybe a little spending money. But now, overriding that, he felt as though some pesky force of Nature was pressing against him, subtly but persistently, like a current, and a chirpy voice like an animated cartoon character was yapping at him—*"Don't do it, Kasp old buddy, listen to me, have I ever steered you wrong?"* Kaspian could have replied that in fact chirpy voices inside your head never steered you any way *but* wrong. Yet in this case he stood there listening, like a dull-witted cartoon sidekick—the big floppy animal that always winds up holding the bomb just before the screen turns into one big animated

What the problem was, partly, was a feeling that it wasn't over yet. Whatever "it" was. The thing that had happened to him on Saturday night, or at least started happening, did not feel yet like a wrapped-up story. Which was odd because Kaspian was *back,* his feet were planted on solid hardwood flooring, the soothing voice of a History Channel announcer mumbled in the next room, there were no mysterious lights or leprechauns in sight. And definitely no dead fathers.

"If you'd like to make a call," the recorded operator scolded him, "please hang up, and try the number again."

Kaspian placed the handpiece carefully in its cradle. He stood there for another minute, staring at the place where the top of Malcolm's head had reached on his thirteenth birthday. Already then he had been as tall as Kaspian was now. You could imagine him: thin as a pencil, nothing but skin and hormones.

Back in the living room, Malcolm lay on his stomach on the sofa, propped up on an elbow, scratching reflectively on a sketch pad. His fingers looked like precision tools. Against his will, but irresistibly, Kaspian thought how different the fingers of the Girl in White had been: pale as milk, so pliable you doubted whether there were bones inside.

Inanna sat in a plump armchair with the *Maine Times* in her lap. The cover article was about home-schooling. There was a picture of a smiling, dedicated mom standing over two kids who pretended to be learning. Kaspian personally knew kids who had been taken out of public school and condemned to a life of full-time family values, and he wondered whether American Youth Academy could possibly be worse.

"Did you get through to them?" Inanna asked.

"Um—" His brain was so scrambled he didn't get at first what she was talking about. "Um, not—"

"The phones have been acting up lately," she said. "Malcolm's had trouble with his e-mail."

Malcolm nodded without looking up. The lines on his sketch pad were coalescing to form some kind of terrified animal—another victim of the killer amoeba, perhaps.

Kaspian drifted closer, watching him work. "Fungi," he muttered.

Malcolm smiled at him, an ironic smile. "Rulers of the Underworld."

"Right," said Kaspian. Then, figuring Malcolm would not take this wrong, he added, "It *is* a little weird, though."

"Yeah, maybe." Malcolm held his Rotel pen vertically, like an exclamation point. "But it seems to me the best stories are always the weird ones. I mean, what the fuck is *Hamlet* all about?"

Kaspian smiled and settled himself on the arm of the couch. He supposed this was another college-level thing: the play of ideas. He kind of enjoyed it.

A knock came at the kitchen door.

Inanna looked up with a happy sort of curiosity. The door opened and a man came in: about 55 or 60 years old, mostly bald with the remaining hair razed to less than a millimeter, wearing crooked aviator glasses and full-body camouflage, complete with a Rambo knife you could have used to field-dress a triceratops.

It was, of course, the same guy Kaspian had seen out in the high school parking lot. Had to be.

"It's Weeb!" exclaimed Inanna, as though nothing could have been more delightful.

Kaspian didn't get it; he didn't get what she and this *Soldier of Fortune* type could possibly have in common. Maybe living in the same Nowheresville town was enough.

Weeb cased the room in a series of quick glances. You couldn't see his eyes through the aviator glasses—this is *night,* you idiot, thought Kaspian—but you got the feeling he was giving Kaspian an extra dose of scrutiny.

"Hiya, Weeb," said Malcolm from the couch.

The man nodded.

"What's up?" asked Inanna. "Have you eaten? Need a beer?"

Weeb took the glasses off. His eyes looked weak, the skin around them pale and saggy. He began speaking with the air of a phys ed teacher, looking hard from one person to another around the room.

"Have any of you people noticed anything strange, anything so to speak out of the ordinary, these past few days? Especially up near the vicinity of Fairy Rock?"

Malcolm's glance flickered lightly, for just a moment, toward Kaspian. He said:

"Like what do you mean, out of the ordinary?"

Weeb propped one leg up on an ottoman. He regarded them gravely.

"*Lights* have been reported," he said. "Electrical anomalies. We've gotten calls from way down-county. And *this* time we've got hard physical evidence. The Hakonnens' peppers have developed malformations, overnight. And you know the Hakonnens: their place is *right* dead center on the ley."

Inanna was smiling and nodding, the way she might have at somebody's story about the antic behavior of his dog. Malcolm went back to his sketch pad but did not appear to be concentrating. Weeb settled his eyes on Kaspian, as though wanting to know—*right now*—just where things stood. Did he recognize him, from out in the ball field? After a couple of seconds he frowned and looked away.

"But the *biggest* news is," Weeb said, back to Inanna, "we've got a confirmed case—*confirmed,* now—of an AE2."

Kaspian heard a note of triumph in the man's voice as he spelled this out—A, E, two—as in, *read, my, lips.*

"What's that?" said Malcolm, laying down his pen and twisting himself into an upright position with the agility of a monkey.

Weeb said, curtly, "Anomalous entity abduction/encounter syndrome. That's recent terminology. We've adopted it in hope of getting past the old debate about the reality status of these experiences. Otherwise, you know, the research tends to get kidnapped by what you might call your fringe types—your conspiracy theorists, your UFO cultists, elements such as that."

Kaspian tried to get a focus on this guy. Clearly he was a kook; but what *kind* of a kook? Did he actually *know* something? Could he possibly shed light on Kaspian's strange experience?

"I guess you've got to be careful about fringe types," said Malcolm, nervously rubbing one arm where the bright blue trisulas were tattooed.

Weeb nodded gravely. He stood poised between the kitchen and the living room with his arms crossed and his feet spread slightly apart, as though ready to spring into action should unnamed malevolent forces emerge from the Defiant Encore.

Inanna lowered her *Maine Times* but did not quite set it aside; she seemed to be withholding commitment. "What's happened?" she said.

Weeb looked at each of them again. As before, his gaze seemed to hang longest and heaviest on Kaspian. Then he cleared his throat and began lecturing in that phys ed teacher's voice:

"Individual cases differ radically. But the core features of the AE2 experience are pretty much invariant. To begin with, you have something we call a liminal or threshold experience, in which some divide, either symbolic or physical, is crossed—for instance a shoreline or the edge of a woods. Or the hour of twilight. Or a *psychological* twilight such as that between waking and dreaming. The point is, some kind of halfway, either/or type of situation is prevalent. This is followed by your initial sighting or intimation, which can take the form of an unusual animal such as a large black dog or cat, but more commonly is experienced as an unexplained light or series of lights exhibiting nonordinary behavior. There might also be noises or mechanical disturbances. Your car might inexplicably shut off. Thirdly, you've got entry or induction—we no longer employ the word *abduction* because this is a controversial term—which may be voluntary or involuntary, and it may or may not involve physical displacement. There are cases of the syndrome occurring to people whose bodies are observed to be physically immobile at the time, as in your classic near-death experience or NDE. Then there are cases in which the subject is observed to be absent, as when children are missing from their rooms in the middle of the night. Fourthly we come to the experience proper, and here is where people tend to be thrown off-track, because this can take just about any form. You can have your talking apparition such as the B.V.M. *Or* you can have a biological entity, perhaps extraterrestrial in appearance— your so-called alien or E.B.E.—though you've got to include here all types of things such as lake and river monsters, hairy beasts, *chupacabras,* and even cases in which no particular entity at all is visible but rather a presence or a being who cannot be directly perceived. Obviously here we run smack into the whole range of mystical and visionary experience, burning bushes and what have you. Not to mention spirits of the departed, goblins, werewolves, and so-called angels. The important thing—"

"You mean," said Kaspian, "like, when you say spirits of the departed . . . you mean, *ghosts?*"

"Anything goes," Weeb declared. Then he raised a cautionary finger. "But understand, this is just Phase 4 I'm talking about: the Encounter. *This* is where your broad variation comes in. By the time we come to Phase 5, the Return, and Phase 6, the Aftermath, then you find that all this apparent dissimilarity collapses back into the core pattern, the structural sameness. Because in 5, you find that the subject's whole sense of time has been distorted or stretched out—he comes down from the mountain and discovers he's been gone 40 days instead of just a couple of hours—and on top of that, his memory is unreliable, simultaneously vivid but fragmented, like a stained-glass window that's been broken and the pieces scattered around on the floor. Then in 6, the Aftermath, you typically start to see the emergence of a whole new pattern of cognitive activity, whether it be psychic episodes or recurrent dreams or unexplained knowledge of some previously hidden truth. That's your AE2, in a nutshell. Did somebody mention a beer?"

"Check the refrigerator," said Malcolm.

Inanna laid the *Maine Times* down, finally. "But Weeb," her voice trailing him as he stepped around the woodstove and ducked under a low-hanging bunch of summer thyme, "what in the world *happened?*"

Weeb returned with a large bottle of Andrew's Bitter, cloudy and pale, which he gently shook, then held at eye level squinting into its mysterious depths. He said:

"You know Gertl Auerbach, that writer lady? Well she was walking back home from the bookshop that other old gal, what's her name, runs down in the village there, she thinks it might have been about eight-thirty or nine o'clock because the fireflies were just starting to come out, and then she says—" Weeb paused to probe into one of the many pockets of his camo vest. He pulled out a notebook, a little better than palm-sized, through which he carefully thumbed. "She *says,*" he resumed, "that a strange feeling overcame her, as though she had just been dozing—though this whole time, mind you, she was walking down the road to that place of hers—and describes the way she felt as like, quote, some loud report or brilliant flash of light had awakened me from a shallow slumber, so that all at once I found myself blinking in astonishment at the world around me, which for a time I failed to recognize, unquote."

Inanna nodded, waiting for more.

Weeb snapped the notebook shut.

"That's it?" said Inanna.

"Not exactly." Weeb took a couple of steps further into the room. He raised the ale to his lips, then stared at the bottle in distaste. "When she arrived home, it was past eleven: 11:18 to be exact. The walk to her house from the village is only about 30 minutes, maybe 45 for an elderly lady such as herself. But this would mean, assuming that she left even as late as 9:00, which is doubtful because it would have been dark by then, that more than one hour, perhaps as much as two, are unaccounted for. This, you see, is wholly typical of the AE2 experience."

Inanna looked at Malcolm and then at Kaspian.

"That's kind of weird," said Malcolm. "I guess."

Weeb took another swallow of ale. "That's not all," he said through the spume. "Later she remembered something. Not a big thing. But something that didn't fit. She remembered being up by the Fairy Rocks—or actually what she said was . . ." (A pause: consulting the notebook again.) "She said quote, I remembered looking down on the Fairy Rocks as though from a moderate height, perhaps a story and a half."

He pocketed the notebook again with a look of vindication.

"Unquote," said Kaspian.

Weeb frowned at him.

"Hmm," said Inanna. She turned a brooding glance toward the History Channel, where it appeared that a new Chancellor had been named following contentious elections in Germany. Celebration was in progress but it did not look like a lot of fun.

"What day was this?" said Malcolm.

Weeb stared into the bottle of ale, contemplatively. "This would have been, according to Gertl, Saturday. Saturday evening. And you see, the anomalous character of the whole incident is borne out by the fact that there's no *way* someone like Gertl Auerbach could have made it from the main road all the way in to the Fairy Rocks in total darkness. And if she *had*, it would have taken *more* than an hour or two. She couldn't have made it home by 11:18. Yet she swears this is the one thing she remembers about that missing period of time."

Inanna smiled at him, tolerantly. "Couldn't she just be mistaken? Maybe she dozed off or . . . or became a little confused. She is getting on in years, you know."

Weeb huffed. "She had a piece just last month," he said, a

trifle defensively, "in the *New York Times Book Review*. She told me that herself."

"Wow," said Malcolm.

"Where are the Fairy Rocks?" said Kaspian.

Everyone looked at him.

"The Fairy Rocks," Inanna began, then balked at the task of explaining local geography to an outsider.

"You go out past the high school—" Malcolm stuck out a long bony arm "—then you head way back into the woods and just follow the power lines. They're called the Fairy Rocks because . . . well, I don't know for sure. They look kind of like, Tolkeiny or something. And there are supposed to be a lot of old stories connected with them."

"New stories, too," Weeb said. He looked at Kaspian for a moment, then drained off the ale. "I take it you're not from around here."

Kaspian shrugged, which was a way of saying that he wasn't really from anyplace, at the moment.

"Kaspian's a camp counselor," Inanna explained. "He's been doing some hiking."

"Which camp?" said Weeb. All friendliness, hearty and gym-teacher style.

Which as far as Kaspian was concerned kind of nailed it. The guy was not just chatting with him. He was conducting an *interview*. At any moment the little notebook was going to pop out.

Kaspian searched for a path through this. He wanted to talk—especially to talk to someone who might be able to answer his questions—but he did not trust this Weeb character.

Weeb appeared to sense his inner debate. He backed off—literally took a step away, toward the woodstove, then dug into a vest pocket and came out with a small card which he flipped expertly toward Kaspian. Kaspian snagged it in the air, like a tiny Frisbee. The card was densely printed in small type: phone numbers, URL's, and at the center, in its own eyeball-shaped frame:

DWIGHT "WEEB" EUGLEY, JR.

Trust for Global Readiness

Weeb tossed a second card toward the couch, where Malcolm received it with enthusiasm.

"Slick," he said, turning the card one way and another, as though something more might be gotten out of it.

Kaspian said, "Readiness for what?"

"For whatever comes," said Weeb Eugley, not taking his eyes off.

Kaspian ran a finger along the edge of heavy-stock paper. His throat still felt dry. He raised his head to find Weeb staring at him, squinty-eyed.

"What are you afraid of, son?" the man said, in a voice that was probably meant to be steady and reassuring. Kaspian felt as though, any second now, the guy would reach over and grab him by the throat.

Inanna saved him. She said in a good mom's voice—not meaning to nag *but*—"Isn't there a phone call you've got to make?"

"Right," said Kaspian. He stepped past the freezer to the scrawled-up wall. Listening to the connection click and hum through—the wonders of a rural telephone system—his mind slipped blurrily, like a sleepless passenger on a bus, through a landscape that was half foreign and half familiar.

The voice on the other end belonged to Walter Gilliland. Hanging around the Senior Staff quarters, pulling gopher duty, sucking up.

"You're in a world of trouble, Aaby," he said. "You've had your stepmother worried sick."

"My stepmother?" said Kaspian. "She's not—"

"A world of trouble," Gilliland repeated, savoring every syllable.

Which at least, Kaspian thought, as he sat outside the pottery shop an hour later, under the sign that said SHARDS, waiting for them to come for him,

was a world whose every sea
and every continent
he knew by heart.

IT was late when the van arrived, after dark and then some, and because the road was so straight, you could see the lights coming for at least a couple of miles. First they appeared on a distant hill, then they dove into a low place and vanished, then slowly they climbed to Kim Hansen High School which was on high ground again, and from there the lights seemed to float, advancing in jerky stages through Sinai Falls in search of something Kaspian had described on the phone as an old Gulf station. He didn't know why he thought Gulf, as opposed to Texaco or whatever. It just popped into his head. Many things were popping into his head lately; some of them he had no words for.

The van was a white GMC with a flag-red diagonal swath along the flank and the designer logo for American Youth Academy, which semiabstractly depicted a young person of apparently male gender with his arms outstretched to form the Y of the Academy's acronym, supporting as if by magic a globe or orb which you had to presume was meant to be, like, the World. Or maybe it was the Sun and the kid was an Apollo-worshiper. Or maybe he was just some poor sucker out chasing a mysterious ball of pure white light, whose nature and meaning could not be fathomed. The side panel of the van rolled open and out stepped the boss of Accelerated Skills Acquisition Camp, a quiet man known as Mr. Orrnyx, whom Kaspian referred to, among his fellow campers, as Herr Direktor. Until now he had had no occasion to call the man this to his face. Mr. Orrnyx looked him up and down, gave a weary nod, and turned to tell someone deep in the shadows of the van:

"It's all right. He appears to be fine."

He motioned Kaspian through the open door, where—still unseen, and thus a little hard to believe in—his Wicked Stepmother waited.

Kaspian turned to flick a wave toward Malcolm, who had been hanging out with him, awaiting the van.

"Take it easy," Malcolm said. It might have been advice, or just good-bye.

"You too," said Kaspian. "Watch out for those AE2's."

Malcolm nodded sagely.

"And hey," Kaspian added, now from the door of the van, "thanks for the t-shirt."

"What t-shirt?"—but Mr. Orrnyx slid the side panel in front of his face like a steel curtain. *BAM.*

Here was the situation. Kaspian settled into the middle seat of the big van, with one empty body-space separating him from his stepmother. He checked her out on the sly (bolt upright, lips pressed together, purse clasped in both hands) but did not make eye contact. Mr. Orrnyx, having evidently ridden beside her on the trip out, now moved up to the front passenger seat, next to Walter Gilliland who somehow had gotten himself chosen to be the driver. Gilliland twisted to face Kaspian; his face looked sickly in the poor light, skin stretched over bones like an oily tarp. "I *hope,*" he said, "this experience teaches you that you can't just run away from your problems."

"For sure," said Kaspian. "If you just *run,* you'll never get far enough. You've got to thumb a ride."

"Drop it," murmured Mr. Orrnyx, addressing Gilliland. To Kaspian, in a louder voice, he said, "Get buckled."

Gilliland put the van in gear. It lurched forward. Kaspian felt like someone being abducted.

"You had your mother worried sick," said Mr. Orrnyx, without looking around.

Yeah, right, Kaspian thought. *Mad as hell* is more like it. But all he said was, "*Step*mother."

"Hm?" said Orrnyx, not registering the subtle but all-important correction.

In the dark corner of the backseat, Carol Deacon Aaby cleared her throat.

"You know, Kaspian," she said—*at last she speaks!*—"it isn't completely necessary to take this attitude. And I also think you owe Mr. Orrinax here an apology. I'm sure he has better things to do than go chasing after runaways in the middle of the night."

Kaspian felt as though she were addressing him from a great distance. Over a walkie-talkie, say. He turned slightly so as to gauge her expression, but could barely make it out in the darkness. Just as well.

"You know, Kaspian," she said, "in a way it's a good thing you went ahead and pulled this. This, running-away-and-staying-gone-for-how-many-days. Because it's given me the opportunity to have a good long talk with the staff there at your camp—and I'm *so* grateful to Mr. Orrinax for taking so much of his valuable time out to sit and hold my hand during this whole ordeal. But Kaspian, in speaking with Mr. Orrinax and other people at the camp . . . well I must say, some interesting things have been brought to my attention."

Kaspian eased his head back onto the seat. It was not hard, with practice, to tune her out. Or at least to convince yourself that you were tuning her out. He focused on the sound of the big engine, the dull flash of trees caught in the headlights flipping by. The van was passing through a thickly wooded area. The north woods; the Dark Forest. A place of danger and magic, where anything could happen.

Really, anything.

"You know I was *hoping*," Mrs. Aaby went on—her tone making it already clear that this hope, like all her hopes, had been sadly thwarted—"that your getting away for the summer would give you a chance to see certain things in perspective. I was hoping that some of those problems you were having in school might have been due to . . . well, the less-than-positive influences you had been exposed to."

She referred, of course—as no one but Kaspian could have

known—to Pippa, the Village Wiccan. On top of Eli, whose mother was a *poet*.

"But *now* I learn," his stepmother continued, "that many of these same problems have persisted, even at camp. What's this I hear about your abusing your internet privileges?"

"It was just an audio file," Kaspian muttered.

"What?" said Mrs. Aaby.

"Yeah," put in Walter Gilliland, taking his eyes dangerously off the road. "An audio file that said, *'Ooo baby stick it in me.'* Which he played over the *entire P.A. system.*"

Despite himself, despite all of them, Kaspian softly laughed.

"I see nothing funny about this," his stepmother said, *"at all."*

"Well at least," said Mr. Orrnyx, in the clear loud voice of a schoolteacher, "that's all in the past, isn't it? I think we can concern ourselves now with what lies ahead. Our only interest is in choosing the course of action that is right for *Kaspian.* Isn't it?" He looked around at everyone, blandly smiling, seeking this minimal consensus.

Yeah, right, thought Kaspian.

"Precisely," said his stepmother, from the shadows.

"Have you given any more thought," said Mr. Orrnyx—to Carol Aaby alone now—"to that alternative we spoke about? There's no need to make a decision immediately, of course. But have you had an opportunity to glance over those materials?"

Mrs. Aaby's features defined themselves as she leaned forward, into the Trekky glow of the instrument panel. They were bland: a round face with a miniature nose like a baby doll's, eyes that appeared wide-open even in sleep, as though continually affronted, and pale brown hair sprayed into submission. Kaspian turned away and cranked a window down, hoping the whoosh of air would make it harder to listen. He nonetheless caught the phrase *very favorably impressed.*

"I'm glad," said Orrnyx. "We're very proud of what we've accomplished down there. In due time, of course, we hope to apply the same formula on a national scale. The facility here in Maine is just one of many that we'll be building up over the next few years—pending of course favorable developments in the legislative arena. But I don't need to bore you with technicalities."

"Not at all," said Mrs. Aaby.

Mr. Orrnyx repositioned himself on the seat, swinging his upper body into view from the rear of the van. This expansive movement caused Walter Gilliland to retract into the driver's seat, elbowed out of the conversation.

"At the present time," Mr. Orrnyx said, "the Virginia campus is definitely our showcase. That's where the Chairman, Mr. Winot, spends most of his time, and it's where we've been able to really get in there and do some intensive fine-tuning of the system. I believe I can truly say that what we deliver in Virginia is probably the most real-world-directed, most outcome-assured investment available in today's educational market."

To this, Kaspian's stepmother could only nod.

"For example," Orrnyx went on, rolling now, "take the question of faculty. Here in Maine, with our limited enrollment, we're only able to offer the most basic range of faculty specializations, such as your traditional Math and Communications Skills and Science Literacy. Whereas down there, at what we call the Field Study Center, we've been able—especially since voucher legislation was signed into law by the governor of Virginia a couple of sessions ago—to really branch out and diversify into some significant areas. Some areas that I think you and Kaspian might have a degree of interest in."

"Yes," said Mrs. Aaby, uncertainly.

"For instance." Orrnyx shifted again, leaning as far back as physically possible into the passenger space of the van. He seemed to be trying to get up close and personal. It would have worked better in a Volkswagen. "There's the issue of counseling services. Now, it happens that a counselor from the Virginia campus is with us at present, on rotational assignment. And should Kaspian need any . . . attention in that regard . . . then of course, while she's with us, it will be readily available. But unfortunately this is only a temporary state of affairs, until such time as our enrollment level makes it possible to provide counseling services full-time."

"Now when you say *counseling* . . ." Mrs. Aaby began, sounding ever so slightly suspicious.

Orrnyx nodded, as though he understood exactly the question she had not managed to ask. "All our counselors are fully trained and qualified to provide a broad range of services, with a strong emphasis on individual needs. They can help a student focus on a particular long-term career path, or equally they can assist with any psychological or, um, group-dynamic situations that may arise."

"I see," said Mrs. Aaby.

Kaspian wondered *what* she saw. He wondered where Orrnyx was heading with this.

"You know, what we could *do*—" Mr. Orrnyx gave them a salesman's smile, a look of rehearsed inspiration—"let's *start* Kaspian on a counseling program, just to see how it goes. For the next couple of weeks, say, while we have the services available. Naturally there would be no extra cost involved. It's all part of the comprehensive AYA package."

Mrs. Aaby settled back into the shadows, taking her private thoughts with her. Kaspian did not actually get what the big deal was. It wouldn't be the first time he'd ever had dealings with a shrink.

"Will there be," his stepmother finally asked, "any sort of New Age guided meditation involved? I've been told that that can be a form of . . . of programming, or brainwashing, or . . ."

Kaspian said, "Yeah, sure. They hypnotize you into having higher self-esteem. Next thing you know, you're out sacrificing babies to the Devil."

"Kaspian Aaby!" she snapped.

"Now, now," Mr. Orrnyx said, trying to restore calm.

From the driver's seat, Walter Gilliland sniggered—a sound so annoying that everybody else shut up. "I'm sorry," Gilliland said soberly, firming up his grip on the wheel.

"There's nothing like that to worry about," Mr. Orrnyx said, with a polished sort of gravity. "Our counselors are carefully monitored. They have no hidden agenda apart from the welfare of the individual student."

It was kind of incredible, Kaspian thought. Herr Direktor was taking his stepmother *so seriously*. As though her crazed notions were actually worthy of discussion.

"I guess that would be all right," his stepmother said. "Just to see how it goes. Lord knows I've tried everything else."

"Of course," said Mr. Orrnyx, oozing sympathy.

He was so smooth that Kaspian couldn't take it too personally. It was just part of the comprehensive AYA package. So he leaned his head against the door panel and listened to the wind whooshing by.

Through the window, between black trees, he could see a scrap of night sky. He blinked to clear his eyes and stared hard out there, into the emptiness. Or was it just emptiness? Was there anything else?

Not much, from what he could tell. A bunch of stars. One bright spot that might be a planet. Hundreds of tiny things, invisible to the naked eye, like communication satellites, beaming made-for-TV movies and Nickelodeon reruns across the trashed and sold-out planet. Space litter chucked by good-old-boy astronauts. That was about it.

No God. No angels.

No spirits of people who had died.

Kaspian blinked. He thought for one panicky instant he was starting to cry.

What's happening to me? he wondered.

Nobody answered.

He peered into the Dark Forest but felt no magic there. He guessed magic and chain saws could not exist in the same place.

It was hopeless, then. He was being transported by alien beings in their gleaming white ship to a place where painful experiments would be performed on him. There was nothing anybody could do.

No Daddy was there to save him.
Kaspian was alone.

THE morning after Kaspian's little outing—which was how the period of his absence would be referred to from now on, and Kaspian saw no reason to object—began, like every morning, with music piped through the P.A. system. It was some kind of march: not a Sousa-type march but something with a thumping drum machine, like NFL halftime music. From the moment it began you had 45 minutes until the chow line opened, during which time ordinary campers could lie around and tap their feet, but kids in the Special Attention Quad, to which Kaspian had been assigned after the sound-byte incident, were required to report to one end of the athletic field, a stretch of sand known as the Grinder, for motivational aerobics. The session was conducted by videotape, fed through a small TV on a rolling AV stand, cranked up so you could barely understand what the peppy video personality was saying. There were 12 tapes in the series, so by the end of the first two weeks you had seen them all and it was easier to follow the instructions without really taking note of them. This left you free to exchange pleasantries with the other SAQ's, except on those mornings when one of the Senior Staff would show up and hang out at the edge of the Grinder, proctoring. This morning started out free of non-prerecorded grown-ups, so Kaspian turned to Hunter Nye, a surfer boy from Virginia Beach whom in a certain way he had come to like, or at least to appreciate, and he said:

"So what's been going on? Did you guys miss me?"

They were executing complicated body bends. Hunter

screwed his head around, like someone about to lose a Twister game, and said, "Yeah, Aaby. I could barely get any sleep. Pisegna kept sneaking over in the middle of the night putting his hands all over me, and there were no witnesses so what could I do? He's such a big fuck I was afraid he'd sit on me and I'd be jelly."

"Fuck you," said Mike Pisegna, indifferently.

"Y-yeah," stammered Ricky Plaster, a skinny black kid from Philadelphia. "I h-heard the two of them out there. G-going at it."

"Yeah, right," said Hunter Nye. "You couldn't hear shit over the squeaking of your own bed because you lie in there pounding it all night."

"F-fuck you."

Kaspian stared at the tiny screen. The figure there—he believed it was female—had dropped into push-up position and was doing something that looked kind of implausible with one leg at a time.

Why is it always sex? he wondered. Always sex. Never a jibe about, for instance, grooming standards, or place of origin, or degree of athletic prowess. Always sex: always this probing and denigrating and ludicrous boasting, day and night. It was like everybody was afraid that everybody else was a bunch of closet queers, or *wanted* them to be closet queers, or was scared shitless of turning out to be a closet queer himself. Or something. Kaspian did not get it. And of course, as he well knew, he himself was as bad or as good at this as any of them, and he didn't get that either.

"Eat me, Nye," he said companionably, straining to bring his leg all the way to *here*.

"All right," said Hunter Nye, leering hungrily. "Whip it out."

Kaspian, worn-out from being up so late, slumped to the ground for a minute. Not even a minute—fifteen seconds maybe—but long enough. The staff proctor had arrived, sneaking up on them while they were down in that contorted position, and now this person wasted no time in yanking Kaspian's chain.

"Come over here, Mr. Aaby," a woman's voice said. "Let's you and I have a little talk."

Kaspian took his time getting to his feet, meanwhile avoiding eye contact. Hunter whispered:

"Hey, Aaby. Who's the babe?"

He was looking across Kaspian's shoulder. Kaspian followed his line of sight to the woman in a staff uniform—suitable attire for the Road to Mandalay. "Beats the hell out of me." He shambled off in her direction.

By the time he got close enough to read her name tag (it said THERA BOOT) the woman was holding out a hand to shake his.

"Hi," she said. "I'm Ms. Boat"—or so it sounded—"and I've been looking forward to meeting you."

Since when? Kaspian wondered. For what? He gave her a vague sort of nod.

The so-called Ms. Boot or Boat regarded him in a way that was part gung ho and part neurosurgery. Kaspian shifted from one foot to the other, but for several seconds she just stood there like, *studying* him. Her eyes had a quality that made them hard not to look at: intense, unwholesome.

"What's the matter, Mr. Aaby?" she finally said. She reached over and cuffed him on the shoulder—pulling her punch in an exaggerated way, so he would know it was just playlike—and gave him a cocky, R.A.F.-officer smile.

He smiled back, halfway. He hadn't intended to but somehow you couldn't help it, like you couldn't avoid her eyes.

Ms. Boot was on the tall side, a few inches higher than Kaspian. She had no breasts to speak of, but her khaki uniform shirt, reefed at the waist, billowed at rib cage level in such a way as to simulate a well-made female body. Her hips were compact and her legs were long and boylike. That was about as much as you could see without getting impolite about it.

"I heard you had quite a little outing," she said.

"Mm." Kaspian shrugged and looked away.

"I'd love to hear about it."

Her voice was so unsarcastic, so plain and seemingly honest, that before he could stop himself he raised his head and caught her smiling at him again. This time he managed not to smile back. He kept on the standard-issue mask of teenage aloofness.

The two of them stood about half a dozen paces from where the other guys were down on their butts with their legs spread apart, twisting to one side and then the other. Aerobics music, something jittery like Gloria Estefan, nattered at them. Hunter Nye motioned to get Kaspian's attention, then reached down and—*daring* Ms. Boot to turn her head—pulled his shorts to one side, laying bare a shadow of pubic hair and an indistinct blob of private parts. Kaspian almost laughed out loud. Ms. Boot took this to mean Okay.

"Good. Why don't you drop by my office, then? It's up in, what's it called . . . the Water Tower Quad? You're not too fond of Defensive Firearms, I hear. So drop by then, and I'll give you a blue slip when we get finished."

Aha, thought Kaspian, finally getting it. This was the counselor that Mr. Orrnyx had been talking about. Here on rotational assignment from the hot-shit campus down in Virginia. (Let's *start* Kaspian on a counseling program, just to see how it goes.) Somehow this wasn't quite what he had expected.

Ms. Boot shot him one more smile—bigger but less real than the others, more of a typical Senior Staff number. I'm not going to fall for this, Kaspian promised himself. She turned and almost marched away on those long legs of hers. Her stride suggested that stiff-ankled goose step you get with hiking boots. I cannot, Kaspian realized, with a certain dismay, take my eyes off. Truly.

"I'd say she's fuckable," said Mike Pisegna, when Ms. Boot was a safe distance up the Grinder.

"D-definitely," said Ricky Plaster.

Hunter Nye scoffed: "As if you asswipes would know." Closer to Kaspian, with a toss of his sun-bleached bangs, he murmured, "So what was that all about? It didn't sound like she was giving you a rough time."

"No." He shrugged. "I guess she just wants to talk."

"Yeah?" Hunter moved his mouth as though chewing imaginary gum. He was short like Kaspian but more efficiently built:

you could imagine that he'd know what to do with a wave, if he ever caught one. "Well, just watch your ass."

He turned away, sauntering off toward the showers. The aerobics tape was still running. Hunter tugged his t-shirt over his head.

"How come?" Kaspian called after him. "Watch my ass about what?"

"Beats me," his kind-of friend said, smirking back at him. "Just be careful, is all. Don't go getting into deeper shit than you already are."

Kaspian did not see how that was possible. He set off toward the showers and then changed his mind.

He wandered away from the Grinder and into the scrubby woods that shouldered in from all sides. The soil was thin, sandy, as though there were a beach nearby. But all it was was grit left behind after glaciers had ground down the mountaintops. He chose a bare spot, sheltered from observation, and pulled Ring Bear out of his pocket. Squatting down, he set the little plastic animal next to a stand of club moss that shot up like a miniature forest. Ring Bear looked at home there. Kaspian wondered why. Had there been club moss growing in the woods behind the house, when he was a little kid? How many things had he forgotten about those days? How much of his own short life was already lost to him?

He thought about what it must be like to suffer from homesickness—to have come here from that sort of place. It was bad, from what he could tell. Ricky Plaster appeared to have a case of it. But was there any equivalent malady that struck campers like Kaspian, kids who had come here from no place and were headed to no place—or worse—at the end of summer? Was there such a thing as homeless-sickness?

He bet there was not.

He was glad.

IN the chow hall, he saw his stepmother sitting up at the head table, next to Mr. Orrnyx. Ms. Boot was there also, but with a couple other Senior Staff types between her and Carol Deacon Aaby, which was good.

His stepmother caught Kaspian watching her. He was making his way down the chow line, picking up his usual chocolate milk and banana, passing on the S.O.S., and she must have figured he was thinking something he was not—such as maybe feeling ashamed of himself, the disgrace he had brought upon the family—because she shook her head at him. Like, her disappointment was so deep it could only be expressed that way, not in words. Like I give a rat's ass, he thought. He turned and, without needing to raise his eyes, worked his way between tables to the corner reserved for Special Attention Quad. Mike Pisegna was gobbling food and everyone else was huddled over some joke.

He glanced back at the head table one last time (Herr Direktor was talking while Mrs. Aaby listened raptly), and just then the SAQ's broke into laughter. Kaspian jerked his head around, irritated—thinking they were laughing at *him*—but no one had even noticed he was there. He felt kind of invisible. It suited him.

HIS first activity block that day was Survival Skills, which he didn't mind. Hunter was off at Water Sports, which Kaspian understood you were supposed to like, but somehow swimming had never gone right for him; he could not get the breathing part down, and something about surrendering himself to the water—the whole-body embrace of it—made him feel helpless, panicky. If his stepmother had really wanted to scare him straight, back when he was still young and impressionable, she ought to have made Hell out to be someplace where, instead of toasting like a damned potato, you eternally drown. Kaspian had lived all his life in a place with long winters and the idea of an underworld full of fire had struck his childish mind as rather cozy. Plus there didn't seem to be too many rules there, as opposed to Heaven which sounded kind of regimented: everybody sitting around on this or that hand of the Father Almighty, et cetera.

But now it was too late because he no longer believed in any of that stuff. He no longer believed in anything.

Well . . . maybe something. Maybe like, the beauty of nature or something like that. If there was any nature left. For him, a believable Heaven would have to be a place with no construction industry. Which would pretty well blackball the congregation of Harborside Baptist Church. Kaspian could imagine the hereafter as a sort of post-Apocalyptic wasteland—only a beautiful waste-land: flowers blooming amid the rubble, like at the end of World War II. Kaspian knew more about World War II than he knew about anything else, having studied it avidly—not in school but on his own, reading and watching videos and doing his home-work in front of the History Channel—for the past year and a half. How he got onto this kick was a story in itself: starting with like, the eighty-seventh time he and Eli had rented *Austin Powers,* when one of them had gotten the bright idea to check out the actual original 007 movies, the ones from the 60's, so they could get more of the inside jokes. Which in turn had kindled an interest in other action/adventure roles played by Sean Connery, including that of Brigadier General Urquhart in a movie called *A Bridge Too Far.* This war story—a thrillingly tragic one—had somehow dug itself into Kaspian's brain to the extent that he sought out, at the town library, a copy of the book with the same title, by one Cornelius Ryan. Who also, as it developed, had written other books on related subjects. And *that,* as the saying goes, was the beginning of the end, where Kaspian's pre-War self was concerned.

The reason he liked Survival Skills, probably, was that he could connect it to this other, larger obsession of his. For exam-ple: when he was led blindfolded into the woods, and instructed to find his way back to camp using only a rough map and a compass, it was easy to imagine being a member of the 101st Airborne, stranded way outside his intended drop zone in the wooded countryside around Sainte-Mère-Église. And so forth.

Other things that they did in Survival Skills agreed with him also. Building fires without matches. Figuring out which wild plants were okay to eat. Keeping warm and dry using only the natural materials around you. Building snares to trap rabbits. He enjoyed such problems because they were definite, they were solvable. The process of solving them—defining the task, imagining possible approaches, choosing the best among them and pressing ahead with it—filled you with a comforting thought: the idea that this is how the world really is, and this is how you deal with it. The world is composed of a great number of problems that in their entirety seem bewildering, but when you take them one at a time you can actually grasp and solve each one in turn. It was a wonderful idea, and Kaspian knew it was bullshit. Yet he enjoyed Survival Skills anyway, just like he enjoyed military strategy games. For a time, the make-believe enemy is real, and for a time you can outsmart and outfight and outmaneuver him. It was cool. It was rewarding. He looked forward to it.

Today, they were scheduled to do a water-crossing scenario. You were trapped on the wrong side of a river (actually this would be just a wide spot of the same old stream) and your task was to get back across without dunking your vital cargo. The cargo was supposed to be antibiotics, needed by members of your party who had fallen sick. But before he could set out with his Jansport stuffed with drugs, Kaspian was summoned aside by the instructor, Mr. Snider, who whispered (as though it was a secret) that his mother had come to say good-bye.

"Stepmother," muttered Kaspian. He bet good-bye was not all she had come to say. But he merely shrugged out of his pack and followed Mr. Snider back to the cabin, where he found his stepmother at a table inside gripping a blue enameled coffee mug. She sat erect, on the edge of a bench smoothed over the years by hundreds of campers' backsides. Mr. Snider had built a fire in the big stone hearth, and the cabin was hot. Sun came in through a couple of windows, filtered by tall pines. Carol Deacon Aaby gave her stepson a selection from her menu of smiles— one that entailed a determined upward compression of the cheek muscles. It made her look as though she had just heard some joyous news that did not concern her personally and was bitter about it.

"Well," she greeted him.

He stood a couple of steps inside the room and let her look him up and down.

"I understand you've already met with this counselor," she said.

He exhaled and stared into the fire. "Not really *met* with."

Mrs. Aaby sipped her coffee, audibly. "I don't suppose you ever plan to tell us exactly what you *did* on this little outing of yours."

"I can't remember," Kaspian said—so readily that his stepmother shot a look at him, as though trying to catch him in a lie.

She was disappointed. Not because Kaspian was exactly telling the *truth*—he remembered *some* things, but nowhere near four days worth. And anyway, what he could remember made approximately zero sense, so what was the use in bringing it up? Except maybe to someone crazy like Malcolm Rugg; but Malcolm was back in Sinai Falls, and Kaspian was here. Acquiring skills.

His stepmother shook her head. "It's a shame in this world," she said. Not specifying what. Stepmotherhood in general, he guessed. Life during wartime. She went on: "Well. I hope this counseling does some good. I hope I'm not making a mistake about that."

Kaspian guessed she was, but not the kind she meant. "I don't think they're going to turn me into a Godless liberal fag," he said, which was kind of meant to be reassuring and kind of meant to annoy the shit out of her. Naturally she only got the second part.

"Why are you so intent," she said, "on *provoking* me?"

He didn't know, truly. Because she was so easy to provoke, he supposed. And because of the *kind* of stuff that got to her. He shrugged. "I don't see what you're making such a big deal about."

Carol Aaby sighed. She rotated her coffee cup between her hands, apparently unaware that she was doing so. Kaspian watched with interest. The cup was like a flywheel attached somehow to her brain, in which gears were revolving. At last she said, "You know, when your father died, I *swore* that I was going to raise you up to be a decent Christian person that he could be proud of. I knew it was going to be hard, with all the temptations out in the world nowadays. But I believed that with God's help, I could guide you through the valley and onto the path of righteousness. Now I just don't know. I don't know whether it's *me* who's failed, or whether it's just . . . maybe in these times, the Few who are chosen just have to stand by and watch the Many be lured astray. Maybe that's one of the trials we must endure. It's just so . . . so *hard* . . . to see it happen in your own *family*."

She was trembling slightly, as though ready to burst into tears. But her eyes were hard, and the trembling probably meant something else altogether: that she was angry, or that she feared her stepson, Kaspian the Lost, was about to rear up and strike her down.

It made him sick.

What he felt like saying was, *What's so fucking wrong with me?* (Screaming in her face, opening the valve on grievances that had been backing up in him for years.) *What the fuck have I done? I'm no worse than anybody else.*

But what he did instead was storm to the fireplace and violently kick a log, causing a storm of sparks to fly in all directions.

Fire and fucking brimstone, he thought.

"Oh, Kaspian." His stepmother had paled to the color of . . . of sackcloth, maybe, whatever that was. Again, though, there was something about her eyes that did not quite fit the rest of the picture. They moved from side to side, casing the floor, as though engaged in rapid calculation.

Then she looked up, straight at him. One possible interpretation of the look on her face is that it was one of *triumph*. She had, once again, given Kaspian the chance to show what an illtempered, ungrateful little wretch he was; and he had taken it. He felt like kicking himself. Or his stepmother. Instead he kicked another log, but his heart wasn't in it.

"I'm going now, Kaspian," Carol Deacon Aaby said. She put her mug down on the table and tucked her purse under her arm and strode to the door. He knew she would not leave with-

out a parting shot and she did not. Turning at the threshold, she
said, "I don't know when we'll see each other again. We'll have
to think about what to do with you between the end of camp
and the new school year. I hope you'll write home now and
then. Your sister NoElle sends her love."

Kaspian wondered, for an instant, whether his stepmother
had ever done any high school drama. It was amazing how little
he knew about her, really. Which of course made it mutual.

He stared out the window at a patch of ground where sunlight lay among pine needles and lambkill until his stepmother
let herself out, and vanished.

A fat, aged red oak tree hulked beside the stream near the widest
spot. From the opposite bank, Kaspian chose a small, nearly
round stone and tied one end of a rope to it, winding this around
and around until it made a nylon ball with a weight in the
center: a monkey's fist. He hurled this across the stream and into
the oak tree, where it wedged in the crotch between two limbs.
Then he tied the other end to a spruce on the near side and
headed across, upside down, hand over hand. He figured this
ought to work.

But the monkey's fist came apart, and the rope gave way a
few inches at a time. Kaspian ended up on his back in the water,
which was cold but not very deep. The lifesaving antibiotic in
his Jansport got soaked, so he guessed the ailing members of his
party were doomed.

That's how it goes, he thought.

"IT'S called passive-aggressive behavior," Thera Boot told him,
cheerfully. "Have you heard that term before?"

Kaspian had not. He stared at a poster of Nick Cave, the
singer and novelist, on the wall of her office, which was in one
of the newer cabins up around the water tower. Nick Cave had
been photographed from a low angle, standing in an elevator
that looked too small for him, holding a book in one hand while

the other fingered a red button all the way down at the bottom. The button was labeled H.

Kaspian had seen this kind of thing before—rock & roll posters taped up behind the desks of high school guidance counselors, so you'd think they were oh so cool. Somehow, though, this did not have the same look about it. For one thing, Ms. Boot did not seem the type to want, or need, to fake it. For another thing . . . *Nick Cave?* I mean, come on, thought Kaspian. Nick Cave is not so much cool as, what—pathological. *Nobody* listens to Nick Cave. The message here was totally different. Kaspian did not know what the message was.

"I don't think so," he said. "I don't think I've ever heard that term before."

Thera Boot nodded pleasantly. "Passive-aggressive behavior is a tool or a modality used by those who perceive themselves to be weak, as a means of getting back at those whom they perceive to be powerful. Understand?"

"I think so," said Kaspian, lying. "Yeah."

"Let me give you an example." Mr. Boot leaned back. She did not use an ordinary desk, but rather a long trestle table, with neat stacks of various things here and there, and a lot of empty space between them. Kaspian sat in a canvas deck chair across from her, far enough back to see her legs stretched out confidently underneath. "Suppose a boss gives one of his workers an order to sweep the office. And suppose the boss does this in a disrespectful manner, in front of other employees, so that the worker feels humiliated. The worker knows that he cannot respond aggressively—he cannot shout back at the boss or refuse to sweep the room. So he responds in the way we call *passive*-aggressive. Perhaps he deliberately sweeps some trash under the boss's desk. Or perhaps, when he's standing by the desk, he covertly brushes against it in such a way that important papers fall into the wastebasket."

"Cool," said Kaspian.

She looked at him. For as long as it takes to blink, then refocus, there was something in her expression besides, or behind, the smile. It passed. "In this way," she went on, "the worker has gotten back at the boss. He has, in his own mind, by his own method of calculation, evened the balance between them. This is his strategy for coping with what he perceives to be the fundamental injustices of his life."

Kaspian got what she was telling him. That his attitude toward his stepmother—seldom openly defying her, and yet failing to cooperate at every opportunity—was a sneaky kind of defiance, in its own right. He was partly pleased and partly abashed to find out there was an official term for it.

Thera Boot leaned forward in her chair.

"So we understand each other a little," she said, grabbing his gaze and not letting go of it with her frank, ice-blue, weirdly intense eyes. "Am I right?"

Kaspian squirmed, which he noticed and did not like. He tried to turn it into a shrug. "I don't know," he said. "I guess. A little."

Personally, he had listened to a few Nick Cave tunes on the sound track from some movie, a confusing movie about angels— he rented it because it had been shot in Berlin—and they sounded to him like something out of a D.A.R.E. presentation: proof of the dire effects of hard-core drug use.

"Good," said Ms. Boot. "I hope so."

She was not pretty. Kaspian's stepsister NoElle was pretty— everyone said so—and Ms. Boot was not like that at all. He guessed she was about 35 and her skin was flawed, slightly pocked from acne, saggy under the chin, unevenly colored. Her lips were narrow and her nose was just, like, there. Even the eyes, apart from their strange gleam, were nothing to squeeze your joystick over. For some reason, though, when you looked into her face you saw and yet you did not register these things. The face as a whole made an impression that did not seem to arise from the raw ingredients it was made of.

He fidgeted in the canvas chair, tried to keep himself still, fidgeted some more anyway.

Ms. Boot affected not to notice. She looked up at the window, maybe checking to make sure it was open. The afternoon had gotten quite warm. Defensive Firearms ran from 1:00 to

3:00, followed by Effective Study Skills. Kaspian could stand to miss both of them. It was nice and breezy in here and there were more painful things to do than look at Ms. Boot's legs. So far it seemed that she had spoken honestly when she said she just wanted the two of them to have a little talk.

"The problem is," Thera Boot said, "a coping modality based on passive-aggressive behavior is guaranteed to get you nowhere. You might cause the boss some problems, and you might have the satisfaction of seeing him get frustrated and knowing you've gotten away with something. But that's the full extent of it. That's all the reward life has to offer you. You'll never *be* the boss, and tell someone *else* to sweep the office. You'll never progress, never advance, never conquer. All you can hope to do is to resist, to obstruct—and even that is probably going to fail you in the long run. People will wise up to you. Passive-aggressive behavior is *sneaky* behavior, and sneaking only works until you get caught."

She watched him with a neutral expression. He knew she was examining him, the way he was taking it. He guessed there was no hope of staying blank. She would take the blankness to mean something; there probably was a psychological word for it.

"What are you thinking about?" she asked him suddenly.

He made something up: "I guess . . . what's the point."

She seemed pleased with this answer. It beat Kaspian why. He decided to go ahead and press it, anyway.

"I mean—what if maybe the guy doesn't *want* to be the boss. He doesn't care about getting promoted. He doesn't *like* telling other people what to do. Like maybe, all he wants is to just, you know, hang on to this job till something better comes along. So then, wouldn't it just not matter to him? If he gets caught, he gets fired, then he just gets another crappy job some-where else. You know? So what?"

Ms. Boot fixed him with those eyes. Her narrow lips did a little sideways thing as though she were going to smirk. Instead, after maybe three seconds, she leaned forward and lifted some-thing off her desk. A section of a newspaper, folded twice. She glanced up from it, then down, then up again.

"If that's the case," she said, "I have absolutely no sympathy for him."

She began reading the paper.

Kaspian could not believe it. Just like that, she was blowing him off. She was done with him.

He waited for her to say something else, to dismiss him, but she did not. She just read the newspaper, and when she got to the place where the article was continued on another page, she unfolded it and shook it out straight. Now Kaspian was invisible to her.

Finally he spoke. "You said you could write me out a blue slip."

She lowered just the top of the paper so that she could look at him. "They're over there," she said, indicating a corner of the long table. "They're already signed. You just fill in the date and time."

He moved down that way and, as soon as she straightened the paper out again, helped himself to seven or eight blue slips—a solid week of sanctioned fucking off.

"Thanks," he called to her from the doorway.

"De nada," she said, without looking. "Come back and chat again, if you feel like it."

"I will," he said, pretty sure that he was lying.

HE woke up sometime past the middle of the night and lay there rocking slightly in his hammock, breathing hard. His skin burned from mosquito bites that he had scratched without knowing it, without knowing anything. The moon was caught up in the tops of rangy evergreens. Kaspian blinked in confusion for half a minute or so, then raked his fingernails up and down his limbs, indulging himself in a frenzy of scratching.

The hammock was strung outside between a pine tree and a post of the cabin he shared with Hunter and Ricky and Mike. Hunter lay in a hammock nearby, a slender cocoon in the moonlight. Kaspian could not remember what had woken him up.

Something must have. He was normally a pretty dependable sleeper, especially in the hours approaching dawn.

It seemed to him that he might have had a dream. The dream might have left him a little shaken up, so that this mood he was in now was really the dream-mood, cut loose from all memory of what had triggered it.

The night was still: breathless. It had not cooled off. He could smell his own body. There was fresh sweat and stale underwear and armpits and, oh fuck, what is this? Kaspian slid his fingers under his waistband and they came up sticky and fragrant, a thick smell like ailanthus flowers. He wiped them on his t-shirt.

He sat up, turning sideways in the hammock, dangling his legs over.

The dream was half gone and half still with him. Not as a memory but as a mood, a state of consciousness. It was something like the way you feel when you break some old treasured object of childhood that you haven't actually played with for several years now. A piercing yet somewhat pointless sense of grief. Desolation lite.

Kaspian slid down from the hammock and wandered away from the cabin like a sleepwalker, restless but lacking a destination, and eventually found his way out onto the sandy, beaten-down athletic field. Maybe the extra space would give him perspective.

There were the usual million stars, gleaming emptily. The air was hushed and tartly scented of balsam fir. In the midst of all that cosmic perfection, Kaspian felt cruddy and hot. His clothes were damp with assorted bodily fluids. Woodenly he tugged himself free of them. The air against his naked skin felt good, but no cooler. And it made his bites itch worse.

You cannot win, he understood.

He supposed this was one of those lessons his stepmother had sent him here to learn.

He rolled his clothes up into a ball, which he lobbed back toward the cabin. He guessed it was as good a time as any for a shower.

The camp was all in shadow, except for a distant Coke machine in a shingled shed, which glowed eerily, white and red, like some glimmer of a far-off, feel-good Otherworld. But darkness was fine with Kaspian: he felt safely invisible, and the moon gave off enough light to let him find his way into the communal wash-up building. This had no electricity but plenty of water, gravity-fed from a cistern and heated in 55-gallon drums painted black up on the roof. On sunny days the water got about as hot as you could stand. He entered the stall and pulled the curtain behind him and he stood there for a long time, letting everything just run off.

He soaped down and rinsed off twice, even the hair. The hair would respond to this by transforming into a substance like steel wool; but Kaspian liked that. He thought it made him look bigger. He turned the water off and realized he had not thought to bring a towel, let alone a change of clothes. Now he was just out here clean and wet in his birthday suit. B.F.D., he supposed.

He stepped outside again. The moon was a notch higher. A breath of air so faint you'd never have noticed it, ordinarily, brushed past his skin and gave him a pleasurable shiver. His scrotum tightened up.

He considered his options. Going back to the hammock, that net of nightly torment, had no appeal for him. He felt his way into the cabin, retrieving his discarded clothes and transferring Ring Bear to the pocket of a clean pair of cutoffs. Then he slipped on a t-shirt that, because it was white, he could tell was the one with the frog. Kaspian had become interested in frogs after he heard they were dying off, apparently due to the intimacy with which they lived in a deteriorating environment. He felt fresh and comfortable with the soft clean clothes against his skin.

He was acutely awake. All his senses were so sharp that the nerve endings fired off random shots like edgy troops in a frontline O.P. He stepped back into the open and looked at the stars and wondered about nothing in particular, just sort of everything at once. What it was all about, whether it made any sense or was just a big accident, an expanding cloud of randomness. He wondered about things like God, distant galaxies, extraterrestrial

life. Angels and aliens. He was certain there was no Devil.
Minor-league demons, maybe. Evil mixed in everywhere with
the good. But no supreme Dark Lord, no Sargon or Satan; not
even many Hitlers. Just a bunch of Bormanns who were not so
much evil as they were malevolently stupid, plus Bohms who
were bullies, Speers who were ambitious, Goebbelses who were
fiendishly clever, and a supporting cast of storm troopers and
concentration camp guards—your basic orcs and trolls—who got
their rocks off kicking people around. Sick but not uncommon.

Then there were the good guys, but these were always off
at a certain distance: they flew over the North Sea at night to
bomb Berlin, then went back to their bases and dance halls.

Propelled by his thoughts, Kaspian ambled through the darkness with no destination in mind, and soon enough found himself
down by the stream, not far from the footbridge. Where it all
started. He could see the water gleaming in yellow moonlight.
Running and hiding. In a big hurry to get someplace else. Kaspian stepped onto the footbridge and walked out to the middle
of it and waited for something to happen. He tried to feel differently, even strained for it. He closed his eyes and tried to remember. Remember anything: that night, or the dream he had had
a little while ago, or the silence he had felt while sitting with
Malcolm in the chestnut grove. He wondered if he was making
any of this up; and if so, how much.

Not the reappearance of Ring Bear, that's for sure.

The funny thing that popped into his head then, for no
reason at all, was Weeb Eugley: the aviator glasses, the camo
vest. Memorized patter about AE2's. All very scientific. All presumably bogus. Kaspian wondered if he had kept the guy's card,
then he knew he had—he had slipped it into one of the side
pouches of his pack, along with his ChapStick and bug repellent
and three condoms he had been carrying around for about a year
now, basically for the hell of it. He wondered now if this was
nothing but a passive-aggressive gesture aimed at his stepmother.
He guessed he had secretly counted on her finding the condoms
and being shocked by it. The look on her face: you could just
see it. Kaspian smiled.

Being sneaky only works till you get caught, Ms. Boot had said. But what if getting caught is the whole idea?

He felt angry, thinking about Thera Boot. He suspected that she was playing some kind of game with him. He was pretty sure now that the whole scene in her office had been part of a complicated head-shrinking exercise—down to and including the handy pile of blue slips, there for the taking. Kaspian bet she had counted those slips, both before and after his visit, so as to calculate exactly *how* sneaky he would turn out to be.

The idea pissed him off. Also in some way it frightened him. Thinking of Thera Boot, those ice-blue eyes flashing unwholesomely, made him feel tiny and transparent and—Let's face it, old chap, he told himself in his Sean Connery voice—horny. Helplessly horny. And therefore madder than ever.

He left the footbridge. He didn't know what he had come here for. Whatever he had once experienced in this place, or imagined he had experienced, was gone now. As lost and gone as his dead father. He turned upstream and followed the path to where the trees thinned down to scattered clumps of alders, and where in the middle of a floodplain sat the dumb little chapel on stilts. The chapel seemed to hover, a green-black shadow adrift in open space.

He climbed the wooden steps, as steep as a ladder. When his weight came down on the porch, the whole structure shifted a bit, its beams adjusting. Inside the chapel, light and dark were reversed. The space under the pitched roof was utter blackness. But all around there were big windows and the moonlight oozing through them seemed oddly brighter here than it had outdoors. Kaspian made his way forward, between the half dozen benches, past the tiny altar, and behind that to the window seat with its foam pillow where the chaplain sat, if he wasn't occupied. It was the only comfortable place, a snug little nook beneath the only stained-glass window in the place, which looked to Kaspian like the summer project of some long-ago camper. It depicted St. Paul being struck by his big revelation, the blinding light from above. St. Paul looked like a cartoon superhero, an idiotic one, down on his butt shielding his eyes from what you couldn't help thinking was a UFO, emitting yellow paralyzing rays. Maybe Jesus was an alien, and all his miracles were just demonstrations of a fantastically superior technology.

Kaspian settled into the window seat and examined the window by moonlight. He guessed that the truth of everything is a mystery. Science tries to explain things and so does religion, but you get the idea that the explanations are just stories. Some guy has a big experience one day, a flash of light he can't explain, and the next thing you know he's dashing off letters to the Thessalonians. Another guy sees the same light and decides to major in Astronomy. But who's to say that either of them knows what he's talking about? Maybe the light was just fucking around with both of them.

It's strange, when you think about it. Probably lots of people have had experiences like St. Paul's, through the ages. Maybe even Kaspian's little outing was similar in certain respects. But most people would be content to keep quiet about it and just try to act normal and pretend it never happened. It takes an altogether higher-level kook to go around proclaiming that God has spoken to him, that he has seen the Light. Kaspian knew he personally was not up to it.

Anyway, God had never had dick to say to him. Even the angel-alien-girl had hardly opened her mouth. And when she did, she tended to repeat herself.

Thinking of the girl made a little bit of Kaspian's dream come back to him. It was like some window had opened in his head and this other view, out toward the dreamworld, became visible. It had been out there all along, waiting. Kaspian's eyes were wide-open and they were staring into that imaginal place.

There had been flying. A spread and flutter of wings. Bitter air in his nostrils, a stench of sulfur. Below, a great city, sprawling without limit, lit by firelight, across a sandy plain.

Berlin.

Kaspian drew a breath. He was remembering now. Or else the dream, of its own volition, was seeping back into him.

He remembered that he had been scared. And there had
been wailing

> *high like wind*
> *shrieking through trees.*

—Make it stop, he had asked someone. Help me down.
Please.

Someone must have heard, they were all around, the air was
full of them. But they did not answer him. And the wailing

> *passed through him like air*
> *through a net. Like a light-saber blade*
> *slicing the empty place*
> *where Obi-Wan has dematerialized.*

Stop dreaming this, Kaspian commanded himself. Stop remembering. Ever what the fuck is going on. And his dreaming
self pretended to obey, but only changed to a different shape, a
different way of imagining. As selves dreaming can do.

He tried to sit up in the window seat, to will himself back
to normal consciousness. But it was useless; the dream was pulling him in now. Through the stained glass, into the jagged ellipsis
of divine light. The mothership was beaming him up. And now

> *the angel came to him.*

She came out of the light—she might have *been* the light,
taking on another form—and she moved to him across a ground
of violent colors that might have been a cloud or might have
been a burning city. Her feet did not move. Kaspian lay curled
in the window seat . . . but no, not the window seat any longer.
He lay on a cold metal table. He lay curled up like a baby and
although his head was turned so that he could watch the girl-
angel approach he could not move otherwise; he was without
external feeling. His heart beat so fast it must be dangerous. His
terror existed like a creature apart from him, a being that had

tapped off all his strength. His face was covered with sweat but the air in the operating theater was cold and the sweat felt like condensation building up on the outside of a glass of ice water.

She told him he had no control in this place and he believed her. She spoke to him without speaking, drifting closer and closer. Her hair was the white of driftwood, aglow under a full moon. The night was the indigo ink of a moonlit sea. Kaspian smelled brine and ozone—odors of a storm sweeping the city clean, drowning its fires—and he closed his eyes and longed to pray. But prayer was not possible here. *She* controlled everything. The bottle of night enclosed him. Nothing could get in or out.

—What do you want? he asked her. What are you doing to me?

She came so near.

She hovered over him and looked down. Pityingly, he thought. But her eyes were not readable; her face was without expression.

This will not hurt, she said to him. Said without words.

Her face did not change. Her stare was unblinking.

Don't be afraid, she said.

—Okay, he said. Suffocating with terror.

Then he felt her hand

touching him

in the most intimate and sensitive of places. Stroking, holding, surrounding him. And his own breath hot and loud, her fingers soft and boneless, the energy that came off her flowing through him and his own life force pouring out. Commingling of fields. Fluids. Ether. Air. The girl's white teeth devouring him. Kaspian floating into her smile. The light within. The Light without.

Exploding.
Starburst.
Forgetting and
sleep.

IT was Walter Gilliland who got credit for catching him. He came into the little chapel and discovered Kaspian asleep—deeper than ordinary sleep, beyond reach of worldly stimuli—under the broken stained-glass window. Yellow and orange shards lay scattered over his face, his limbs, all around. Gilliland tried to rouse him (Kaspian would hear about this afterward, *in detail*) but after a while gave up and went to find Mr. Orrnyx. The two of them returned and, at Orrnyx's direction, Gilliland fetched water from the stream and dumped it over Kaspian's head. Even so, it took him a couple of minutes to return to something like waking consciousness. In the meantime he lay opening his eyes and closing them—for a long time there appeared to be no difference—until he noticed first the brilliant sunlight streaming through the empty space above his head, then two other people in the chapel. Finally the broken glass. He sat up.

"He appeared to be under the influence of drugs," Walter Gilliland testified an hour or so later, standing rigidly before Mr. Orrnyx's desk. "I shook him as hard as I could and he didn't even blink. *That* would explain why he can't seem to remember how the window just *happened* to get broken."

Mr. Orrnyx nodded absently, as though Walter Gilliland's opinions amounted to jack shit.

Kaspian muttered, "What do *you* know about the influence of drugs?"

"Enough, Mr. Aaby," Herr Direktor said resignedly.

Kaspian slumped back down in the hard wooden chair and gave Gilliland a treacly smile.

"It also would explain his *attitude* problem," Gilliland said.

"Thank you, Walter," said Mr. Orrnyx. He nodded toward the door. "I think I can handle things from here."

Walter Gilliland snapped to attention, started to leave and then paused. "I will get progress points for this, won't I?"

Orrnyx waved him off.

The door bumped shut. The camp director's office was strictly Adirondack—rustic this and rough-hewn that—ornamented only by such discreet appointments as a nautical clock of gleaming brass that chimed out the watches every half hour, a Craftsman table lamp, and a lithographed portrait of Jasper C. Winot, founder of American Youth Academies.

"Well, Mr. Aaby," Orrnyx said. "You certainly show a high degree of imagination in the variety of challenges you present to us. First it was a series of relatively minor infractions. Then, when those failed to gain you whatever it is you are seeking— is it merely attention?—we embarked on our little five-day outing. And now, to that list, we have added vandalism and unauthorized absence from morning formation. Where do we go from here, I wonder?"

"It was only four days," said Kaspian.

Herr Direktor cocked an eye. He shot Kaspian a look of irritation—barely a fissure in the mask, but something.

"Ms. Boot tells me you were less than cooperative in your session yesterday," he said, his tone perfectly flat.

"I didn't know it was a *session*," said Kaspian. "I thought we were just like, talking."

Mr. Orrnyx waved a hand—a signal, Kaspian guessed, that he did not wish to waste time quibbling. Whereas Kaspian had all the time in the world.

"Let's be square with each other." Herr Direktor leveled a gaze that was frank in its boredom. "I promised your stepmother that by the time you left ASAC, you'd be ready to buckle down and focus on your studies. I was hoping that, like most of our Special Attention campers, you'd respond over the course of

time to our standard program. Now I'm forced to conclude that
additional steps will be necessary. You seem to have some
agenda, perhaps related to your situation back home, I don't
know, that drives you to rebel against anything and everything,
even against those of us who are trying to help you. You leave
us no choice now but to customize a unique solution to meet
the needs of your own particular case."

He fell quiet and just stared at Kaspian for half a minute or
so, as though letting the import of his words sink in. The trouble
was, from where Kaspian sat, his words meant nothing. He just
cranked them out, like simulated speech from a computer. They
had no import at all and neither did Herr Direktor. In Kaspian's
mind, if nowhere else, the rules had changed.

"Starting today, Mr. Aaby, you will be assigned to galley
duty beginning 90 minutes prior to the start of every meal and
extending until cleanup is accomplished, at the discretion of the
Galley Chief. During the interim periods, if any, between mealtimes, you are to report to Ms. Boot's office for further assignment as she deems appropriate. This will be an *opportunity* for
you, Mr. Aaby, to take some strides toward gaining an understanding of yourself and your position in today's society. Should
you choose not to avail yourself of that opportunity, I'm sure
Ms. Boot will be able to suggest many other ways to occupy
your time. Mr. Gilliland has volunteered to, ah, *mentor* you. I'm
sure you can imagine what form that might take."

Kaspian was impressed by the crudeness of this. He would
have expected another 15 or 20 minutes of We Care About You
before the fist came down.

Well, live and learn.

"Can I go now?" he said.

Mr. Orrnyx flicked an eyelid. He seemed to have been looking forward to some kind of argument.

"There is also," he said, "the matter of reimbursing ASAC
for that window you broke."

Kaspian stood up. He couldn't take just sitting there anymore. "I didn't break it. I told you that."

Mr. Orrnyx shook his head. "Mr. Aaby"—with like, profound disappointment—"the window was broken. You were in the chapel alone. There is reason to believe you might have been under the influence of a controlled substance."

"I was *NOT.*"

Mr. Orrnyx leaned forward, the two forearms below his Banana Republic safari shirt, immaculately creased, coming to rest on burnished oak.

"I will not tolerate being treated with disrespect," he said—making a show of how calm he was.

"I DIDN'T BREAK THE FUCKING WINDOW," said Kaspian. And he felt his immediate future shatter with the finality of all that colored glass. The pieces of it fell around him.

Mr. Orrnyx smiled. "Very well," he said. "You have made everything perfectly clear now. I appreciate that."

Then he turned away. His chair swiveled and bobbed like the belly turret on a B-29. He was finished with Kaspian. His eyes were fixed on something outside the window. But just at the end, before Kaspian dragged himself out, he said in a voice that sounded almost cheerful, "You can tell that to the Marines."

WHY should they have believed him, though? Kaspian asked himself this—he had plenty of time, splooshing a mop around the galley floor—and the only honest answer was that they shouldn't have. Circumstantial evidence was the least of it. Every single thing about Kaspian—posture, attitude, disciplinary record, tone of voice, all the way through his so-called little outing—sent a consistent message to the world, and the message was, *I am a total fuckup.*

The estimated cost of replacing the window was set at $400, which Kaspian felt was a little steep.

On the other hand, maybe he *did* break the thing. It beat the hell out of him. Only, in that case, why were there no cuts on his hands? And why had the shattered glass fallen *inside* the chapel?

Nobody had thought of that. Even Kaspian had not thought of it at first, and now he guessed it didn't matter; he had given up

on trying to convince them of anything. They wouldn't listen; or
maybe it was that he no longer wanted to talk. Maybe he had
gotten comfortable with this big bad outlaw role he found himself cast in. Maybe he *liked* hanging out in the galley. If nothing
else, people tended to leave him alone now. He could kind of
appreciate the novelty of that.

HIS SAQ buddies, except Hunter Nye, were giving him a hard
time in ritual fashion as they passed down the chow line. It was
high noon on a hot day. Kaspian stood there behind steam trays
of instant mashed potatoes and soggy French-cut green beans,
holding a long-handled serving spoon and wearing a little white
cap and a kitchen apron that hung nearly to the floor. He felt
like a dork. Ricky Plaster said, "C-could I have some e-extra
gravy, please, mister?" though there was no gravy, and Mike
Pisegna winked at Kaspian and said how cute he looked in that
dress, meaning the apron. Hunter Nye smiled sympathetically in
his sideways fashion, glanced around to see who was watching,
and said, "Can you steal any of those ice cream bars or what?"

Kaspian guessed he could.

"I'm ditching Firearms," Hunter said. "I'm going to tell
them at the dispensary my stomach is upset. Meet me down by
the gatehouse if you get some time."

Kaspian nodded, and Hunter slouched off toward the table
in the corner. He walked in a cocky way, sort of pivoting at the
butt, that Kaspian had tried unsuccessfully to imitate. Maybe it
was a surfer thing, a method of locomotion especially suited to
lugging your stick across the sand. Kaspian did not admire
Hunter, nor wish to be like him, but he did envy Hunter's
absence of self-doubt. Hunter was a certain definite person in a
certain definite place. When he boasted, the way everybody
boasted, about girls, his words had a ring of authenticity. Once
he had said, about an older girl at camp, "I wouldn't fuck her
with *your* dick"—and Kaspian marveled at how it sounded so
believable, that Hunter was actually in a position to pick and
choose.

Kaspian's closest thing to a girlfriend had been somebody he met freshman year, Dee Dee Burger. They met backstage during a rehearsal for *Carousel,* in which Kaspian was an extra and Dee Dee was Billy Bigelow's little girl, the one that will never walk alone. The following summer, one year ago, Kaspian had ridden his bicycle daily to the Burgers' cottage at Lake Mahatowondoc, where they had taken boat rides and splashed in the water even though Kaspian could not actually swim. Dee Dee's bathing suits never seemed quite big enough and Kaspian felt as though he had spent hours staring at the one or two pubic hairs that always stuck out of them. He fantasized about floating up to her, under-water, and pulling the bottoms down. On the lake there was a shady inlet where they would dock the boat and make out, sheltered from view by low-hanging ash trees. He had gotten erections so hard and prolonged that his dick would be sore afterward, but kissing was as far as it ever got. Then the summer ended, and although he had thought he was in love with Dee Dee Burger and could not live without her, somehow when school got started he quit wanting to hang out with her. Anyway her parents hated him and she was actually, when your dick was soft, kind of a moron. So it was over without really having ended in any definite way or at a particular time. Kaspian had spent the whole year since wishing they could have gone ahead and had sex, nonetheless. Because then he would have *done* it, whereas now, as things stood, the whole thing had been sort of pointless and he felt rather stupid about it.

He was remembering Dee Dee Burger, thinking about other ways it might have gone, when Ms. Boot came down the line. She stood before him for several seconds while he stared (with that third eye, maybe) at Dee Dee's white thighs and the stretch of blue fabric between them. When he flashed on to Thera Boot he found her watching him in amusement, almost smirking. Though this was impossible, he felt certain that she had been reading his thoughts.

"What should I have?" she asked him.

He did not understand.

"Beans or potatoes?" She was smiling brightly at him, showing the edges of many teeth.

He blushed. He did not know why. Thera Boot's smile was nonchalant and girl-like. The ice in her blue eyes glinted under the fluorescent lights of the chow line. Today, instead of a staff uniform, she wore a loose-weave maize-colored blouse with her hair pulled back into a short ponytail. She looked, in Glassport parlance, like yacht trash.

"They both suck," he said. "I'd say the potatoes suck less."

She stuck her plate out. He gathered up a big scoop and plopped it on. She seemed to find this highly entertaining.

"It must be hot back there," she said.

Her eyes were saying something of their own. All he could think of by way of reply was, "Yeah, no kidding."

She glanced over him, up and down, as though checking for sweat. Checking for something. "Maybe you'll get a chance to cool off later."

"May be."

It was beyond him. Her attitude was almost flirtatious. Perhaps she was mocking him, the fix he was in, but it didn't really seem like that.

"Well if you do," she said, "why don't you drop by my office. All right? There's something I'd like to talk with you about."

She turned, swinging her food tray around fast. She glanced back just long enough to say, "See you, Kaspian." Like a prediction.

He was not sure whether the unanswered questions here made him feel like blowing her off, going down to the gatehouse and smoking cigarettes with Hunter Nye, or whether it made him more eager than he might have been to finish the cleanup, so he could stroll up to Ms. Boot's office near the water tower. For the rest of lunchtime and a while after that, he wondered which of these he was going to end up doing, and why.

HUNTER Nye said, "The way I look at it is, you probably were so happy to get out of here that it was kind of like getting drunk. You ever gotten drunk?"

Kaspian nodded. Then he shrugged. He had had some beers, which made him want to vomit. He had felt uncoordinated. He was not absolutely sure this qualified as getting drunk.

"You forget things," said Hunter. "The next morning, it's like none of it ever happened. Even the parts you do remember don't seem real. Probably it's like that when you get out of here for a while—you feel so good you sort of go crazy, then when you come back it's such a downer, like waking up with a hangover. Nothing you did when you were out there makes any sense."

"That's for sure," said Kaspian.

He had decided to tell Hunter the story of his little outing, to the extent that it was tellable. He figured that Hunter—being a surfer, and therefore very center-of-gravity-oriented—might provide a sort of ground wave on the reality graph.

"Okay," said Hunter, eyes averted rightward in thought, left hemisphere taking over the problem. "What *do* you remember?"

Kaspian narrowed his eyes so as to blur his vision, which failed to convey the sense of warped intensity he was trying to bring back into his mind, though it did make the blue patches of sky blur in a cool way with the backlit, jewel-green undersides of maple leaves. They were leaning back on the narrow stoop of an old building made of fieldstone. It lay on camp property, but at a distance from the main complex. Hunter and Kaspian called it the gatehouse because they couldn't figure out any other purpose it might have served. It served now only as a landmark in Survival Skills and a place for Hunter and Kaspian to lay low. The stone walls kept the place cool all day long. Hunter had declared, when Kaspian first led him down here, "This would be a great place to bring a chick." *Exactly* this attitude is what made Kaspian think Hunter would be just the person to confide in.

"The first thing I *remember*," he said, speaking slowly so as to get it straight in his own head first, "is waking up on that rock. I thought it was just like, the next morning. Then I found out it was *four days later*. But nothing had happened in between, it felt like."

"Yeah?" Hunter looked at him with a serious expression—not disbelieving, but cautious and attentive, like a detective. He wanted the facts; he wanted to get to the bottom of this. "No. You *have to* remember something."

"I do," said Kaspian. "But it's not like ordinary remembering. I don't know how to explain this. Things *come* to me. Into my head, like. Like I'm making them up. But I *couldn't* make anything like that up. No possible way. It was way too . . . too *big*. Too real. Realer than right now."

"Aha." Hunter picked up a stone and weighed it in his hand. "Realer than now. But not like ordinary remembering." He tossed the stone into the woods, listening while it whickered down. "Would you say it was like, a dream?"

"No. Well—maybe a little. There *were* some things screwed up about it. Like sort of, parts that don't fit together right, like something's been cut out in the middle. So when the next thing happens you think, whoa, what's *this* about, how'd *this* part get in here. You know what I mean?"

Hunter smiled sarcastically. "Did you consume any unfamiliar mushrooms there in the woods?"

"Ha, ha. No I did not. It was dark, I was just walking. That's what's weird: I wasn't doing *anything*."

"Why me, right?" Hunter flipped up his pack of cigarettes hard, so that a couple stuck out, and extracted one with his lips. A second one he handed to Kaspian. Camel Lights. Kaspian stared at the thing in his fingers until Hunter gave up and blew the match out.

Kaspian took a shallow drag, unaware until he did so that the Camel wasn't lit. Hunter laughed. Kaspian told him how he had stepped from the woods into the open field, that night. How the light had come. How he had felt that the light was aware of him.

"How?" asked Hunter.

"I don't know. I wasn't thinking like that. I was scared shitless. Among other things."

The fear came back to him now, strong enough to make him sweat. Yet he could not remember having made the slightest effort to turn around and get the hell out of there. He couldn't remember even thinking about it.

"Now see," said Kaspian. "That's one of the things that's screwed up. Because wouldn't you think a normal person would have at least *thought* about running?"

Hunter maintained a courteous silence: he failed to point out that they were not dealing here with a normal person.

The light had changed then—become fuller and more complicated—and Kaspian tried to describe this to Hunter. "Everything was spinning around," he said. The words meant nothing now, or they meant something slight and uninteresting. But at the time, this cognition « *everything spinning around* » had been cosmic in its seductiveness, its infinite power to draw you in.

"Then I saw my father. My father is dead. I *knew* he was dead, I wasn't losing my memory or anything. But there he was, spinning around with everything else. Dead. With this totally, like, just plain, how-ya-doing smile on his face. As if you were bumping into him at the grocery store. Only, dead."

"Okay," said Hunter, signaling T for time out. "I got the dead part. Was this recent? Are you still like, grieving over it? That would explain a lot."

"No it wouldn't. Besides, it happened a million years ago." Kaspian felt irritated though he was not sure why. "Actually, let's see, nine. Years ago. When I was six."

"Aha."

Hunter drew on the cigarette slowly and deeply, holding it between the thumb and finger like some kind of cool movie guy. Kaspian knew that if he tried this himself, it would look ridiculous; but for Hunter everything worked.

"Maybe the dad part doesn't mean anything, then," Hunter said. "Maybe you were filling that in."

"I was not filling anything in."

Hunter raised his hands. "Hey, okay."

"Okay."

Kaspian breathed in and out, wondering how crazy it sounded. How crazy it was. He looked across the overgrown pasture past the gatehouse, festive with purple loosestrife and

Queen Anne's lace, to the rusted cow fence that marked the boundary of Accelerated Skills Acquisition Camp. He looked hard at Hunter—because this was specifically the part he wanted to run the reality check on—and he said:

"Then, these three little men came out. They looked like leprechauns. Not *exactly,* but short and sort of costumey-looking, like that. And they took me down into this place where I met this, um, girl. In white."

In his mind, "girl" was bracketed by quotation marks, because he knew she was something else, really. He just did not know what.

Hunter heard him out, with no expression on his face. He flicked the remains of his cigarette dangerously into the yellow field grasses, wiped his hands on the skinny butt of his jeans, and said:

"I knew it."

Kaspian stared at him. "Knew what?"

"There had to be a girl involved."

"Well, actually she was . . ."

Hunter raised a hand. "Look—I'm sorry if this sounds mean, but—*of course* there was a fucking girl. Nobody would *buy* it if there was no girl."

Kaspian didn't get it. "That's not the point. Nobody's buying it *now.*"

"You are," said Hunter, "obviously." He punched Kaspian on the arm. "Okay, so: what *happened* with the girl?"

"I'm not exactly sure. See there are two separate parts, only they may or may not go together. One of them *might* have been only a dream." A particular, embarrassing kind of dream. He was not sure he wanted to get into that with Hunter. "Then suddenly I'm waking up and it's someplace else. And even though I have *no* idea where I am, I just *know* that like: I'm back. Ta-da!" Kaspian stuck his hands out, mocking theatricality, then dropping it. "I just wish I knew how it ended."

Hunter thought about this. "Maybe it's not over yet. Maybe it's still going on."

Kaspian started to ask what he meant, but Hunter narrowed his eyes and said:

"Yeah." This train of thought seemed to please him. "Maybe like, off in that other reality or whatever, time runs a different way because it's a whole different dimension—sideways to this one or some shit. And over there, it's all *still happening.* You're still there. Part of you. Only it's a part that nobody can see from *this* dimension."

Kaspian squinted, trying to imagine it. He could; but then again he couldn't. One objection was that no matter what might or might not be happening in some other dimension, things were the way they were in this one. So in the end you could just figure, So what? He said as much to Hunter.

"How do *you* know, Aaby?" Hunter poked a finger into his chest. "How the hell does anybody know what the true story is? How does anybody know there *is* a true story? Maybe it's all just . . . you know, one from Column A and one from Column B."

Kaspian rubbed his chest. He wondered what this thing was Hunter had about physical contact. He said, "I don't get it."

"I'm not sure I do either," admitted Hunter. Which made Kaspian trust him again.

"Here," Kaspian said. "There's one thing more." He dug into his pocket until his fingers touched Ring Bear. The little plastic toy was nose-up; you could feel the slight indenture of his mouth.

At the last moment, Kaspian decided Ring Bear was too personal to share. It came from someplace too far away or too deep, the cobwebby corners of his childhood. From a different pocket he pulled the business card he had been given by Weeb, the kook in camouflage. TRUST FOR GLOBAL READINESS.

"Here," he said, handing the card to Hunter, "you can have this. The guy claimed to be an expert."

Hunter examined the card minutely, as though checking for fibers. Then he stuck it in his own rear pocket, safe against his bony ass.

"Thanks, Aaby," he said. "I'll hang on to that."

As they were walking back, up the overgrown drive from the gatehouse, Kaspian said, "Don't tell anybody else about this. Okay?"

"Sure," said Hunter.

This sounded a little too casual to suit Kaspian. He stopped walking and stood there until Hunter stopped too and turned to look at him.

"Promise," Kaspian said sternly.

"Sure, I promise," said Hunter, with approximately the same degree of solemnity as before. "What's the big deal, anyhow?"

Kaspian couldn't begin to answer. One big deal was everything he did not know. The Mystery. Either what had happened to him was an event of profound, possibly divine significance, or . . . or else it was like some stupid hoax, a practical joke cooked up by . . . well, by who, though? Or *else* he was just crazy. In any case, it wasn't something to go blabbing about.

Kaspian was pretty sure already that people thought he was weird. Back in Glassport, his only friend had been Eli, a shrimpy science nerd. If word got out that he had been like, abducted by little green men—or worse, that he *believed* such a thing— the social consequences were too horrible to contemplate.

"Just keep it quiet," he told Hunter. "I'm trusting you."

HE slunk back to the chow hall only 15 minutes late for dinner prep. His job was to scrub a billion carrots and throw them into a giant pot filled with boiling water. It was while he was doing this—lost in the steam that rose from the pot, filling the galley like a hot cloud—that he had an idea what Hunter had meant about, How does anyone *know* there's a true story? He gazed into the steam and thought maybe there are many stories, or many versions of the story, the way there are a million remakes of *Dracula*. And none of them is the *real* story, in the sense of one-and-only; but some of them seem closer than others, and no matter how many versions you've seen it's always interesting to check another one out. Someday, you think, they'll get it exactly right. But really you know that's impossible.

★   ★   ★

AFTER chow-time, as part of his new, post-window-breaking
regime, Kaspian reported to the Data Lodge—a name he thought
was stupid—to click his way through the latest episode in an
interactive soap opera called *Hanging with Billy and Jamal*. The
software was proprietary stuff. While it loaded, the screen filled
with a wallpaper pattern composed of endless iterations of the
AYA logo—that *Y* like outstretched arms, beseeching a globular
mothership, *beam me up*—across which floated a quotation from
Jasper C. Winot, Founder and C.E.O.:

> "There is nothing anybody can do for me
> that I can't do better for myself."

Kaspian had watched the sign-on screen so many times now
that the words and the ratcheting sound of the hard disk and the
arresting black & red & white graphic evoked in him the visceral
sensation of having his brains sucked out.

A week had passed since his talk with Hunter at the gatehouse. Nothing seemed to have been affected by it. The two of
them goofed around as they had done before, traded vulgar comments, snuck a cigarette now and then. Kaspian had expected
Hunter to bring the matter up, but he had not. Maybe he was
thinking about it. Or maybe it had just settled into his head with
all the other crazy things people had told him along the line. It
is a strange world and everybody in it has got a story.

On the computer in the empty office, the two animated pals,
tan and medium brown, were discussing what to do with some
time off they had, lucky bastards. But before Kaspian could really
get into it, the door behind him opened and Thera Boot
strode in.

She stopped a pace away from Kaspian. He turned in his
chair to look up at her. On-screen, Jamal was saying how he
wanted to get down with some of his older brother's friends,
who were having a party. They gonna be *ladies* there, he exuber-
antly confided. Ms. Boot looked out of breath. Her face was on
the pink side. Some of her blond hair had escaped the barrette
and was limned by the ceiling light like dry grass. Her eyes

stretched wide, radiating intense but undifferentiated energy into the room, like so much white noise. Kaspian absorbed some of it; it tingled in his stomach. For a couple of seconds Ms. Boot said nothing, only gazed blankly at him.

"Is there like, something I should know?" he ventured to ask.

"You could say that." Ms. Boot returned to herself, though the eyes stayed much as before. "There's been quite an unexpected development. A *positive* development."

From the computer a smooth, newscaster-type voice said, "Now what would *you* do, if *you* were in Billy's shoes?"

Kaspian turned to check on what Jamal had gotten them into. Billy and Jamal took turns playing lead fuckup from one episode to the next, and sometimes their annoying friend Diego got into the act. On-screen, Kaspian saw Billy's troubled face, and beneath it a list of possible things to do, *Click on your choice*— go with Jamal to the party, tell him you've got too much homework, ha!, and various weaselly alternatives—but Ms. Boot broke it up.

"You can close that down for tonight. Tonight, we have something a little more interesting for you to do."

Kaspian sighed, as melodramatically as one of his role-playing amigos. He did not want to do anything interesting. He was perfectly content tagging along to Jamal's brother's party.

"Come along now," Thera Boot commanded him. "You've got a real experience in store. Mr. Winot *himself* has come to pay us a visit, and he wishes to speak *personally* with you."

It took Kaspian a moment to grasp who Mr. Winot was— he had never heard the name spoken aloud, and had imagined it might sound French. But no, it sounded as incorrect as it looked, like it had been misspelled on the birth certificate. Ms. Boot called to him again, louder this time, but Kaspian kept his eyes on the computer screen, gazing at Billy's troubled, dumb-ass face—which, with its freckles and bad haircut and other trappings of Average American Kidhood, not to mention its cartoonish expression of total bewilderment, bore a strange resemblance to Kaspian's own.

"Why does he want to talk to *me?*" he asked Ms. Boot.

She looked down at him with an expression he could not exactly place. It might be the look a proud country hausfrau on her way to the fair gives to a basket of killer tomatoes.

"We'll have to see how it goes," she told him, laying a hand on his shoulder—a hand that, Kaspian would have sworn, you could feel the blue sparks prickling out of. "But if I'm not mistaken, you're about to become a star."

As in the movies? wondered Kaspian.

> No: as in the sky:
> hot gas exploding
> into nothingness.

part 2
VIRGINIA

I went to the Garden of Love,
And saw what I had never seen:
A Chapel was built in the midst,
Where I used to play on the green.

And the gates of this Chapel were shut,
And Thou shalt not. writ over the door;
So I turn'd to the Garden of Love,
That so many sweet flowers bore,

And I saw it was filled with graves,
And tomb-stones where flowers should be:
And Priests in black gowns,
were walking their rounds,
And binding with briars, my joys & desires.

—William Blake, *The GARDEN of LOVE*

THE thing he would remember was the cars.

He had never seen so many cars, not even in Glassport at the height of tourist season. But what he would remember was not just the number of them, nor their newness—you hardly saw anyone driving a car more than three or four years old—nor the amazing speed at which they moved in their endless formations. What he found most remarkable of all was the vastness of the landscape that had been given over to them. It was as though the cars were some higher species, a unique breed whose requirements took precedence over those of humanity, so that the best and most beautiful lands were reserved for them, separated from the human pens by tall concrete sound barriers that were overgrown with honeysuckle and ivy, paved to a smoothness like that of perfect snow, soot-gray snow, and decorated with lights that gleamed even at midday, forming brilliant red and green X's—this lane open, that lane closed—and with signs that bore the names of places you could never see but only imagine somewhere behind the walls, past the long slow curve of the exit ramp. Falls Church. Vienna. Winchester. Fair Oaks. National Rifle Association. Centreville. Manassas National Battlefield Park. Strange names and somehow enchanted ones, exotic places where the people lived who drove the shiny cars, where they shopped and played with their children. Kaspian wondered what the kids were like, what language they spoke, what kind of clothes they wore. He wondered this even though he knew that all kids are alike, they spend their lives watching the same shows at the same time on identical TV sets. He did not understand how you could know this and yet still wonder, as he wondered again now, what kind of world this was that they had brought him to, what strange kind of people he would meet here. Would they think he was a dork, coming from some nowhere town in Maine? Would they even talk to him? Do the toilets flush the same way down here? Are there angels lurking in the woods? Or aliens? Are there any woods left to lurk in?

He supposed he would find out soon enough.

THE van ferrying Kaspian and a younger kid named Vernon, who had bunked in one of the other SAQ cabins, peeled off the interstate onto a highway with many lanes that appeared to go nowhere. They plugged along in heavy traffic through a desert of parking lots and strip malls and auto dealerships. After a couple of miles they turned onto another road with just as many lanes but no traffic at all. Here the land opened out a bit and you could see clusters of trees between office parks—oak trees mostly, taller and stouter than those in Maine. A mile down this second road the van braked and turned between two stone columns, on one of which a bronze plaque read AMERICAN YOUTH ACADEMIES and on the other, SUDLEY FIELD STUDIES CENTER. A winding driveway led them through a stand of trees to a shaded parking area. Kaspian glimpsed a swimming pool and a cluster of one-story buildings through elaborate land-scaping that featured azaleas and red-leaved barberries. A few stands of native cedar had been preserved, their wizened and rippled limbs giving the place a long-settled atmosphere.

The driver—a young black man who had spoken not one syllable—came around and opened the side panel. Kaspian stepped out, then Vernon, into a blast of Virginia sunlight, hot as a furnace. The air felt denser than anything Kaspian had ever tried to heave in and out of his lungs before. There were smells in it—decaying pine needles, the tang of smog—he wasn't accus-tomed to. When he turned to grab his pack out of the trunk, he found that the driver already had taken it, and Vernon's too, and was trudging away with them, down one of the many paths.

Vernon gave Kaspian a puzzled look, then smiled and shrugged, somewhat comically. He seemed like an okay kid, maybe twelve or thirteen. Kaspian thought of asking him some fellow-jailbird-type question—What're *you* in for?—but held back because the two of them had not really gotten to know each other on the flight down; then later, in the van, maybe because the driver wasn't talking, they had ridden in total silence. It felt weird now, being in this unfamiliar place together.

"Maybe we should follow him," Vernon said, staring up the path where the driver had gone. The black guy was lost from sight now, along with their luggage.

Kaspian looked the other direction, down the drive that led to the wide empty road. "Maybe we should just split."

Vernon glanced at him quickly, like checking to see if he was for real. The kid had red hair and a small nose that made him look like Opie on *Andy of Mayberry*.

Kaspian realized, then, why he had not wanted to talk to Vernon before, and why he was now coming off like such a hard-ass. It was because of Hunter. Hunter's betrayal.

THAT was exactly the word—*betrayal*—that had flashed in Kaspian's mind, when he figured out what must have happened. He did not especially want to think about it again now, but there was no way not to.

Thera Boot: she had been in on it. She had been, *must* have been, the driving force, both before and after she came striding into that empty office where Kaspian was hanging with Billy and Jamal, the cyber-fuckups. Ms. Boot had hustled Kaspian's butt out of there and across the Water Tower Quad to a small lodge with a big stone fireplace and a rack of moose antlers on the wall. And there, in rustic splendor, Jasper C. Winot, Founder and C.E.O., was holding court.

Around the lodge Kaspian recognized most of the Senior Staff types he knew—Orrnyx and Mr. Snider and the galley chief and a couple of others. The only kid present, besides Kaspian, was Vernon, who seemed already to have had his official audience, or whatever, because when Ms. Boot came in dragging Kaspian behind her, Jasper Winot nodded toward Vernon and said, "Thank you, son. It's been very informative." The kid gave Kaspian a nervous glance and went over to a stiff-backed chair, where he sat like a chastened puppy dog. Then Jasper Winot brought his full attention to bear upon Kaspian.

Winot was a runty little guy, round in the middle. He wore white chinos and a white denim shirt with cowboy-style trimmings, strung together with a bolo tie around the neck. He gnawed a cigar, knocking ash in the general direction of the big open hearth behind him. What hair he had was shaved down to a yellow-white stubble that looked abrasive to the touch. He sat not in a chair but on a wooden stool, the kind of thing you'd milk a cow on, probably. His back was erect and his chest puffed out but he was runty nonetheless.

Jasper Winot said, "And this would be . . ."

"This is Kaspian Aaby, sir," said Mr. Orrnyx. His voice sounded eager and weary, at once.

Thera Boot stepped forward and there was nothing tired about her at all. Her excited state, which had made her come off as flustered back in the office, now made her seem electrically alive. Her complexion looked better than usual by the glow of the fire. Kaspian remembered how attractive he had found her at first. She was still attractive, he guessed. She still had the legs. But he had begun to see other things about her as well.

Ms. Boot said, "This is one of our more *challenging* cases." As though the case in question was not standing close enough to bop her in the butt. "The subject, a 15-year-old male—"

"I can see he's a *male,* ma'am," said Jasper Winot. He chuckled and glanced around at Orrnyx, who gave him a pained and dutiful grin.

"The subject," continued Ms. Boot, stirred but not shaken, "came to us with an anecdotal history of intrafamily tension: early death of the mother followed by the father's remarriage, resulting in sibling rivalry with an older female from the stepmother's prior union. The father himself has been deceased for a number of years, and the subject consequently feels himself to occupy a second-class status within the household. This has both expressed itself through and been exacerbated by mounting difficulties in coping with the public school environment. Most recent grade completed, ten. This summer marks his first experience with ASAC or AYA. Since arriving, the subject has allied himself with a trouble-prone element and has repeatedly been found in violation of camp regulations, usually of a minor nature. However, immediately prior to my arrival, the subject absented himself for a period of five days—"

"Four," muttered Kaspian. "Damn it."

Jasper Winot glowered across the room at him, which was a little scary.

"—and when he *returned*," Ms. Boot went on, "he claimed to have no recollection of where he had been or how his time had been spent. A standard chemical-abuse screening was negative. No evidence was noted of physical injury. The family from whose home the subject finally reestablished contact was unable, or unwilling, to provide amplifying information."

Jasper Winot nodded. He leveled a gaze upon Kaspian. Pardner to pardner. "Where'd you run off to, son?" he asked, in a tone of voice so cordial you could have poured it on a waffle.

"The moon," said Kaspian. "It was really neat. They're still talking about Neil Armstrong up there."

"That'll be *enough*, Mr. Aaby," snapped Orrnyx.

"He has been unwilling to talk to *us*," Thera Boot said. "But to another *camper*, with whom he's on confidential terms, the subject related a long and very colorful story that included an incident of abduction by unknown, nonhuman entities, an encounter with a being whom he perceived to be the spirit of his biological father—deceased, as I mentioned—and a further encounter with a figure he describes as being quote, a girl in white, kind of like an angel."

She glanced aside at Kaspian with a smile. A cat smile. As though she expected, after that, to get stroked.

Jasper Winot opened his eyes. Really opened them now, as

though at last they had found something worth looking at. With a thumb and finger he rotated the cigar in his mouth like a propeller shaft.

"Kind of like an *angel*," he said.

Thera Boot—who Kaspian wished would just shut up—said, "I've compared his statement, as reported to us by the other camper, who is considered to be a reliable informant, with the available literature on this phenomenon. What I found was a remarkably high level of correlation with a pattern identified by Dr. Kenneth Ring at the University of Connecticut, who—while not passing judgment on the reality status of the reported, so-called abduction experience—has constructed a profile of what he terms the *encounter-prone personality*. Our subject's case history, as well as the results of psychometric screening here at ASAC, suggests a strong one-to-one correlation with Dr. Ring's indices of encounter-proneness, particularly in the area of family background and early childhood trauma. I want to stress, however, that my investigations to date have been strictly preliminary. Nonetheless the conclusions reached so far appear solidly based, and I'm confident that the subject would make an ideal candidate for the Model Remediation Program."

Kaspian stood there, slightly behind and to the left of Thera Boot. Despite his anger, he felt too dizzy with surprise to try anything like shoving her into the fire.

Jasper Winot was conferring, in quiet tones, pivoting on that cow stool, with the people around him—in particular with a nondescript man in a trim gray suit who had been standing all this while beneath the moose antlers, a shadowy place. He looked like an extra from *The Godfather,* one of those swarthy types in the b.g. waiting to kiss the capo's ring. As Winot spoke to him, the man dipped his head in a series of short nods, finally murmuring some response of which all Kaspian caught was, *"no doubt in my mind whatsoever."*

Winot said, "Good!" at his usual volume and turned to Orrnyx. "Parental authorization taken care of?"

Orrnyx said something but Kaspian didn't catch it. In his inner ear, the word *betrayal* was bleating like a car alarm, while in his mind's eye flashed the smirking face of Hunter Nye. Who had kept Kaspian's secret for maybe three or four days before blabbing it to Ms. *Boot* of all people.

Well, he thought, it's my own stupid fault. My fault for trusting him. For trusting anybody.

"Kaspian."

He clicked back to the present to find people looking at him: Mr. Winot among others. Ms. Boot had spoken his name.

Jasper Winot said, "Is this an aftereffect of his abduction?"

"No," said Mr. Orrnyx, "Kaspian is, um . . ."

Always like this. It didn't take a psychic.

Thera Boot murmured near Kaspian's ear: "Mr. Winot was just asking if you would be willing to tell us about your . . . encounter."

Kaspian looked around the room. The staff drones, the C.E.O., the snapping fire, the earthly remains of a moose. He tried to think rationally but in such an atmosphere it was not easy.

"I'd *mighty* like," Mr. Winot said, rotating his cigar, "to hear more about this *angel*."

Kaspian said, "She wasn't really an angel. I don't think."

A mistake, perhaps. Because once he had opened his mouth, he could never quite manage to shut it again. His tragic flaw. Now he supposed he might as well just tell them, let everybody hear it straight from him in its entirety—or its entirety minus Ring Bear, the only secret left—and not in pieces broken off and spun by Hunter Nye. Hunter the Horrible. Hunter his closest-thing-to-a-friend.

WHEN the younger kid, Vernon, suggested again that they go follow the black guy, it seemed to Kaspian that there was something anxious, something maybe plaintive in his voice. He turned and looked down into the Opie face and gradually came out of the trance he was in. He realized that Vernon was afraid to take a step up that path, or anywhere, without Kaspian along. The poor kid was alone here—well, they were both alone here, but

Vernon was only twelve or thirteen years old. He hung close to Kaspian the way a scared infantryman hangs close to a tank. Not usually your best move, because it's a bigger target and tends to draw fire. But still, you have to pity the poor little bastard.

"Okay," Kaspian said. "Let's figure out where our bags went. I've got some shit in there I can't afford to lose."

A little profanity goes a long way in these cases. Vernon bucked right up.

"Yeah," he said, trying to get his voice deep. "Me too."

They started up the path. Vernon fell into step and you could see him smiling, a tiny sideways smile. Kind of like Hunter's. Kaspian pressed his lips together. He did not want a sidekick. But by the time they reached the end of the path, where a low fence separated them from the swimming pool, perfect fake aquamarine in color, and Vernon drew a breath and said, *"Cooool,"* looking up at Kaspian like he needed some confirmation, even of this, it seemed kind of clear that he had acquired one.

THEY had come on a Sunday and Kaspian figured that's why no one was around. The black guy turned up, eventually, in a cinder-block building that appeared to be some kind of maintenance shed. Everything was painted the same colors: beige and money-green. The driver sat at a table with two other guys, also black but a few years older, and all three of them looked up at Vernon and Kaspian standing in the door.

"Left your bags over at the *intake* center," said the guy who had driven them from the airport—the first words they had heard him speak. "Gal working over there'll give you the keys to your rooms."

"We each get a room?" said Vernon, in Opie-like surprise.

The three black guys looked at him and at each other and they smiled.

"This is a first-class place," one of the older men said. "This is the *Sudley* Center. Mr. Winot *himself* stays here, sometimes."

Kaspian got the distinct idea that this was a joke, but he

could not tell what kind—a black joke, or a Virginia joke, or a
shit-job-employee-working-on-Sunday joke, or what.

The driver stood up. He was muscular but not very tall, and
his motions were deliberate. There must have been something
in the two boys' faces that made him feel sorry for them, because
he walked unhurriedly to the door and grabbed a ball cap off a
hook there and said, "You all come along with me."

Outside the cinder-block building he told them, "My name's
Ronald," then headed off without waiting to hear what theirs
were. Either he already knew or he didn't want to. Vernon
looked at Kaspian and gave his shrug and Opie smile again. They
followed Ronald through the compound, which was practically
a maze—low buildings tucked into the remnants of old woodland, with rolling fields in the middle and a web of brick-paved
walks tying everything together. You couldn't get a clear picture
of the size of the place, but it seemed to comprise at least a few
acres of what Kaspian imagined was primo real estate. As they
turned from one path onto a longer and straighter one, Ronald
told them:

"This used to be a club—sort of a private recreation spot.
Mr. Winot bought it lock, stock and barrel. Right here," pointing at the sidewalk, "this used to be the third *base* line."

Kaspian looked down. Ronald had a way of speaking with
emphasis but no particular expression, so you couldn't tell if he
felt one way or the other about this. The bricks in the sidewalk
were pretty new. They were laid in a herringbone pattern, and
no moss had crept in between them. Maybe this place had
stopped being a recreation spot not very long ago.

The intake center resembled a motel lobby. A blond-haired
girl maybe a year out of high school stood behind a counter and
appeared to be expecting them.

"You must be *Vernon* and *Kaspian*," she exclaimed, in an
amazing accent. "We were *wondering* about you two."

"Wonder no more," said Vernon, so quickly that Kaspian
guessed he must be quoting something. There are certain kids
who speak chiefly in quotations, from movies or whatever, and
Kaspian hoped Vernon was not one of them.

"You working hard?" Ronald asked the girl, whose name tag read Kaylla.

"Hardly working," she said. She had begun keying things into a terminal and didn't look up. Kaspian noticed his pack on the floor at the end of the counter, and went over to check it out, though in truth there was nothing that could have gotten broken, and little enough that he even cared about. He would have hated to lose the new t-shirt—the one from Inanna Rugg's house—but that was about it. Vernon came over to join him and it turned out that the kid owned a boom box, which had been jammed into a carry-on bag. Ronald stood around for a minute or so, then must have decided that nobody needed him for anything, because he turned and left. At the door he paused just long enough to say, "You all be good," which provoked an automatic laugh out of the girl.

"*Here* we go," she said finally. She slid two piles of objects across the counter at them. "Here are the keys to your rooms. And here is a map of the Sudley Center. And here is a booklet that contains useful information, including dormitory regulations and instructions for third-party billing of calls from the phone in the Student Lounge. Now this here is your orientation package, which you'll want to go over carefully, because it contains your schedules for the next week and also our Code of Honor. You'll find a copy of the Code posted as well on the back of your bathroom door. Please remember to study this because it's the single most important document you'll ever read here. Mr. Winot composed it personally himself."

She beamed at them. Kaspian scraped his orientation material into the open top of his pack. The room key jingled on its chain, secured to a large red plastic disk bearing the familiar logo. He motioned to Vernon and the two of them left without a word.

"Just go *right*," the girl was saying as the door pulled itself shut.

Kaspian turned left. He and Vernon walked into a field that sloped down to a small pond, not much more than an oval of cattails and muck. The edges of the pond were raw clay, reddish in color. The grass had been left to grow tall and coarse around it. Large insects buzzed through the stalks. Kaspian plopped himself down and learned that the ground here was a lot harder than the ground in Maine. There was little topsoil, just more of that clay, with cracks running through it where the sun had baked it dry. The afternoon was so hot it was like sitting in a sauna.

Vernon knelt beside him and stared at the little pond. After a while he said, "No frogs."

Kaspian heard the disappointment in his voice and felt badly for him.

"What did they send you here for?" he asked the kid, after all.

Vernon turned to him but kept his eyes lowered, concentrating. "I've got attention deficit disorder aggravated by a severe situational reaction to adolescence. When I hit puberty they had to change all my medications. And there's a *suspicion*," he said, raising his brows significantly, "that I'm bipolar. I've got a family history."

He ticked this off like he was proud of it; like it was something that gave him a sense of distinction or singularity.

Vernon pointed at Kaspian. "And *you've* got an encounter-prone personality, right? Plus a history of acute but not exceptional family problems."

"Ha," said Kaspian. "You got it, I guess."

"That's cool," said Vernon. Like he really meant it.

Kaspian stretched out on his back. The sun splattered ionizing particles all over his face. Insects he had never seen before zoomed over him. A stalk of some yellow wildflower, broken and dangling, hung lamely near his hand. Kaspian plucked it and brought it to his nose, but it only smelled like dust. Lying still, you could hear a windy roar of traffic not far away.

The pond had no frogs in it.

There was nothing good here at all.

"I am a sovereign individual and I am responsible only to myself, and to the Power that made me.

"My life and well-being are my responsibility and no one else's.

"There is nothing anybody can do for me that I can't do better for myself.

"Life is a serious business. Like any business, it can succeed or fail, prosper or go bankrupt. Whichever way it goes, the credit or the blame is all mine.

"I will talk straight and deal square with those both above and below me.

"If I am in trouble, it's up to me to get out. If I've got problems, I can't look to anyone else to solve them. If I'm lost, I'll keep going till I find my way.

"No one can hold me down or oppress me, because I have sovereign power over myself.

"The best time for me to do anything is now."

KASPIAN closed the bathroom door. He crossed the room, flopped on the single bed and took his shoes and socks off. His toes scratched the rough red wool blanket. The room was small and spartan but the air conditioning sure felt nice.

"I don't think I get it," said Vernon from over by the wardrobe, which stood open to reveal shelves stocked with neatly folded uniforms. "What's so important about that? What does it have to do with honor?"

Kaspian shrugged.

Vernon said, "I hope they don't make us memorize it."

Kaspian chuckled. The things this kid worried about.

"I wonder what kind of games are on here." Vernon opened the lid of the portable computer that sat on Kaspian's desk—the only thing there besides a banker's lamp. If this was a concentration camp, it was an unusual one. A *high-class* one, as Ronald's buddy had said. Vernon exclaimed, "Nothing! No games! Nothing but *educational* stuff."

He drummed his fingers on the desk, whose surface was protected by a glass plate, so you couldn't scratch your initials in it.

He said, "I wonder if there's anything on the one in my room."

Kaspian snapped, *"They're all a-fucking-like"*—which came out sounding meaner than he intended. It wasn't Vernon that was on his nerves. "Get a *clue*. The rooms are alike, the computers are alike, the uniforms are alike. *Everything* is alike. That's because we're such sovereign individuals we've all got to be treated like a bunch of little clones."

Vernon looked stung. "Oh—" His eyes fell to the computer screen. After a couple of moments, new light came into them. "Hey, you think there's a way to get *online?* We could *download* some games. Maybe there's an LAN and we can play Dark Forces."

Kaspian had never heard of this.

"It's like *Doom,* only in the Star Wars universe. You run around blasting imperial storm troopers."

"Sturmabteilung."

Vernon looked at him but said nothing.

"The S.A.," Kaspian told him. "Those were the real stormtroopers. They wore brown, though, not white."

"Oh." Vernon closed the computer. He looked disconsolate. The hard drive spun down and locked with a tiny click. "I guess I'll go get unpacked." He walked to the door and Kaspian was sure that he didn't really want to go, didn't want to be over in that chilly room all by himself, with only his boom box for company and a portable computer with no games on it. And one red blanket, and one standard allotment of gray-and-white uniforms. Vernon looked at Kaspian out of the side of one slitted eye, but Kaspian just didn't feel up to doing anything or saying anything to let Vernon know it would be okay to stick around.

As far as he was concerned, Vernon could do whatever he wanted to. It was his own damned sovereign life.

BREAKFAST was served restaurant-style, with no choice other than dairy or nondairy, by a young black woman whose name tag said Vonda. Kaspian showed up fifteen minutes past the appointed time, 7:10 A.M., on the schedule in his orientation packet. The other kids—23 of them, mostly boys—were already seated, four to a table, alike in their gray uniforms. Kaspian took the only chair that was left. Vernon sat across the room and smiled nervously in his direction but neither of them waved or anything.

Uncomfortable quietness was the order of the day. You heard silverware scraping on plates. There were no instructor types: only Vonda and a bunch of scrambled eggs. The dining room was decorated with sepia-tinted lithographs of Civil War incidents such as the battle of the *Monitor* vs. the *Merrimac*. Kaspian couldn't remember which was which or who won; it wasn't his war. The First Battle of Manassas was represented by "Stonewall" Jackson, Brig. Gen. C.S.A., staring flintily from a large white horse.

The three other kids at his table were mostly done eating and not inclined to talk. One of them, however, made introductions. This is Todd, that's Jeremy, over there is Brenton. Kaspian had forgotten these names and the faces that went with them even before he scraped the last bit of red jam out of the plastic pack and knocked down his orange juice and got out of there. He had decided firmly that he no longer wished to know more than was necessary about anyone. More to the point, he wished no one to know more than was necessary about him.

It was not clear yet how long he was going to spend down here—whether this was a permanent transfer or just a temporary gig, what was going to happen in the fall when the regular school year started, et cetera. He guessed it was up to his stepmother. But he did not intend to call her and ask. She would choose her time to communicate with him and that was fine. Until then, everything was provisional. He was committed to nothing, wholeheartedly.

A Welcome Aboard speech was given by the *Godfather* extra who had hung under the moose antlers whispering to Jasper Winot. Winot himself was nowhere to be seen. Who was to be seen— the very person Kaspian did not wish to see—was Thera Boot, sitting primly up at the front of the classroom along with half a dozen other grown-ups in nice professional clothing. Ms. Boot looked different than at ASAC. Kind of like a classy restaurant hostess now, Kaspian thought. Her hair had been fixed in a more formal way and she wore a black dress with prominent gold jewelry. *Dressed to kill* was a phrase that came to his mind, and although he wasn't sure precisely what this meant he thought it sounded right.

The *Godfather* guy introduced himself as Jason Aracos. "What we're embarking on here," he said, "is truly one of the most exciting experiments in all of American education today. And each of you is going to play an active role in it."

Vernon, a couple of desks away, rolled his eyes back, his mouth hanging slackly open: dead of boredom. Kaspian could not help but smile.

"You're not just students here," said Mr. Aracos. He managed to sound enthused and droidlike at the same time. "You're not just going to sit back and passively absorb depersonalized information. You are all *active collaborators* in a process that we call Individualized, Outcome-Assured, Unlimited-Expectation, Skills Advancement. Now let's take that one word at a time."

Kaspian could just *hear* those 23 other voices straining against their respective larynxes, desperately trying to say, *Let's not.* But Aracos was unclued. He turned to the whiteboard and began writing it down: one word at a time, exactly as he had threatened.

Thera Boot was staring. Right at Kaspian, right this second. She took her eyes away as soon as he looked at her, but he had seen it well enough.

What is *up* with her? he wondered. She uncrossed her legs and crossed them again the other way, and he could not keep himself from watching that.

To get his mind anywhere else, he turned sideways in his chair. The desk between him and Vernon was occupied by a girl, black-haired and sort of punkish looking. You could see piercings all around her ear but there were no rings in them. She wore little makeup except a tiny rim of black eye shadow—this might be where the punk look came from, plus the mown-down hair—and her skin was very pale, nearly white, like she never got any sun. Kaspian didn't think she was pretty, and did not want to get caught looking at her, so he twisted his head to scope out the rest of the room.

It was, he supposed, the classroom of tomorrow. Every desk had a USB cable, and some of the kids, having lugged the laptops from their rooms, were jacked into it. There was an oversized monitor up front and a number of smaller ones recessed into one side wall, plus a laser printer, a scanner, and a color Xerox machine. Totally Road Ahead. In place of your usual inspiring posters stuck on the walls, the wall monitors displayed an assortment of web sites of varying degrees of nerdulocity, such as a video record of somebody's effort to break the Guinness world record for number of living hamsters crammed into a biscuit tin, whatever that is. NO HAMSTERS WERE HARMED IN THE MAKING OF THIS SITE, dancing Java-enhanced graphics declared.

"When we use the term *individualized*," Jason Aracos told them, admiring his writing on the whiteboard, "we mean we have left behind forever the paradigm of the one-size-fits-all curriculum. When we say *outcome-assured* we mean that we are able to deploy a variety of proven learning modalities, and to insure that no student is left behind as we move forward on the leading edge of the educational wave. By *unlimited expectation* we mean that we remove the shackles of so-called classroom egalitarianism, the mentality that says no student is destined to rise far above any other. But the most important words of all are *skills* and *delivery*. Because we don't just promise to fill your heads with abstract knowledge. We promise instead to give you the mental power tools that will enable you to cut your way through the complexities of modern life in the real world, which I'm here to tell you can be a pretty tough place."

Aracos turned to face the room again. He took a few moments to move his eyes around, from one person to another. Kaspian exchanged a quick glance with the girl next to him. She did not smile.

"And what we promise," Aracos concluded, "we deliver."

The girl's lips moved, and Kaspian wondered what she had said. Some smart-ass rejoinder, he hoped.

Aracos introduced Thera Boot as the Director of Student Services. She stepped up to the small podium looking excited.

"I'll be meeting with each of you personally in the next few days," she said. "And I'll be asking you to fill out some forms and answer some questions, and you'll probably think it's all a waste of time."

She paused, as though expecting people to laugh at this. Aracos, seated now, smiled encouragingly.

"But let me explain one thing," Ms. Boot went on. Her tone and her expression grew serious. Kaspian thought this made her chin look smaller.

"What we are doing here," she told them, "is of the utmost importance, not just to you, and not just to American Youth Academies, but to the very future of education in this country. We're setting out to demonstrate that if you take the aggressive, problem-tackling philosophy that characterizes our most successful corporations, and you apply this mental attitude to the field of education, then you can raise the speed and quality of skills acquisition just as reliably, and as dramatically, as you can raise the level of profit on a balance sheet. We know this to be true because AYA is proving it every day in classrooms around the country. But there are still many who cling to old ways—who have not been privileged as we have to see this process at work. And of course there are vested special interests committed to preserving the outmoded mass-education paradigm. So our Chairman, Mr. Winot, has decided we need to offer compelling, *dramatic* proof that what we offer here is so *much* more powerful than anything in the chaotic, dissension-ridden public arena . . ."

She paused, as though lost in her own words. A couple of pieces of hair had come loose and she seemed to sense them dangling there; she ran her hands along the sides of her head, getting everything in place.

"You have been brought here," she told them, "you have been *selected,* I should say, from all parts of the country, precisely *because* you all, every one of you, have shown yourselves to be such challenging individuals—challenging at least within a conventional educational structure. Each of your cases is distinct—some of you have required extreme disciplinary intervention, while others have simply been unresponsive to a wide range of instructional techniques. Some of you have unique, um, therapeutic requirements. But what *all* of you represent is a cross section of that large and growing population of students who—in traditional schools, with ordinary teaching resources—are nearly one hundred percent guaranteed, as Mr. Winot puts it, to succeed in failing."

Kaspian looked around the room at the other kids slouching behind their desks with a new sense of appreciation. A whole roomful of losers. The finest money can buy. He knew about Vernon—that long diagnosis ending with maybe bipolar—but he wondered now about the rest of them. What were *they* here for? He wondered about the punkish dark-haired girl.

"Mr. Winot wants to prove, once and for all," said Thera Boot, "that the innovative methodologies being developed at AYA are so powerful, and so dependable, that they will succeed even in the case of a student population as . . . as *problematic* as any in the nation. And he wants to prove it *here,* close to the Nation's Capital, where crucial decisions are being made every day that will determine whether or not we as a society have the courage to embark on this exciting new voyage into the future of education—whether we will enlist the dynamism of the private sector in the task of educating our youth—or whether we will cling to an antiquated system that has failed and will *continue* to fail, as long as it is held hostage by politicians and entrenched interest groups."

Kaspian felt himself, unwillingly, sitting more upright at his desk. Thera Boot had this quality of pumping out vibes that you couldn't hide from. They filled the air and passed through the furniture, like invisible fields of electromagnetism around power lines. It made Kaspian uncomfortable to contemplate. He was squirming a bit, adjusting the way his pants fit around the crotch, at the *exact* moment when the girl beside him turned and looked at him. She looked first at the hand that was tugging at his uniform and then up at the rest of him.

Kaspian was too embarrassed even to acknowledge it by looking away, so he just stared back at her. His eyes were empty, or so he hoped.

The girl looked pretty blank herself. Her irises were gray amidst the black makeup and black eyebrows. Her skin was taut and smooth, and her arms seemed very long, tapering down to abnormally narrow wrists. The fingers were small and their nails had been bitten or broken off.

Girls wore a uniform here very similar to the one for boys. Instead of gray pants they got a skirt. The red tie was reduced to a ribbonlike affair, the same color and material. Even the shoes were identical. This uniform gave the dark-haired girl, who was still not pretty, a boyish look and a slightly haughty one. She jerked her head away finally without smiling, though *after* she had done so she gave a slight, twitchy nod—like a form of communication had passed between her and Kaspian, a silent agreement on some issue. Maybe that Thera Boot was not worth listening to. Maybe that any kid who was bad enough to get sent here couldn't be *totally* bad. Or maybe neither. Kaspian hardly knew any girls, and the ones he knew he had known all his life, so they hardly counted as *girls* in the sense that had lately risen to concern him—the sense that would be assumed, for instance, by Hunter Nye.

Welcoming Aboard proceeded. Each of the faculty members was introduced and had something to say. They sounded pretty much alike, though Kaspian felt that a couple were more benign than the others: a plump, light-skinned black man named Alphonso Crewe, who was in charge of Physical Development, and a soccer-mom type named Helen Craig, who ran Literacy Attainment.

For lack of anything else to do he tried to summon up a state of resentment at being tagged as a kid doomed inevitably to, quote, *fail to succeed,* unquote. It might be true and it might not, but the thing was that these people were not in a position to decide, because they hardly knew him. Ms. Boot had talked to him what, maybe four times? And she had given him a few role-playing scenarios to click around in, during which the computer no doubt recorded and classified his responses. Then suddenly, *voila:* she comes up with this "encounter-prone personality" thing. End of story.

He ought to feel angry, he supposed. Yet the more he thought it over, the less it bothered him. For one thing, as rash conclusions go, this one was kinder than a lot of what he got from his stepmother, being free of any reminder of what Jesus died for. Moreover, being tagged as an all-but-lost cause might turn out to be an advantage. Because now, any remotely non-boneheaded thing that he did or said would be taken as proof of the genius of AYA teaching methods, and the staff would be pleased with him.

Across the room Vernon was up to some furtive shit with Brenton, a crater-faced kid from Kaspian's breakfast table. They appeared to be exploring alternative uses for the networking cables.

Kaspian looked out the windows. These were high on the wall, giving a skewed vision of oak limbs with yellow-white sun on them. His thoughts drifted, as they always did sooner or later, to the memory of his little outing. He considered it half-mindedly, out of habit, the way a kid probes with his tongue the hole left where a tooth has come out. Kaspian touched lightly upon the memory and it did not hurt; it did not make his heart thump in panic; all it did was fill him with a puzzled and empty feeling, an ill-defined sense of loss.

That weird nighttime journey seemed very far away. It had

shifted around in his brain to someplace settled and abandoned. Compared to the bizarre, teeming, hard-edged landscape of northern Virginia, Kaspian's memory of a place like a giant indoor jungle, with fake-looking fruit hanging low on vines, and a girl who seemed to float beside him without moving her limbs, seemed like an okay deal by comparison. He remembered— though blurrily—moments of nightmare dread, but somehow that felt less real now, less of a threat to him, than this classroom presided over by boring people in business clothes who wanted to like, deliver an exciting pedagogical product.

He missed something that Jason Aracos, back at the podium, said. Suddenly around him everybody was in motion. The girl at the next desk was on her feet and looking down at him. She must have caught the zoned expression on his face, because she gave a funny quiet laugh. Then as Kaspian struggled to untangle himself from his chair, she stuck a hand out. The gesture was clear: he took the hand and she hoisted him to his feet.

"Is your name really KASPIAN?" she asked him, looking down at his name tag.

Kaspian did not answer but glanced at the girl's name tag. "Is your name really CHARITY?"

Around them people moved toward the door.

"What's going on?" Kaspian asked the girl, who was standing with her orientation packet held against her chest. Her feet were wide apart and Kaspian thought again that she looked boyish and . . . and *spunky,* like Pippi Longstocking.

"First break," she said. She opened her orientation packet and pointed at a tiny rectangle on the weekly schedule. "Seven minutes. Then we go to Opportunity Block 1."

Kaspian had not glanced at the schedule; he considered this a measure of personal integrity. He followed as the girl threaded her way between desks. The two of them were the only people left in the room.

"Do we all go to the same place?" he asked her.

She paused to regard him. "No-o," she said, her intonation rising toward the end of it, like a word in Chinese. "We follow our *Personal Action Plans.* Aren't you paying any attention at all?"

Kaspian said, "Not actually."

She flashed him an exaggerated, talk-show smile. "I've always admired that in a person." Then she stepped out into the hallway in a manner that made Kaspian think of the word *flounce*.

He did not really care for her attitude. He suspected that she might be destined to become his friend. He wondered whether, under the circumstances, this was advisable.

OUTSIDE, after the last Op Block of the day, Kaspian saw Ronald, the black guy who had driven him and Vernon from the airport. This afternoon, under a blazing sun, Ronald was steering a lawn mower around. He covered the sloping field in big swooshes, like a Stuka strafing the countryside. His shirt was off and tied loosely around his neck, and his skin was shiny as a sea stone with the tide splashing over it.

Kaspian waited for Ronald to notice him so he could wave. The air was so hazy that he doubted it was safe to fill your lungs with. After Ronald made another pass without acknowledging him, he turned up the walk and trudged toward the student lounge, where there was a soda machine.

The sidewalk took him past the swimming pool, through the older part of the complex where the buildings looked relatively cheap and unassuming. Ronald had said this used to be a recreation spot, and here you could believe that, among these no-nonsense structures of plywood and cinder block. Nobody but Kaspian seemed to be out of doors and you could not blame them. He walked by the utility building where the three guys had been hanging around the other night, but the door was closed. From a lumpy mound of old boxwood, a shrieking of sparrows arose.

Kaspian felt suddenly, senselessly, afraid. He did not know of what. Of nothing. Yet the bite of fear was so sharp, so unmistakable for anything else, that he took a step backwards, then another step, until the stiff branches of boxwood pressed against him from behind. He let his weight ease into them, so that the boxwood supported his upper body, yielding only a little, embracing him with those arms of tiny, strange-smelling leaves.

Right away, he heard footsteps coming up the sidewalk. Voices too: a man's and then a woman's, then the man's again. Kaspian felt certain the woman was Thera Boot. They were already so close that if he stepped away from the boxwood, into the middle of the sidewalk, it would be like he was lunging out at them. That would be too weird and he would have no explanation for it. He guessed he was more or less locked in to a strategy of keeping out of sight.

The inside of the boxwood was hollow, like a deep green tent. The ground underneath was naked and tramped down. Kaspian guessed he was not the first kid who had discovered you could hide in here. He settled onto his haunches while the footsteps and the voices passed by. And though he was not *trying* to listen—he was trying to hold still, that's all—there was no way not to overhear at least a little bit.

Ms. Boot said something about tracking the parameters. The man said "Yeah" a couple of times. He made a compound vowel out of it: yea-uh, yea-uh. His voice sounded impatient, like he wished Ms. Boot would cut right to the calf-toss. It was not hard to guess that this was Jasper C. Winot.

The footsteps paused, a little past Kaspian, and the man had a few things to say that Kaspian did not pay close attention to. His mind was busy with the possibly interesting fact of Ms. Boot and Mr. Winot talking alone together, in quiet voices, like conspirators, after Winot had kept himself out of the picture all day.

"I tell you," the Chairman said, "this is going to happen no matter what I have to do to *make* it happen. You follow what I'm saying?"

When Thera Boot answered, though her words were less distinct and Kaspian did not catch them all, he got the clear impression that she was sucking up. She said something like, "That's what you have to do in your position," emphasizing *you* and *your,* referring to Winot, in a way that Kaspian hoped he would remember clearly, because he had never heard her talk like this before. It made her sound kind of pathetic, and Kaspian thought he might enjoy thinking of her this way.

"The stakes are just too high," Winot said, "to have that damned Colonel distracting Ruby at a time like this. These committee hearings are going to be all-important for us. *All*-important, hear me? The whole darned legislative package is going to come off the rails if the hearings don't go well for us. We can kiss vouchering good-bye, at least for the current session. That's why we've got to protect Ruby's credibility. She may be a fanatic, but she's *our* fanatic. And the *last* thing we need is for her to open her mouth in open session about some damn Secret Brotherhood in the Skies or ever-what-the-Christ that fool has got her lathered up about."

Ms. Boot murmured something in a reassuring voice, and the two of them moved out of Kaspian's earshot.

When they were gone and he extracted himself from the boxwood—whose smaller parts turned out to be brittle, with a strong attraction to Kaspian's Velcro hair—he felt very much like an older version of Harriet the Spy. In other words, an idiot.

MANY things happened next but nothing in particular. There were classes and meetings and tests. Meals were edible. Kaspian got used to wearing the same clothes every day. A week passed and then another week, and by now it was Labor Day and other kids—regular students, Kaspian supposed, as opposed to Model Remediation types—began showing up. Jasper C. Winot vanished from sight again. Thera Boot kept to her office, calling in kids one at a time for Individualized Program Planning, an ordeal that evidently took a whole day. Kaspian's turn had not come yet.

On the first few evenings, after supper, Vernon came over to Kaspian's room, even though the two of them seldom had the same homework assignments. Kaspian would sit at his desk, not saying much, while the younger kid chattered and bounced around on the bed. After that, Vernon started spending more of his time with Brenton and some other guys from the West Coast.

They looked to Kaspian like stoners but he supposed that might be just the look. He made up his mind to feel relieved about not having Vernon, with all his restless energy, hanging out in his room every night.

Two things, maybe, qualified as noteworthy events during this period. The first was a call from his stepmother.

It came at an unusual hour, late enough that Kaspian was done with his homework and just hanging out, waiting for it to be bedtime. Mr. Crewe, the Physical Development teacher, came to tell him he had a call and he could take it in the student lounge. Kaspian was filled with a miserable sort of anticipation by the time he crossed from one building to the other and picked up the phone, an old heavy one from the Ma Bell era. He could hear a TV going at the other end, *The 700 Club*. They were doing a news wrap-up but you could still tell it was CBN because even the news had that tone of barely restrained indignation.

"Hello," he said, unhopefully.

"Kaspian!" his stepmother exclaimed. "How are you?"

The enthusiasm in her voice made him wince. The problem was, she could go from this extreme to some other one within the space of a sentence or two. If she would just settle down to a level of seminormalcy, it would be a lot easier to take.

"I'm okay," he said. He could hear already that his voice was coming out snide or sullen or some other teenage way. He tried to clamp down on it. "How are things back home?"

"Oh, you know how we are up here," she said, brightly. "The weather's simply been beautiful. You wouldn't believe how much traffic there's been through the village the past week. It's been ideal for the petition drive—so many people out on the sidewalks. In fact I saw your friend Eli a couple of days ago—that boy is always out there, in front of the library, isn't he? with all those other young so-and-so's. He said to tell you hello. And he asked whether you were coming home soon."

Kaspian waited. He hoped that his stepmother would answer this question, because it was something he wondered as well. Finally he said, "So what did you tell him?"

"I told him it all depends."

Her tone had changed. It had changed abruptly, as it tended to, and now sounded stern and even threatening. He knew this particular voice and hated it.

"Depends on what?"—he could not help asking even though he knew that she wanted him to, that she had set him up for it.

"It depends on what kind of reports I get from your teachers down there. Among other things."

"What other things?"

"You know what I'm talking about."

Usually he did—he prided himself on his ability to see through her like the glass of a television screen—but now he wasn't sure. He frowned at the telephone. "No. What *are* you talking about?"

She drew a breath in, hissingly, like she was sucking it through the fiber-optic line.

"I'm looking for a *sign*," she said. "Not just words, but factual evidence. That you've had a real change of heart. That you're willing to *work,* for a change, at bettering yourself. You know, we're put on this Earth for but a short time, and it's up to us to make the most of it. The Lord can't do it for us."

"Sure He can," said Kaspian. "He's all-powerful, right? He can do anything he wants to."

He knew this was goading her and that he would pay for it. But it was a reasonable point, wasn't it? And anyway he was only talking. He thought that on the telephone that is what you're supposed to do.

"Oh, Kaspian, Kaspian." Her voice had the cheesy sound of an actress overdoing it, like in one of those Charlton Heston movies. Oh, Moses, Moses! "You know, since your father died, I've done everything I could—*everything*—to raise you the right way, into an honest decent person. And all I've ever gotten in return has been back-talk and rebellion. You simply refuse to do what anybody else does, to just fit in and get along. You've got to be *different*. You've got to stick out. It makes me so *evil*."

This was an expression of hers. It meant something like, so

consumed by righteous rage that she could not be held accountable.

"Well, gosh," said Kaspian, "if you're so evil, then you don't have a whole lot of room to talk, do you?"

Why was he doing this, poking her right in the sore spots? He didn't know—it was just something he did.

"Now you *listen to me,* young man. It's costing me a lot of money to send you down there, even taking into account the scholarship."

"I've got a scholarship?" said Kaspian. "Hey, wow."

"It's not an *academic* scholarship, I can tell you that. It's based strictly on financial need, since this so-called great country of ours does not make it easy for working parents to send their children to the school of their choice. Not *yet.* Though that's going to change, let me tell you."

"Maybe you should start another petition," said Kaspian. "When you get done with the fag-bashing campaign."

"Don't use that kind of tongue with *me.* And for your information, I have every *intention* to. It's important to keep our coalition together. *However,* that's not what I called to talk to you about."

"I figured."

"What? You said it figures? Well, let me tell *you* what figures, young man."

The conversation lurched on, from bad to really bad, until finally Kaspian just laid the phone down and walked away from it. There were other kids in the lounge now and they looked at the telephone that still had his stepmother's voice coming out of it. He left the building and stepped outside, where the evening sky was clouding over and a dull breeze was coming up from the southwest, following the line of the Blue Ridge Mountains. Back home it would already be autumn now, but down here it seemed like summer was never going to stop.

Beyond a certain point, Kaspian thought, nothing his stepmother said to him had a noticeable effect. You reach a level of saturation, and everything after that just washes over the top. It was like the two of them just slipped into roles that had become familiar and even perversely comfortable, speaking lines they both could have delivered in their sleep. Someday maybe one of them would do something really surprising—pull out a secret weapon, like, and finish the other one off. Until then, it was same-o same-o.

None of which prevented Kaspian from feeling so disheartened that he walked out into the field, sat down with his knees drawn up, and lowered his head onto them. After a while he pulled Ring Bear out of his pocket, and the two of them hung there together in the heavy Virginia evening. Which was stupid and childish, he knew, but still did not feel the same as being alone.

THE second noteworthy thing that happened during those first weeks was not an event, actually. It was the girl.

Her name *was* Charity. Truly: Charity Ann Laird. It was a funny name because it was full of short *a*'s—just like Kaspian Anders Aaby. The two of them kind of bonded over that, laughing about it even after there was nothing novel or amusing anymore. Laughing because it came as a relief.

Her eyes were such a strange color: pale gray, not at all what you expected with her very dark hair. The hair was as short as Kaspian's but with none of the curl; instead it jutted out straight this way and that, leaving exposed her narrow, swan-white neck. Her arms were so long and thin, the wrists and fingers so breakable-looking, that those were the things he stared at. He was not sure whether it was a sexual thing. He believed that sexual things usually concerned themselves with other parts of the body. But while there was nothing wrong with the other parts of Charity's body (the phrase *Charity's body* gave him a particular feeling which *was,* he was pretty sure, a sexual thing), he did not feel inclined to stare at them. He guessed he would figure all this out as he went along.

They did not spend a lot of time together. They had three Op Blocks in common, two on Tuesdays and Thursdays and one on the other days. The weekend portion of Kaspian's PAP was devoted chiefly to outdoor activities, most of which were boys-only. So it came down to free periods and personal time, of which neither of them had a great amount.

Anyway, he did not know what he was doing or what he was feeling, truly. It got to be easy, though, after that first day, to sort of drift over to where Charity was, and just kind of *be* there. Usually she had some remark to make. Kaspian said little himself, but she didn't seem to mind. She was the kind of person who touched you at times—on the arm, or with her elbow, or anything—just as part of interacting with you. Kaspian had not known many people like this; it was the opposite of how his family acted. At first he was surprised but soon he got used to it. He noticed that she did it with other people, too, not just him. He noticed his own disappointment in that.

They did a couple of minor things together. He showed her the small pond that had nearly dried up. They scrunched down among the cattails trying to find frogs there and to identify insects. Charity told him she came from Glen Burnie, Maryland, not far from here, but that she hated Virginia. He told her he came from Maine and hated Virginia too, at least what he had seen of it.

"It's very 60's here," she said. Her head gave a twitch sideways, as though she were tossing her little bit of hair. He didn't know what she meant. His expression must have showed that. "Technicolor," she said, sweeping an arm out, taking in wide horizons, "but bleached out a little. You know, *Lawrence of Arabia. Some Like It Hot.*"

Her spine was straight as a rifle barrel. But her eyes had something small and almost pleading about them. Like she knew her opinions were smart, but she *really* wanted him to agree with her.

"The 60's aren't actually my decade," Kaspian said. Then he was about to tell her that the 40's were, and about the WWII thing. Only she smiled too fast and declared, "Then Virginia's not your state." Blinking in sort of a dumb way, like the words had jumped out accidentally.

He laughed: she surprised him.

On a Sunday afternoon they played tennis. Kaspian had hardly ever held a racket in his life and she creamed him, even though she complained about how shitty the equipment was. The balls were worn and flat. She showed him how to bounce a ball on the face of the racket, which strengthens your wrist. While he did that, counting the bounces, she slammed serves into a concrete wall with a stripe painted at net level. She half-hummed and half-chanted a song that he didn't recognize.

It felt a lot different than being with Dee Dee Burger, his onetime sort-of girlfriend. With Dee Dee, the situation had been pretty unambiguous. It had all been focused, like sunlight through a magnifying glass, on making out in the boat. With Charity, there seemed to be no focus at all. There was this space between them that was basically vacant, and they watched each other across it—they *touched* each other across it—but neither moved in to occupy it, and Kaspian guessed that was fine. It felt fine. But it felt uncertain, too. He worried that there might be something he didn't get.

Now and then a day would pass without them talking or spending time together at all, except for sitting near each other in class. On those days Kaspian would watch her—careful not to get caught doing so—studying the tiny hairs on the back of her neck, her bare forearms, her nervous fingers tapping the desk, and he would wonder again what she was here for. Or to put it another way, what was the matter with her. She must be a problem kid in some respect, to have been *selected,* as Thera Boot said, for this program. But she didn't seem that way. She seemed like a pretty good student who was just bored or directionless. She had a peculiar sense of humor, and a certain twitchy quality, but everything seemed safely within the big lump in the middle of the bell curve. He supposed he could just ask her, except that the times when he was thinking about this were times that she seemed disinclined to talk. When she felt like talking he didn't feel like thinking anymore.

He decided that this was not going to bother him. He decided that everything that kept them apart was good—it was good because it left them both safe, unexposed to emotional risk—and that everything that brought them together was good, too. The situation was a no-loser.

He should have recognized this as the flashing neon danger signal that it was.

THE Sudley Center grounds were crowded now, in the first weeks of September, or at any rate they seemed so after the emptiness of August. Most of the newly arrived kids were younger than Kaspian, K-through-8-aged. They seemed, on the whole, to know their way around, though now and then one of the lost ones would come up and ask Kaspian for directions. Get them while they're young, he thought. Something about the way they all looked—from one of the higher spots you could gaze across the rolling grounds and see them by the dozens, each wearing his or her gray-and-white Jack & Jill costume with the bright red tie: like a Mr. Rogers neighborhood version of *Hitlerjugend,* outdoorsy little pricks—made Kaspian feel not so much sorry for them as worried about what they were going to be when they grew up. Either hell-raisers or robots, he guessed.

And yet in a certain way he was one of them. Right down to the red tie. He ought to be asking these things of himself.

His turn with Ms. Boot for Individualized Program Planning came when he wasn't prepared for it. Not that he ever would have been; but the day in question was the coolest one so far, only in the 60's, with a vigorous breeze down from Pennsylvania, and Kaspian could almost imagine what autumn might be like down here, if autumn ever happened. It felt wrong in every way you could think of to spend a day like this sitting across a table from Thera Boot, trying not to let those unwholesome eyes get ahold of you. But the little gopher who found him at the chow hall and handed him the square of blue paper turned and left before he could come up with any excuse to send back, so he guessed he was caught.

He never sat with Charity in the dining room—the thing between them seemed out-of-context there—but usually he positioned himself so that he could look at her, anyway. Now as he crumpled the blue paper, which said to report for testing by 8:00 A.M., and raised his head to check the clock, which said 7:43, he happened to lock eyes with Charity at her usual table, backed up against a movable partition that separated the M.R. area from the rest of the room. He noticed something funny about her eyes, like modest alarm, which puzzled him at first. The he realized that what he was seeing was a kind of double reflection: his own bummed-out vibes bouncing off her consciousness like short waves off the ion belt, then coming back to him. Kind of strange to think that the world works that way. Kind of cool, too. He smiled at Charity and that *really* made her look worried.

He was in that same kind of halfway-there, halfway-not mood—which might also have been an effect of the change in the air, the foretaste of fall—when he plodded up to the door that said Director of Student Services. It faced out onto a brick plaza covered by a pressure-treated pergola, from which strands of honeysuckle hung so low you had to brush them out of the way as you walked. Kaspian wondered why the groundskeepers didn't trim this above head level. Perhaps because Ronald or whoever's job it was rather liked it this way. Kaspian did too: it gave the place a New Orleans feeling. On Ms. Boot's door a handwritten sign said KNOCK THEN ENTER. He ignored the first part.

The office was as small as Kaspian's bedroom and looked temporary: a field headquarters on the road to higher ground. Ms. Boot had placed her desk diagonally in one corner. There were two chairs and a small table against an opposite wall. The poster of Nick Cave was gone, and instead there was one of a young-looking long-haired guy identified in squiggly psychedelic letters as Nick Drake. One Nick at a time, he thought. The current version looked barely older than Kaspian himself, looming toward the fish-eye lens with a soft white hand out, empty, asking for something.

Ms. Boot was on the telephone. When she spotted Kaspian she first looked annoyed, then indifferent, and finally waved for him to come in, all without pausing in what she was saying.

"You can ask anybody," was about all Kaspian heard of this. Then, "I've got to ring off now. Somebody's here."

Her voice on the phone was different yet again: different than when she spoke to him, and different than when she had been sucking up to Jasper Winot. He guessed she had a voice for every audience. She was still smiling about something that was none of his business when he picked one of the empty chairs and flopped down in it. He pressed his head back against the wall and stuck his legs out, trying to get relaxed.

"So how *are* you, Kaspian?" Ms. Boot asked.

On the table beside him lay two sharpened pencils: one yellow and one green. He took the green one and bumped its eraser down, again and again, like a pile driver.

"Okay, I guess," he said.

"How do you like the Sudley Center?"

He kept his eyes away from her. He guessed that she was not really making small talk; that where Ms. Boot was concerned, everything was *about* something.

She went on, just as casually, "Making any friends here?"

He shrugged. "Kind of. Not really friends. I mean, I know who the kids in class are, anyway."

"So I've heard," she said. Then she sat still and waited for him to look at her, knowing that he would. She knew he would need to know what she meant by this, and when he turned she continued: "I've heard you've gotten to know one person in particular. A student named Charity Laird."

Kaspian did not want to talk to Ms. Boot about Charity Laird. It bothered him even to hear the name spoken by her. He said nothing and wondered what he looked like, sitting there with his mouth locked shut. Could she tell he was getting angry? He guessed she could tell everything, even stuff he didn't understand himself. She was a professional.

"I just want you to be careful," Thera Boot said. "It's very important that you watch out for your own feelings, and also that you watch out for Charity's. She's a very sensitive person. Very delicate. There was some doubt as to the wisdom of sending her here, to a mixed setting. I personally assured her parents that everything would be fine, that their daughter would be perfectly safe. I know you want that also, Kaspian. Am I right?"

She was not going to trick him into agreeing with anything. He continued to sit there, remembering that the last person who had urged him to be careful was Hunter Nye. It had been good advice, only Kaspian had not quite understood it, had not grasped what he needed to be careful of.

Finally he said, warily, "What's the matter with her?"

Thera Boot nodded: satisfied, evidently, to have gotten a response from him. "Nothing is the *matter*," she said slowly—of course he had not meant it that way, and she damn well knew it—"but as I've told you, she is a very fragile, delicately balanced person. I don't want her to be hurt for any reason. I don't want any student here to be hurt. That's why sessions like this are so valuable—they help us understand each person's unique needs and desires."

Kaspian said, "I'm not going to hurt her. I don't even know her all that well."

"That is exactly," Thera Boot said, pouncing on this, leaning across her desk, "my point. You *don't* know her all that well. It's doubtful that you ever will. That's why it's *so* important that you be careful."

She paused to give his brain some time to soak that up. Then she picked up an assortment of papers—they seemed to consist of several distinct sets, distinguished by color—and rapped them a couple of times, edge down, tidying the stack. She shot him a smile and leaned forward, holding the papers out. For an instant, her pose and that of the rock star on the wall echoed each other; though the great difference between them was that Ms. Boot looked strong and confident while Nick Drake looked lonely and weak.

"I guess you've heard all about this by now," she said.

Kaspian took the papers, thinking that at least you had to appreciate Ms. Boot's way of dealing with things in a crisp, businesslike manner: moving from one thing to the next without fuss. He bet that on a hot date, when the proper moment arrived, she would just come out and say, Let's fuck now, shall we?

(What *was* it about her that made him have thoughts like this? She seemed to encourage him, God knows how, to act more cynical and roughened, like a make-believe grown-up. Which at first had been kind of exciting. But now he was used to it and he wished she would turn those eyes off.)

"For you, however," she told him—putting a certain edge on *you,* pricking his attention with it—"I want to try something a little different. Instead of the usual questionnaire, I've obtained a special . . . a *customized* personality inventory. It's not a *test,* exactly. It's more of a classification tool. It was developed by a professor of psychology named Kenneth Ring and is used for certain categories of individuals—"

"Encounter-prone?" asked Kaspian.

She smiled at him, with a trace of surprise. "Why, yes."

She appeared, Kaspian thought, not to remember that he had heard every word she had spoken to Jasper Winot back in Maine, in that lodge with the moose antlers. He had heard about this psychologist, and this diagnosis Ms. Boot had made, the encounter-prone personality bit. She must have been so focused on impressing Der Chef that she was oblivious to everything and everybody else. He found this kind of amusing.

"So," she said, taking charge again, "I've recently been in contact with Professor Ring, who has kindly sent me a copy of the special personality inventory he has administered now to several thousand evaluees, many of whom have had . . ."

She paused as though searching for a precise clinical term.

"Little outings?" Kaspian suggested.

". . . contact experiences," Ms. Boot continued, in a measured tone, "similar in some respects to your own. And many others of whom have not. As I say, this is not a test. There are no correct answers, or incorrect ones. We are simply looking here for certain *patterns* in an individual's background, in his personality and temperament, that have been shown to be . . . associated . . . with the phenomena under consideration."

It sounded to Kaspian as though she was carefully not saying something. He looked down at the multicolored papers. The top page bore the heading

OMEGA PROJECT BATTERY
Identification Sheet

"What phenomena?" he asked her. He wasn't even sure what the word meant. He thought it ended with an *N*.

"Well, oddly enough," she said, more down-to-earth, like she was leveling with him, "in its original form, the inventory was designed for use with regard to near-death experiences. You're familiar with those? In which a person briefly . . . ? Good. Well, over time, it was found that individuals who are prone to *those* experiences, which have been fairly well documented now, are *also* prone to certain other, more controversial ones. Professor Ring was the first to note the correlation and to develop this analytic tool for gauging an individual's level of general encounter-proneness."

Kaspian flipped through the pages. The second was titled Background Information Sheet. It was followed by Experience and Interest Inventory (2 pages), Omega Childhood Experience Inventory (2 pages), Omega Home Environment Questionnaire (3 pages), Omega Psychological Inventory (4 pages), Omega Psychological Changes Inventory (3 pages), Omega Life Changes Inventory (2 pages), Omega Religious Beliefs Inventory (1 page), and Omega Opinion Inventory (3 pages). Quite a bit of work. He looked up at Ms. Boot, who was watching him in a funny way, expectantly or something. He guessed she was as new at this as he was.

"So what do you think?" she asked him. "Ready to give it a go?"

He looked at Nick Drake, who struck him as a total feeb. "What for?"

Thera Boot's brow creased.

"I mean what's the point? What is this stuff supposed to tell you? Whether my childhood was fucked up, or I've got strange ideas about aliens and UFO's, or what? I just don't get why you want me to do this."

"Well." Ms. Boot brought her elbows to rest on the surface of her desk, leaning forward with her shoulders hunched up. "I suppose I could say—without knowing, of course, what the actual results will be—that it should at least tell us a couple of important things. One, it will tell us whether or not you do fall within the category—which represents a rather slender percentage of the general population, by the way—that is considered to be encounter-prone. And two, it will give us a certain, shall we say, scale of weights and balances, with which to weigh the . . . the report of your contact experience. Which has remained impressively consistent in both its versions, the one you gave us yourself and the one relayed by your friend at ASAC."

Kaspian pressed his lips together. His *friend* at ASAC. The treacherous Hunter Nye. A cold realization fell upon him.

"You want to know whether I'm lying," he told Ms. Boot. "You're trying to figure out if the whole thing is just like, some bullshit story a stupid kid made up."

Her face, held flatly before him, was the perfect German mask.

Kaspian settled deeper into his chair. He riffled the pages of the OMEGA PROJECT BATTERY. At last, without looking at Ms. Boot, he said:

"Okay. That's cool. We'll see if I'm making it up."

It was something he kind of wanted to know himself.

QUESTIONS are revealing; they can tell you, for instance, precisely what your interrogator does *not* know. But the pages spread before Kaspian were a puzzle, the kind of puzzle where you can fill in blank after blank and still have no clue as to what the final answer is.

When I was young, I loved to spend time alone in natural   T F
    settings.

As a child, I felt that I had a "guardian angel" or special   T F
    spirit friend that watched over me.

When I was a child, I was often "off in my own world."   T F

When I was a child, I nearly died.   T F

The true-false items went on and on, down the page and
onto the next. While Kaspian thought his way through them,
Ms. Boot settled back with a glossy magazine, *Vanity Fair,* and
seemed to forget him. He wished he could do likewise.

The second section, Home Environment Questionnaire, was
somewhat different.

In responding to these questions, simply circle the appropriate number
according to these definitions:
    4=always
    3=very often
    2=sometimes
    1=rarely
    0=never

Did your parents ridicule you?   4   3   2   1   0

When you were punished as a child or teenager, did   4   3   2   1   0
    you understand the reason for the punishment?

As a child or teenager, did you feel disliked by either   4   3   2   1   0
    of your parents?

Was your childhood stressful?   4   3   2   1   0

Ms. Boot shifted her position—hitching one long leg up
onto her desk and moving her foot to some inaudible rhythm.
Maybe a Nick Drake tune. Her expression changed also as she
progressed through the magazine. Sometimes she sat with her
head bent raptly forward, while at other times it tilted back and
her eyes seemed to stare without focusing. She was oblivious
of Kaspian. He could have pulled Hunter Nye's old trick—
whipping his dick out—and she wouldn't have been any wiser.
He moved on to Psychological Inventory, the longest section
so far.

Please answer these items by circling the appropriate number following each statement according to the following scale:

    1=strongly disagree
    2=disagree
    3=neutral
    4=agree
    5=strongly agree

Sometimes I have blank spells when I do things with- 1 2 3 4 5
out being aware of what I've done.

Sometimes a part of me just wants to laugh hysterically 1 2 3 4 5
at everything.

When I was younger, I had an imaginary playmate as 1 2 3 4 5
a companion.

I think I have agreed to having medical treatments I 1 2 3 4 5
really didn't need.

After three pages of this, he moved on to the Religious Beliefs Inventory, whose instructions read:

Since your interest in UFO experiences, would you say that you are *now* more or less inclined to agree with the following statements or that you hold the same belief as before? If you are more inclined to *agree* with a given statement, please write *A* in the space; if you are inclined to *disagree*, write *D;* if your opinion is the same as before, write *S.*

"Um," he said.

Ms. Boot lifted her head, inattentively. "Is there a problem?"

"Well." He held the paper up. "I don't actually *have* an interest in UFO experiences. And it says here—"

"Yes. I'm familiar with what it says." She lowered her magazine. "The way it was related . . . your contact experience has what is known as a *structural similarity,* at least, with a typical UFO encounter. The lights; the mysterious swirling object; the sudden appearance of unidentifiable beings."

Kaspian shook his head. "So what, though? I still don't have an interest in UFO's."

Ms. Boot mused for a few moments. "Let's say this, then. Let's take that part of the questionnaire to mean, *Since I had my unusual experience*. All right? The purpose of the inventory is not to measure your interest in UFO's but rather to make a before-and-after comparison of your beliefs. Do you understand?"

"Sure. I just don't buy it."

She smiled as though to let him know that his attitude was not going to bother her. "Let's just take the test anyway, shall we?"

"You said it wasn't a test."

She only picked up *Vanity Fair*. And Kaspian, as she must have known he would do, went back to answering questions. He was too far in now.

____   The essential core of all religions is the same.

____   I believe there is a heaven and hell.

____   The Bible is the inspired word of God.

____   A universal religion embracing all humanity is an ideal which strongly appeals to me.

It was funny: he felt right at home here. And it was funny too because he realized that in some way, his beliefs actually *had* changed since the night of his little outing. They had sort of crystallized.

Before, his total lack of belief in like, *everything*—religion especially—had been a matter of principle: a way of positioning himself vis-à-vis his stepmother, who believed in *exactly one thing* and believed it with brutal certainty. But now . . . it was different, sort of. Now it was more like, he *knew* his stepmother was wrong. That her narrow ideas were mistaken. He thought back to that morning with Malcolm, down in the chestnut grove, the silence around him. That was a definite thing: you could believe in that. Everything had sort of fit together and made sense, in a way that he couldn't explain either now or then. It was only a feeling. But a solid feeling, nonetheless. A belief.

That was a change, for him.

If there had been a Comments section, he might have written some of this down. But there were only questions, endless dozens of them.

The final part was called Opinion Inventory and it was similar to the one before, except spacier. Our home is earth, but our destiny is the stars, for example. There is a plan for our universe. If extraterrestrial life exists, it does not necessarily bode well for humanity. I have come to feel that I am part of a much larger "field of intelligence" than I previously believed. Kaspian poked his way through, agreeing here and disagreeing there, but mostly undecided. Finally he slapped the green pencil down and straightened the stack and slid it across the table, in the direction of Ms. Boot. She looked up at him.

"All done?" she said. "That wasn't so terrible, was it?"

He shrugged, which was preferable to coming right out and agreeing with her. He said, "Do I get to know the results?"

"We'll discuss your answers, and any pattern that seems to emerge from them, if that's what you mean. I'll need to go through the literature first. This entire field of study is in its infancy, so I need to caution you that in all likelihood nothing definitive will emerge. But yes—I'll certainly let you know."

Kaspian nodded; he guessed that was fair enough. He rose to leave, but then—following some momentary impulse—he stopped beside the door and asked her:

"Does this school make a lot of money?"

Ms. Boot looked annoyed. "Not really. It's a demonstration facility, primarily. A showcase for AYA's pioneering methodologies. It's not intended to be a profit center."

"Then where does it all come from?" He waved his hand around, to show that he meant everything: swimming pools, computer labs, counselors reading glossy magazines. "Is Winot just superrich, or what?"

Thera Boot gave a trim little smile. "I'm sure I wouldn't know. I believe his primary holdings are in agriculture, in the upper Midwest. Cattle ranching, on a large scale. Education is a more recent interest—an outgrowth of his involvement in politics out there, the battle over tax reform. He believes that property owners are being bled dry to overfund a school system that does a poor job of teaching the wrong lessons to other people's children."

Kaspian guessed this was a direct quote. For some reason, the answer satisfied him. He had been puzzled by how he fit into the picture here, but now that he saw the picture in a broader way—some wealthy cattle-butcher out to change the world—he guessed the answer was that he didn't fit into the picture at all.

Which could be nothing
but fine.

HE dreamed of being a boy. A *real* boy, too young to know jack about anything.

He was in a place . . . an orchard. Old trees. Fallen apples lying around. Wind and kites. The color red, as in apples; as in the leaves of a swamp maple down by the wastewater treatment plant; as in the leatherette cover of the Bible on a special table in the hall.

Kaspian running. Tugging the string, the kite so high. Wind in his Velcro hair.

Leaves raining around him.

Something falls from his pocket. A toy?

He stops and searches for it among the colored leaves. Kite forgotten, dematerialized. Out in a field now. Lonely place, far away from home. Searching and searching. Red leaves and yellow and orange and brown.

Kaspian yelling. Tiny voice like an instrument, like a sawtooth wave from an oscillator, down and up and down.

Daddy I can't find

What? Kaspian turns in his sleep, aching to know.

The boy in the field is lost. Leaves rain around him. No one comes when he cries.

Knock at the door.

Kaspian twisted in his blanket. Where has it gone, down under the leaves? What will he do if he can't get it back again? The door opened and light fell onto the bed, onto his forehead, where sweat sparkled.

"Hey—Kaspian?"

He blinked. Already forgetting. Grasped, but failed to hold it.

"Are you awake?"

Vernon stepped into the room. The door clicked behind him. Dark again, with only the pale blue light before dawn at the seams of the curtains. The younger kid was fully dressed, uniform tie and everything, with his hair slicked down from the shower. He radiated awakeness.

Kaspian moaned.

"Did I wake you up?" said Vernon, coming over toward the bed. He sat on the corner of it, head moving around in the semidark with the alacrity of a bird. "Sorry, dude. I can't get used to how long it stays dark down here. I guess it's farther west, huh? So the sun doesn't rise as early? Even though we're in the same time zone and everything."

"Vernon." Kaspian's voice came out thick, gummed up in the throat. "What are you doing here? What time is it?"

The bed jiggled as Vernon's weight moved up and down, almost bouncing. The Opie eyes flashed with a light of their own, a weird light. "Which league are the Orioles in? National or American?"

"I do not *know* what league the Orioles are in," said Kaspian. He kind of liked the way his voice sounded now. Deep and slow. He wondered why it wasn't like this during regular waking hours. He sat up in bed and tried to straighten the covers, but Vernon's hold on the corner made this impossible. Air moved across his chest, which was damp with sweat, and he shivered. "Vernon, why are you awake? What the hell are you doing here?"

He did not mean to be unfriendly and Vernon did not seem to take it that way. Actually Kaspian was almost glad to see the dumb kid, who at least was a fellow Mainer. If not actually a friend.

"I'm just awake." Vernon waggled his shoulders. "I always wake up kind of early. It drives my mother crazy. Drove."

A reflective look passed over his face, then was gone.

"Yeah, well," said Kaspian, climbing out of bed and heading to the bathroom, "there's no moms here. Right?"

His usual morning erection was not happening today, perhaps because his body was too confused. Out in the room he could hear Vernon moving the chair by the desk. He closed his eyes.

Immediately: the leaves.
Bright red, huge. Bigger than his tiny hand.

He reached hard for the memory but it vaporized again.

Vernon was sitting at his desk fiddling with the computer. He did not look up when Kaspian came back in and started pulling on his uniform, the same as yesterday.

"You haven't got *Wolfsschanze*," Vernon said, sounding more dismayed than Kaspian thought was strictly necessary.

"I haven't got anything. What's *Wolfsschanze*?"

Vernon shrugged. One of his hands tapped a drumbeat on the desk while the other worked the trackpad, probing Kaspian's hard disk. "Some kind of werewolf game, I got it from Brenton. I can't figure out how to get past the chimney sweep."

Kaspian pulled his belt tight—a black leather belt with a slightly larger-than-necessary brass buckle engraved with the AYA logo—and noted that while his waist had not changed size, his pants seemed too short. He wondered if he was having another so-called growth spurt. The last one, such as it was, had happened about three years ago, right when he was trying to figure out how to survive middle school, and had provided the occasion for an epic battle with his stepmother over the selection of a replacement wardrobe. He firmly believed that the loss of that battle had cost him much ground in his drive to become socially acceptable.

"Brenton's a fucking stoner," he said.

"No he's not," said Vernon. "Not here, anyway. How can

anybody be a stoner in a place like this? You think we're copping drugs off like, Vonda at the chow hall?"

"No," said Kaspian. He was a little bothered by Vernon's use of the word *we*. "I figured maybe Kaylla at the intake center. You know, the brainless white-trash type: always a reliable source of controlled pharmaceuticals."

Vernon looked blank. "Brenton's not a stoner," he said again. "He thinks maybe you are. I told him you're not."

"How do you know I'm not?" said Kaspian.

Vernon looked worried; scared almost. Kaspian felt bad about it but there was just something about that Opie face, and about the very *irrepressibility* of this kid, that brought out some dark urge to act like a bad-ass.

"Ha," said Vernon finally. He stared forlornly at the computer screen, as though despairing of finding a source of entertainment. "I might as *well* get into drugs. I don't see what difference it would make."

Kaspian didn't understand. He stared at himself in the mirror on the closet door. No matter how much he practiced, he could not make the tie come out right. It wasn't even as though he really cared; but nonetheless it was frustrating, like repeatedly losing at solitaire.

"Here," said Vernon. "Let me show you."

The boy came over and stood in front of Kaspian, undoing the last screwed-up knot and starting from scratch. "First you have to adjust the length of the two sides."

Kaspian didn't want to listen. "What do you mean?" he said. "About what difference it would make."

Vernon pressed his lips together and looped one end of the tie around the other. He seemed very small and very young, this close up. The freckles and the white shirt gave him a choirboy look. He said, "I mean, with all the drugs I'm taking already. I don't see what difference a little bud would make."

"A little *bud?*" said Kaspian, hearing the cool Left Coast in this.

Vernon blushed. Maybe he thought he had gotten the terminology wrong.

"There's Ritalin," he said, hastening back to familiar territory, "and something called Paxil which I'm not really sure what it's for. And those two upset my stomach so I take another thing for that. And then last week they started me on something new, like lithium but it's not called that. It's supposed to help make the ups and downs more flat."

He illustrated the process with two hands held flat horizontally, squeezing something nine inches high down to something two inches high.

"Jesus," said Kaspian.

Vernon stepped back, motioning for Kaspian to look in the mirror. The knot, a full Windsor, was perfect. Kaspian looked as sharp as any of the clones.

He turned to Vernon, seeing now in those flashing Opie eyes a certain unnatural gleam. "So you're saying, you take these drugs, then you take *other* drugs to control the side effects of the *first* drugs, and now they've given you something *else?* Who is it that decides these things?"

"Well, my mom," said Vernon, "to start with. And the doctor back home. And I've got this counselor I go to—went to— every other week. And when I started at ASAC I had an evaluation with Ms. Boot, and she was the one who recommended Paxil. Then when the test results came back—"

"Test results?"

"You know. The multiphasic personality thing. Didn't you get one? When the results came back they said—"

"*Who* said?"

"Ms. Boot. And also Mr. Crewe, during my Adjustment Block."

Kaspian nodded. He himself did not have an Adjustment Block—perhaps because nobody wanted to sit down and talk to him, one on one, for a whole hour—but he had heard about them. Charity had one.

"Anyway," said Vernon, "they looked at the results and they said that now they understand why my personal advancement resources are so underexploited."

"They *said* that?" said Kaspian, though of course he knew

they had, in just those words. Vernon was good at recording such things.

Vernon nodded. "So they started me on this new medicine, and it really seems to work, because now my resource-exploitation rate is showing a strongly positive delta."

Kaspian was relieved to see that at least Vernon had the sense to grin at this—like he had some idea of what a bunch of crap it was. Maybe they hadn't caught him young enough. "So what's it feel like," he said, "taking all that stuff?"

Vernon shrugged. "What's it feel like not to? It's good, I guess. I find that I'm able to concentrate better in class."

Again, it sounded to Kaspian as though the kid was repeating something he had heard.

"That's cool," said Kaspian. Though he wondered. When his own test results came in, would Ms. Boot have a little pharmaceutical surprise in store?

Vernon looked restless, or maybe he just wanted to drop the subject. He came over and sat on the bed, his usual spot, and said, "So you going on the field trip or what?"

"Isn't everybody?"

"Not if you've got too many regress points. Brenton's already up to nine this week. One more and he's buried."

Brenton Brenton Brenton, thought Kaspian. Stoner or not, it was hard to tolerate the guy. He definitely was not a positive influence on Vernon.

(Right: and *you* are?)

"I think it'll be cool," Vernon enthused. "We get to see the Tomb of the Unknown Soldier."

Kaspian closed his closet door. He tried to remember if there ever had been a time—ever—when a thing like the Tomb of the Unknown Soldier would have excited him. The effort gave him a funny, vertiginous feeling, as if he had suddenly gotten old and was having trouble recalling his distant youth.

"It'll be cool to get out of *this* place for a while, anyhow," he said.

Vernon nodded happily, eagerly, Opie-like. The stupid little twerp.

★   ★   ★

HE saw Charity out in the field later that day, but she was with
a couple of her girlfriends. Kaspian just stood and watched them
from a distance, though he had been hoping to get a chance to
talk to her. He wondered what Charity would think about Vernon, all the drugs he was taking. He wasn't sure why this bothered him so much—it was none of his business, actually—but
his mind kept coming back to it. He kept thinking that he
saw new things, different things, in Vernon's behavior, even his
appearance—a different sort of roundness in the shape of his face.
Maybe it was crazy. All in Kaspian's head. Like so much else.

Though not everything. Damn it. Not everything.

On the way back to his room he ran headlong into a parade
of grown-ups, being drum-majored up the sidewalk by Jasper C.
Winot himself. There were seven or eight of them in all, not
instructors but older and better-dressed people who might have
been business pals of Der Chef. A bunch of well-heeled go-
getters. Kaspian hustled his butt out of their way before they
flattened him.

"I try to impress upon *all* my people," Winot was saying,
waving an arm that almost smacked Kaspian on the forehead,
"the classroom is a marketplace, just like any other. The commodity of value is knowledge. And if we can get the students
to *regard* knowledge as a commodity—something they can acquire, add value to, and trade at a profit—then the whole process
of education takes care of itself."

One of the others, a middle-aged woman in a red dress, said,
"That *sounds* well and good, Chopper. But what does it mean
to the teachers on the front line? You're going to have to spell
it out persuasively if you want to move the fence-straddlers. We
sit up there every day listening to finely tuned rhetoric, from
both sides of the aisle, and let me tell you, the opposition is
slicker than owl shit. They've got the studies. They've got the
statistics. You need something a little more compelling than the
genius of the marketplace."

Winot stopped walking, turned to face the woman in red,
and gave her an extraspecial smile. Kaspian could tell from half

a dozen paces away that the cattle baron was not going to let
owl shit go unanswered.

"Ruby," he said, "you are a great American and a stellar
Representative, but I wonder if you've been spending too much
of your time up there on the Hill. Let me just throw an example
your way. Down at our Richardson campus—"

"That's in Texas?" a man said.

"Texas." Winot nodded. "Down in Richardson, Texas,
we've got a pilot program utilizing something we call Achieve-
ment Points, or A-chiPs. Now, these A-chiPs are tokens, like
real money, and students can earn them any number of ways.
For instance by getting good grades on tests—three chips for an
A, one for a B—or by doing an excellent science project, or by
turning in an outstanding English report. Extra work is treated
as overtime and paid at a higher scale. Students can also be *fined*
A-chiPs, for disrupting class or failing to turn in homework.
Now these A-chiPs, the actual tokens themselves, can be spent
at the school store, or fed into the Pepsi machine, or used to
quote unquote *buy* special privileges such as time in the campus
swimming pool. *That's* what I'm talking about, the classroom as
a marketplace, knowledge as a fungible commodity. That's a
lesson they'll *never* teach in the goddamned public schools."

His listeners, the flock of well-dressed grown-ups, were silent
for a few moments. Then the man who had spoken before said:

"But that's in *Texas*."

"That's in Texas," confirmed the woman in the red dress,
Ruby, glancing quickly around the group, as though taking a
quick poll by eye contact.

"It could work *anywhere*," said Winot.

Another woman said, more quietly, "But doesn't that create,
within your school, a situation with haves and have-nots?"

"Just like *actual life*," Winot said, almost thundering now.
"No different! Haves, have-nots, do's, do-not's, winners, whin-
ers, also-rans, could-have-beens, never-wases—no different! It's
the way the world works! How else are we going to *teach* these
kids that?"

The woman in red reached out and patted his arm. "You'll

do all right, Chopper," she said. "But you need to tone down your delivery. Think *microphone*. Think *C-SPAN*. The hearing room has excellent acoustics and there's absolutely no need to shout."

Winot stood looking at her as though he were torn between thwacking her on the rump and giving her a big cowboy hug. Finally he let out a breath and said, "Aracos tells me I ought to let the professionals do my talking for me. He says we're funding this damned PAC, this Committee for whatever, Choice in Free Schools or hell, no, it's something like that. So we might as well let it do its thing. But I say, you need that *personal* touch. You need that passion, that sense of genuine up-by-the-bootstraps enterprise. After all, there are some things money can't buy."

"That's true," spoke the entire chorus of grown-ups, nodding their well-groomed heads as one.

Ruby of the red dress said, "You know, Chopper . . . I wonder if you might enlist the students themselves in this, somehow. Speaking of that personal touch."

"What do you mean?"

"I'm not sure." She had a thoughtful look on her face. "Is there any way I might meet some of them personally?"

Winot gave her that special smile again. "For you, Congresswoman, all things are possible. I'll have Aracos speak to your staff and we'll see what can be arranged."

He laid a big hand on one of her shoulders, and they set off walking again. Within a few steps Ruby slipped out from under the hand and went on her own way.

THE day of the field trip was a Tuesday late in September, and though it was still hot and the leaves had not started to turn—except for some sumacs that flashed scarlet along Interstate 66, beside the Metro tracks—you could see a change in the angle and color of sunlight, and it was clear that autumn was on its way even to Virginia, even to these endless wide runs of pavement, the sound barriers overgrown with Boston ivy, the squat glass office boxes, the town-house complexes with naked concrete foundations set on plots of eroding clay: this land without topsoil.

They were traveling—all nineteen kids whose regress points totaled fewer than 10, which unfortunately included Brenton and the Left Coasters—in an almost brand-new minibus, stark white except for American Youth Academies in black and red. Ronald was driving. The bus flew smoothly over the perfect highway, its tinted windows blocking out most of the objectionable stimuli, sights and sounds and smells, from the outside world. You could see in a place like this how the term *environment* might take on a negative, even an offensive connotation, and how some of these glass boxes might be filled with professional lobbyists working hard to save honest Americans from exposure to its effects.

Kaspian remembered from the hours his stepmother spent tuned to CBN that the addresses to which you were always being urged to write for information, or to express your support for this vital work through your fully tax-deductible contributions, quite often included a post office box in Virginia somewhere: Lynchburg, or Fairfax, or Virginia Beach, or Arlington, through the last of which the minibus was gliding right now. It was as though he had finally been delivered to a kind of strange, behind-the-cameras Promised Land. Then the highway broke into the open and you could look across the Potomac River and see Washington, D.C.

Washington was different; you could tell that right away. It looked very green, with the famous monuments rising from a girding of trees. The bus moved too fast for Kaspian to get more than a passing look. Yet, in a way, that was all he needed, because the sights of Washington were so familiar from books and movies and TV news; you felt like you had seen them a hundred times before.

Still, though. There was something about *being* here.

Even through tinted glass, and the blue-gray haze of morning, those white marble buildings, and the sand-colored hard-on of the Washington Monument, built of huge chunks of Indiana limestone, and the dark polished rectangle of the Reflecting Pool, over all of which the early sun threw shadows of great American elms, gave Kaspian a feeling he had not expected today: a rush of energy upward from his diaphragm, like he had felt on some coal-black night long ago under the stadium lights at a Portland Sea Dogs game, when the crowd rose to sing the "Star-spangled Banner." His daddy had set the tub of popcorn down and lifted Kaspian up and the little boy had become one with the night, the crowd, the brilliant lights, the soaring off-key music.

He probably had not thought of that night for more than half his lifetime; but it came back to him now, for a few seconds so intense they brought him a kind of agony. Then they passed, and when the memory ebbed it seemed to dissolve like a movie fade to another memory, some dream he had recently had. He strained for it but that was like grabbing handfuls of smoke.

By this time the bus had plunged down from the interstate into a complicated series of exit loops that took them, eventually, to the tour-group parking area at Arlington National Cemetery. A roadway where traffic zipped by stood between them and the Potomac. Away from the river, the land rose to a tree-covered hill, at the crown of which stood an old Virginia mansion of exactly the sort Kaspian had imagined finding all over the place. Below stood an up-to-date visitors' center anchored to the landscape by a tree-lined colonnade. It was all very classy in that democratic, Park Service style.

The bus rolled to a stop and the nineteen kids, plus Mr. Crewe and a math teacher called Ms. Velásquez, clambered out. This was the first chance Kaspian had had all day to get close to Charity. She had ridden in the dead-last row, along with some bombed-out girl from Cincinnati, whom Kaspian judged at a glance to be a fellow victim of hard-core Christian parenting. Now, as the group ambled in loose formation over the parking lot, he drifted back to where the two girls were fastened together talking in low voices and rolling their eyes.

"Hey." Charity shot a greeting at him from a few paces off.

He could not tell if it was a warning to keep his distance. The other girl studied him through heavily made-up eyes. She had long straight hair of no nameable color and wore pentagram earrings, and on the whole looked as though half of what she knew in life she had learned from renting *The Craft*. Kaspian could have told her a couple of things if he could have brought himself to care enough.

"Hey," he said back to Charity.

"Kaspian, this is Jill," she said airily. "Jill, Kaspian."

"Pleased to meet you," the other girl said, like a dope. Her eyes floated in their own tiny puddles. Kaspian wondered what custom blend of medication *she* was on.

They fell into step, Charity in the middle. The rest of the group had gotten ahead of them—you could see little Opie up there, darting from one pack of kids to another, totally up-polar today—but Mr. Crewe and Ms. Velázquez were among the more laid-back of the faculty, and they seemed content to let the kids ramble.

The day was nice. Sunny and not really hot, with a few cumulus clouds in a sky that was bluer than usual, as though an overnight wind had blown some of the pollution away. Only, it was weird how loud the background noise was. The planes into National Airport came right down the river every two or three minutes with an unbelievable roar. But even without that, the traffic sounds never stopped; they merged from all directions into a steady, mechanized rumble, as though the entire urban area was one titanic machine, grinding impersonally onward, as unstoppable as Rommel's tanks.

Kaspian and the two girls followed the others into the visitors' center and passed immediately out the doors on the opposite side, giving onto the cemetery itself, which from here looked like nothing but a big old leafy park. Charity had snagged a map which she and Jill studied while Kaspian strolled ahead to the end of the sidewalk. From there a winding road led up the hill in two directions, and inconspicuous signs directed you to points of major interest. The girls caught up with him and Charity said:

"Jill wants to go see the JFK burial site. There's an eternal flame there."

Kaspian had no interest in JFK. And eternal flames made him think of his stepmother. Then again, he did not have a particular interest in anything, except hanging out with Charity. This Jill was a major inconvenience but it seemed she was part of the package.

He said, "I was kind of thinking about the Tomb of the Unknown Soldier."

"I like that name," said Charity. She smiled magically, and raised a skinny hand to rake through her coal-black hair. The gesture made her look little-girlish and pert. "But hey—we've got all day, right?"

"Just till lunch," Jill said, "remember? Then they're taking us to that other place."

"Oh, yeah," said Charity. "But at least then we get to ride the subway."

Kaspian had not heard about any of this: his firm policy about schedules. "What other place?" he said.

"Oh, you know," said Charity. And she and Jill set off up the hill like they knew where they were going.

It occurred to Kaspian that if Vernon joined them, there would be a better sort of balance—two and two—plus he'd have somebody to talk with. But the rest of the kids were still inside the visitors' center, and the girls were getting ahead of him. Off on a tangent of their own. He guessed there was nothing to do but follow.

The morning was starting to get a little warm.

UNTIL you came this far you tended to overlook the fact that this place was—surprise—a humongous graveyard. Suddenly you stepped around a bend of the road and the fields rolled out before you, endless grids of modest white stones, the nearer ones softened to greenish-gray and blurred with age. Men of all ranks and services were interred here together, no grave site better or different than any other—though Kaspian thought he personally would have liked one shaded by the gigantic elderly trees along the roadside. The hill ran down into a dark but pretty ravine with a creek at the bottom. Nearby another road forked right. Just ahead of them, a shuffle of elderly tourists disputed over the reading of a map. Their voices seemed loud here because the atmosphere was so still and quiet, despite the traffic and the intermittent airport noise. Not somber, exactly. But peaceful. A feeling that lulled you, a sense of some deep strength abiding in the ground.

Kaspian thought that in some way, standing here in Arlington Cemetery reminded him of sitting in the chestnut grove in Sinai Falls. Just letting the sun fall. Soaking up the silence.

Fields of consciousness. That was Malcolm's phrase. And something like it had popped up on the Omega Battery: field of intelligence. Only this field was covered with grass and had rows of marble tombstones everywhere.

The girls came to a stop by a heavy cable that blocked off the patch of woods around the ravine. Jill dug through her purse. Charity was talking. Kaspian was too far back to hear what she was saying, and he chose, for now, to keep it that way.

Back home, the graveyard where his father had been buried was also on a hill, though a very different one. It was steep, exposed to the north wind, with a view of Mount Wabenaki and of the state highway running up toward Dublin, hedged by trees on the east side where you might otherwise have gotten a glimpse of Cold Bay. There was one bench in a isolated, windy spot. Kaspian had never seen a soul come to sit on it.

Personally, he had picked out a tree. It was a fat old maple with a cleft in the middle where a limb had been ripped down by a storm, and if you were tall enough, or had your daddy to lift you, you could settle down into that cleft and keep snugly hidden. At the same time you could see almost everything, the entire cemetery. In particular you could see the small granite pillar, rough on three sides and polished smooth on the fourth, that marked the final resting spot of Edward Karssen Aaby. It was as close as Kaspian generally liked to come to that place. Though unlike his stepmother, who made a big show of setting out pots of geraniums a couple of times a year, and was fastidious about stray grass shoots poking up around the base of the gravestone (which was stupid because his father, as Kaspian definitely recalled, had hated to mow the lawn above all other things, claiming to *like* the way grasses looked when they grew tall and floppy), at least he did go by the cemetery now and then. He climbed his tree and hunkered down and kept watch.

He was never tempted to do that thing you see in movies: where people sit by the grave and have these intense conversations with the dead guy, filling him in on late-breaking news around the old house, their eyes leaking tears while they try to bravely smile. Kaspian couldn't imagine that; not in real life. Up in his tree he would sit and remember stuff, thinking hard about exactly how it had been. Trying to bring the reality of his daddy back—not in a weird occult way, as a ghost or anything. Just as a good, clear memory. That had gotten harder as the years went by; but still he climbed up there and tried. It was a peaceful thing: melancholy but soothing. He could have stayed in the tree all day but usually clambered down after a while because it came to feel, even in summer, with no wind off the mountain, too cold.

As a child, I was able to look into "other realities" that   T F
    others didn't seem to be aware of.

When I was a child, I could see what some people call   T F
    fairies or "the little people."

When I was a child, I nearly died.   T F

THE girls called to him and he walked over.

"Jill's got to use the bathroom," Charity informed him.

Jill was staring out in a different direction in such a way as to arouse Kaspian's suspicions.

Charity continued: "You want to go on with me and look for JFK? Because otherwise I'm just going to head back."

Kaspian shrugged. "Sure. JFK. That's cool."

Jill said good-bye to them and headed back toward the visitors' center, but only got about halfway up the hill before the rest of the group came over the crest, the kids now leading Ms.

Velázquez and Mr. Crewe. Vernon was at the front of the pack and Kaspian waved to him, but the kid wasn't looking; he was dashing about yelling something, and Mr. Crewe was trying to restrain him, though not making a big deal of it. You had to smile. Charity said:

"Come on. Let's go before they see us."

She took his hand—he hardly noticed, she was so slick about it—and led him right down into the ravine, where Kaspian was pretty sure you were not allowed to go. They made their way up the creek bed, which was less beautiful at closer range. The pale rocks were sharp-edged and unweathered, as though deposited here not long ago by a bulldozer, and there were tiny bits of litter such as candy wrappers lying among the multiflora roses that shot their arching canes everywhere, snagging your clothes. Kaspian's shoes and socks got wet.

But it was great. It was a rush to follow Charity, who plunged ahead so heedlessly that her legs got seriously scraped by rose thorns. One of these came whipping back at Kaspian and punctured his pants leg, drawing blood that seeped into the gray twill, and when he yanked himself free he saw that Charity was laughing—perhaps not at him, perhaps just at everything. One of her legs was bleeding, too, on the knee and above that, as far up her thigh as you could see, but she didn't appear to notice or to care. Kaspian caught up and she took his hand again and they climbed the opposite embankment, sloping sharply up to a different road.

Several paces shy of the open space ahead, she stopped. There was no sign of anyone. The two of them were hidden by a thicket of mulberry trees. The ravine they had just climbed out of seemed to mark a natural divide, separating one part of the cemetery from another. For a minute they stood there plucking leaves and rose thorns out of their clothing; then they turned and started picking through the other person's clothing too, like chimpanzees grooming each other on the Discovery Channel. Both of them laughed about it, without having to say a word. Together, they got it.

Just then a pickup drove by. It was painted in National Park

Service colors, green and brown, and its bed was loaded with
lawn maintenance equipment. The three black guys riding up
front failed to notice Charity and Kaspian. Excellent.

He turned back to her, but she turned quicker. Before he
could quite understand what was happening, she kissed him.

It was a serious kiss. Her mouth pressed onto his at a twisty
angle, and her lips opened and her tongue moved between his
lips, though not far. He tried to do something, to turn his body
and put an arm around her, something normal, but she broke
off and looked away. Her face was pink. She bit her lip, still
damp from the squishing of mouths.

He expected her to say something—it always was she who
did—but Charity only stood there fidgeting. So Kaspian figured
it was up to him; it didn't seem right to just leave it at nothing.
All he came up with was:

"Hey."

That got her to look at him. He was not sure what her
expression meant; it was a little crazy, and her eyes were open
wide.

He said, "Can we do that again?"

"Oh," she said—more an exhalation than an actual word.
"God, I was afraid—"

He took her shoulders carefully with both hands and pulled
her close and kissed her lightly on the neck. It felt like the
greatest and wisest move he had ever made. The warm smell
rising up from under her shirt was something you could live
forever on. She hugged him back with a strange kind of almost
ferocity, a desperation.

He wanted to take it slow, really slow—partly because he
was surprised and a little disoriented, mostly because he wanted
to make every tiny step of their coming together go on for
eternity—but Charity was tuned to a higher frequency, or something. She kissed him on the mouth again and this time she
pressed her body up against his, hard enough that he could feel
the bones of her pelvis. Needless to say he got an erection so
large his heart could barely pump fast enough to maintain the

needed blood pressure. He felt dizzy; he needed to sit down. It was fine with Charity.

The ground was covered with fallen leaves, and under that was gravel. He and Charity more or less stumbled to a spot among the roots of a beech tree, its massive trunk defaced with dates and initials. Kaspian knew they were hidden from the road but he felt awfully exposed nonetheless, to Charity if no one else. They looked at one another for a couple of seconds, scoping things out without speaking their many uncertainties aloud. She was biting her lip again. Her gray eyes were not looking into his but at the rest of his face, his neck, his shoulders. What was the verdict? Before he could even wonder they were kissing more.

He wanted her so much he felt deranged about it. He almost wished they would stop for a minute, talk a little, anything. He wanted to touch her wrists that he had stared at so long and so longingly. Instead he was running a hand across her back, then forward to brush the side of her breast.

This brought him to a personal frontier: the outer reaches of his explorations with Dee Dee. It would have seemed incredible, an hour ago, to imagine that he might have gotten so far again, so quickly, in such a place as this. It would have been fine with him to hold up here awhile. But Charity drew herself back and opened the top buttons of her shirt. Then before he could grasp what was happening, she pulled it off over her head. She unfastened her bra and was suddenly naked from the thin white waist upward.

Kaspian went frog-eyed. He couldn't stop staring even though he knew he was doing it. Charity's breasts were like nothing he could have pictured in his head. They were smaller and paler, with nipples brown and . . . and like *nipples,* with little pointy ends and everything. He was almost afraid to touch them. As it turned out that did not matter. Charity unbuttoned his own shirt—he got around belatedly to helping her—and when his chest was bare she pressed herself warmly and tightly against him, and you would not *believe* what that felt like.

He groaned in ecstasy. Until now, for some reason, he had

been keeping perfectly quiet, even holding his rapid breaths in check. So was she, which was notable because usually she talked. There was something efficient and purposeful about her actions.

It all happened so quickly. She brought his hands behind her, under her uniform skirt, to cup around her bottom. She lifted herself up a little and straddled his legs in such a way as to press down against his groin, settling in for a long deep kiss. Kaspian was unnerved by the obvious fact that she had done this before, while he had not. He felt out of his league, though on the whole they had gotten way beyond the point where a thing like that could have bothered him. They were at the point now where Kaspian's whole awareness was centered upon a certain urgent need he had, a pressure that felt strong enough to make him explode on the spot if it was not quickly attended to.

It was attended to. Still perched above him, her legs apart and squeezing him from the sides, Charity rose on her knees a little and undid Kaspian's pants. She took him in one small cool hand and it was over so fast he felt like a fucking *plane* had come in too low and flattened him. He collapsed against the beech tree, spent and shivery from top to bottom.

Charity leaned forward against him, breathing hard, rocking very gently and humming to herself like a child. Her hand was still around his dick, in all the mess there; and then, as he floated in a blissed-out daze, she turned her face just enough to look into his: making sure it was okay, like.

He gave her a weak, but he hoped a happy, smile.

He said, "I . . . I . . ."

"Yeah," she said. "Sure. I bet."

She snuggled back into his chest. Her head was hot against him. Sweat cooled on his skin. Kaspian looked up through the beech leaves at the blue Virginia sky, empty of mysteries. He kissed her hair and he thought how strange it was, in the dankness and shade of an endless cemetery, to feel so explosively alive.

VERNON said, "Where did you guys go? Mr. Crewe was looking for you."

Kaspian walked beside him feeling too much a stranger to himself and to the world to communicate with Mayberry right now. Every single thing in the universe, including the cracks in the cement walkway and the crabgrass sprouting through them, emanated pulses of mellow energy, like the ringing of subtle chimes.

"I'm starved," said Vernon. "I can't wait to check out the subway, can you? It's supposed to be so cool."

Kaspian was ready to believe anything. He glanced behind them at the straggly line of kids leaving the cemetery, heading for the Metro station. They resembled a platoon of victorious but weary infantry, trudging to an assembly point. The two chaperones hung about halfway back, while in the rear guard Jill and Charity dragged their heels as though hoping the rest of the group would forget about them. Charity raised a hand, pointing at something across the river. Kaspian turned his head but could not figure out what. On the water, two narrow, low-slung boats were being rowed fast by teams of college students, slicing upriver toward Georgetown University, whose towers rose like a medieval fortress behind Key Bridge.

"Look!" called Vernon. "A train's coming in."

He had already reached the entrance to the Metro, which was above ground here. From the crosswalk, the train looked like a U-boat, easing into its pen. This is the moment, as everyone knows who has seen *Das Boot,* that R.A.F. dive-bombers show up.

"Does it cost money to ride this thing?" Kaspian asked.

"Didn't you get your fare card?" said Vernon. He fished in his pocket and produced a rectangle of stiff paper with a magnetic strip.

Kaspian shrugged. It was hard to remember anything about the world he had come from. All he wanted to do was find a nice bit of grass to lie down on. With Charity. Resting her head on his chest. Or no: just lying there, next to him. The two of them knowing that they were together, that everything was fine.

Kaspian discovered a fare card in his own shirt pocket: a mystery how it had gotten there. He and Vernon clocked into the station and of course little Opie *had* to go running to the very end of the platform to stare down the tracks, which plunged into a tunnel that bored its way downriver beneath the Pentagon. Kaspian caught up and the two of them watched a train pull out of the station and vanish down the hole. As it whooshed by, the air current got so strong that the metal guardrail and some hatch covers protecting electrical equipment began to rattle noisily. Vernon shouted:

"It's like a special effect! Flying saucer landing!"

Kaspian smiled. He patted the little idiot on the shoulder.

Behind them, the other kids and their chaperones trooped into the station. Jill and Charity were with them—which Kaspian found, to his surprise, came as a weird kind of disappointment, as though he had expected them to ditch the field trip and take off on their own, now that everything important had been taken care of. *Somebody* ought to, he thought. The city's right there.

Instead everyone stepped aboard the next westbound train, and soon they were lost in the dark under Virginia, going rapidly to lunch.

AT a place called Ballston, five stations down, they emerged into an instant city of office buildings and apartment houses, all of exactly the same height and none more than eight or ten years old. Mr. Crewe, wielding a map, conducted them to a brick-and-glass box that might have been chosen at random, and they rode elevators to a seventh-floor lobby where a nicely dressed young woman smiling like a flight attendant sat behind a huge curving desk between palm trees. Behind her a wall display said

COUNCIL FOR ACADEMIC FREEDOM AND CHOICE IN AMERICA

"The banquet room is *just* down that hall," the young woman said. "Washrooms are on your left. I hope you all enjoy your visit with us today."

Mr. Crewe nodded and turned aside, blinking a couple of times, as though dazzled by the brightness of her smile. He motioned the kids down the hall, tucking his shirttail more tightly around his corpulent middle.

"Sounds like they're expecting us," Kaspian heard him murmur to Ms. Velázquez.

The banquet room was not as impressive as the name implied, though it did have a pretty good view of Interstate 66. Kaspian and Vernon picked a table as close to the windows as they could get. Charity and Jill settled down near the door and were joined by another girl and an older kid from Nebraska named Ewan, who had a bad complexion and a bad attitude. Kaspian would not have guessed he was queer except that Ewan had lost no time in telling everyone. It was like his one big distinction, plus the zits that flared all the way down his neck. Charity had such excellent taste in people to hang out with. Kaspian wondered how he himself had ever come into the picture. And he wondered where, from Charity's perspective, he fit now.

While he was thinking about this and staring across the room, Vernon succeeded in getting the attention of Brenton and a couple of his buddies. These guys came over and sat down. Besides Brenton there was an iron-pumping peroxide victim called Phil and a more or less humanlike entity known as Foo Bird who was this gigantic, like, Samoan or something.

Lunch was laid out quickly by a staff of Hispanic people. Kaspian had expected ethnic diversity down here, but his expectations had been slightly off the mark, in that what he imagined was the type of social puree you get on a successful TV sitcom, everybody all blended up. Instead he had found a pattern of stratification, like an exotic Jell-O dessert that you make in layers or swirls. He supposed it was no big deal, but it surprised him: that's all.

Vernon opened up a little tin candy box—Altoids, the Curiously Strong Mint—and dumped out an assortment of pills. He swallowed them one at a time, between bites of food. Kaspian supposed that was how he had been told to do it. Brenton was laying down a valley-boy rap about some German tourists he had stood next to on the train. He described their haircuts in detail. Kaspian didn't care to listen so he slid his chair back until he could look down from the window into a triangle of land wedged between the interstate and two other roads that crossed at acute angles. There was water down there, and cattails, and red-winged blackbirds. All around them, noise and traffic. Kaspian wasn't sure whether to feel heartened or dismayed by this tiny, hemmed-in remnant of nature; then he realized that what he was looking at—without question, because he had seen them a hundred times before—was a beaver pond.

The dam the beavers had made (—where had *beavers* come from, around here?—) choked off the flow of water through what probably had been nothing but a low pocket of land scooped out by bulldozers. The water entered through one giant metal culvert and exited through another. But with the dam in place, the water had backed up and now it lay there, stagnant and brown. You could even, from seven stories up, pick out the places where trees—ailanthus and mulberry—had been chewed down for building material. It was pretty amazing.

In his distraction he had failed to notice the latest arrivals. At the far end of the room, where a row of chairs sat behind a small lectern, half a dozen grown-ups had gathered. One of the guys, shorter than average, with his back to the kids at their tables, threw his head back and gave a hearty laugh. By his buzz cut and his good-old-boy manner, Kaspian recognized Jasper C. Winot. Beside him, sharing his laughter though more discreetly, stood Ruby the Congresswoman. She still wore red, but only a blouse today, under a steel-gray suit. Jason Aracos lurked nearby, looking, as usual, almost translucent.

Brenton went from German tourists to a Swedish exchange student whom he claimed to have fucked over the summer before they shipped him off to *this* shit-hole. His coarseness made Kaspian lose some of his appetite. He picked at the food, which had that trucked-in-by-a-caterer quality that you find at weddings and other special occasions. Was this a special occasion? He stared up toward the front of the room, and at that moment Jasper C. Winot came over to the lectern and got his mouth all over the microphone and said:

"Good afternoon, boys and girls."

It came out loud and garbled, like a bomb going off inside someone's epiglottis. Foo Bird, the giant Samoan, grinned and said:

"Boys and girls. You don't hear *that* shit every day."

Kaspian thought this betrayed a glimmer of evolved sentience. He decided to stay tuned.

At the microphone, Jasper Winot said, "I was very glad to learn that your group *happens* to be visiting our PAC offices today. Because we're privileged to have also as a special guest this wonderful lady here to my left, who is a member of the United States Congress. Do you believe that?"

"Nope," said Brenton.

The Congresswoman took a little step forward, beaming, and Winot went on:

"Let me introduce the Honorable Ruby Rijowski, who represents my own home state of North Dakota. She's a real hero— or should I say heroine—in the fight against excessive government interference in the rights of free citizens to choose what kind of education their children can receive. And I've been telling the Congresswoman about *you* all, too. I've told her how you've come here from every part of this great country, some of you with a history of problems that would make my own boyhood out in the badlands look like a Sunday-school picnic, and how we're just doing everything we can, every darned thing we can *think* of, to help you put all that behind you and achieve a level of success that would just *amaze*—let me tell you, I can see the looks on their faces—just *amaze* the teachers and school board officials and—"

At the table, Foo Bird whispered, "That's the Black Helicopter lady."

"What the fuck are you talking about?" said Brenton, loud enough that Mr. Crewe shot a warning look from two tables away.

Foo Bird nodded earnestly. He had blue-black hair that was only long in front, and when he leaned forward it fell down over his eyes. The gesture of tossing it aside had become a reflex with him, punctuating his speech. "She's the one that held hearings about the black helicopters. You know: the *black helicopters*. She called all these government officials in, Air Force officers and whatnot, and they all said, We don't *know* anything about a bunch of black helicopters. And she said, I don't believe you— next witness. She didn't use those exact words, but that's what it amounted to. I watched the whole thing on C-SPAN."

Up at the lectern, Jasper Winot moved aside, making way for Congresswoman Rijowski, who Kaspian thought—seeing her now on public display—was a mighty unremarkable-looking woman, though she did seem sure of herself. She stepped right past the lectern and out nearly to the first row of tables, close to where Jill and Charity were sitting.

"I congratulate you," she told them, in a voice that needed no amplification, "on your good fortune, to have escaped from the public schools alive."

A couple of kids laughed, but not at Kaspian's table.

"She used to be a minister," said Foo Bird. "Lutheran, I believe."

That explained it, Kaspian thought. He felt like joining the conversation now. "Did you know," he said, "that Martin Luther was a virulent anti-Semite?"

"Who the fuck was Martin Luther?" said Brenton.

Foo Bird said, "No fooling."

"Yeah," said Kaspian. "And he was wildly popular with the peasants, who would flock to see him when he traveled from town to town. In all of German history only Adolf Hitler drew larger crowds. But then when the peasants revolted? Because they were all stirred up by Luther's speeches? He betrayed them and sided with the wealthy landlords, and there was *huge* amounts of bloodshed. It set the stage for centuries of blind obedience by the German masses."

Foo Bird nodded with a twisted smile. Like, he could dig that. "So how do you happen to know about Martin Luther?" he said. "For a report or something?"

Kaspian blushed. "I don't, actually. I know about Adolf Hitler."

"Him I've heard of," said Brenton, irritably.

Congresswoman Rijowski was talking about her girlhood, which sounded pretty dull. She gestured with both of her arms, not just the hands but everything from the shoulders down: you could see her up in the pulpit.

Suddenly, like a talk-show host working the audience, she stepped out between the tables and said, "Why don't some of you kids tell me about yourselves, where you came from, how you happened to get here. Chopper Winot tells me this program you're in is highly selective. Who wants to go first?"

"*Chopper* Winot?" whispered Vernon, with an Opie grin. "What a dumb nickname."

Foo Bird nodded. "It's from when he was doing battle with the unions in his meat-packing business. He cut so many jobs the union finally called a strike, which is exactly what he was hoping for, because he shut down the plant and opened a new one in a right-to-work state. They started calling him the Chopper."

Kaspian was growing impressed by this kid, who looked like nothing but a head-banging blimp.

Up front, Ruby Rijowski called upon all her ministerial energy, trying to persuade some loser to introduce himself. What does she think? Kaspian wondered. We're going to stand up and recite the whole list of screwed-up things we've ever done?

To his amazement, at the table nearest the Congresswoman, Charity Ann Laird rose shyly to her feet.

What is she *doing?* Kaspian thought. He felt strangely panicked.

Slowly Charity turned to face halfway toward the Congresswoman and halfway toward the rest of the audience. In a wavering, little-girlish voice she said:

"I was raped by my clarinet teacher."

You could feel the air sucked out of the room, like a hole had been blown in a spaceship.

Congresswoman Rijowski seemed a little taken aback. A lot taken aback. She murmured something about how that was simply *awful.*

"It's a cow-shit lie," muttered Brenton, with vehemence.

"How do you know?" said Foo Bird.

Kaspian just stared at Charity, who was on her feet but now visibly quivering.

Brenton said, "Her brother offed himself, is what happened. She told that other cunt, Jill—that's how I heard about it. I guess she got all like, tizzied out over it. But I mean, she wasn't even the one that found the body."

Kaspian looked more closely, and he decided that Charity's quivering might, in fact, be an effort to control her laughter. It was a good act, though, if Brenton was telling the truth. For sure, it had done a job on him.

The Congresswoman moved on past Charity's table, as though eager to get beyond all that. "Now who else would like to tell me how they got here? You know, as an elected Representative, I'm always interested in hearing about the lives of real people. It's so easy to fall out of touch, here inside the Beltway."

"Tell her something," Vernon urged Brenton. "Or *you*," he said to Foo Bird.

The giant Samoan, or whatever he was, only smiled.

"Fuck that," said Brenton, scornfully. The way he shifted in his seat, though, made Kaspian think he was chicken.

Suddenly, taken by the impulse, with no time for sensible thought, Kaspian stood up. He had to practically jump in the air to get Ruby Rijowski to notice him, but finally she said, "Ah, here's another one over here. What's your name, young man?"

"Kaspian," he said. "Like the prince? Only with a *K*. And I got—I was abducted by like, these strange little guys. Sort of like leprechauns. And I was missing for four days."

Around the banquet room, there was snickering, followed by outright laughter, though it was scattered and sounded uncertain. The other kids seemed more interested in how the Congresswoman would react than in what Kaspian had to say. Probably they all assumed he was lying. *We're all liars here, aren't we?*

At first, Ruby Rijowski did nothing. She stood there, a couple of tables away, staring at Kaspian, taking the measure of him.

Then she said—no longer in a pulpit voice, but with church-coffee sincerity—"I find that highly interesting. I'd love to hear more about it at a later time. Thank you for sharing it with me." Then she turned back to working the room.

Kaspian sat down, not quite knowing what had happened: why he had done it, or why the Congresswoman had passed over it so smoothly. The answer to the first question came when he noticed Charity smiling at him from across the room. When she caught his eye she made a quick OK sign with her thumb and forefinger. Like, job well done.

The answer to the second question did not come until somewhat later.

THEY had to change trains, from the Orange Line to the Blue, to get back to Arlington Cemetery where the bus was parked. The transfer happened at a station called Rosslyn, the last stop before the train slid under the Potomac River into Washington. There was an escalator, the highest and longest Kaspian had ever seen, leading up from the platform to the place where you punch in and out. Vernon insisted upon riding up this escalator and down again. Like, just to do it. Kaspian demurred. He was a hick, but not *that* much of a hick.

"Anyway, you'll probably miss the train," he said.

"So what?" said Vernon. "There'll be another one."

The kid was acting crazy, anyhow. Kaspian guessed it was all the pills he had taken at lunch, kicking in. Let him run it off.

"I'll be back," said Vernon. Then he was gone, up the long escalator. Kaspian got distracted by a train pulling in and a load of passengers in business clothes rushing past him.

"Kaspian!" Mr. Crewe called from somewhere deep in the crowd. "Vernon! Let's go!"

At the end of the station, a strip of light flashed blue. The train in the station was the one they were supposed to be getting on.

"Okay!" Kaspian called back. He stared up the escalator, looking for Vernon. It was difficult because the damned kid was so small. Finally Kaspian saw him coming down—still a long way up, though. On the platform, the crowd was boarding the train.

Kaspian waved both arms over his head to get Vernon's attention. Vernon saw him but misinterpreted the gesture. He waved back, shimmying comically back and forth.

Well, so what? thought Kaspian. There'll be another train. He turned to signal Mr. Crewe to go ahead without them. But in the huddle of passengers he could not make the teacher out.

By the time Kaspian turned back around, Vernon seemed to have flashed on to what was happening. He was moving down the escalator at a quick trot, first one step at a time and then two. Kaspian shook his head and shouted, "Never mind! We're going to miss it anyway!" But Vernon couldn't hear him.

The kid was coming down fast. He was coming down too fast. Kaspian saw that the steps were farther apart than Vernon could handle with his short legs; he was losing his balance and, in effect, falling forward. The only way he could stay on his feet was by moving faster and faster ahead, trying to keep up with his own center of gravity. He was forty steps up, then thirty, then twenty, plummeting toward Kaspian at the bottom of the escalator. Kaspian felt something twist in his stomach.

Vernon kept it together until he was only half a dozen steps away from the bottom ramp. At that point, the angle at which his body tilted forward became impossible. His feet slipped off the metal steps and he flew outward at incredible speed and almost landed right at Kaspian's feet. He actually hit first on the second-to-lowest step of the escalator, one shoulder crunching down and then the head. The escalator kept moving and sort of dumped Vernon like luggage off a conveyor belt. He slid forward, carried by his own momentum, until his crumpled body collided with Kaspian's shoes. There was a trail of blood from the escalator onward. Nearby a lady screamed.

Kaspian bent down and touched his stupid friend

> but it was only later,
> back in his room,
> he started to cry.

THE weather stayed perfect for a couple of days—not yet really fall-like, but a definite break from the heaviness of summer—and then it started to rain. It rained for nearly a week, off and on. That was possibly the worst distinct period of Kaspian's life, that he could remember anyhow, because there was no way to break out of it. Back home he would have been able to go back behind the house into the woods that sloped down to the wastewater treatment plant. He had done this so many times that the sound of that chugging equipment—a system of giant rotors, stirring the sludge—automatically put him in kind of an absent, broody frame of mind. But here in Manassas, Virginia, he could only lie in bed listening to the rain drum down. He understood that some people consider the sound of rain to be soothing. But this particular downfall made Kaspian feel trapped and afraid.

In the middle of one long night—maybe his third night running of getting zero in the way of sleep—he stood up and pulled on some clothes, regular clothes and not the uniform, and went outside. He took the boom box with him, out into the rain.

The boom box had been a dilemma. It was sitting on Kaspian's desk when he got back from that horrible trip, that unthinkable day. He had walked into his room like a zombie—lost to the world and to all the people temporarily alive in it—and then he had seen this fucking *boom box,* and that had been just too much. He had sort of folded up on the floor and sobbed like a little kid, in a way he hadn't done in years. The image of Vernon setting the boom box there—little Opie prancing in first thing that morning, excited about the field trip, tuning the radio in to DC 101, pestering Kaspian until he got up—would not leave his head. He tried entombing the boom box at the bottom of his closet, under the mass of dirty laundry. But that was like the Edgar Allen Poe story where a guy buries a murdered body but can still hear its heart beating. He considered turning the box over to Mr. Aracos, to be shipped back to Maine with the rest of Vernon's things; but he found that he was not willing to give it up. He clung to it, for all the misery it caused him.

So this particular night, maybe a week after Vernon's accident—that was the term people used, *death* being apparently too extreme—he got up and walked out into the rain with a pair of cutoffs on, carrying the boom box and letting its cord trail behind on the ground. The night was dark, but there was an overall pinkish glow in the sky from all the highway lights. He made his way through the maze of buildings and azalea bushes until he came to the sloping field, and wandered out there feeling his way to the dumpy little pond. The grass under his feet was so thick and tough it felt like walking through somebody's flower bed, after they've cut the stems back for winter. Kaspian thought about how he hated Virginia, even the plants that grew down here. At the bottom of the field he discovered that with all the rain, the pond had filled up and was not just a puddle anymore. The place where he had once knelt down next to Vernon, swatting at alien insects—that was only five or six weeks ago, but Jesus did it seem like forever—now stood ankle-deep in water.

Kaspian waded out into it. It felt good, in a mucky sort of way. It made him feel connected to something. He went far enough out to get some idea of where the middle of the pond was, the deepest part. Then he aimed with care and tossed the boom box in that direction. It hardly made a sound over the slashing rain. Kaspian was soaked by this time, and for some reason that was a kind of relief. As much as getting rid of the boom box, it made him feel freed or cleansed of something: whatever it was that kept him locked up in his room every night, unwilling even to hazard a trip to the student lounge to see what was on TV.

He stood for a while, thinking nothing, enjoying the sense of having lost track. Then it somehow became time to go, so he turned and lifted a foot from the muck and glopped it down again. As he did so, he felt movement beneath it—quick and slithery—as though he had nearly stepped on something alive.

Curious, despite the weirdness of the situation, he bent down. The slithery thing moved again: hopping clean out of the water right below him and landing a couple of feet farther away.

It was a frog. A genuine kiss-my-ass, believe-it-or-not frog. After the second hop Kaspian lost sight of it—but that's what it had been.

He got back to his room eventually, hardly knowing what he had done or how to feel about it. But for the first time in maybe three nights, he climbed into bed, still dripping wet, and crashed hard into deep, uninterruptible sleep.

THE sound of rapping on the door finally caused his eyes to snap open. They opened before he was really all the way switched over to consciousness; some dream was all jumbled up with his waking perceptions, to the point that he had no belief whatever that when Thera Boot came in and sat on the edge of his desk, staring down at him in bed, she was for real.

But she was for real. She adjusted the position of his chair so that she could prop her feet up on the seat of it. Other than that, she did nothing at all, and said nothing: only waited for him to decide to acknowledge her.

He tried not to. He rolled over in bed and pulled the covers up and just lay there, hoping she'd go away. Not for a moment did he expect her to, but they can't kill you for hoping. Eventually he gave up. The pressure of knowing she was there, staring at his butt through the covers, was more than he could stand. It interfered with normal breathing. He rolled back over and said, "What time is it?"

"Eleven forty-three," she told him. "You've slept through all your morning blocks. Including an appointment with me, which you also *forgot* to attend day before yesterday."

He propped himself weakly on his elbows. His regular morning hard-on was a prominent feature at the center of the bed, your proverbial tent in the blanket. Thera Boot glanced down that way with no effort to hide that she was looking. Kaspian decided—who knows how he was deciding things in those days—just to let it stand there. Let her stare at it all she wants. This decision, the self-consciousness of it, made the erection more intense. He flopped back down onto the pillow, embarrassed but stubborn.

"I know you have a tendency to blame yourself for things," Ms. Boot said. "I assumed you were having a rough time of it when you skipped the memorial service and declined to attend the group counseling sessions. Which were not optional, by the way. That's why I scheduled a personal, one-on-one block—I thought perhaps you'd feel more comfortable in that setting. Now you've skipped two of those. I really don't know what you expect, Mr. Aaby. You're in a relatively fortunate situation here. But out in the world at large, there is generally no one who is willing to reach out to you. Now, do you mind if we just sit and talk for a while?"

It seemed to Kaspian that she was being a little rough on him. But maybe it was calculated; maybe she was trying to snap him out of his funk. For all he knew it might work. She was a professional and might have a knack for such things.

On the other hand, she ought to know damned well why he hadn't felt like sitting in a classroom through some touchy-feely group weeping binge, listening to a bunch of girls talk about their *feelings,* while a counselor—Ms. Boot, no doubt—lectured them soothingly on the nature of grief and the importance of getting through it, of not falling into despair. Kaspian knew all about this because there had been a suicide at his high school last year and he had been through the whole nine yards, even though he hadn't even been friends with the kid. He was not about to sit through any of that again. Above all not with Ms. Boot presiding.

He propped himself up again and found that his hard-on had gone away.

"Excuse me," he said, and rolled out of bed, clammy cutoffs and all. Let Ms. Boot puzzle over *that*. He padded into the bathroom and peed for about five minutes straight. He felt like he had been asleep for a month. When he came back out, she had opened the curtains, and a little bit of sun was slanting in, falling in globs between oak leaves. The rain was over.

"Sit down," she told him, and he obeyed her, right on the corner of the bed where Vernon had always sat. He even tried bouncing the way Vernon had bounced, but he was too heavy to make it work right, to achieve that manic springiness.

Ms. Boot examined him with her eyes. He wondered if she really was a psychologist—like with a degree and everything—or just a guidance counselor putting on airs. The way she comported herself in moments like this made Kaspian feel that *Doctor* Boot was a real possibility. There was a certain authoritative force behind those probing eyes. Not for the first time, Kaspian reflected that this was a person you did not want to get on the bad side of. He wondered why, in that case, he could not keep himself from fighting her every inch of the way.

"What did you mean," he asked her, "when you said I blame myself for things? I don't blame myself for Vernon. I don't blame myself for shit, actually."

"No?" she said. She smiled at him. Truly smiled, right now, like she was happy about something. But then he supposed this was all just part of her routine, her little black bag of mind-tools. "Whom *do* you blame, then?"

The correct answer was, Nobody. But Kaspian, possessed by the usual devil, said, "Well as a matter of fact, I kind of blame *you,* a little bit."

She opened her eyes so wide it was almost worth it. It gave him a few seconds to ponder what there was about those eyes that was so unhealthy for growing boys.

"Me personally?" she said at last. "Or *us,* the Staff? Or just authority figures in general?"

Kaspian pressed it. "No, I mean *you.* Wasn't it you that gave him all those pills? He was taking like, five or six separate things. I watched him, that day at lunch. *That's* what screwed him up so bad. He was hyper even before. But the last couple of weeks, he was hopping all over the place. He couldn't keep still for a minute. Didn't you even notice?"

Ms. Boot waited to make sure he was finished. Something changed about her expression but Kaspian could not have said what the difference was—a tightening of the facial muscles, an imperceptible flaring of the nose. She seemed to be looking down at him from a greater height than just the glassy top of his desk.

"I think," she said slowly, "you're accusing me in order to purge yourself of your own guilt. You were his friend, an older friend who had assumed the role of a surrogate brother. You took Vernon under your wing, and you made him a kind of disciple. He was beginning to mimic your mannerisms and your patterns of speech."

"That's not true."

"You can sit with me and watch the videotapes of his counseling blocks," she said. She spoke with growing force, though her voice stayed reasonably quiet. "I noticed it immediately, and I'm not the only one. Other people were wondering whether your influence on him was appropriate, given your respective backgrounds."

"What other people?"

She blew it off. "I have *always* followed with the utmost strictness *all* applicable guidelines concerning the administration of psychopharmaceutical therapy. You are *far* off-base in your accusations, and anyone would agree with me about that. But I understand that you're just speaking out of guilt and out of grief, so I'm willing to overlook it. Once. But I'll tell you frankly, Kaspian—I am starting to get my fill of your obstructive attitude. Not on my own account. But I have to consider the well-being of *other* students, after all."

By *other*, Kaspian thought, she might have meant other students besides him. Charity, for instance. Or she might have meant other students besides Vernon. In other words, *people you haven't killed yet.*

He turned angrily away. He felt like ripping the pillow apart.

But he knew that anything he did—anything he even said— would just become another little entry in some folder in Ms. Boot's filing cabinet. He told the wall, "I am *not* guilty. I am not blaming myself. You're an idiot if you think that. Maybe that's a standard thing that you think always applies whenever some kid dies, but it doesn't apply to me."

"I know you would like to believe that." Her voice became softer. "It's part of your mechanism of self-image protection, to feel that you're *different* from everyone else, that ordinary laws don't apply to you. But trust me, Kaspian. Grief is a universal human experience. It follows certain patterns, like everything else. Certain governing principles apply. I can help you under- stand what you're feeling and what you're *going* to feel, weeks or even months from now. That's why I came here to your room. That's why I'm taking *my* time out to talk with you."

As opposed to what? Kaspian thought. Brownnosing Jasper Winot? Flipping through *Vanity Fair?* He glared at the wall.

"For instance," she said, "take the death of your father. I know you've never quite gotten past blaming yourself for that. Perhaps the present crisis can help you to resolve some of those older issues. After all, that was a primal experience for you: a rite of initiation. It was your first awareness of death, and it was devastating to you. Quite naturally so. No child could be ex- pected to comprehend or to assimilate such a loss. You were what: six years old at the time? Nonetheless, the fact that you were *not* able to assimilate it continues to cloud your feelings, even today."

Kaspian did not feel clouded. He felt as clear as bulletproof acrylic windows in an armored car. He turned upon Ms. Boot and he said:

"I. Do not. Blame. Myself. For. My father. Dying."

She shook her head. "Tell me, then, why you feel such anger and resentment toward your stepmother."

"What does *that* have to do with anything?"

"Ah. Getting a little complicated, isn't it? That's why these things are so hard for a person to understand. A person needs help sometimes, help from a knowledgeable outsider. To answer your question, what it has to do with anything is that your anger toward your stepmother represents a transference of blame for the death of your father."

"Transference my butt," said Kaspian. "She did kill my father. I mean, not really *kill* him. But she made him so unhappy he just sort of . . . lost it. The spark, whatever. She'd do the same to me, too, if I let her."

"I see," said Ms. Boot, in a way that made Kaspian regret having opened his mouth, or rather not having closed it. The tragic flaw again. "So you've never reflected upon *why* your father decided to remarry? You've never understood *who* he was trying to be a good father to, by providing a substitute mother? Of course you have, Kaspian. You know that you are, at the bottom of it, the motive force. Not just in your own life, but in your father's life as well. Thus, by implication, in your own emotional equation, you are the motive force behind his death. You have carried that knowledge—which is *false* knowledge, I hasten to say—in your subconscious since early childhood. You wish to eliminate your stepmother because she serves to remind you of it, by her very existence. And today, when confronting the death of a friend, though it occurred quite by accident, you cannot escape that old, deeply ingrained pattern. This death, you feel, must somehow have been caused by you. Something you did, something you failed to do. A word you might have spoken. A different place you might have stood. These things must be going through your mind and causing you *tremendous* pain. And all I want you to understand is that I *know* how badly you feel, because it's part of the *pattern*, you see. It's—"

"Would. You. Please. Shut. Up."

Kaspian rose from the bed and walked across the room to the window. He stared at the grounds of the former recreation spot, where some of the clones were done with lunch and soaking up the sunshine. He saw Foo Bird and Brenton and wondered idly what those two could possibly have in common, enough to want to hang out together. Maybe coming from California was enough. He guessed it had been enough for him and Vernon to have come from Maine.

"Okay," he told Ms. Boot. "Maybe you're right. Okay? I'll have to think about it. Now can I please just like, be by myself? Please?"

She slid her butt off his desk, which was all he wanted. "I hope you *do* think about it," she told him. "And I hope you'll come talk to me, when you feel ready to. Believe it or not, I'm here to help you. That's my job."

"Right," said Kaspian. "Fine."

"And also . . ." She paused long enough to make him wonder, despite himself, what could possibly be left to say. "We never talked about the results of your Omega Project Battery, did we? They're fairly interesting, I think. Perhaps you'll think so as well. If you come by, we can discuss them."

That was all.

Kaspian stared far away while she let herself out.

HE did not believe a word of it.

Not that she understood. Not that she was there to help.

Not that there was anything he could have done, or that he *thought* there was anything he could have done, even subconsciously.

Not that he was tormented by something that had happened way back when he was six years old.

And not—above all not—
that he had killed
his daddy.

WHEN he finally left the room that afternoon, he felt as though he had been indoors for a long, long time. He felt like he was crawling out of some Underworld, and was not quite ready for the sights and sounds of quote, reality, unquote. He looked for Charity but she was still in her Physical Development block. Her schedule had changed lately and so had his. Now they did not overlap at even one point. Kaspian would have bet money this had not been the computer's idea.

To kill time until dinner, he dropped by the student lounge, where he found Brenton and Foo Bird playing All-Star Hockey. Brenton appeared to be plastering the giant Samoan kid, whose reaction time was slow. Kaspian watched for a little while until Brenton got bored with winning so lopsidedly.

"*You* want to go a couple rounds?" he said to Kaspian, without even asking Foo Bird. Kaspian shook his head. Brenton slapped the side of the game and said, "Well shee-*hit*," and walked out the door. Foo Bird smiled in a crooked manner, shaking his head.

"What an asshole," said Kaspian.

"Yeah," said Foo Bird. "I know. But I love the guy."

Kaspian studied Foo Bird's expression, but it was difficult to read; the face was just round and quiet.

"Want to play?" Foo Bird asked him.

Kaspian said, "Sure," and they faced off with the little plastic-and-metal guys in their long grooves. They whacked the puck back and forth without notable effect. After blowing one practically locked-up shot, Kaspian said, "What the hell kind of name is Foo Bird, anyway?"

The big kid nodded, as though to indicate he was taking this question under advisement. He rammed the ball down the rink, passing it neatly from a guy on the left to a guy on the right, only to lose it before Kaspian could even find his goalie's lever.

"We suck," said Kaspian.

Foo Bird nodded ruefully. "It's a nickname," he said.

"Yeah, like—no kidding."

Foo Bird was not kidding. "Haven't you heard the joke?"

"What joke?" said Kaspian.

"If the foo shits, wear it. Haven't you heard that?"

"No," said Kaspian. "I mean, I guess now I have."

"That's just the punch line. Ask around, everybody's heard it. I'm not going to tell it to you because I'm sick of it. My real name is Fuad. That's an Arab name. My dad's from Jordan. My mom's from the Big Island. That's basically the story. It was Brenton who gave me the nickname. We grew up together in Pasadena."

"No kidding?" said Kaspian.

Foo Bird slammed the puck and accidentally scored. It seemed to please him, though you could only surmise this from the scantiest of clues.

Kaspian thought Foo Bird was a strange guy, but not an unlikable one. His manner was pleasant enough. You got the feeling he did not like to talk about himself. Yet he did not mind talking, per se. Like that other day at lunch.

That other day. Kaspian turned aside, forgetting the hockey game for a moment, dealing with this stab of pain right in the heart: a physical fact and not just a metaphor. His heart hurt. He winced and liquid squeezed out of his eyes.

Foo Bird said, "Are you okay?"

"Sure," said Kaspian. "Maybe I need to get some air."

He walked slowly out the door. The sun was low, and errant leaves were blowing around—small ones, mostly, from the buffer strip of woods between Sudley Center and the highway. The big oaks overhead were still drab green. Kaspian didn't realize

Foo Bird had come outside with him until the big kid spoke from just a couple of steps away.

"He was your buddy." Then nothing for a few seconds. "I'm really sorry. You must feel sad."

Kaspian turned to look at him, but the sight was no different than usual. "Thanks. He was a good kid. We used to hang out sometimes."

Foo Bird nodded. He stood still—not as though he was waiting, but just as though he had chosen not to move.

"It *is*," said Kaspian, calming down some, "kind of a stupid name, though. Foo Bird."

"You think?" said the big kid, as though this were an interesting opinion. "I look at it as a form of camouflage."

That almost made sense. Kaspian thought it over. He wondered what his own camouflage consisted of. Or whether he had any.

"Well, I'll see you around," said Foo Bird. He turned and went back inside the student lounge. Kaspian waved to him, knowing he couldn't see.

CHARITY did not come to dinner. Kaspian left the chow hall and hunted for her every place he could think of, her room, the tennis court, the gym. Eventually he tracked her down in the largest building at the Center, a panelized void that served as an assembly hall, a theater, and on weekends, a nondenominational chapel. She was just sitting there under a skylight in a folding metal chair, reading a book by what remained of the used-up light of day. The book turned out to contain poems by Christina Rossetti, which meant nothing to Kaspian.

"Hey," he called across the room to her. His voice echoed.

"Hey," she called back.

Everything was cool. So far.

Still, he approached with care. She could be moody and she did not like to be crowded. These things were just about the extent of what he knew about her, except for all the physical characteristics he had memorized, and the story Brenton had told about her brother committing suicide. She sat at a long table, the fold-up/fold-down kind. Posters for an antidrug campaign were laid across it. She went on reading her book while Kaspian picked a place to sit: not too close, not too far.

She was the one who was supposed to talk first. That's the way it had always been, but now, as she continued to read without looking at him, Kaspian guessed things maybe had changed. He couldn't think of any way to break the silence that would not sound obvious and dumb. But after a while the emptiness of just sitting there got to him. He stood up and embarked on a tour of the room, scuffing his feet on the waxed and polished floor.

Charity said, "You don't have to make a scene. I'll pay attention to you, if that's what you want."

He didn't get it. It was like she was mad at him.

"I don't need *attention*," he said.

She closed her book. In a stagey voice she pronounced: *"Life is not sweet."*

He had to strain his already overloaded cognitive facilities to decipher this: she was quoting from the poetry book.

She took a dramatic couple of steps, falling down on one knee and striking a pose that reminded him of the tarot card with the naked girl on it, The STAR.

> *"One day it will be good*
> > *To die, then live again;*
> *To sleep meanwhile: so not to feel the wane*
> *Of shrunk leaves dropping in the wood,*
> *Nor hear the foamy lashing of the main,*
> *Nor mark the blackened bean-fields, nor where stood*
> > *Rich ranks of golden grain;*
> *Only dense refuse stubble clothe the plain:*
> *Asleep from risk, asleep from pain."*

Kaspian said, "I've never seen anybody actually *declaim* before."

She cracked up. Kaspian was a little surprised because he hadn't meant it to be *that* funny.

"Truly, I haven't," he said. "That was very good. So I guess, maybe, you're into acting?"

Something about her seemed to loosen, like a knot was untied. She shook her head. She executed another couple of steps in that stretched-out, stagey way, bending her knees sharply and keeping her weight low with a very straight spine, and belatedly Kaspian got it that she was a *dancer*. He wished she would go on just moving her body like that, so that he could sit and watch her; but now she discarded the pose and fell into a kind of slouch. Staring at him: waiting.

He said, "You know what I saw last night?"

She shook her head. Kaspian had come to stand under the skylight now, and it was she who was off in the shadows. Her pale gray eyes looked spooky there. Her entire form—seeing it now abstracted by dusk—had a certain feline quality, an efficient fitted-togetherness, that was missing from, say, Thera Boot's.

"What did you see?" she asked him, indulgently.

"A frog."

She smiled. "Are you sure?"

"Of course I'm sure. I live in Maine."

"You lived in Maine."

The formulation sounded wrong but he could not find a way to actually disagree with it.

"Anyway. It was down at the pond. Remember the pond?"

She looked at him like, What a question. Though they had only been there once.

"Show me," she commanded.

She spoke in a voice that he wanted very much to obey, to submit to. Only, the pond . . . he wasn't sure if he was ready for that again, so quickly, after his little ceremony last night. What if the stupid boom box was lying there half out of the water?

Charity wasn't waiting. She walked to a set of double metal doors, barely glancing over her shoulder to see if Kaspian was coming.

Well, at least she checked.

He made a point not to race to the door after her. He noted

with appreciation that on her urgent frog quest she had taken not the nearest exit but the one that lay on an axis leading to the pond. One straight-ahead female there.

By the time they got to the bottom of the field, you could see the first stars. Kaspian missed doing "Star Light, Star Bright." So many things about childhood are so *cool*—so magical and fun. Why can't you keep on *doing* that stuff—why do you have to outgrow it? You do, though. Then you feel like you're faking it if you try doing "Star Light, Star Bright" again.

Still, you could dig that first little speck of gleaming thermo-nuclear radiance.

Charity said, "My feet are all wet."

"From the grass? Mine too."

The thought arose in him to do something impulsive—take his shoes off and go wading out, like—but couldn't get up for it. His impulsiveness must have shot itself off for the time being. He stood uncertainly, caught between childhood and now.

"So where was this frog?" she said.

"Hm?"

His head had floated off somewhere—over toward the higher ground across the field: dark tree shapes against the afterglow of sunset. Charity's face appeared suddenly up close, piercing his thoughts. She kissed him before he had time to get ready for it, even to think about it. Out of nowhere she was opening her mouth to his and just as suddenly she broke off. Kaspian's heart did a triple backspin followed by a belly flop. The Hungarian judge is giving it a 3.5.

"I said, *Where was this frog*."

He shrugged. "I have no idea. It was pitch dark."

"Then *how* did you *see* a frog?"

He assumed a historically accurate posture, reenacting the crime. "I was kind of turning around like this, and I was taking a step, and when my foot came down I heard this *sscchhllooop*"— unrealistic but evocative muck sound—"and this *frog* hopped out right from under my foot, otherwise he would have been squished. I felt it because I was barefoot."

She frowned gravely. "You were barefoot."

He nodded; he didn't want to explain.

"But you didn't squash him."

"No way. I saw him again. He hopped."

"What kind was he?"

"I couldn't tell. *It was dark.*"

"You don't have to flame off at me."

"I wasn't—" He felt like Foo Bird, reacting too slow to Brenton's slap shots. He *hadn't* been flaming off, though he could see how she might have taken it that way.

"So how's your new schedule?" he said.

She gave him a frowny look; this was way off-topic. He tried again.

"I mean, are you all right? I just haven't seen you or anything. I'm only *asking* because I *care,* I'm *interested,* okay?"

"Right. You really sound it."

He felt like screaming. He only knew one way to talk. Maybe it was a smart-ass way, but this was not English as a second language: it was his only tongue. Yet obviously the words were coming out of his brain with a certain polarity and going into hers with another, refracted by a number of degrees.

"I'm so fucking sorry," he said. The sad thing was that this was true, he was sorry, honestly, about a whole bunch of things. Too many, perhaps: so that no single one of them could claim much of his energy any longer. The effort of making himself clear to Charity—after having failed with his stepmother, his teachers, a couple of ministers, and countless professional kid-listeners—seemed pretty much foredoomed. He sighed. "Look, I've been having kind of a hard time, too, okay?"

"I never said you hadn't. I waited for you last night and you didn't come."

"I didn't know you were . . . where? Where did you wait? How was I supposed to know?"

"Right there. Where I was tonight. Which proves you could have found me if you looked."

He opened his mouth. But what? He was supposed to tell her how he had been too freaked with grief and terror to risk coming out of his room? He closed his mouth again.

She turned away. It was dark enough now that her pale skin had a glow about it, a halo effect, as though you were seeing the pure whiteness of her aura. He wanted so much to reach out and touch her. He could so nearly recall the exact smell that had risen out of her shirt that day—that day—in Arlington Cemetery: even the memory of it was so intense that he felt a twinge of weakness in his legs.

Yet a distance greater than mere units of space—something like the distance between dreaming and waking—lay between them. The distance had always been there, the empty middle, but before, it had been their meeting ground. Now it was No-Man's-Land.

"I don't see any frogs," Charity said.

At first hearing, it sounded petulant. But on the replay, it acquired a brokenhearted sound like a scratchy old vinyl LP.

"You don't just *see* them," he told her. "That's not how it works. You have to really *look*. Like this."

He squatted down and surveyed the ground as best he could in the dying light. It looked too high-and-dry here, so he waddled a few steps closer to the pond. Charity watched him tentatively, biting a finger, seeming to withhold judgment as to whether he was for real. He tried to keep steady, like you do with an animal: no sudden moves. There was no *way* he was going to locate a frog in this light, or rather nonlight.

Liminal.

The word tapped his inner ear with a papery resonance, like the tight skin of a tambourine. He remembered hearing the word before, though he did not, for the time being, remember where. It had to do with thresholds. It was a name for those places and times when strange things, unexplainable visions and visitations, occur. Kaspian realized that he was at just such a time and a place now: the edge of a pond, the fuzzy beginning of night, the No-Man's-Land between him and Charity. On one side of him were love and gentleness and human warmth; on the other, things too bad to even think about.

He understood then what he wanted to show her, what he needed to prove to her, and it had nothing to do with a frog.

In the grip of this weird, penumbral inspiration, he looked up at her from his squatting position and said, "Do you believe in angels? Or like, other worlds, other dimensions?"

She laughed. He could not make out her expression and couldn't be sure what kind of laugh it was. "You mean like what you said that day at lunch? *I was kidnapped by little green men.* That was *so* good."

"Kind of," said Kaspian.

He knew it was pointless. But he stood up and looked past the pond into the dark trees beyond. There was nothing distinctly physical to see there, and yet you could see *something.* He pushed his mind harder, trying to summon up the appropriate semidementia.

"I mean, kind of like magic," he said, staring off in that peculiar way. "You know, alternate reality. I knew this witch once. I mean, this woman who was a witch. Anyhow—like, there's two different realities? Or maybe more. And you can sometimes slip over to the other one, or open up a little passageway to it. That's what magic is about. And religion, too, I guess."

He was getting nowhere; that was obvious. Yet after a moment Charity said:

"Sure. I believe that."

"You do?"

She moved closer to him. Close enough that he could see her face better, the small pert nose, the eyes that glowed like fairy fire.

"I believe," she said, "that there are more things in heaven and earth, and all that. If that's what you're asking."

It was, but not exactly.

More exactly, he wanted it to happen again. *It,* the experience, the vision, the AE2—whatever it had been. He wanted it to happen with *Charity,* to both of them together.

Only the good parts, though. None of that blinding terror and other shit.

He chuckled, shaking his head. He knew it wouldn't work that way. It would never work where or when or how you wanted it to.

And yet.

"Here," he said. He stuck out his hand, and as if by magic—this would never have worked five minutes ago—she took it into hers, holding on tight and unquestioning, and allowed him to lead her closer to the pond, until they could look down into the luminous, dimensionless, disklike blur that was part water and part reflected sky and part distilled adolescent yearning. The blur was not a specific thing but an area of jumbled definitions. You could see shapes inside it, colors, anything. He squeezed Charity's hand and she squeezed back: a more-than-natural phenomenon in itself.

"Say something," he told her.

"Like what?"

"Like . . . something spooky. One of your poems maybe."

"Spooky!" she repeated, as though pleased by this word. She dropped his hand and took a step forward so that her toes were right in the water, and she raised two skinny arms that you could faintly see up toward the first night stars.

> *"I shall not see the shadows,*
> *   I shall not feel the rain;*
> *I shall not hear the nightingale*
> *   Sing on, as if in pain;*
> *And dreaming through the twilight*
> *   That does not rise or set,*
> *Haply I may remember,*
> *   And haply may forget."*

Kaspian wondered what this meant, but didn't want to snap the mood. He looked beyond her into the shadowy woods, as he had looked into other woods in Maine, another evening, when a light had come out of them. He wished so hard for that light again. Or for *something*.

Can you wish without knowing what for?

Kaspian remembered that as a small kid, still at the "Star Light, Star Bright" stage, sometimes you saw the star and you rushed out the words so quickly that no particular desire had time to swim up into your conscious thoughts. And yet, somehow, the wish—the great secret Wish at the center of your little being—was always there. As a boy, he had never had any doubt of that, or thought for a second that he was doing "Star Light, Star Bright" for nothing. Deep in his mind, some ideal happiness, a dream of perfect fulfillment older than even his long-ago babyhood, was always there, always being wished for. His whole life, in some strange way, was nothing but an acting-out of that wish, a yearning by twilight for that barely imaginable happiness. It was the same now.

For some unmeasured time—only a couple of minutes, maybe, or a good deal longer—the act of remembering this, glimpsing again the bright, dreamy figment he had wished for as a kid, held Kaspian in a kind of trancelike suspension. He forgot, among other things, that the unspoken wish had never come true. That instead of progressing toward happiness, his childhood had been blown apart as if under a rain of mortar shells, falling one after the other, his father's death and his stepmother's step-by-step demolition of his little-kid illusions.

He looked at Charity, who had been watching him.

"I'm so sorry," she said. "I'm so sorry for you that he died."

He didn't get who she was talking about, not at first. That's how out-of-it he was. He moved into her arms like a soldier in full, disorderly retreat. She held him and the night air felt cool all around their small circle of warmth.

After that they walked out into those dark woods, where no mysterious light appeared, but where Kaspian experienced something unbelievable nonetheless—something he had thought about with mounting intensity for the past couple of years, but

could never have imagined
being as great
as it was.

YES.

Kaspian opened his eyes and he thought: It's true. It's real.

Yes.

He sat up in bed feeling more clearheaded than he'd felt since he was a little kid with nothing to clutter his brain. The sun was barely up; there was time to take a long hot shower before breakfast.

He pulled Ring Bear from the secret place in the drawer where he stayed—*where he lived,* Kaspian allowed himself to think, because nothing was impossible today—and carried him into the bathroom.

In a pirate voice, hale and blustery, he said, "It's you and me, Bear."

Hearing the words, Kaspian felt certain that he must have spoken them before, long ago, in his Karl Jaeger persona, in a make-believe grown-up.

"You and me," he said again. In just a Kaspian voice now; thoughtfully. "We're inseparable."

He put the little animal down and wondered how much, or how little, he would ever remember.

When he stepped into the shower stall, just before the water hit him, the complicated mixture of smells left on his body from the night before rose into his nostrils and—

"Whooah, *YES*"

—he yelled out loud in a rush of good feeling. Then the water ran over him and he squirmed under the hot-hot stream that ran down his neck between his shoulder blades and into the center channel along his spine. He felt completely, perfectly alive.

He made plans and resolutions. He was going to start showing up on time for all his Op Blocks. Even the counseling block Wednesday afternoon in Ms. Boot's office. She was not going to get to him anymore. He was going to sit with Charity at mealtimes, and he was going to make friends with Foo Bear, even if this meant training himself to tolerate Brenton. He might call his new friend Fuad, his actual name. He was going to send postcards to his stepmother—this might forestall her from phoning to check up on him—and perhaps even one to his stepsister at Bob Jones University. He was going to sit down and write a letter of condolence to Vernon's parents, telling him that their son had been a good kid, promising to remember him always. Then he would figure out how to send e-mail from the system here, and get back in touch with his buddy Eli back home. Eli and Kaspian had sort of a falling-out toward the end of last school year; but that was way back then, and Kaspian felt like a different person now. A totally different person.

He dropped by the student lounge and picked up his latest weekly schedule, which had lain for a couple of days in his cubbyhole. He noted how clear and attractively laid-out the graphics were: you could easily see how your time was going to be divided. You could plan ahead. He looked forward to sitting down and aligning his schedule with Charity's, scanning for blocks that overlapped and empty spaces that they could find ways to fill, together. The two of them. A team.

Everything was good. His uniform fit comfortably. His full Windsor knot came out halfway decent, and the memory of Vernon did not hurt him so much, only made him sad, and sadness is an aspect of life, an ingredient in that magical stew that you have to taste all together, for everything is stirred up and irreducible.

Outside the door of the student lounge, on his way to the chow hall, he bumped into, of all people, Jason Aracos.

Aracos looked at him strangely, as though Kaspian were like, wearing a ridiculous hat. Kaspian looked back, too solidly planted on new ground to be disturbed by this shadowy, murmuring functionary.

"Excuse me, Mr. Aracos," he said. When Aracos did not yield his position in the middle of the sidewalk, Kaspian placidly stepped around him. He halted when the man said:

"I'd like to have a talk with you. If I may."

Something in his voice . . . a faintly heard warning, like an air-raid siren off in a village miles away.

"What about?" said Kaspian, guardedly. He hoped this dweeb did not plan to screw up his perfect day.

Aracos said in a very flat voice, like the words meant nothing to him, "Charity Laird tried to kill herself last night. She swallowed a large number of pills. Her friend Jill discovered her and alerted us and Charity was taken to the hospital, where I'm told she's in satisfactory condition. Jill tells us that Charity was with you last night. That she was with you until quite late. I'd like to ask you a few questions about that. If I may."

IT was not possible. Kaspian was sorry but it was just not.

Admittedly, his ideas of what is possible and what is not had undergone some serious revision lately. But for Charity to kill herself, or try to kill herself, or *want* to kill herself—after last *night,* after what happened, the two of them . . . that absolutely was not. He would never believe it.

"What kind of pills did she take?" he asked them.

They were sitting in Mr. Aracos's office. Thera Boot was there. The office was large but lacking in personality.

Aracos started to speak but Ms. Boot said, "What difference does that make? It's doubtful that they *would* have killed her, if that's what you're getting at. But it's also doubtful, in fact highly improbable, that Charity herself could have known that. We're treating this as a serious attempt and not merely a gesture."

That hadn't been what Kaspian was getting at. He was getting, or trying to get, at where the pills had come from. Like, whether they had been prescribed by Ms. Boot, or were something Charity had gone out of her way to get her hands on. It seemed like an important point, but Ms. Boot had missed it, and Kaspian figured that was just as well. He wanted zero further confrontations with authority figures.

The questions Aracos wanted to ask him amounted to a stern but blessedly quick grilling as to what he and Charity had done the night before: what they had talked about, whether she had given him anything like a hint. Kaspian was too stunned to shake the questions off, though he didn't exactly give straight answers to them, either. The two adults must have recognized his astonishment for what it was, because they didn't press him. They could see that Kaspian knew nothing, that he had not even *begun* to see it coming, and they accepted this. In fact, his ignorance did not appear to surprise them. He thought about that, and when it was his turn to speak, he tried to probe it a little.

Had *they* known such a thing might happen? Was there something about Charity's *case,* as Ms. Boot would have called it, that flashed a red light? Had she, for example, ever pulled such a thing before?

He didn't ask any of this straight out. Rather he just sat there and tried to keep the conversation, such as it was, going a little longer. They made no objection to this, seeming to accept his presence in the room as a natural part of the situation. Which probably only proved how terrible things were, like the stunned abeyance after an air raid, when you sit among your neighbors, nobody saying much, trying to pool the little bit of hope there is among the bunch of you, waiting for the all-clear to sound.

It was too bizarre. Kaspian had woken up with the smell of a girl who might have been dead by then clinging to his body. And even though she was alive, she might as well be on a different planet. *The hospital.*

For a few more minutes, he sat there without speaking, while Ms. Boot and Mr. Aracos quietly conferred. He didn't even try to listen. Finally Mr. Aracos looked up and told him he could go.

By then he was ready.

*   *   *

IT was not far to the hospital. There had never been any doubt, since the word first dropped like a 500-pound bomb, that Kaspian was going to take off for there. The only questions had been, where was it, how was he going to get there, things like that. Practical, real-world concerns. In other words, jack shit.

As it turned out, Prince William Hospital was just a mile or so farther up the main highway, away from the interstate. Kaspian tried hitching a ride, but when none was forthcoming, he hiked to the nearest convenience store and they gave him directions. The whole trip took a half hour.

The hospital reminded him of a fleet of cruise ships, old ones and new ones, all gleaming expensively with their rows of identical cabin windows, anchored in a bay of parked cars. He guessed Charity would have been transferred by now from Emergency to a regular room. So he chose an entrance in one of the older parts of the complex marked Inpatient Reception, where he found a long desk with a lot of women sitting before computer terminals.

He spoke her full name aloud for the first time since she had told it to him, and he had repeated it, delighted by the sound. In this place it sounded less delightful. He guessed that even the most potent invocations lose their power when uttered under fluorescent lights. The receptionist glanced up from the screen with a bland face full of competent, professional friendliness.

"She's in F-151. That's over in the Fones Building? Psychiatric and in-residence recovery? It's an access-limited area. Are you a member of the immediate family?"

"Her brother," he said, without expression.

"Well, you just go out through that door at the end of the hall. You'll be asked to present a photo I.D. at the nursing station."

He thanked her. He tried to formulate a plan while he walked from one building to the other. From the many times he had seen this sort of thing done on television, the chief lesson was that you should act like you belong there. You bide your time until everybody is preoccupied (for instance, talking to their boyfriends on the phone)—then you make your play. But as soon

as Kaspian stepped into the Fones Building, he was confronted by a young male nurse in green hospital garb stationed at a counter looking over a small waiting area. There was no place to lurk inconspicuously. So Kaspian walked up to the counter and repeated Charity's name, and that he was her brother.

"And *your* name is?" said the nurse.

Kaspian came close to stopping to think. Idiotic: she had never told him her brother's name, and he had not had the sense to have a made-up one ready. The only name he could say fast enough was his own.

"Like the *prince?*" exclaimed the nurse, who struck him as gay, though what did Kaspian know? "That was such a wonderful series. I went out and read all the books."

"Me too," said Kaspian. "Actually, I didn't care for Aslan."

"Wasn't he *bossy?*" said the nurse. He smiled at Kaspian in a way that Kaspian wasn't accustomed to. It reminded him slightly of a certain look that Thera Boot sometimes gave him.

He took a risk. "Do you know if she's okay? My sister? Is she sleeping or anything? Because I don't want to like, disturb her. I know she needs her rest."

"Why don't we go see," said the nurse.

He stepped briskly from behind the counter and led Kaspian around a corner and onto a quiet hallway that ended in a bank of windows through which sunlight poured into a small recreation area. At Room 151 they halted, and the nurse eased the door open a foot or so, enough to glance inside. The lights were off but the curtains were open, and you could glimpse some dogwood trees outside.

"I'm sure she'll be happy to see you," the nurse said quietly, stepping aside. Before he left he told Kaspian his name was Patrick, and they shook hands.

Then Kaspian passed through the space-time portal to the distant planet where Charity lay.

WHAT was so alarming was how different she looked. He had been with her less than twelve hours ago, been with her intimately, and the Charity in this bed hardly looked like the same person at all.

Her eyes were closed. Her face was thin and the wrong kind of white: tinged with cream-yellow, like the potted narcissus you buy in winter at the grocery store. That face, and the skinny arms that lay like sticks of fallen wood on top of the blanket, and the close, spiky haircut did not make her look like a punk anymore. They made her look like an inmate at a forced-labor camp. When Kaspian got close enough to really *see* her, he made an involuntary noise, a tiny outburst of dismay. It wasn't loud, but Charity hadn't been asleep after all. She opened her eyes and looked right at him.

"Hey," she said. "I figured you'd come."

Her eyes didn't look too bad—they weren't like, sunken or anything. And her voice sounded pretty much the same as always. Tired, was all.

"Jesus H. Christ," he told her. But he didn't know what to say next. He sat down on the edge of her bed, inevitably reminding himself of Vernon. For some reason, and this was odd, he also reminded himself of his own father, coming to tuck little Kaspian in. He sensed that all these things, all these people, were connected somehow, himself included—himself especially—but there seemed no way to make sense of it.

"Did they give you a hard time?" Charity asked him.

"Who? Why?"

Stupid questions, he immediately thought. She had the sense not to answer it. She raised one arm from the elbow and aimed a finger out the window. "There's a pair of cardinals out there. Somewhere. The female comes to sit in the dogwood tree. But she never stays long."

"How can you tell which is the female?"

"Don't you have cardinals in Maine?"

"Sure, but—I guess I've never been too much into birds or anything."

She gave him a look. Like she had detected a grave flaw in his character. "It's their coloring. The male's is more intense."

She paused and then added, "It's the state bird. Here in Virginia. You're not allowed to kill them."

"You mean," trying to be funny, ha ha, "you're allowed to kill everything else?"

"Sure," she said. "Only in season, though. But that's not so bad, because nigger season lasts all year long."

Her tone was bitter, close to angry, but too emptied-out to make a go of it. He wondered if she was pissed that the pills hadn't worked.

How do you go about asking a person why she has tried to poison herself? Was it even any of Kaspian's business? Did she still want to die, or was it just a way she had felt last night?

Last night. That was still the strangest part, where Kaspian was concerned. Because he had gone to bed so happy, so filled up with feelings for her that he supposed probably added up to love, plus pleasure and gratitude and a measure of incredulity. Always that requisite withholding of belief. On the Opinion Inventory, Kaspian had had a lot of trouble circling A for "agree" with many of the statements, especially the big ones: I believe there is a higher power guiding my life; or There is a plan for our universe. On the other hand he hadn't been willing to chuck those things by circling D, either. Because disbelief is just another form of belief, like Satanism is upside-down Christianity. And for sure, his caution, his instinctive agnosticism, had been proven out. Because look: no sooner had he come to believe in the existence, in his own life, of *one good thing* . . .

Charity said, "Thanks for coming to see me, anyway."

"How do you mean, *anyway?*"

She smiled, which wiped away some of the labor-camp look. "I mean, *despite* the fact that I have turned out to be another problem for you."

Her tone was self-mocking but Kaspian did not buy that. "No you're not," he said. "You're . . . I mean, I . . ."

Now would be the time, he told himself. If he was going to make a statement to her—*I love you,* or any variation—now would be the time to do it. She might even be asking for that. Some reassuring tenderness.

The trouble was, his lack of belief ran even to stuff like this. He wasn't sure he understood anything about love, or about the things that people call love, which often turn out, in cases he had witnessed, to be more like a long-term emotional flu. After a while the fever breaks, unless it kills you first. Maybe what he felt for Charity—all the warmth and attraction and the at-homeness in her company and the exultant afterglow of last night—had more to do with his gonads than with his heart. How are you supposed to know?

Instead of saying anything he took one of her hands and raised it to his mouth and kissed it.

"You scared me shitless," he said.

She gave him a wry, shadowed kind of smile, but a seemingly for-real one. He was not going to live up to her expectations, but at least he was there; he had come for her.

"Plus," he said—though it had not been his plan to mention this—"I couldn't believe . . . I mean, after what happened. Because I thought, or I felt, or whatever, that everything was *so,* I mean, totally *wonderful.* Seriously. I'd never . . ."

"I figured that."

Kaspian looked down and saw that his hands were shaking. "Figured what?"

"That you'd never. It was pretty obvious."

"Yeah, well." He was blushing and he knew it. He turned aside but she held on to his hand—didn't pull, but definitely held on to him—so that after a couple of seconds he turned back. She was staring up at him, her eyes brighter than before. She looked so sad and so beautiful. Like she was wasting away from some Victorian ladies' disease. He wanted to kiss her but first to scoop her up gallantly into his arms.

"If I tell you something," she began, then stopped. She was biting her lip, which was one of the dozens of tiny gestures that he had memorized. "If I tell you something, will you promise, and I mean *swear,* that you'll never tell a living soul for the rest of your life?"

Kaspian nodded.

"Then do it," she said.

"Do what?"

"What I said. Swear that—"

"Oh. Okay: I swear I'll never tell another living soul for the rest of my life."

She turned her head away, huffily. "You're going to have to say it like you mean it, or I'm not going to talk. I've only told one other person, ever, so like, I know it's not hard for *me* to keep my mouth shut."

Kaspian adjusted his position on the bed, sliding closer to her, so that his thigh was up against hers, exchanging warmth through the blanket. He said it again, and he did really mean it, whether or not his voice came out that way. He guessed in the end she would just have to decide whether, or how much, she trusted him.

"All *right,*" she said, practically before he got the words out. "Now this is about last night. About what we did. Okay? But it's not about *us.* Or at least, I don't mean it to be."

He nodded. He didn't get what she was saying, but wanted to encourage her.

"I've only done that a couple of times before. Well . . . a few times, more than a couple."

She stopped and looked at the wall of the room, where a television was mounted on a bracket so that you could adjust the angle. Kaspian looked at her neck. A swan princess neck, long and white.

"The thing is," she said, "it was a while ago. The times I did it before. Back when I was younger. And I never thought . . . I thought, and I told myself, that I was not going to do it again. Not till I was completely grown up."

Kaspian saw where this might be heading. He felt frightened now, because what she was trying to say might be hard or embarrassing to hear, and impossible to respond to. Beyond like, Gosh, that's terrible.

"So you mean," he said, "it happened when you were *too* young? Like a little girl?"

She shook her head. "I was . . . that doesn't matter, that's not what I'm talking about. The *person.* Who I did it with. I mean, I *loved* him, not just in that way. And he's gone now. And I know it was probably wrong that we did it, but it's . . . kind of, all I've got left of him. You know? And what I thought, what I meant to do, was . . . was be *loyal,* I guess. Even though he's gone. And even though—"

She stopped talking with a finality that suggested that she meant to stay stopped.

Kaspian straightened his spine a little. Suddenly, he understood. And as usual with understanding things, right away he wished he had just stayed in the dark, because it was a lot better that way.

"What was his name?" he asked her, gently, or so he hoped.

"Jonathan," she said, starting to cry now. "His name was Jonathan."

"It's okay," he told her, leaning down.

"It was just the two of us," she said. "We were together all the time. We did *everything* together. Not just that."

"I know, baby," he said. He pressed his face against hers, side to side, feeling the tears on her cheek.

He didn't know where the *baby* came from. It sounded like a dumb movie line. She circled her arms around him, joining them behind his shoulder blades, and didn't so much hug him as hang on to him. As in, for dear life.

IT didn't really explain anything, he thought later.

If she had had a thing with her brother, a sexual thing—and then for whatever reason, maybe related to that or maybe not, her brother had killed himself . . . that didn't really explain what had gone so badly wrong last night. It didn't explain why, after making love to Kaspian, Charity had gone back to her room and swallowed a handful of pills. He kept going through it in his head, on the long walk from the hospital to the Sudley Center and for hours after that, asking the same questions again and again. And in the end he decided that what she had told him, her great secret, did not explain a single fucking thing.

On the other hand, what did? At least it made him under-

stand her better. And as Malcolm had said, the coolest stories are
the weird ones.

He still didn't know if he loved her. But he made a decision,
that he didn't care. He was going to act and think as though he
did. His life was locked up with hers; they'd gone through
forced-labor camp together.

The war—whatever strange war this was that was killing off
people all around them—had been brutal to them both. Charity
had lost a brother and a lover; he had lost first his dad, which
was all that his family amounted to, and now stupid little Opie,
his friend.

But there was more. There was him and Charity, still alive
in the middle of all of it. They had done magic together; they
had wished upon a star. Then they had stepped across the pond,
and taken their clothes off, and lain together on the hard Virginia
ground. They had breathed each other's breath. They had told
each other secrets.

These things couldn't mean nothing. Kaspian believed that.
For that, he would have circled the big A.

THE following week, with Charity still in the psychiatric ward—
for *another* Vulcan mind probe, as she said, though Kaspian
thought she sounded oddly hopeful about it, like maybe this one
would turn something up—was a busy time for him back at the
Sudley Center. With no one left to brief him, Kaspian was forced
to examine the schedule himself. He felt like a gypsy reading
chicken entrails.

There was going to be another field trip, and this one required getting ready for. The day of the trip itself, Thursday,
was blocked off with the unhelpful title Student-Led Outreach.
The days leading up to it were front-loaded with blocks devoted
to the U. S. Constitution and Bill of Rights, the Separation of
Powers, the Founding Fathers, Church and State, and Congress
at Work: Contemporary Front-Line Issues, the latter of which
was not objectionable because it entailed many hours of watching
C-SPAN. Kaspian had never done this before and it reminded

him of the public-access station back home, where sometimes they stuck a camera in a high school classroom and just left it on, so that parents with nothing better to do could get an idea of where their property taxes were going.

On C-SPAN, the camera kept running while members of Congress sat grumpily in a wood-paneled hearing room, putting their buffalolike heads together, whispering off-mike to lean and hungry staffers, and shuffling through reams of legal-size paper, all the while listening to testimony from a succession of witnesses who came to fidget at a table behind gigantic microphones. Kaspian tried to make sense of what the hearings were about, but too many issues appeared to be intertwined. It was hard to tease them apart and get to the heart of the matter. But from what he could tell, the Honorable Members were having the same problem themselves.

Kaspian surmised that a conflict was going on, a long and bloody one—not in the hearing room but out on some broader plain of battle, to which the people giving testimony referred now and then by the phrase *Beyond the Beltway*. Often they gestured with one arm while they said this: sweeping widely, communicating vastness. After a while Kaspian came to think that this place, Beyond the Beltway, must be a definite physical location, despite its vague-sounding name—like Kosovo, which just means "field." For the sake of convenience he applied to it the mental image of Manassas National Battlefield Park, to which his Phys Dev group was bussed for cross-country practice on Mondays, Wednesdays and Fridays: part open and part wooded, with hills and rolling meadows and widely spaced stone walls, a landscape suitable for massing troops and artillery but also for concealment, infiltration, flanking movements and deadly enfilades. You could fight many kinds of battle there; and indeed, the two Battles of Manassas had been very different contests, with different outcomes. Nothing was predictable beforehand; it all depended on how things went.

How things were going in the Battle Beyond the Beltway was anybody's guess. Kaspian could not make heads or tails of it from staring at C-SPAN.

For instance. Here was a teacher from Salem, New Hampshire. She seated herself at the witness table and said she had come to speak in behalf of "children caught in the middle." She talked about the burden imposed upon hardworking families by legislators sitting in a chamber far away who think they can solve problems by throwing money at them. She spoke of "the sacred and time-honored principle of local control." Just before she was politely cut off—her allotted time having run out—she had begun to evoke a heart-wringing picture of a family forced to give up its home and move to a distant, strange community in order to escape "an alien value system forced upon the schools by some federal task force."

Next came another teacher from New Hampshire, a town called Franklin. She told the Committee that she had come to speak in behalf of "the children frozen out by our present method of funding." Kaspian could not tell if these were the same as the children caught in the middle. The new witness talked about crumbling schools and low teacher salaries and an inadequate local tax base. She said, "We need to find a way to spread our money around more evenly, so there are no longer pockets of wealth and poverty within a few miles of each other."

One of the Representatives, a woman in a red dress, broke in to ask the witness whether this didn't amount to "robbing Peter to pay Paul." Kaspian recognized first the biblical reference and then—with a rush of excitement that he felt dumb about, afterward—Jasper Winot's friend, Ruby Rijowski. So she really was a Congresswoman. Some things are hard to believe until you see them on TV.

The teacher from Franklin, New Hampshire, said, "Maybe more like Robin Hood. But when the rich are *so* rich, as they are in this country, and the poor are so *very* poor . . ."

"But don't you see," asked Ruby Rijowski, "that that is *exactly* the inequity which our Educational Freedom Initiative is designed to redress? By providing voucher and tax credits to working families so that *they* can enjoy the same range of choices that better-off families *already* possess."

The Chairman, a resigned-looking old man from Iowa, re-·

minded his colleague from North Dakota that this week's hearings were reserved for open testimony, and that the time for
debate would come later. Ms. Rijowski smiled and said she
looked forward to that.

Kaspian was deeply confused.

Conflict, he thought he understood. Open warfare, the clash
of opposing forces, cries and explosions, mounting casualties,
panic and dismay, the deep problems of generalship, the critical
importance of morale—he could have written a book about this
stuff. But the Battle Beyond the Beltway did not seem to obey
the laws he had learned. To begin with, you could hardly tell
who the warring armies were, or what each of them represented.
They actually looked and sounded rather alike. Worse, it seemed
there might be more than two of them.

Then there was the problem of figuring out which side you
were on. Was Kaspian one of the children frozen out, or the
children caught in the middle? Both? Neither? The tangle of
interlocking questions frustrated but also intrigued him.

As soon as the opportunity arose—this happened on Tuesday,
during his Physical Development block—Kaspian approached
Foo Bird and asked him to explain, in simple terms, what was
going on. He figured somehow that Foo Bird would know.

The big kid—whom Kaspian continued to think of as Samoan rather than an Arab-Hawaiian from California—dug
through a bucket of neon-green tennis balls, searching for a couple that weren't flat.

"It's the House Education Committee," he said, casually
squeezing a ball hard enough to implode it. "They're considering
legislation to scrap the traditional method of funding schools
through local property taxes. The Republicans have introduced
a bill that would establish a nationwide school voucher system,
and put public and private schools on a more equal footing, as
far as access to public revenue is concerned. It would also prevent
the Federal government from mandating certain things like educational goals and curricula, by reserving these matters for local
jurisdiction. The Democrats and the teachers' unions are screaming bloody murder because they say it will be the death of educa-

tional equality. They say the public schools, especially in poorer areas, will be left to wither on the vine, and a permanent underclass will be created. The Republicans argue, though, that—"

"Who's right?" said Kaspian.

Foo Bird looked at him as though the question were nonsensical. Or as though Kaspian, in asking it, had betrayed an unbelievably childish naïveté. The look shut him up.

"Our own Jasper C. Winot," said Foo Bird, with what sounded like a hint of sarcasm, "is scheduled to testify, later this week."

"Oh," said Kaspian. He knew better now than to ask something idiotic like, For what side?

They headed out to the tennis courts together. Most of the other kids, team-sport types, were playing soccer, so he and Foo Bird had the courts to themselves.

"I heard about your girlfriend," said Foo Bird. "I hope she's all right."

She's not my girlfriend, Kaspian started to say. But he stopped himself. He had made a resolution about this. He said, "She's fine. I guess."

"Yeah, well," said Foo Bird. "From what Brenton says, I gather she is not a carefree individual."

"What did Brenton say?"

Foo Bird just walked over to one side of the tennis court and said, "Want to volley for serve?"

"What's that mean?" said Kaspian.

Foo Bird gave him a giant Samoan smile. "You serve first," he said. "You *do* know how to serve, right?"

"Fuck you," said Kaspian. Who then double-faulted.

It turned out, however, that Foo Bird was at least as bad as he was, tennis-wise, though the big kid did enjoy a certain advantage in understanding the rules, as well as being hip to the common wisdom of the game, such as how to respond when the other player rushes wildly toward the net, brandishing his racket like a battle-ax. Nonetheless Kaspian, by wild and unconventional maneuvers, was able to eat him up across the court.

"You are without a doubt," Foo Bird panted, "the worst player I've ever been beaten by."

"Thanks," said Kaspian. He strolled to the other side of the baseline, juggling two balls in one hand, with a triumphant swagger.

"Seriously," said Foo Bird. "You're so bad, your actions are completely unpredictable. It's an interesting approach."

Kaspian was only half listening. "So . . . what's Winot testifying about?"

"At the hearings? Who knows?"

Foo Bird stood, awaiting Kaspian's serve, like a human wall. Like Stonewall Jackson in the dining room. *Rally behind the Virginians!* Kaspian tossed a ball up into the pale sky, whammed it as hard as he could, and watched it crash into the net about six inches off the ground. The next one he dumped sloppily into the middle of the box and Foo Bird smashed it into his stomach.

"Ha," Foo Bird said. "Sorry."

"Yeah," said Kaspian, lining up for another serve and this time, to his own surprise, nailing it.

Foo Bird made no comment, just assumed the wall position on the other side of the backcourt. Then—as Kaspian was tossing the next ball up in the air—he came out with:

"It's strictly business for Winot. He doesn't care shit about politics."

Kaspian blew the serve but didn't mind; he was instantly interested, more so than in tennis. He dribbled the backup ball. "How do you mean, business?"

"For Winot, it's in his best business interest to discredit the public education system as thoroughly as possible. It's a marketing issue. See, Winot has been going into states where school-voucher systems are in place, and he's been opening up AYA campuses like you open up McDonald'ses. He offers a standardized product, at a fairly low cost, and he's got the packaging and sales angles down pat. He's way ahead of his competitors in those respects."

Foo Bird twirled his racket, which looked a couple of sizes too small for him. He went on more expansively:

"See, most of the competition—your big-time private-sector operators—are geared toward taking over existing school systems and running them under contract. Winot is the only one pushing the franchised-school angle. He's the only one geared up to rush into a statewide market as soon as it opens up and to totally dominate the field right from the beginning. Now with this legislation pending on a *national* level, he's salivating. Over the past year he's been moving into states that he wouldn't even have looked at before."

"Yeah," said Kaspian. "They've even got an AYA up in Maine."

"Exactly. See, he wants to establish a presence, to develop liaison with the local education honchos, get past the initial learning curve. That way, as soon as legislation is enacted—*if* it's enacted—he's poised to jump."

Kaspian thought this over. "Is that bad?"

Foo Bird gave him the Look again. "Is it good? Is it anything? It's *business,* is all. There's a lot of uncertainty. Who's going to come out ahead, apart from a handful of private-school entrepreneurs, and maybe property owners who will see their taxes go down? Who's going to come out behind? The N.E.A.? Brown-skinned kids in the barrio? No one really knows. That's the political side. Strange bedfellows, and all that. The art of the possible."

"How do you know this stuff?" said Kaspian.

"I watch TV," said Foo Bird. Absolutely deadpan. No way to know whether he meant this to be funny or not. He maintained his perfect equipoise so far as to add: "C-SPAN."

Kaspian won the game on his next shot. Foo Bird came walking toward him and for a moment Kaspian feared bodily harm—the strong silent type turns out to be a *very* poor loser—but all it was was time to change sides of the net.

"One game to two," said Foo Bird. He sent a powerful serve blasting a couple of inches long, without seeming to stretch his muscles all the way out. Kaspian guessed he could achieve, at least theoretically, sufficient ball-velocity to knock you down. Foo Bird said, "Actually I was an intern for a while. I was in this program called Capital Encounter. We worked part-time in an office, stuffing envelopes and whatnot, and in exchange we got to *experience the workings of the American political system at first hand*. Then I got kicked out."

He served again successfully, but Kaspian, quite by accident, tapped an unreachable return.

"Ha," said Kaspian. "For what?"

"Long story," said Foo Bird.

"Cool."

Kaspian was ahead—by how much, he was a little vague about—when the Phys Dev block ended. They didn't ring a bell to signal the change of classes here; instead, some genius had modified a bronze-faced outdoor clock to chime in accordance with the daily schedule. Its tones were tastefully dull.

"Want to finish the set or quit?" Foo Bird asked him.

"And a *set* is, again . . . ?"

Really he knew and he was goofing with Foo Bird's head; but the big kid got the idea. Foo Bird took flight, flicking a sign-off with his undersized racket. Kaspian thought, What an outrageous guy.

ON Wednesday, the day before the trip, a letter came from his stepmother. He saw it lying in his cubbyhole in the student lounge like a little greeting from the Unabomber. He managed to transfer it from the cubbyhole into a notebook without injury, but it detonated later, during lunch, possibly from pressure. Kaspian felt the impact even before the envelope was all the way open, just by running a finger along his stepmother's iron-fingered crease.

The note began with pleasantries and small talk, mostly concerned with her anti-gay-rights referendum drive back home. Three separate people, she said, had signed her petition with the name of the *identical* movie star. This made her wonder about the movie star. Kaspian read at a deliberate pace, resisting the urge to skim ahead to the point. He knew there had to be a point, there never was not. His stepmother commented on the change of season ("It's getting black as Pitch"—evidently she took this to be a place, a demonic subbasement—"by 5:00 in the afternoon") and on the prospects of his old high school team, the Windjammers, in football this year. Stuff like this she knew he didn't care about, but she seemed to have decided that he *should* care, like normal people do.

"Now as to this girlfriend of yours," she wrote, getting down to it so abruptly that Kaspian was caught by surprise, despite reading slow. "I want you to know that while I am glad to hear you've finally taken an interest in girls (for a time there I had my doubts) I do hope you're not getting all hooked on this one particular girl who I hear is a very disturbed young person. Take it from someone who knows, there are many fish in the ocean. You have always had a knack for picking the real kooks to be friends with, but when it comes to girls I think you should at least give yourself the benefit of choosing someone you would not be ashamed to bring home to meet myself and your sister."

He crumpled the letter. Where does she *hear* this stuff? he wondered. Suspicion fell naturally upon Ms. Boot.

The rest of the note, which he uncrumpled and flattened out on the lunch table, consisted of routine admonishments: do your homework change your underwear type of thing. She saved one final twist for the P.S.:

"I am pleased to hear that you have put that episode last summer behind you. That was highly upsetting to all of us and it is a relief to know that the tests have come back negative. I pray for you every night and at Church."

Kaspian tossed the note with the lunch debris into a plastic hopper. It had to be Ms. Boot, he decided. That bit about test results was the clincher.

Outside, the day had grown snippish. The wind seemed to fall from overhead, swooping down on you by surprise. Some of the kids, stretching the dress code, wore AYA ball caps, black with the logo in white and red, and these were getting blown off, causing the kids to scurry and drop their books. Kaspian ambled along a path that skirted the swimming pool. He could see Kaylla, the airhead blonde from the intake center, bustling in from her car, trying to hold her hairdo in place.

He was on his way to a counseling block. He had skipped the last two, and Ms. Boot had repaid him by coming to his room, catching him in bed with a hard-on. God knows what she would do next time. He reached the courtyard where honeysuckle stems whipped wildly from the pergola, and star-shaped gum leaves scooted over the brick pavers, giving the place an illusion of abandonment. The hand-lettered sign that said *Knock Then Enter* hung like a warning, missing only the concluding phrase, *Ye Who Dare*. Kaspian was a few minutes ahead of schedule and he figured that might help him get the jump on her.

Music was playing: you could hear it through the door. Kaspian paused to listen. It was strange music, not in itself but in that he could not reconcile it with anything he knew about Ms. Boot. There was an acoustic guitar and a mellow, depressed-sounding male vocalist, and behind them rose and fell the kind of dubbed-in studio strings that go with the sappy music dumb girls listen to. But whatever Ms. Boot might, in her innermost self, be, it was not a dumb girl. Kaspian listened through the end of one song and partway into another, which sounded the same. Then he entered, as usual, without knocking.

Ms. Boot sat on the floor. Photographs lay scattered around her, and pieces of paper, and a miscellany of other stuff—stamps and rubber bands and half-used pencils—that suggested that she had been cleaning out her desk drawers. There was also a cardboard box and a four-CD compilation of recordings by Nick Drake: the pale-skinned youth with the open hand.

Ms. Boot looked up when Kaspian came in, but she did not greet him. She smiled for a second, then went back to examining the photographs and other stuff scattered on the floor.

Was this one of her games? Some sneaky psychological exercise designed to draw a response from the unsuspecting evaluuee?

Kaspian didn't think so. He couldn't say why, but he got the idea that he had managed, by showing up early—maybe by showing up at all—to catch Ms. Boot like, being herself.

"Want me to come back later?" he said. Playing a little game of his own.

"No," she said, as he figured she would. "No, that's all right. I was just . . . Is it one o'clock already?"

Kaspian shrugged. He plopped into the chair where he had sat to take the Omega Project Battery. "So who's this Nick Drake?" he said. "An old fave of yours?"

She gave him that uncharacteristic smile again—strange and rather private. "Not exactly. As a matter of fact, I had barely even heard of him when he was still alive."

She started to collect the things from the floor and place them in the cardboard box. Kaspian thought she was done answering his question but then she went on:

"There was one song they used to play on the radio, and I thought it was pretty, but I wasn't knocked out by it. Then when I actually saw a *picture*—" She gestured toward the poster on the wall, the fish-eye-lens shot. "I thought, Good *golly*. But by then he was gone."

Kaspian thought the sadness in her voice was a little too sharp to be caused by a dead folk-rock singer.

"Were you ever married?" he asked her, out of nowhere.

She looked like he had thrown a stick at her. "Why did you say that?"

"I don't know. Just wondering, I guess."

"No, really. What put that question into your head?"

"Why?" he said. "*Were* you?"

She rose from the floor and jostled the cardboard box at him. "These are my former husband's things," she said. "I was just going through them. He left them in a writing desk in the living room, and I've been schlepping them around for *years*. I hardly ever think about him anymore, otherwise. But I'm very interested to know what made you choose this particular moment to inquire about my marital status."

"Maybe I'm getting psychic," said Kaspian. The idea pleased him, though he didn't believe it.

Ms. Boot said—with apparent seriousness—"That may be.

It's been reported in the literature. But it would not be entirely consistent with . . . other factors in your case."

Kaspian stuck his legs out and crossed them, left over right. "Such as?"

Ms. Boot tossed the last of the past-life flotsam into the cardboard box, then stood up and reorganized herself. The process was smooth and efficient. Within seconds, before Kaspian's eyes, she turned back into her old confident self.

"Such *as*," she said, meeting his eyes frankly, "your over-abundance of imagination. Not for its own sake: your imagination appears perfectly healthy and within normal parameters, simply the mark of a lively creative intellect. But in the context of the Omega Battery, it turns out to be a *negative* indicator of encounter-proneness. That is, people with active imaginations are *less* likely, for reasons no one knows, to report UFO sightings, near-death experiences and a broad range of other anomalous phenomena, than people with nonimaginative temperaments. Something as simple as reading fiction regularly is a negative indicator. Also, having been fond of fairy tales as a child. Whereas, a person who says that as a child he actually *saw* a fairy—that's the whole other side of the coin."

She gave him an ironic smile that showed, at the very edge, a hint of something like uncertainty. Not your usual Thera Boot thing.

"On the whole, then, Kaspian, you do not register very high on the scale of encounter-proneness. Of course we're only speaking in statistical terms, which can be misleading. But in Doctor Ring's studies, these indices have been borne out over time. So where does this leave us?"

She folded her hands on the desk and watched Kaspian as though waiting for him to come up with an answer. Only as far as he was concerned, this left him no place different than he had been all along. He glanced up at the poster of Nick Drake, who had looked somewhat ghostlike even when he was alive.

"I guess he must have killed himself, huh?" Kaspian said.

"Who?" Ms. Boot frowned. Then, getting it, she said, "That was the coroner's verdict. But you know the British—they're never as anxious as we are to get to the bottom of things. They seem to be comfortable with a certain level of ambivalence. More so than I am."

She lifted the top sheet of paper from a stack, and beneath it Kaspian saw his own multicolored questionnaire. Ms. Boot studied the page in her hand which he supposed must be the score sheet.

"Do you know that word—ambivalence?" she asked him. "Going two ways at once? Your battery profile is a case in point. On the one hand, family background . . . your childhood doesn't seem to have been *terribly* happy, does it?"

No . . . but on the other hand, yes, thought Kaspian. Yes before, and no after. Was this ambivalence?

"That's a *positive* indicator. A stern religious environment likewise. But in other respects . . . we don't seem to observe, for instance, the marked personality change that, according to the literature, typically follows upon these experiences."

"So what did you tell my stepmother?" he said. "That I had like, *failed the test?*"

Ms. Boot flicked a hand and said, "Not much. We're required by company policy to share with parents or guardians the results of any evaluations we conduct. I advised your stepmother that while the nature of this battery is not such as to render definite, clear-cut findings, it would *appear* that your personality does not conform to the pattern of encounter-proneness."

"So, what are you saying? It never happened?"

She leaned across her desk. "*Something* happened, Kaspian. I want you to know I believe that. Our only question is, what was the *nature* of that happening? Was it a genuine anomalous encounter? Or might it have been, shall we say, a *projection*—something that emanated from within you, perhaps as a result of psychosocial stress? This is not to downplay the significance of the episode. It merely brings it, so to speak, back down to earth."

"Where was it before?" said Kaspian. "In the sky?"

"Well you know, your story does contain many of the standard features of a UFO sighting."

"*I* never said that."

"No, perhaps you didn't, but—"

"I wasn't even going to *tell* anyone except for that asshole Hunter. But I *know* it wasn't something I made up. Unless I could make up . . ."

His hand rested on Ring Bear, an irregular lump in the pocket of his uniform pants.

"Make up what?" said Thera Boot.

"Nothing."

She leaned back in her chair again, thoughtfully. "Let me ask you this. Have there been any . . . recurrences? Any follow-on episodes like the first one? Since you got back from your little outing, have you experienced any other periods of time you can't account for? Or any of the other unusual aspects of the original experience?"

Kaspian felt a certain helplessness. Because except for the broken window, which he did not want to get into again, the plain answer was no.

Not only no, but *fuck* no, Kaspian thought. Even when he *tried* to make it happen—that evening by the frog pond with Charity—there had been nothing. Not even a wall you banged up against: just blankness. As though the Girl in White and the three little guys and his dead daddy had not just gone away, but totally ceased to exist. Receded into unreality.

"You see," said Ms. Boot, speaking almost gently, "in virtually all anomalous encounters that have been investigated in depth, it appears that *recurrence* is a consistent feature. The follow-on experiences need not replicate the original. Often there is an abrupt transition from, say, a so-called alien abduction to claims of newly acquired psychic powers, or of having been cured of some chronic medical problem. Or conversely, subjects report having *developed* problems—headaches, nosebleeds, even a small number of grave illnesses like ovarian cancer—following their initial episode. But the most common thing is for the original experience to repeat itself. One-night stands, so to speak, are unusual in this field."

Kaspian didn't like the way she was talking now. As though she understood better than he did. Not that *he* understood the first thing about it. But damn it, *he* was the one it had happened to.

"I think we can feel *comforted* by the battery results," said Ms. Boot. "Because by all indications, your experience was not as . . . as *extreme* as we might otherwise have thought."

"What a relief," said Kaspian.

And she smiled at him. Totally not getting the sarcasm.

"So," said Ms. Boot, relaxing a bit, stretching her long legs out. "Are you looking forward to the field trip tomorrow?"

"Oh, yeah," said Kaspian, trying out a new voice filled with secret, inaudible ambivalence. "Definitely. I can't wait to see what Washington is really like."

She kept smiling. Not with that weird, vaguely erotic intensity. Just a teacher smile. That's a good boy, like. "I'm sure you'll find it educational," she said. "You and Fuad in particular."

"Foo Bird?" he said. "Why us, in particular?"

Ms. Boot hesitated. Kaspian got the idea that she had relaxed a little too much, stepped over some line. "Because the two of you have been . . . selected . . . to attend a special function. While the others are up on Capitol Hill. It's quite an opportunity. I hope you'll make the most of it."

The Nick Drake CD finally played itself out. Ms. Boot punched the amplifier off.

"You'll like D.C.," she said. "It's a place where things happen. Anything is possible there, you get the feeling."

Kaspian said, "I can hardly wait."

ON the telephone, Charity's voice sounded bummed.

"I don't know what's going on," she told him. "They're done with the workup but they won't release me. I've spent the day in the rec area playing cards with this sweet old lady who's crazy as a hoot owl. Canasta——have you ever heard of that?"

"On Nick at Nite, I think," Kaspian recalled. *"I Love Lucy."*

Charity laughed: a brief, bitter exclamation. "It's like they've made up their minds to keep me here but nobody will tell me why. The only doctors I ever see are these cute resident guys making their rounds, and *they* are radically without a clue. Plus Ms. Boot of course."

"What do you mean?" said Kaspian. "Plus Ms. Boot."

"Well, she's a doctor. And she comes by every day."

"She's a *real* doctor?" asked Kaspian. "I sort of wondered."

"Wonder no more. She's got this little clip-on name tag she wears when she visits. *Seriously* professional."

"Hm."

Silence oozed though the open connection. They had been talking for a while—Kaspian hunkered down in a corner of the student lounge, his back to the room, keeping the phone tied up—and now even though he could find little else to say, he hated to break it off.

"Do you miss me?" Charity said, in a fake little-girl voice.

"Sure," he said, annoyed and then puzzled: it wasn't like her to *ask* a thing like that. Another reason to worry. "I miss you a lot. Why?"

When she didn't answer, he mused aloud: "I wonder what's going on."

"*Nothing's* going on," said Charity, her distress now clearly audible. "That's the whole thing. I'm just here, like, *sitting.* Playing canasta."

"Is it fun?" said Kaspian. "Canasta."

"Sure, if you're Ethel Mertz. Kaspian, I want to get out of here. I want to see you. I want to *breathe.*"

"Well, probably you don't want to make the field trip to D.C.," he said, in case this might cheer her. "We couldn't hang out together anyway. I've got some special place I'm supposed to go to."

"Uh-oh," she said.

He waited but she added nothing. He let it go.

Behind him, Brenton was agitating to use the phone. He poked Kaspian between the shoulders and said, "Come on, asshole. *Say I love you, good-bye.* Don't let a cunt keep you tied down all night."

"Yeah, like I've got a lot else to do," said Kaspian crossly.

"What?" said Charity.

"It's just Brenton," he told her.

"Oh," she said, in a voice so quiet he had to play it back in his head, listening for hidden meanings. "Jill likes him," she tacked on.

"Figures."

Then silence again, which made Kaspian conscious of the pressure from behind him.

Finally she said, "That was fun, that night out by the pond."

He guessed she meant splashing in the water, looking for frogs. It was funny how that seemed disconnected, now, from all that came later: the soaring and the crash.

"Maybe we can do it again," she went on—her voice again very small, drawn-in—"when I get out of here."

"You'll get out of there," he assured her. (Who had said she wouldn't?) He spoke like someone making a promise. But he was in no position to make promises, so he tried to slide out from under it. "Can't you get your parents to call up and just, *order* the hospital to release you?"

"Ha, my parents." This was evidently a whole other topic. "They'll go with anything AYA tells them. Especially if it's like, that I'm *diseased* or something—they'll definitely believe *that*. But if you tell them I'm *okay,* they want a second opinion. I could spend the rest of my *life* in here, as far as my parents are concerned."

"You'll get out," said Kaspian, with determination.

"Oh," she said, sounding miserable, "I want to. I want to see you."

"You'll see me," he said.

And this time he knew it was a promise,

and he knew he would
do anything
to keep it.

part 3
THE DISTRICT

The little boy lost in the lonely fen,
Led by the wand'ring light,
Began to cry, but God ever nigh,
Appeard like his father in white.

—William Blake, *Songs of Innocence and Experience*

RONALD drove the AYA minibus right up to the curb in front of the Carl Albert House Office Building like he owned the place, undeterred by the heavy stream of pedestrians, the crush of cabs, the Capitol Hill Police cruiser nosing its way up the street, or the sawn-off figure of Jasper C. Winot planted in the striped crosswalk waving his arms like some kind of demented air traffic controller, impatiently signaling the bus to halt. Kaspian thought that Ronald—whom he was watching from two seats back—made a taut little grimace when he caught sight of Winot, but he couldn't be sure. The imperturbable black guy slipped the bus into park and popped the flashing red lights on.

"You all watch your steps," he called back to the kids who were already leaving their seats. "Just keep together there till somebody tells you what to do."

Ms. Boot, a chaperone today, bounded to the sidewalk as soon as the doors opened. She strode directly to Winot and the two of them fell into discussion. Winot gestured with a finger blunt as a cigar, aiming it at Ms. Boot's right breast. She was done up like Emma Peel today: tight black pants with her hair loose and shook-out-looking. As Winot talked, she nodded earnestly and looked so pumped-up you expected her to karate-chop a pedestrian any moment now. Kaspian turned his head away in mild disgust.

A couple of blocks off, the dome of the U.S. Capitol building rose through some scraggly linden trees and over the nearby rooftops. It was a cool sight but Kaspian guessed he was not going to see much more of it. Ms. Graham, the other chaperone, touched his shoulder and told him to stay seated; she said the van would be leaving soon to take him and "another student" to "a different destination." Then she disembarked and the other kids filed after her. Brenton gave him a poke as he went by and said cheerfully, "Have a nice life!" Soon the bus was cleared out except for Kaspian and Ronald and Foo Bird.

The giant Samoan kid was midway toward the back. When he saw Kaspian looking around he nodded slowly but did not move to change seats. He only turned to look out the window like he was sorry he wasn't going where the other kids were. Outside you could see them milling around fecklessly, some of them going over to check out an Asian street vendor presiding over a gaudily adorned cart, while Ms. Graham tried vainly to muster them into disciplined ranks. It was an impossible task, even though their numbers had been thinned not just by Foo Bird and Kaspian staying behind, but also by the larger-than-usual number of kids disqualified by their regress-point totals from making the trip. Ms. Boot remained huddled with Winot, while Ronald just stared straight ahead through the windshield.

That was the situation. It was a little too static for Kaspian's taste. He slid over to the window, which opened, though you had to push it hard. Ronald didn't notice or didn't care, so Kaspian shoved at it until he could stick his head out.

Along with taxi horns, traffic noise, and general urban blare, he could distinctly hear Jasper Winot's voice, issuing what sounded like marching orders to Thera Boot:

"—cut that happy bastard off right at the knees."

The merciless Washington sun revealed fissures in his face. Ms. Boot nodded eaglerly. Winot wagged the stubby finger and went on:

"Then do whatever you have to. Use all your—"

Kaspian missed a word or a short phrase here. Then he heard loudly and clearly, 5 x 5:

"You have my blanket authorization."

Ms. Boot looked like a kid, all but squirming with pleasure.

Kaspian loved seeing her act like such a toad. She said something inaudible and Winot shook his head.

"That doesn't make a hill of beans. *Ruby* takes him seriously. It's a big-league distraction from where she *ought* to be heading. But I'm leaving it to you, now, to keep that snake in its hole. Distract him, feed him a couple of prairie dogs. Hear me?"

Kaspian guessed that anybody who cared to listen heard him—for what it was worth.

Abruptly, Winot strode across the sidewalk to accost Ms. Graham, and Thera Boot, looking quite merry, reboarded the bus.

"You've got that other address?" she asked Ronald.

"Yes, ma'am."

"And you know how to find it?"

Ronald didn't answer, just pulled the lever to shut the door.

THERE are secret ways through Washington. Ronald steered the minibus down a broad avenue that ran parallel to the Mall. It was just past nine o'clock but already tourists were out, blocking the sidewalks, getting in the way of commuters hurrying from bus stops into those halfway-familiar-looking buildings on both sides of the road. Kaspian glanced up a facade capped with a carved-stone relief that showed two beefy guys surrounded by globular produce, over the legend FRUITS. A sign read Department of Agriculture. They crossed a wide street and circled a giant construction site with the Washington Monument sticking out of it, looking strangely naked.

After that something happened to the road, for the van soon was curving up a gorge with low bluffs of granite on the left and a creek coursing through a dank, muddy hollow on the right. Traffic was sparse; you did not feel like you were in a city. The sides of the gorge had a sculpted look: dynamite followed by a century of weathering. Out of the rich bottomland tangled woods grew thick and green as a jungle, even in October. The trees arched overhead and in places joined together high above the traffic lanes, which narrowed to squeeze between the abut-

ments of an old bridge decorated with sculpted Indian heads and
guarded at each end by buffalo. Nestled into the hillsides east
and west, you could glimpse grand, old-fashioned buildings that
Kaspian imagined might be foreign embassies. In London during
the war, twelve shadow governments had operated out of town
houses and hotels. Kaspian wondered what the point of embassies
was anymore, when there were no wars or alliances or international intrigues, and hardly even any countries. He wondered if
Daimler had an embassy somewhere, or Sony. Those would be
back on the Virginia side, he guessed.

The parkway divided, and divided again, each time becoming
smaller and less traveled, the woods growing denser and closer
until it was like you were passing through a tunnel. The scenery
would have been attractive, perhaps even beautiful, if it hadn't
felt so much like a murky, congested underworld. Like the cata-
combs of the Green Witch in the C. S. Lewis story, which
Kaspian preferred in its *Wonderworks* version. He hated, though,
the part about the prince, his namesake, who was such a little
feeb.

Very soon then, the bus turned off the parkway onto a road
that emerged from the woods into a deserted-looking residential
quarter. Ms. Boot leaned over Ronald's shoulder saying, "It
ought to be right around here someplace," but Ronald ignored
her, just braked and turned up a long driveway. It rose steeply
and curved to the right, asphalt gray and crumbling, leading in
a hundred yards to a big stone house, hemmed by massive white
oaks, with a greenhouse on one side full of colorful blurs Kaspian
imagined might be orchids, not that he would know. Five cars
and an official-looking (but unmarked) panel van occupied the
available parking space. Ronald paused to consider this problem
and Ms. Boot, fairly leaping to her feet, said:

"Let me out. Here, right here. I'll go up and make sure
they're ready for us."

Ronald pulled the lever with no expression. When the door
opened the red lights came on, giving Ms. Boot's stepping-down
a portentous aspect. Ronald then decided to back the minibus

onto a stretch of lawn that looked like it had been used for that purpose once or twice before.

"Okay, men," Ronald said when the bus had stopped. "I guess this is where you get off. Tell the lady in there I'm going to be heading up to the 7-Eleven for some coffee, in case she's asking. She can get me on that *cell* phone if she needs to."

The two boys exchanged a look, and Kaspian wondered if Foo Bird was thinking along the same lines he was: that Ronald was ditching out on them, leaving them to their fate.

When the big kid came abreast of the driver's seat, he turned and said to Ronald, in a tone of perfect formality:

"I guess this is good-bye."

For an instant, Ronald looked at him as though his head was cracked. Then he laughed and said, "Shit. You fellows. Go on, now."

Kaspian smiled. He thought, it's funny how you can like somebody without really knowing them.

Dislike them, also.

They walked up a stone path to the front door, which was recessed in a portico and surmounted by a Gothic arch, like a modest old-money fortress. *Festung Washington*. On one side of the door a brass plaque read

PAUL F. CARPATHIAN
Lt. Col. USAF (Ret.)

while on the other side another plaque, similar but less verdi-grised, read

TRUST FOR GLOBAL READINESS
Group Potomac Headquarters

Foo Bird pointed to this, as though posing a wordless question.

Kaspian frowned. He knew he had heard about this organization but could not remember where, or what. He put his hand on the door and was turning the handle when Foo Bird said:

"Don't you think we ought to ring the bell?"

"No."

Foo Bird put a large hand on his shoulder. "This is what I admire about you, Aaby," he said. "Your lack of restraint."

The door opened on a large empty hall. Sounds of conversation came from a room at the far end, while a television muttered in a sunny parlor that opened through French doors to one side. The air in the house felt chilly, with a faint smell of cleaning agents. In midhall, a broad staircase had been blocked off by one of those felt-rope arrangements they use to manage the crowd at movie theaters.

"This seems like kind of a strange place," said Kaspian, drawing a little closer to the giant Samoan.

Foo Bird lowered his brow. They advanced together toward the room with the television. Inside, three men and a woman—not Ms. Boot—lounged on chintz-covered furniture staring at a big-screen rear-projection model tuned to C-SPAN. It was the same Congressional hearing, apparently just coming to order for another day of testimony. The camera impassively scanned the hearing room, taking in Congresspeople huddled with their staffs, pages dealing out paper like floppy poker cards, witnesses milling about in the visitors' gallery, and finally a small crowd of uniformed teenagers being herded into two rows of seats that appeared to have been reserved for them.

"Blow me," said Kaspian.

The three men and one woman in the TV room turned to look at him and Foo Bird, who stood just inside the door. Neither of the boys looked back: they were absorbed in watching the other kids from AYA taking their places among those gathered to testify before the House Education Committee. Ms. Graham bustled among them officiously, pleading with them to sit down and behave. Meanwhile Jasper C. Winot, who for some reason appeared taller on TV than in so-called real life, conferred in the foreground with a woman in a red dress. The camera came to rest on them, and after a few seconds C-SPAN helpfully put up a caption in blue and white: "Rep. Ruby Rijowski (R.—N. Dakota)."

"Do you two gentlemen need any help?" one of the men in the room asked Kaspian and Foo Bird.

"We're just waiting to see Colonel Carpathian," said Foo Bird, smoothly.

The man nodded—"I see"—though he continued to look back and forth between the two of them for several moments. At last he turned away.

Kaspian was impressed—especially by how Foo Bird had guessed that none of these guys was Carpathian himself. Only after a bit of study did Kaspian pick up the clues: these people had the air of staff lackeys about them. Like the minor court of adjutants and secretaries and bodyguards hanging around the anteroom of any headquarters. Waiting for the call.

On television, the Chairman banged the hearing into session. C-SPAN switched to Cam 1, a fixed angle taking in the row of Members ranged along the proscenium. Ruby Rijowski sat three places to the right of center. Still, you noticed her. Like a cardinal.

Kaspian wanted to talk but he did not want to do it here. He nudged Foo Bird and they stepped into the chilly hall.

"Can you believe that?" Kaspian whispered. "We could have been on TV!"

"No we couldn't."

"What do you mean?"

"We're here," said Foo Bird. "And they're there. It was obviously planned this way."

Kaspian didn't see anything obvious. He didn't even know where *here* was, in practical terms.

"Don't you see what he's doing?" Foo Bird said, in a voice that, for once, seemed to contain some emotion—*barely* to contain it, as though the pressure of his feelings threatened to burst the lid.

"No," admitted Kaspian. "What?"

"He's dragged in all the nice, well-behaved students as *living proof*—don't you love that phrase?—*living proof* of how wonderful his schools are. He'll say, Look, I've got kids here who were so tough that other schools gave up on them, their parents gave up on them, their blooming *places of worship* gave up on them. But see, I've got them all dressed up in natty uniforms and when I say Jump, they say How high? You cut me loose from these pesky regulations and give me a national school-voucher system and I can do this for *your* kids, too."

"Oh," said Kaspian. He supposed it did explain things. Among them, why *he* had been whisked out of camera-range. Perhaps also why Charity—having mouthed off to Ruby Rijowski that day at lunch—was locked away in a psychiatric ward: a thought that truly pissed Kaspian off.

It did not, however, account for Foo Bird. Maybe the giant Samoan was just too smart to be deemed trustworthy.

"*Here* you two are," exclaimed Thera Boot, hustling toward them from the distant end of the hall. "I just dialed Ronald and he said he was off at a 7-Eleven somewhere."

Her smile glimmered the way glass containers do when the refrigerator light comes on.

"If you'll just follow me," she said; "the Colonel is very anxious to meet both of you."

A fire blazed in the gigantic hearth that, with its buttressing of bookshelves, took up a wall of Paul Carpathian's smoking room, throwing off so much unnecessary heat that a window-mounted air conditioner was blasting on Max Cool to keep the place bearable. Even so, the room felt pressurized, and cigar smoke made it worse.

Carpathian sat in a big leather chair with one shoulder to the fire. He looked like a former dictator living in genteel exile. He wore khaki pants and a patterned rayon shirt, one hand resting on a walking stick though he didn't seem to be planning to walk anywhere. He looked old enough to be a Colonel but not sufficiently battle-hardened. Opposite him, bracketing the fire, sat a proper-looking lady who might have been a few years his senior, dressed like him in tropical mode, complete with a wide-brimmed safari hat that threw the upper part of her face into shadow.

Ms. Boot said loudly—as though extra effort were required to penetrate the air of the room—"Colonel, these are the two young men I was telling you about. Here is Kaspian Aaby, and here is Fuad Suleiman."

The Colonel rose to shake hands. His frame was gaunt, almost bony, beneath the slack layers of clothing. His face was about two-thirds beakish nose.

"Mr. Suleiman, Mr. Aaby," the Colonel said, "I'd like to present my life partner, Amanda Marks."

"Amanda Marks-*Morrow*?" asked Foo Bird—so quickly that it sounded like a quarterback barking an audible. "The futurist?"

The lady in the opposite chair smiled and gave a slight nod.

"Yes, dear, I am," she said.

"And these," said Carpathian, gesturing over a shoulder toward the end of the room farthest from the fireplace, where you might have expected to see hunting trophies but saw instead an up-to-date law library, "are two recent and *valued* additions to our staff. Over there is Candice Goldblum, our Director of Communications. And *this* gentleman is Dwight Eugley, who has *just* accepted an appointment as Chief, Corps of Investigators. Both of them bring us the kind of real-world expertise that we're going to need in the difficult times ahead."

Kaspian turned and gazed through smoke and intervening obstacles (an areca palm, a ceiling-mounted orrery of the solar system, and a sumptuously furnished, though untenanted, parrot cage) toward Ms. Goldblum, who looked like a professional model with a degree in theoretical physics, and Mr. Eugley, who looked like, and was, fucking *Weeb,* the camouflaged weirdo Kaspian had met a long time ago in a hippie farmhouse in Sinai Falls, Maine.

That, Kaspian realized, was where he had heard of the Trust for Global Readiness before. Readiness for what? he had wondered.

And Weeb had answered: *For whatever comes.*

Kaspian managed to swallow his surprise, waiting to see if Weeb would recognize him. They had met just once, and Kaspian had changed at least three times over since then. The red tie and gray flannel trousers were the least of it.

Weeb, for his part, had changed only to the extent of swapping his field uniform for Headquarters mufti: an olive-drab gabardine jacket with parallel rows of black metal buttons, and baggy pants stuffed into butt-kicking boots. From his jacket he extracted a small, dog-eared notebook, through which he flipped unhurriedly. He stopped at a certain page, scrutinized its contents, looked up at Kaspian, and nodded.

"Well," said Carpathian, all gung ho, "now that we know each other, let's get down to it, shall we? Our friend Ruby Rijowski tells me that you two have had some remarkable experiences. Amanda and I would *love* to hear about them."

"Not Ruby, dear," his life partner said from her chair across from his. "It was Jasper who discovered these young men, I believe."

"But Ruby said *she'd* met them," the Colonel said, sounding miffed. "I could have sworn—"

"Ruby *met* them," Mrs. Marks-Morrow said, smiling gently, "but she didn't *interview* them. She wisely chose to leave that to the experts." Here the safari hat tilted sideways a few degrees, roughly in Weeb's direction. "Fortunately, she was able to prevail upon Jasper to make the young men available—that's where *he* comes in. I assured Ruby she could count on our continuing gratitude and support."

"Ah. Just so." Carpathian gave a stiff, martial nod. He turned to Kaspian and Foo Bird. "Well, gentlemen. Let's not shilly-shally around. First I want to tell you why we're so interested in hearing—in detail—whatever you may be able to tell us about your, ah—"

"AE2's," suggested Weeb.

"Quite so. Exactly. It's because, until such time as the governments of the world come to their senses, *we* find ourselves in the uncomfortable but exciting, very exciting, position of being as it were an advance guard, manning a forward base camp, facing a vast and unknown host whose intentions are hidden from us, but which may *very* well turn out to be less than friendly. I won't tell you much more than that right now because I don't want to prejudice your own accounts. But I will say this: you boys may be in a position to provide us with information that could prove to be of crucial importance not only to us, and not only to all humankind, but to all the generations that will follow, on this planet and perhaps many others."

Mrs. Marks-Morrow nodded deliberately, with an indecipherable expression.

Kaspian didn't know what to think. Apart from the obvious: that Colonel Carpathian was a nutcase. But Foo Bird said, "I'm afraid you're going to be disappointed. At least where I'm concerned."

The Colonel nodded, understandingly. "Your experience doesn't *mean* anything, is that what you're thinking? It's strictly a *personal* thing? These are very frequent comments we hear from our interviewees. But let me give you some of the benefit of our wider perspective. You might recall the parable of the blind men trying to describe an elephant. One feels the leg and says the beast is like a tree, another the ear and says it's like a blanket, and so forth. Now gentlemen, I mean no disrespect whatever, but each of you is in the position of those blind men: you've been *gifted*, if I may use that term, with a certain limited perception of something too big for any one observer to grasp in toto. Yet by amassing and collating *many* isolated perceptions like yours, we might expect an overall picture of the elephant to emerge. Do you see what I'm getting at?"

Kaspian looked at Foo Bird. He could not help wondering what sort of strange encounter the big kid had had—whether it was anything like his own; whether a Girl in White or a dead relative figured in.

He also wondered what possible usefulness his own half-baked story might have for Colonel Carpathian or Weeb Eugley or this mysterious Trust for Global Readiness.

"I don't think *I* see what you're getting at," Kaspian said. "Or maybe I do, but . . . Do you guys think we're about to be invaded by *aliens* or something? And you're trying to get ready for them? Because what happened to me . . . it's got like, *nothing* to do with that. *At all.*"

Colonel Carpathian smiled indulgently. "Yes," he said, "I have no doubt that it seems that way to you. And perhaps, indeed, your experience will have nothing in it to further our understanding. On the other hand, the forces arrayed before us are nothing if not masters, absolute masters, of camouflage, of brilliant disguise, of well-masked infiltration. Perhaps you've heard Winston Churchill's remark about truth being so precious . . ."

"It should never appear unless surrounded by a bodyguard of lies," said Kaspian.

The Colonel gave him a slight bow. "Just so."

"Is there any question," Amanda Marks-Morrow asked, "of medical releases? Parental permission? Anything of that kind?"

Thera Boot spoke up quickly: "I've been given blanket authorization."

Satisfied, Mrs. Marks-Morrow settled back into her private shadow.

"Shall we give it a go, then?" asked the Colonel, of the room at large. He reconnoitered with a hawkish eye, meeting no opposition. "Very well. Let's give it a go."

THEY advanced in formation up the hall to the wide staircase blocked off by felt rope. Kaspian dropped an anchor outside the TV room, where a clutch of his fellow M.R.'s were crowded into the C-SPAN camera frame. Two of them sat, and five more, including Jill and check this, *Brenton,* stood in the immediate vicinity of Jasper C. Winot, who was chewing up the microphone with some bullshit story about a family in California having their hopes rekindled and the love of their only son restored following their discovery of the Third Way™ offered exclusively by American Youth Academies.

"Now if I may, Mr. Chairman," Winot said, "I'd like to ask a few of these lucky young people to tell you their own unrehearsed stories, in their own words."

C-SPAN switched to Cam 2, a close shot of the Chairman, who looked a bit irked. He glanced at his watch and recognized the Member from North Dakota. Ruby Rijowski—back to Cam 1—said she would very much appreciate hearing these fine young Americans testify of their own volition. The Chairman gave up. Ms. Boot nudged Kaspian in the ribs and said, "Come along, Mr. Aaby. This ought to be fun."

Indeed, she was smiling. She was having fun already.

With reluctance—or something deeper than that, an instinctual misgiving—Kaspian let himself be pulled away. His final glimpse of C-SPAN contained the translucent image of Jason Aracos, materializing like a ghostly special effect behind Winot's shoulder and murmuring off-mike into his ear.

One of the court-follower types—a blond guy who dressed too neatly, in his mid-30's—stood holding the felt rope aside. He shot Kaspian a look that was almost impolitely curious, as though he were staring into a cage at the zoo.

They climbed to the second floor. Up here the rooms were dark except for a bathroom (door cracked, glimpse of sumptuous appointments) and an L-shaped room at the rear of the house, which Kaspian entered in the wake of everyone else.

In the nearest leg of the L stood a dark wooden conference table; in the other, a grouping of two upholstered chairs and a sofa, with a coffee table and a large shelf stocked with audiovisual equipment. Paintings (landscapes, dreamy, neo-Luminist) hung on the walls. Tall windows stood with drapes half drawn, giving you a glimpse of the white oaks pressing against the aged, ripply glass. The Colonel and Mrs. Marks–Morrow and Candice Gold-blum seated themselves at the table, while Weeb Eugley and the blond adjutant walked over to the AV shelf. Thera Boot conducted the two boys—taking each by an arm, practically dragging them—toward the sofa.

"Who'd like to go first?" she asked.

Go first for what, neither kid asked.

Ms. Boot turned to Foo Bird and said, "Why don't *you* sit here, then."

She motioned to one end of the sofa. Foo Bird flopped

there, in an expanse of burgundy chintz that yielded deeply to his body weight.

"And you," Ms. Boot told Kaspian, "can sit *here*"—nodding to one of the armchairs—"until it's your turn."

Kaspian made a point of crossing to the wrong chair. But the gesture was lost on Ms. Boot, who turned to Weeb and said in her most professional voice:

"What's your procedure?"

"Multimodal," he said crisply. He took one soldierly stride toward the sofa, where Foo Bird sat looking utterly blank. "Young man," Weeb said, "is there any type of music you prefer?"

Foo Bird shot the tiniest glance at Kaspian. Then in a voice ringing with conviction he declared, "I am fond of the later works of Alfred Schnittke, especially the Concerto. Of the Eastern Bloc composers, I feel he is the most brave and resolute. Górecki is also good, though many people put him down too facilely as a Mystical Minimalist, on the sole evidence of that one long Symphony. But listen to the String Quartets: much greater darkness and ambiguity. You might mention Shostakovich here but I think he belongs to an earlier canon."

Weeb heard him out, then turned to the attentive adjutant and said: "Classical."

The blond guy flipped through a row of CD's on the shelf and pulled out something by Tchaikovsky, which he inserted in a player. Then he handed a pair of headphones over to Foo Bird. The music was cranked loud enough that you could hear it coming through the tiny speakers. *Swan Lake,* Kaspian thought. Or maybe *The Nutcracker.* One of those stories where things turn into other things.

Foo Bird adjusted the headphones to his oversized skull, appearing (to Kaspian) rather pleased with his performance; though from the frown that crossed his face when he pulled the headphones on, you got the idea Tchaikovsky did not agree with him.

Ms. Boot joined the Colonel's party at the conference table. Weeb took the armchair Kaspian had rejected. The adjutant handed him a different kind of headset than Foo Bird was wearing, a telephone-operator type of thing. He settled back into the stuffings of the chair, making a show of getting comfortable.

"Just relax now," he spoke into the tiny microphone, looking at Foo Bird. "Can you hear me well enough?"

Foo Bird nodded.

Weeb turned to Kaspian, doing something with a little knob at one ear. "Now just watch. You'll see there's nothing frightening about this at all. What we do is, we patch in a subliminal relaxation tape underneath the clearly audible music. The effect of the two sound sources going at once is to bring about a gradual dissociation between two functional regions of the brain, the sensory-processing apparatus and the deeper memory centers. I can speak to *you* now, off-channel, without Mr., ah—" consulting the notebook "—Mr. Suleiman becoming distracted by my voice. In a little while, I'll be able to lead Mr. Suleiman through a simple regression exercise in which we will tap directly into his subconscious powers of recollection." He turned back to Foo Bird, turned the knob at his ear, and said, "Now why don't you just settle back into the couch there and put yourself entirely at ease? Feel free to stretch out, if you like."

The adjutant, at this cue, spun a rheostat to dim the room lights, then handed a fluffy pillow to Weeb who laid it next to Foo Bird on the sofa. Foo Bird gave the pillow a skeptical glance but otherwise remained impassive.

To Kaspian's amazement—not happy amazement, either—everything happened just as Weeb described. Within a couple of minutes, Foo Bird appeared to grow drowsy; he eased himself lower into the cushions, big legs sticking way out. Weeb pushed the pillow a little closer and this time Foo Bird accepted it, arranged it behind his head, and closed his eyes. In a matter of seconds, his body sagged as though he had been drugged.

Weeb shot Ms. Boot a foxy smile.

"Impressive," she said. "Has any monitoring been done of cerebral function during this procedure?"

"Pronounced alpha," said Weeb. "Diminishing beta, though with upward spikes. Left-right parity subject to strong surges in either direction. Overall coherence along both axes increasing to a plateau, followed by a characteristic pattern of cycling. To my knowledge, no one knows what any of this means."

Ms. Boot nodded. Kaspian thought it was odd that not knowing what any of this means was of so little concern.

Weeb turned to Foo Bird and began speaking in what passed, for him, as a soft and reassuring voice. "All right, um, Fu-add. I'd like you to go back to the night of . . . 10 June of this past summer. You were up on a hill, I believe. A hill overlooking the city."

Foo Bird murmured something that nobody caught. Weeb looked at the adjutant, who now wore a set of headphones of his own, connected to a video recorder. Kaspian scanned the room and discovered a camera lens peeking like an eyeball from a recess in the ceiling. The adjutant pointed to a sound-level indicator and shrugged.

"I'm sorry," Weeb told Foo Bird. "I couldn't quite make out what you said."

"Mount St. Alban," said Foo Bird more loudly. His voice was irritated, and what bothered Kaspian was that you could *tell* that. The stone wall had cracked.

"Okay, you're on Mount St. Alban," said Weeb, looking at the adjutant, who gave him a thumbs-up. "Can you tell me what time it is? Are you alone? What is the nature of your surroundings?"

Foo Bird started talking in a mumble, then seemed to remember to speak up. "I'm alone, yeah," he said. "The other guys are back at the dorm boning for finals. It can't be too late because it's still sort of light out. I'd say eight o'clock, maybe eight-thirty. I'm in . . . it's like a yard, with walls around it."

"Good, good. Excellent. Now just stay relaxed. Let's stay with that moment a little while. What do you see in your immediate vicinity?"

"Trees. Mostly trees. Somebody told me they're the oldest trees in Washington. And down in front of them there's a statue of George Washington, up on a horse. I can't see him too well. Behind that there's a wall. Semicircular."

"Good. What else? Are there any sounds? Smells? Lights?"

Foo Bird's face wrinkled up as though he were straining to bring it back. "Roses. I think I can smell roses. I can't hear . . . I mean, there's traffic, but otherwise it's pretty quiet up here. It *feels* quieter than it *is,* if that makes any sense."

It made perfect sense to Kaspian but he did not want to betray that. He was freaked out by what was happening now— above all that Foo Bird was being so cooperative, as though his will to resist had been outflanked. In this helpless state, the giant Samoan sounded much more like an ordinary kid, no wiser or more clued-in than anybody else.

It was hard to escape one obvious conclusion. Kaspian's own defenses were likely to be no better than Foo Bird's. He would fall like Holland.

"What happens now?" asked Weeb.

Foo Bird stirred on the sofa. Something appeared to discomfit him.

"There's an animal," he finally said.

Weeb glanced back in the general direction of the Colonel and Mrs. Marks-Morrow. The lady nodded inscrutably under the cover of her hat, while the Colonel leaned forward, anxious lest he miss anything.

"I don't know *what* it is," Foo Bird went on. "First I thought it was a cat. But now it looks too big to be a cat. I think it might be a dog. A dark-colored dog. Black I guess. But I don't know . . . it *moves* like a cat."

"Where is it?" asked Weeb. "Can you tell what it's doing?"

"It's right there on the wall. It's moving toward—*Jesus*. It's got like these, glowing red eyes! It's looking *right at me.*"

His whole body moved. Writhed, practically. Kaspian could barely keep still in his own seat, so powerfully did Foo Bird's distress communicate itself.

"No wait." Foo Bird bit his lip. "Now it's just . . . it's sitting there. On the wall, like it's waiting for something. Fuck, I hope it doesn't look at me again."

He sat with his eyes squeezed together, both feet twitching hard like he was suffering an attack of palsy.

"Now it's . . . I think it sees something else. Yeah, look. There's something down there in the woods. The cat, whatever it is—it's going down from the wall. Jumps down there so fast you can hardly follow it. Now I've lost it in the bushes. Maybe I can see better from the gazebo. Wait a minute."

The muscles in his face and neck showed strain.

"There. *Wuwwoo.* I can see the eyes again. That's all I can see now. Way back in the trees. I don't know what to do."

Weeb said, "Do you feel like you ought to follow it?"

"No way," said Foo Bird.

"Why not?" said Weeb.

"Well, because . . . I mean, shit. Did you *see* that thing?"

Weeb looked at the people around the conference table. The Colonel gave him a purposeful nod. To Foo Bird he said, in a firmer voice, "But you *do* follow it, don't you?"

Foo Bird did not answer directly. His body started twisting again and he made a quiet noise almost like a whimper. Kaspian hated to watch this. Truly hated it. But what could he do? Despite himself he was as hooked as any of the others.

"Okay," said Foo Bird. His breath came rapidly. "Okay. I'm down in the woods. I'm down in the woods. I can't remember walking here, but . . . I don't see the cat anymore. It's gone, I think. But there's . . . something else. Something close to me, even though—even though—"

His breathing stopped. Every muscle up and down his large frame was tensed. Kaspian held his own breath in sympathy.

"Yes," whispered Foo Bird. "I see it. *I see it.* Jesus I can't believe it but I *see it with my own eyes.*"

"What do you see?" said Weeb.

Every single person in the room appeared to lean forward in his or her seat.

"It's like . . . it's kind of like . . ."

Suddenly Foo Bird ripped the headphones off his head. He sat upright and stared around the room, his eyes passing from face to face to face. He looked like someone jerked abruptly out of sleep, fuzzily adjusting to real time. At last he declared:

"Tchaikovsky."

Kaspian gave a slight, nervous laugh.

Foo Bird shook his head. "I *hate* Tchaikovsky. Whose idea was *that?*"

Weeb and the adjutant exchanged accusatory glances.

"Damn," said Foo Bird. "For a minute there, it was all coming back. Stuff I hadn't remembered before. But then . . . the *Waltz of the Sugar-Plum Fairies?* Do you truly expect a person to remain hypnotically susceptible through *that?*"

Ms. Boot said, "So you do recall the session up to that point?"

"Quite clearly."

Foo Bird's dignity was about him once more, and Kaspian was glad.

"Could you . . ." Ms. Boot hesitated, looked at Weeb, then went on: "Do you think you could continue your . . . your narrative, without hypnosis?"

Foo Bird tossed the long front locks out of his eyes. "Perhaps. But I'm not sure I care to. The episode does not seem to have been a pleasant one. I'm not sure I *should* remember any more."

"What do you mean, should?" asked Ms. Boot.

Foo Bird did not answer at first. Then he said, thoughtfully, "Maybe there's a reason I've forgotten these things."

"'You bet there is," said Weeb. He signaled the adjutant, who switched the recording equipment off. "We find," he told Ms. Boot, "that it's better to interrupt a session, or even break it off entirely, rather than press too hard."

She did not look chastened. She said, "Shall we do *him,* then?"—pointing to Kaspian with all the consideration you would show a lump of cellophane-wrapped beef.

Weeb leaned back in his armchair. "We *find,*" he said, "that what is often most productive is to engage in a frank discussion *with* the subjects about what they've told us, what we're hoping to learn, and other aspects of the investigative procedure. After all, it isn't *us* that's running some vast clandestine experiment, using them like human lab rats."

"Who is it, then?" said Kaspian. "Scary aliens? Guys in Black?"

From the other end of the room, Colonel Carpathian said gruffly, "I wouldn't joke, young man, about matters you don't begin to understand. I'd wait until I knew a little bit about what's really happening in the world. The danger we all face."

"I wasn't joking," said Kaspian. "I was *asking*."

Mrs. Marks-Morrow laid a hand on the Colonel's arm. "Perhaps, dear," she said soothingly, "you could have Mr. Eugley brief our guests on the mission of the Trust. That might help them grasp what we're trying to accomplish here."

"Just so," said the Colonel. He rapped the table with his walking stick. "Weeb? Would you care to take the floor?"

Weeb looked momentarily panged at having to give up his armchair. Then he rose heavily to his feet, took out his notebook, and read:

"The Trust for Global Readiness, founded in 1969, has as its primary mission the tracking, study and evaluation of any and all phenomena suggesting the presence, on or near Earth, of advanced nonhuman intelligence, especially as it poses or may pose a threat to the well-being of *Homo sapiens*. It is not the desired purpose of the Trust to act unilaterally in meeting such a threat. Rather, the Trust intends to make available to National Governments and credible NGO's, on a selective basis, information gleaned, together with an overall strategic assessment and recommended courses of action."

Weeb licked a thumb. He flipped the notebook leaf.

"*However*—this is paragraph 2—*However,* bearing in mind the unpredictable nature of the political process, and the characteristic slowness of governments to act, the Trust *shall be ready*—this is in italics—*shall be ready to undertake on its own*—end italics—direct action in response to a fully evaluated threat."

He gazed slowly up one leg of the L and down the other.

"Not the most comely prose in the world," said Foo Bird. "But I suppose it makes its point." He gave Kaspian a look nobody else in the room would ever decipher: Samoan Face Language for *I think these guys are dangerous.*

Kaspian wasn't sure. To him, Weeb seemed like just another eccentric Mainer, probably a military retiree, who had latched on to some weird thing to keep his mind active. Back home in Glassport, one of the neighbors had taken up African drumming and then, a year or so later, radiant subfloor heating, the advocacy of which he carried out with religious fervor. Such passions did not seem altogether different to Kaspian than Weeb's thing for UFO's. Or whatever it was. Including this air of expertise, which you could acquire on any nameable subject during the course of one Maine winter.

"So it *is* scary aliens," Kaspian said. "Right? That you guys are worried about."

He could sense Carpathian's hand cinching up on the walking stick. But Weeb only looked at him the way a police officer giving a driver's-safety presentation looks at a smart-mouthed student—with a conspicuous show of good humor, as though to say: Laugh now, kid. I'll be seeing you around.

"When you speak of aliens," Weeb said, "I assume you're talking about four-foot extraterrestrials with large black eyes. Or perhaps your education has come predominantly from science fiction movies. Bug-eyed monsters from Mars. In either case, the answer is no. We are not worried about aliens."

At the conference table, Amanda Marks-Morrow nodded her head, a modest motion made grand by the fanning of her giant hat brim.

"You see," Weeb went on more loudly, as though encouraged by this show of approval, "we consider these so-called aliens to be secondary phenomena. A sideshow. We're interested in the primary phenomenon itself, the thing that lies *behind* aliens."

Kaspian shot a face-signal at Foo Bird: like, Maybe you're right.

"To tell you the truth," said Weeb, "we don't *believe* in aliens. That is to say, we don't accept them at face value as the occupants of interstellar spacecraft. We believe they're, so to speak, *generated*. Or you might say *projected*. They're not literal biological entities in the sense that we are. They may have a physical basis or they may not, but they're only manifestations of some deeper control intelligence. And *that's* the thing we're trying to pin down."

"Have you pinned it down?" Kaspian asked.

Weeb shook his head. He had a funny smile on his face. "Not in a way that we can take to the newspapers and say, Look here, this is what's happening to our planet. But we have a theory."

He glanced toward the conference table. Colonel Carpathian murmured something to Mrs. Marks-Morrow, who said, "I don't see why not. The truth must come out."

"Go ahead," Carpathian told Weeb. "Speak frankly."

Weeb turned back to the little audience consisting of the two boys and Ms. Boot. "Our theory is that the physical appearance of so-called aliens is generated in the moment they become visible. How this occurs is unknown. Some interaction with the mind of the witness might be involved, a feedback relationship, but the generating power is always in charge. This accounts for the extreme mutability of the aliens' appearance—no two sightings are exactly alike, even in multiple-witness scenarios—but beyond that, it provides a screening function, causing so-called scientific observers to conclude that aliens, quote, are not real. As I've said, we agree that aliens are not *literally* real, yet we find incontrovertible evidence that they are *phenomenologically* real. That is, there are tens of thousands of documented cases of their appearance in all parts of the world, even though their specific physical form and their concrete actions and speech, if any, are highly variable. Not to say wholly absurd.

"The problem for *serious* investigators, then, is to make sense of these seemingly incompatible facts: the reality of the phenomenon, and the inconsistent or even self-contradictory nature of the evidence. Toward this end, the Trust for Global Readiness has undertaken a rigorous analysis of the broadest sampling of first-person data we can obtain. And that, young men, is where *you* come in."

He ended by looking straight at Kaspian. Who figured now that Weeb *must* remember him from Maine, from Inanna Rugg's living room. And yet Weeb had not acknowledged or even hinted at this in any way. It was like a secret between the two of them.

"What our analysis shows," Weeb went on, looking away, "is that the forms assumed by so-called aliens do not just vary randomly. Instead they show a distinct pattern of clustering, and a tendency to drift over time. By clustering I mean that within a given time frame, these forms revolve closely around central themes, somewhat like moons orbiting a planet, or—this is a better comparison—subatomic particles moving in indeterminate clouds about a nucleus. For example, the alien type known as the Small Gray represents a sort of gravitational center, an ideal form around which many sightings cluster, though if you closely examine the actual sighting reports, you always find inconsistencies. One observer will see three fingers, another six. No one sees five.

"By drifting over time, I'm referring to the well-known pattern of a certain alien type prevailing for a decade or two, only to be superseded by a different type. Actually it's more complicated than that, with many types and subtypes emerging and fading, and dissimilar types swapping traits. But to take the most clear-cut example, you had your Nordic type that dominated from the 50's into the early 60's, then the emergence of both your Large and Small Grays from the mid-60's onward. Neither was dominant at first, but over time the Large Grays diminished in importance while the Small Grays are currently—though I might add, temporarily—so prevalent they're sometimes considered synonymous with the term *alien* itself."

"What's a Nordic type?" said Kaspian.

"Oh, you know. Tall, slender, blue-eyed, blond- or white-haired, generally human-friendly, often bringing warnings of some impending catastrophe, sometimes perceived by witnesses as semidivine in character. They haven't *quite* vanished—now and then they still pop up, sometimes in a good-cop bad-cop scenario vis-à-vis the Small Grays. But on the whole, they belong to a different era. Your *parents'* generation," he added, smiling indulgently.

Kaspian was pretty sure Ms. Boot was looking at him. He

worked hard at not glancing her way. It didn't take a genius to see that this Nordic type fairly well nailed his Girl in White. Who might or might not have done something intensely personal to him on an operating table.

"As theories go," said Foo Bird, spread out across a good portion of the sofa, "this one doesn't seem to explain much. You still haven't addressed the problem of what these things *are*."

Weeb nodded. "True enough. We don't know what Small Grays are. But we do know what they're *like*."

He paused for effect with one finger pointed toward the ceiling. Toward the sneaky video eyeball, in fact.

"What," said Foo Bird, mechanically giving him his cue, "are they like?"

"They're like *Schwartalfen*. Dark Elves. And the Nordics are like Light Elves. The Reptoids are like dragons and the Robotics are like a type of dwarf described as having skin like metal. Every alien type, and every subtype, and every observed permutation, has its parallel in worldwide lore of mysterious, often supernatural beings who have coexisted with human beings for millennia. The most striking parallel is not appearance—the most variable of traits—but a deeper correspondence of structure and function. I would summarize it this way: Aliens, like elves, have no regard for the laws of science, which they violate with impunity, thereby leading—you might even say *tricking*—respectable scientists into disbelieving in them. And *yet,* they have the strictest regard for the universal laws of fairy lore, which have been examined and codified for over a century, and which both elves and aliens obey *to the letter*.

"Let me tick a few things off. Number 1, they appear erratically, favoring remote places and liminal situations while, number 2, shunning any effort to capture them, whether bodily or on film. Number 3, they come and go with inexplicable suddenness, in the blink of an eye. Four, they are typically small in stature, though exceptions abound. Five, they have an unhealthy interest in human reproduction, while 6, their own reproduction is somehow enfeebled. This leads to 7, their not-well-explained need for the vitality or life-force of human beings. Fairies you know often take midwives, abducting them if necessary, though typically the woman goes willingly. Aliens are beyond all that, so they're less fussy about who they take, and their prurient obsessions are masked by science-babble, genes and mutations and so forth. But in each case, the act of *taking human beings*— this is number 8—whether by force or otherwise, to assist in reproductive functions, is a strong common thread. Which leads to 9, the creation of hybrid offspring, who inherit some of the weakness of the nonhuman parent, as in the famous story of Tam Lin, the half-fairy boy, or your recent reports of spindly infants aboard UFO's. Finally 10, the gift, the payment. Or conversely, the curse, the *touch*. Both elves and aliens tend to leave some kind of mark, physical or otherwise, on humans who interact with them. This is usually an equivocal sort of thing. Fairy gold tends to vanish, or turn into something worthless, just like the advanced knowledge revealed by aliens—the gold of the Information Age—usually turns out to be a bunch of bunk. But not *always*."

Weeb stood there, apparently pleased with himself, as though he had just wound up a killer summation to the jury. Kaspian and Foo Bird exchanged silent Samoan expressions, but it was Ms. Boot who finally spoke up.

"So what are you saying?" she asked. "Aliens are nothing but fairies?"

"*Like* fairies," he corrected her. "So *much* like fairies, it would be irresponsible to ignore the parallels. Because obviously a structure of this depth and complexity has some deeper meaning. It *might* mean that the whole alien phenomenon is part of a vast deception—the aliens appear to us in a way that ordinary people find easy to accept, and scientists find easy to ignore, because of its subliminal familiarity. Therefore our attention is diverted from what's *really* going on. Or—a second possibility— it might mean that the whole body of fairy lore, dating back thousands of years, is *itself* a fuzzy record of this same pattern of interference in human affairs over a very, *very* long period of time. One way or the other, we're speaking about an intelligence or a power that possesses intimate knowledge of human nature and human habits of thought. That fact alone should be alarming enough."

"Alarming enough for what?" asked Kaspian.

Weeb frowned at him as though Kaspian was being obtuse. "Alarming enough to justify, at the very least, a heightened level of concern."

Kaspian said, "Oh."

There was silence for a few moments. Then Colonel Carpathian exclaimed:

"Well, I don't know about anybody else, but personally, I could stand a bite to eat. What say? We can have some sandwiches made up, and carry on with our work here on a full stomach."

Kaspian felt no hunger and even less desire to carry on with this. He found Weeb's rap to be *possibly* interesting—he would have to think it over to be sure—but did not relish at all the prospect of changing places with Foo Bird, slipping those headphones on, having his subconscious strip-mined while the videocam rolled.

As usual, nobody bothered about what he wanted. The blond adjutant went around the room asking people what kind of sandwiches they liked. When he came to Kaspian he said only, "Mustard or mayonnaise?" The smile on his face you could have cracked a lock with.

"Same as you're having," Kaspian told him.

In the milling about that followed, Foo Bird went to stand by a tall, half-draped window. Kaspian joined him there and they stared down at the greenhouse with its bright blobs of color. If you figured it right, you could jump out the window here and go crashing through all that glass.

"Does it seem to you," Foo Bird said quietly, without looking in Kaspian's direction, "that these people have gotten ahold of something? Or that something has gotten ahold of them? Namely a case of collective psychosis?"

Kaspian laughed, but he shut it off quickly, not wanting to draw attention. "Oh, I don't know," he said. "It makes as much sense as anything else. I'd say it's a little ahead of Creation Science."

"I don't believe that."

Foo Bird said this in such a way that Kaspian stopped. Not stopped anything in particular but rather dropped his own thoughts and tuned into the Samoan Channel, the quiet current under the waves. Foo Bird was looking at him steadily but on a slant, 45 degrees off, his head still pointed down toward those imperiled orchids. "My case doesn't fit. It's an anomalous anomaly. Their theory explains nothing."

"Why?" said Kaspian. "What was it you saw? I mean, is it too scary to talk about?"

Foo Bird shook his head. "On the contrary. It was only a person. There was nothing in the woods but an ordinary person. I'm sorry if I startled you back there with my histrionics. But I needed to get unhypnotized. I needed to shake myself out of it. The situation was growing uncomfortable."

Kaspian marveled at such self-possession. "So you were just faking it, the whole time?"

"Oh, no," said Foo Bird. "The memory itself was genuine. Those *eyes*."

He shuddered but Kaspian couldn't tell if this was only for effect. "So the black cat—that was real?"

"Or dog. Or whatever. Yes, it was there. Was it *real*, though—that's a whole other question."

"But then it went away? And there was nothing but . . ."

"A person. A homeless person, in fact. A guy who called himself Ben the Lama. He told me his life story. I walked a mile or so down Massachusetts Avenue with him, past the Naval Observatory. Then the guy—this was rather remarkable—turned out to be living in a stretch of woods between Mass Ave and some little back street at the bottom of a hill. There was wild bamboo down there that had escaped from a garden, and Ben the Lama, who I gathered was your basic brain-damanged Nam vet, had built himself a little bamboo hut."

"You actually *went* with this guy?" said Kaspian.

Foo Bird shrugged. "I couldn't say no. It wasn't all that dark, with the lights around the Vice President's house."

This is great, Kaspian thought. Such embroidery. Could it be true? What did *true* mean? He no longer felt certain about the reality status—a chance phrase he'd picked up lately which already was proving useful—of anything. "Okay, so you followed this guy to his hut."

"Right. And that's about all there was to it. I listened to his life story and then he got into this thing about the Supreme Court—he was an Associate Justice for a while, you know—and after that I said good-bye and came out on the other side of the woods, the Woodley Park side. Not all that far from here, as a matter of fact. Anyway, that was it. My anomalous encounter. Except for one other thing."

Kaspian said, "Don't tell me. A girl, right?"

"Shh." Foo Bird glared at him. Behind them, the grown-ups had gathered around the conference table in the opposite prong of the L. "Not a girl. It's stupid, actually. This guy, Ben the Lama. He knew all these *things* about me. Nothing major, just tiny dumb stuff. Names of my friends back when I was a kid. Stuff like that. Who my favorite singer is."

"Who?" said Kaspian.

"Shut up. Are you listening? It was like a party trick. One pointless detail after another. I never asked him how he was doing it—I could tell he *wanted* me to, like that was part of the routine—but I never did. And he never came out and said a word about it. It was just like, out of nowhere he'd scream, *Your grandfather built a fallout shelter.*"

"Did your grandfather build a fallout shelter?" asked Kaspian.

"Figure it out. *Yes*. I wouldn't be telling you this if it wasn't *yes*. This idiot was always right but the whole shtick was so indescribably vapid. Like a *tired* party trick. I mean think of it. Ben the Lama. With his collection of vintage comic books, all wrapped up in plastic. Right there in his bamboo shack. Down the hill from the Vice President's house."

"Only in America," said Kaspian.

Foo Bird stared blankly at him and then chuckled. He looked relieved to have told his story to someone. Kaspian knew the feeling.

"So now you see," said Foo Bird, "their theory doesn't fit *my* experience, at any rate."

"Sure it does," said Kaspian. "If you run into an ugly old crone—in a story, I mean—she *always* turns out to be the Queen of Fairies, or something. This sounds like the same deal. You ran into a homeless person, and he turned out to be—"

"A homeless person. A slightly *psychic* homeless person."

"I think it fits. Nevertheless."

Foo Bird fanned this suggestion away with one big hand.

"So listen," said Kaspian. "You never told me how you got kicked out of that program you were in. Unless this is prying. See, I was kind of thinking it might have had something to do with . . . your experience. But I guess not."

"It's not prying." Foo Bird held his eyes fixed on some infinity-point outside the window. "I just had some . . . difficulty, for a while. Emotional difficulty. Adjustment problems. I couldn't keep up with my studies. I became . . . disruptive. It was only an episode."

"When was this?"

"In the summer. July. It's a tough season, out here."

"Everywhere," said Kaspian. He patted the giant Samoan's shoulder. Foo Bird gave him a sideways smile.

"Ah, provisions at last!" exclaimed Colonel Carpathian.

There was much shuffling but little enthusiasm from the other end of the room. "I think we ought to get going," said Kaspian quietly.

Foo Bird did not at first seem to have heard him.

"Seriously," Kaspian said, keeping his voice still and his eyes casually in motion. "I think we ought to get out of here. These guys give me the serious creeps. *Now* is our best shot, while nothing's going on. I don't want to wait until I'm like, drugged and helpless."

Foo Bird gave him a clinical stare, weighing this outburst of paranoia.

"I think you're alarmed over nothing," he said. "I *hope* you are, because I have no intention of going anywhere. I'm not a scofflaw by nature. I follow the rules, ordinarily. The other thing was just an episode."

"Right. So are you coming or what?"

Foo Bird only stared at him.

"Well listen," said Kaspian. "Here's the deal. I'll wait for you at the bottom of the driveway for about ten minutes. I might be off in the bushes somewhere, but I'll keep an eye out. You can come if you want to."

"Come where?" said Foo Bird.

Kaspian hadn't thought of that. It hadn't seemed to matter. Now he felt his momentum falter.

"Why do you want to leave?" asked Foo Bird. "I mean, truthfully. Do you really think something bad is going to happen? Or do you just feel inclined, generally speaking, to *get away?*"

Kaspian shrugged. "When the fairies take you under the hill, you're not supposed to eat their food. If you do, you'll never make it back."

Foo Bird withheld comment for a moment. Then he said, "I hope you make it back."

"Yeah, thanks," said Kaspian. "Me too you."

They parted, cool and friendly, like that.

THE bathroom was only a dozen steps down the hall, but by the time he got there Kaspian could hear footsteps behind him. It did not take a lot of imagination to picture the blond adjutant tagging along, keeping him under surveillance. Well, screw that.

Once inside, he closed the door and turned the latch of the heavy lock. He closed the drain in the bathtub and opened the faucet to a steady trickle that sounded like someone pissing. The window was a bitch and a half to open. He flushed the toilet, opened the tap to a loud spatter, and went out feet-first, belly-down, scraping his balls on the sill.

He hit the ground hard but did not seem to have broken anything. He found the AYA minibus out front on the lawn, with Ronald nursing his paper cup of 7-Eleven coffee, heavily involved in the *Washington Post* sports section. His body jerked when Kaspian thumped on the windshield.

"What's up?" Ronald said, levering open the door.

"Take me someplace," said Kaspian. "Quick."

Ronald sized him up. Heaven knows what he saw in Kaspian's eyes. After a moment, he nodded and said, "Get on down there. Keep low so nobody sees you."

Kaspian dove behind the front seat. Ronald revved the van and started down the drive. When he had rounded the curve, out of sight of the big stone house, he said, "All right, now. Where *exactly* do you want to go?"

Kaspian hadn't a clue. He was alone in a strange city. Maybe a stranger city than he had thought. Just then, the cellular phone in Ronald's pocket went off.

"Ron Griffith," he answered it. He glanced at Kaspian while listening to the voice at the other end. "No, ma'am. I'm just up the road a ways. Keeping the *driveway* clear, if you see what I'm saying."

Kaspian breathed in and out.

"Yes, ma'am," said Ronald. "Yes, ma'am, I surely will." He clicked off the connection and told Kaspian, "She wants me back."

"Great," said Kaspian. "Fucking great."

Ronald opened the door and it looked like that was going to be that. Suddenly a thought seized Kaspian—probably a hopeless one, but a thought nonetheless.

"Can I use that phone?" he asked.

Ronald looked at him thoughtfully, then pulled the cell phone from its pocket and handed it over.

When Directory Assistance came on, Kaspian said, "Malcolm Rugg? Like a carpet, only with two G's?"

There followed the longest pause in the history of telephonic communications. Finally the operator said in an overworked voice, "Please wait for the number," and Kaspian closed his eyes and

he made that secret wish
that is always inside you
waiting to be remembered.

"I kind of feel like I should keep out of sight," Kaspian told Malcolm.

Malcolm accepted this; or at any rate he did not question it, merely said in that case Kaspian should not go *right*, because that would take him out to Connecticut Avenue. He should go *straight*: just walk across the road and get on the discontinued part of Klingle. Kaspian wondered how he would know which was the discontinued part of Klingle, but Malcolm said, "Just cross the road and go *straight*, okay? I'll meet you under the bridge."

They hung up after maybe 90 seconds. And yet Kaspian felt as though some great and powerful thing had been bestowed upon him—a miracle, or a chain of miracles: that Malcolm's number had been listed; that he had been home; that he had known *exactly* where Kaspian was, just from Ronald telling him the street name (Porter, a quarter mile west of Rock Creek); and that—with no questions asked, no pause for thought, like this was the sort of thing that happened all the time—Malcolm had proposed to meet Kaspian and bring him back to his apartment, where, as Malcolm put it, "everything will be cool. Only I hope you don't have nice clothes on because I've been doing some painting." Kaspian said he was wearing a uniform. Malcolm said, "A *uniform*. Wow." Then Ronald took the phone away and Kaspian found himself out on the street. Which at least now he knew the name of.

He did not know much else. But that was his usual situation, right? It had never mattered much to him and did not matter now, except insofar as a feeling of importance had come to attach itself to his movements and his decisions, beginning with his making up his mind that they were not going to do to him what they had done to Foo Bird. Kaspian figured that his private memories—however screwed up, implausible and unhappy they might be—were his own inviolable territory, his landlocked and winter-stricken Poland. He was going to defend them if he could.

He fingered Ring Bear in his pocket, partly for comfort and partly out of simple habit. It was funny how you could get used to an impossible thing, come to accept it as a natural part of the world. Probably you either had to do this or go crazy trying to figure everything out.

Kaspian guessed he was safe: he had figured nothing, with a big *N,* out.

He stepped quickly across Porter Street. He kept going down a sort of ramp to a smaller road that plunged into heavy woodland. The pavement was in terrible shape: chunks of concrete broken loose, weeds growing out of the gutter. He guessed this must be the discontinued part of Klingle. Now it only remained to find the bridge he was supposed to meet Malcolm under.

He took a breath and expanded his chest and looked about him. It was a good day. He was ready. *For whatever comes.*

THAT crazed illusion passed quickly enough. This was no city road. It was a movie set, a post-Apocalyptic urban wasteland. Kaspian had always loved movies like that and to his eyes Klingle Road was beauty itself. Down the left side a chain-link fence topped with triple strands of barbed wire was being digested by honeysuckle. Overhead towered hardwood trees Kaspian did not know, probably seven or eight stories tall, except there were no buildings to give you a sense of scale. The trees arched and folded their limbs together high in the air, blocking most of the sky and straining the sunlight down to a yellow-green concentrated essence that dribbled onto just certain spots. All kinds of invasive plants lapped it up. Jewel weed was in flower, little vulvas of purple fading to pinkish white. Virginia creeper infiltrated the shattered pavement, crossing the center line, trying to root. Downy seed puffs of hawkweed blew loose at the slightest stirring of air.

From the look of things, the city had kept patching this road for many years, laying asphalt on top of the concrete where it failed, then had given that up too and abandoned the place. But this had happened so long ago that the posts of the guardrail, set in asphalt, having settled over the years, now sagged over at 45 degrees, and in one place, next to a drain hole, the asphalt had just *melted*—turned gooey in the summer heat and shape-shifted, a road becoming a river, flowing halfway down the slope. At the bottom lay something between a ditch and a stream, wide but empty except for a foot of dirty water. All kinds of shit had been dumped down there. Real shit, no doubt, amid the old boots, tires, plastic store bags, rotten outer garments worn to death by homeless people, a shopping cart full of newspapers that were turning autumn leaf colors, smashed-up household appliances, plastic toys that were still bright, still glowing in the jewel weed, and indescribable other things well along toward melting into the breast of the Great Mother. Kaspian walked past all this with a perky stride until he came to a wall.

It was just three preformed concrete barricades, dropped across what was left of the road. One of them was set at an angle, so that you could zip through the gap on a bicycle. Kaspian paused long enough to check out the graffiti. It was high-quality work: elaborately wrought initials, and the words EAST SIDE BOEEZ GONA GET U. The other side was more abstract. Apart from DISCO DAN in black, the elaborate spray-work was done in bright colors, chiefly neon yellow and an intense cobalt blue: a sort of guerrilla mural, too surrealistic for Kaspian's eyes to follow.

He stood by the barrier, hesitating. Until now, it had not occurred to him that coming down here, to a forgotten part of an unknown city, might be dangerous. Probably not, probably everything was cool. Otherwise Malcolm wouldn't have told him to come this way. Right?

He went forward. Past the wall, into the deeper shadows

beyond. He looked hard through the woods but saw nothing that looked like a bridge: only trees and garbage and underbrush. Then he realized that he could *hear* the bridge—not just ahead but above him, up in the forest canopy. The sound of a bus roaring through its lower gears, picking up speed, came down from there. But it was not for another hundred paces or so, around a slow curve the road was making, that he actually saw what he had come for.

The bridge was a giant thing, grand as an ancient aqueduct, soaring on concrete legs. Way, way up at the top, maybe eighty feet above where Kaspian stood, he could see traffic and tiny pedestrians crossing behind an ornamented railing painted bright green. The tallest trees barely topped the plane of the bridge deck, which was easily four lanes wide, so that up there it was open and sunny and hot-looking, all the colors more intense.

It was weird to stand down here by yourself. Kaspian wasn't scared, especially. But he decided what he would do was hang back a little, not directly under the bridge but close enough to see if anybody showed up. He was glad of this almost right away, because he saw that there *were* people there, already.

It was two guys, one tall and one short. He hadn't noticed them at first because they were off the road up a bare dirt slope where one of the giant bridge columns was anchored to the earth. For some reason there was a *door* sunk into the mass of concrete, and this door had been opened up or (more likely, he guessed) broken down, and that's where the two guys were, one of them leaning in the doorway and the other standing outside it. For the next couple of minutes, Kaspian kept such a tight watch on these guys that he forgot to maintain a rear guard, and all at once the sounds of footsteps and careless voices made him spin around to see half a dozen teenage kids coming up behind him. Instantly he thought: *the East Side Boeez.* He was standing in plain view from that direction, and when the kids spotted him they shut up.

Four of them could have been called black, though actually they came in such various shades that for the first time Kaspian saw some logic in the alternate term, African-American. Another was white with flaming red hair and the last was unclassifiable in a way that reminded him of Foo Bird. They struck Kaspian as tough-looking and a couple years older than himself. He wondered how hard it would be to turn and scramble up the hillside, in case they made a move. No way, he decided: if they wanted his pale young ass, it was theirs.

But as they got closer—staring at him the whole time—he saw that they were about his own age, and maybe not so tough after all. What made them look otherwise was the way they carried themselves, how they moved through the semiwild landscape, plus a calculated dishevelment of their clothing, which was not much different than the stuff Kaspian would have worn if he hadn't been forced into uniform. On top of everything, they were carrying *schoolbooks*. As they passed Kaspian (which seemed to take forever) the shortest one gave him a very slight nod.

An unexpected thought came to him: that if he lived here, and he went to their school, these guys might be the very crowd he hung out with. They looked about right. And what the fuck were they doing out of school at this hour, anyway? Clearly they were Kaspian's kind of people.

By the time they were gone, the two guys under the bridge had also disappeared, and the door in the concrete block was closed. Kaspian guessed he was alone again, but soon he heard gravel being kicked loose and bouncing through dry leaves, and he thought, *Now* what?

It was Malcolm, coming fast down the hill on the other side of the stream.

Malcolm looked the same as ever—skinny and somewhat crazed—but at least here in D.C. he wore a shirt, its sleeves long enough to cover those blue rings tattooed around his upper arms. His black hair flopped chaotically as he blew down the hill, half sliding and half hopping, with his arms flung out like branches heaving before a sudden wind. Reaching the bottom, he gave Kaspian a wave and turned upstream, making for a place where a giant sycamore had collapsed, spanning the dirty water. Kaspian went that way to meet him. Finally they came together in an open spot where sun fell in a triangular patch bounded on one side by the immense shadow of the bridge.

"You found it," said Malcolm.

Kaspian said, "Where did *you* come from?"

Malcolm pointed upward. From here, the traffic sounds took on deeper and somewhat metallic sonorities, their vibrations absorbed and transformed by the bridge. "Connecticut Avenue."

Ah: the Sunlit Lands, from which Kaspian had been warned away.

"You look different," said Malcolm. He smiled quizzically, as though trying to make out what the difference consisted of.

"Thanks," said Kaspian. He knew it hadn't necessarily been a compliment. But from his standpoint, *different* translated to *less like a know-nothing punk.* He would accept that. "Kind of a cool place here."

Malcolm's angular face lit up. "It's *great,* isn't it?" he said, beaming boylike enthusiasm. "I come here all the time to do field studies."

"For your comic?" said Kaspian. He remembered the giant killer amoeba.

"I'm calling it *sequential art* now. That's easier for my faculty advisor to handle. Here, come on. I'll show you some stuff."

He started off, passing under the bridge, beckoning Kaspian to follow him. It was kind of amazing: not a word about what emergency had led Kaspian to call him out of the blue.

Kaspian hustled after him and they passed under Connecticut Avenue. It seemed to mark a sort of divide. On the other side, you could see apartment buildings set high on the slope, their upper stories lost in the trees. The road itself was slightly less dilapidated, and the woods around them were dense but not so jungly. A short distance ahead, beside a second concrete barricade, the two men who had been hanging out under the bridge were climbing into a D.C. government utility vehicle. Kaspian reflected that once again he had thought things were a certain way—like he had descended into a dangerous Underworld—but reality had turned out different: this Underworld was inhabited by teenagers trudging to school, and maintenance crews making their rounds, and a young artist hunting for inspiration.

Malcolm spun off to the right, where a cast-iron fence in seriously bad condition bordered the road, capping stonework half buried in surging ivy and periwinkle. Malcolm picked a spot where a section of fencing had collapsed. There you had to leap a ditch and scramble up a dirt bank, but the way was worn clearly enough to suggest that other people had come this way before you. Once off the road, the path continued in two directions, following the line of the old stone wall. It looked like a deliberate thing, not just some foot-run worn by trespassers. Malcolm struck off and Kaspian followed him into a kind of open, emerald-green hollow beneath enormous tulip poplars, with rhododendrons fifteen feet tall leaning down from farther up the hill and forming their own subcanopy. The path led to a tiny amphitheater carved out of the slope with tiers of gray stone and a stage that was mostly grass, scuffed to bare soil in the middle, like somebody still used it.

"What is this place?" Kaspian asked finally.

"It's a school. Foreign students, mostly. Before that I guess it was somebody's house."

Kaspian could not see buildings anywhere. They walked a little farther until the rhododendrons got into a territorial shoving match with some kind of huge-leafed bamboo, and ivy piled up a foot deep on the steep bank, irrupting here and there with fountainlike clumps of daylily foliage, and you could begin to make out a row of houses on the far side of the hollow. Here Malcolm paused beside a stretch of wall whose stones were completely encrusted with a life-form Kaspian would not have dreamed of trying to classify: reddish-brown and droopy, damp-looking, almost like seaweed, with a texture that reminded him of the skin that forms on instant pudding in the refrigerator.

"Feel it," said Malcolm, running one of his own fingers gently across the stuff.

It felt totally dry. Like bread crust. Almost the opposite of how it looked. Very weird.

"I *think* it might be a lichen," said Malcolm. "You know, there are lichens that aren't part algae, but part photosynthetic bacteria instead. I'm kind of thinking this might be one of those, with rhodoplasts instead of chloroplasts. I'm basing a new character in my comic—I mean, my sequential art project—on it."

"A character?" said Kaspian.

"The senior senator from North Carolina."

Malcolm spoke so seriously, engrossed in his study of the droopy life-form, that Kaspian couldn't tell whether to laugh. He laughed anyway, and Malcolm gave him a funny little smile. The way his eyes sparkled made him look very young despite the growth of black stubble on his face.

"Want to go to my place?" he asked Kaspian.

"That's probably a good idea."

Malcolm didn't ask why. He just nodded and set out walking again. The path was so overgrown as to be almost impossible to follow, but they thrashed ahead until they came to a rise of stone steps laid into the slope, which they climbed to a higher terrace where the ivy had been weed-whacked. Just beyond that was a long curvaceous driveway. Farther up the hill, you could see sand-brown buildings and open lawn, and a sign in international symbol-language depicting children crossing a road. As they followed the driveway out, a van came rolling in, its windows crowded with students who all looked Chinese. Malcolm waved and the driver waved back. One little girl, about nine or ten, stared at Kaspian like he was Mork from Ork. He flashed her the peace sign and she began energetically whispering to her seat-mate.

The sign at the front gate, where the cast-iron fence was in immaculate repair, said Washington International School. Why can't I get sent *here?* Kaspian wondered. Instead of American Youth Academies, Inc. The Third Way. The classroom of the future. The front line in a long and terrible war, whose stakes are high and whose outcome hangs on decisions being taken far from the field of battle—somewhere in this vast, strange, scary and yet magical-seeming city.

THE walk to Malcolm's apartment was all uphill. Kaspian would never have thought that D.C. was such a hilly place. He remarked on this to Malcolm, who cheerfully said, "Where we're going is the highest point in town. The Soviets built their new embassy there, back in the Cold War, so their antennas could pick up *everything*."

"I see," said Kaspian. Not his war. The neighborhood they were passing through was beautiful, he guessed: big old houses surrounded by gardens, each with its discreet home-security sign. They crossed Reno Road, narrow but full of speeding traffic, and after another couple of blocks Kaspian happened to glance to his left, then came to a stop. The whole empty space at the end of the street, plus the sky all above that, was filled with an enormous Gothic structure that looked like a medieval fortress. "What's *that?*" he asked.

"That's the Cathedral," said Malcolm. For some reason this made him grin, the way you do when you're reminded of something good.

Even from a couple of blocks off, the building was so huge it crowded your field of vision. The great churches of Western Europe had been mostly blown all to hell by the Allies in 1944, on the grounds that they afforded excellent lookout posts for the defending Germans. Kaspian imagined training a three-inch field gun on this soaring, intricately carved tower, with its gargoyles and pediments and machicolations and all that other medieval stuff. *BLAM.*

He found Malcolm watching him patiently. Wondering, but not too much. They set off again without talking and came out presently to Wisconsin Avenue: back to the Sunlit Lands again. Malcolm's apartment was not far beyond that, in an unprepossessing building next to a liquor store that appeared to be a shrine to the Washington Redskins. They climbed to the third floor— Malcolm springing ahead of him, jangling his keys—and entered a small room connected with other small rooms, with metal casement windows looking out over a crowded streetscape. The air smelled like turpentine and linseed oil. From one window, in the dining room, you could see the Cathedral again, and other churchy-looking buildings clustered around it. Kaspian picked a chair and flumped into it.

The apartment was packed. Malcolm's art stuff—easels and

boxes of supplies and comic panels propped against the walls—
took up most of the living room, at the expense of ordinary
furniture, while the dining room was jammed with books that
overflowed their shelves and collected on the floor in piles,
growing like stalagmites. There was barely enough free space to
accommodate a dinky café-style table-and-chair set. Malcolm
turned on stringy, ululating Middle Eastern music while Kaspian
scanned the titles of the nearest stack.

"You've got an awful lot of books here about God," he said.

Malcolm squeezed by, heading for the kitchen. "Those are
mostly my roommate's," he said. "His name is Geoff. He's studying to be an Episcopal priest. That's why we're living in Cathedral Heights."

He came out of the kitchen with two Pop-Tarts, one of
which he offered to Kaspian. Then he sat down and said, "Actually, we're more than roommates. I hope you're okay with that."

It took Kaspian several moments to understand what this
meant. *"Ohhh,"* he said, when he got it. Then he felt dumb
because he didn't want Malcolm to think that the *ohhh* meant
anything. "Sure," he added quickly.

The truth was that he was okay with it, he was fine with it
in fact, but he was something else as well, something he couldn't
pin down. Surprised? Mildly freaked? Amused? (Because what
would his stepmother say, caught up in her petition drive?)

Malcolm munched his Pop-Tart and nodded in time to the
music, which was rhythmical but bizarre, somewhat like the entertainment at Jabba the Hutt's desert palace. Kaspian said, "Do
you have a TV?"

"In the bedroom," said Malcolm, with his mouth full.

Kaspian followed him there and, however hard he tried, he
could not shake his mind free of the fact that he was entering a
room where *two guys slept together*. It was weird but he could not
help imagining that. The way he found to deal with it was to
think about himself and Charity: the things they had done together,
and how none of those things, if you took it by itself, meant
anything at all—you had to look at the whole picture, the feelings
involved et cetera, which no outsider could possibly do. From that

perspective, the physical acts changed into something else. It wasn't like they hadn't happened—they *had* happened and Kaspian's heart beat faster when he remembered them—but they hadn't meant what they would mean if you watched them in an X-rated movie.

After thinking this through, he felt like telling Malcolm again that everything was okay with him, but that would have been stupid. Malcolm handed him the remote and Kaspian sat down on the floor (not *the bed*) and flipped to C-SPAN.

The hearing was no longer on. C-SPAN had moved its coverage to the Senate, which was in session, though hardly anybody but some pages seemed to know about this, because the chamber was almost empty. A couple of bald Senators with red neckties stood conferring in front of the President protem. Kaspian tried to imagine these guys with faces of red-brown lichen, and found it surprisingly easy to do.

"So what's going on?" Malcolm asked him at last. He flopped down on the bed and stretched out with his head propped up by an elbow. On an end table behind him sat a 20-gallon aquarium, jammed with plants and snails and algae but no fish.

Kaspian didn't know what to tell him. How much, or from what angle. He said, "I guess I've run away, kind of. Not for good. But till I can get some things figured out."

Malcolm nodded as though this were perfectly sensible. After a moment's thought he said, "Can I help? You looking for a place to crash?"

You've already helped, Kaspian started to say. But then he remembered how Malcolm had been there before—been *waiting* there, almost—that other time he ran away. That night he had ditched ASAC and wandered out into the Maine woods, to end up four days later lying on a rock in the sun. He looked at Malcolm now: skinny as a stick, rings in his ears and nose and eyebrows, hair like a black floor mop. Malcolm with his secrets and his fungi and his esoteric knowledge. And he wondered why these unscheduled journeys through strange woodlands always ended with *this* guy at the end of them. He was like a tour guide to the Dark Lands. Kaspian eyed him and, dead serious, asked:

"How do you know when something is real?"

Malcolm, of course, did not find anything non-sequiturish about this. Agreeably he said, "Like what?"

"Like . . . a thing you remember. Or a thing somebody else remembers. How can you tell? Because sometimes it seems like, this *can't* be real, I must—or whoever, this other person must—be making it up. But at the same time, how could you be making it *up*? I mean, you *couldn't*. You could never imagine a thing like that. I mean, some stuff, you just know is impossible. Because it's too stupid, or it's against the laws of physics or whatever. So then . . . then how can you *remember* it? How come it feels so much like it really happened? But if it *is* something you only imagined, then . . ."

. . . *then where did Ring Bear come from?* is what he was thinking. He closed his mouth. He was quite certain that nothing he had just said, or could ever say, made any sense at all.

"Those are all very good questions," said Malcolm. "Very old questions, also. Difficult to answer."

"You're telling me," said Kaspian.

"But *not*," said Malcolm, "impossible."

Kaspian looked at him. "Not?"

"Definitely."

Malcolm looked rather serene, laid out there. He looked like he was right where he belonged. Kaspian envied him. He envied everybody in the world who was not confused and fucked up. Who had found a place for himself and was lounging around in it.

"Okay," Kaspian said. "Okay, if it's not impossible to answer, then what are the answers? *Where* are the answers?" He almost added: Mister Know-It-All.

Malcolm leaned over and tapped Kaspian lightly at the center of his forehead. The old Third Eye.

Not that again, Kaspian thought.

Then Malcolm rolled himself into a sitting position and said, "Want to see my slime mold?"

"Yeah," said Kaspian. "I truly do."

Malcolm rose from the bed. "Come on," he said. "It's in the bathroom."

★   ★   ★

THE bathroom was tiny and it seemed to Kaspian that the slime mold had been given an inordinate amount of floor space. It lived in a giant Tupperware salad bowl among some moldy leaves. To Kaspian it just looked like a yellowish blobby mass, not much to get excited over, though it did possess a certain appealing grossness, like the green yuck on Nickelodeon. Malcolm demonstrated how he kept it moist with water from the fish tank.

"It's not ready to be fed," he said. "Too bad. That's a trip."

"You *feed* it?" said Kaspian.

"Sure." And Malcolm explained the process, which involved old-fashioned rolled oats soaked beforehand in buttermilk. You place the food a slight distance from the slime mold, "then the *cool* thing," Malcolm said, "is to observe how the organism senses the presence of food and extrudes a pseudopod in its direction, eventually engulfing it. Kind of like a python."

"So is this thing an animal?" asked Kaspian. "Or a plant? Or what?"

"Right—it's an *or what*. That's what's so cool about it. I've modeled my protagonist on it."

"What's that?"

"The hero of the story. He's kind of a wandering philosopher. He evolves and acquires knowledge by absorbing new genetic information."

"Ah, yes," said Kaspian. The best stories are the weird ones.

Malcolm closed the Tupperware lid. They walked back out to the living room, where the Middle Eastern music seemed to be going on an eternal loop. In place of regular furniture there were some cushions here and there about the floor. Malcolm sat on one and drew his legs up, assuming his Shiva pose. He appeared quite comfortable that way. Kaspian paced around, looking at what there was to look at. Which was plenty, and all of it was stuff he had never seen before.

"But to answer your question," said Malcolm—and Kaspian thought *which question*—"I'm not sure there's such a big difference between what's real and what's made up. *Everything* is made-up, to begin with, isn't it? That's why the universe is called

Creation. Because, in theory, it's all just something that popped out of the mind of God."

That doesn't help a whole lot, Kaspian thought. Especially if you suspect that God Himself might be a crock. He picked up a package of incense that lay among tubes of acrylic paint on a table and gave it a sniff. "Mmm, patchouli," he said, in his ordinary smart-ass voice.

"Sandalwood," said Malcolm.

"I'm not God, though," said Kaspian. "Neither is Foo Bird. If *we* make something up, that doesn't make it real. That makes it, like . . . made-up."

Malcolm stared at him as though he had made an important point. "*Foo Bird?* You mean as in, *If the foo shits . . . ?*"

"Why has everybody heard that joke but me?" said Kaspian. "He's just a kid, okay? What I'm saying is, if *we* make something up—"

"Yeah, I get what you're saying. I don't know. Creation is a godly prerogative. If any of us is able to create something, then we're doing a godlike thing, right? I mean, even . . ." He brushed his hand sideways, indicating the comic-book panels along the wall beside him. "Doesn't the act of creation, of making this stuff up, make *me* a god, in my own little way? Because these things, these pictures, they *are* real—aren't they?" He thumped a finger against one, to prove it. "Even though they just came out of nothing, they just swam into being out of my mind somehow."

"Yeah, but . . . maybe so, but, you can't just make up something that's *impossible,* and have it suddenly become real. For instance, suppose like, you made up this story about Evil Leprechauns. That doesn't mean there's really such a thing as Evil Leprechauns."

Malcolm looked at him with great interest. "You've met leprechauns? Was this down here, or up in Maine?"

"*No,*" said Kaspian, pissed at this damnable open-mindedness.

"Then how," asked Malcolm smoothly, "do you know there aren't any?"

"That's stupid. Because if there were, they wouldn't be hanging out in the woods waiting for some asshole teenager to come along. And they wouldn't take you down to a secret place under the Earth. It's too dumb to even be on *Highlander*."

Malcolm looked as though he still wanted to hear more about the Evil Leprechauns, but he kept quiet about it.

"I'm sorry," said Kaspian, "I guess I'm just sort of . . . thinking out loud. *Too* out loud."

Malcolm said after a moment—as though he too were thinking out loud, in his own direction—"I don't know if you can put limits on creation like that. I mean, when you say, There can't be any this, or They wouldn't do that. The whole point of creation is that it's something *new*, right? Something that didn't exist before. Which means that any act of creation breaks through some kind of previous limitation. It changes the laws of what's possible. Maybe the new thing *is* stupid. In that case, probably the creation doesn't last, it doesn't hold up. But that doesn't make it unreal or nonexistent. Just . . . ephemeral."

Kaspian wasn't sure he followed this. Malcolm read that on his face.

"It's like virtual particles," said Malcolm. "You know? That're always frothing up out of the Void. Usually they just, *pop*, annihilate themselves in a couple of nanoseconds. But it's a statistical thing. There's a certain small probability that they'll last longer, and a smaller probability that they'll last longer than *that*, and a teensy-weensy probability that they'll still be around for the Big Crunch. See, *everything*," waving around the room, "comes out of nothing, and goes back there. Every electron, every particle. Nothing definitely exists in physical form, it's all just a big dance of possibilities. If you measure the energy in a certain way, at a certain instant, then a certain thing takes shape. But it could have gone some other way. You shape the world around you just by being in it, observing it, thinking about it. And the world shapes you."

Kaspian shook his head. "This is *way*—" And he made an over-the-head gesture, skimming his Velcro hair.

"Yeah, for me too," admitted Malcolm. He shrugged. "But

all I'm saying is, I'm not sure this question of reality is so clear-cut as people think. From what I've read, the world *looks* pretty solid, but it's really a bunch of empty space filled with energy. And when you look at what energy is, it's just a bunch of inter-locking *fields*. And fields are nothing but, like, relationships across space and time. So the heart of so-called hard physics is actually pretty nebulous. And what *I* think is, the question of what's ultimately possible and what's not is an open book. You can make up anything you want and write it down there. Most of what you make up is probably ludicrous. But now and then something clicks. Even the ludicrous stuff. I mean—"

He turned bodily toward Kaspian, dramatic in his earnestness.

"*Look at the world,* man. Just look at the fucking world. Does it *seem* to make sense? Does it *look* like it's run by logic and reason and the laws of fucking physics? Or does it look like something that a bunch of crazy gods have slung together, with-out ever bothering to consult each other? Tell me that."

Kaspian could answer that question without bothering to think. The one thing he knew about was World War II. And World War II had proven beyond a doubt—though he had never found a historian willing to come out and say this—that the world is dangerously, even fatally absurd. Things happen all the time that make no sense at all, even to the people who cause them. Both Hitler and Churchill attributed everything to some-thing called Providence, which Kaspian deduced is kind of like God, except even more fuzzy and indefinite. There is no such thing as Providence, really—it's just a manner of speaking—which means that the very people who were supposed to be in charge of things, running the show, were themselves convinced that the show was being run by something that was not a thing at all. In other words, by No-thing. And this mighty No-thing had redrawn the maps of the world, wiped out entire popula-tions, changed the direction of history, and given know-nothing kids like Kaspian something cool and horrible to read about and play computer games based upon. In fact, you could say that the War had happened for the *benefit* of Kaspian and kids like him. Because to be a know-nothing was to be a knower of No-thing, the great agent of causation, the motive force behind the War, and therefore presumably behind everything else.

"I think you're exactly right," said Kaspian.

"You do?" said Malcolm. He gave his boyish smile again. "Wow."

They hung out listening to Middle Eastern music for a while, then Kaspian asked if he could use the telephone.

Malcolm narrowed his eyes, Shiva-like. "It's in the kitchen. And while you're in there, could you get me a Pop-Tart?"

CHARITY sounded sleepy, or perhaps groggy. Dazed with drugs.

"How was the field trip?" she said. "Aren't you back early?"

"I'm not back," he said. "And I'm not on the field trip."

"Mm?" There were rustling sounds and he imagined her propping herself up in bed. He imagined the warm smell of her rising from the bedclothes.

"I split," he said. "They sent me, me and Foo Bird, to this other place. Foo Bird thought it was just because they didn't want us on television. But I think it was something else. There was this guy—"

"Television?" said Charity, like she was still trying to wake up.

"C-SPAN," said Kaspian. "It's part of this whole plan of Winot's. But look, it's complicated, I'll tell you when I see you. I was just calling to find out how you're doing. Are you feeling okay?"

"I wish I was out of here," she said, in a pouty voice. "I wish I was back home. Back in Glen Burnie. I mean, I'd miss *you* if I was there, but . . ."

"Couldn't you just talk to your parents? Ask them to pull you out of AYA?"

"They'd never do that. They think it's so *wonderful*. It's like they've memorized all the glossy brochures. They keep telling me how *lucky* I am, all the *opportunities*, the excellent *facilities*, the *Staff*. Nothing I say is going to make them change their minds."

"They need to see it on the news," muttered Kaspian.

"What?"

"Nothing. Just . . ."

"I don't know why I feel so *sleepy* these days. I wonder if they've put me on some new medication."

"Don't you know?"

"They just bring in the little paper cups and I swallow whatever is in there. It's the only thing you can do. If they think you're not cooperating . . ."

She trailed off. Kaspian guessed she was speaking from long and bitter experience. He felt terrible for her. He wondered if she remembered that he had promised to get her out of there. If so, she had the tact not to mention it.

"I guess I'll let you go," he said after a while.

"*Ohh,*" she murmured, in a make-believe whiny voice, like a child being told to take a nap.

"I love you," said Kaspian.

And check it out: now that he had finally gotten himself to say the words, Charity did not seem to grasp their significance.

"Love you too," she said, in an automatic way, like the little girl being told nighty-night.

Kaspian rested the phone in its socket and stood there for a moment, feeling as though the conversation had not really happened. It was like he was remembering it through a gauze of dream, or imagination. Which actually kind of fit.

THE next call was to the Sudley Center, where Kaylla, the dumb blond receptionist, answered the phone.

"I'd like to leave a message for one of your students," Kaspian told her—altering his voice as far as possible, though there was minimal likelihood that she would recognize it, or indeed that she had the faintest memory of who Kaspian Aaby was. Which made two of them. "His name is Fuad Suleiman."

"Ah, you mean Foo Bird!" Kaylla exclaimed. So much for her cluelessness. "And whom shall I say the message is from?"

Once again, Kaspian had failed to get a fake name lined up. As quickly as he could he said, "Prince. Just tell him Prince called, okay? And let me give you a number."

He read the digits off Malcolm's telephone, hoping they were the correct ones, and not left over from some previous apartment.

"I'll surely do that," said Kaylla, her voice as fresh as paint. "Now you have a wonderful day, all right?"

Back in the living room, Malcolm was sketching. Still seated in his lotus pose, he held a drawing pad against one knee and moved a pen back and forth in quick, slanting strokes, giving shadow and dimension to what appeared to be an especially vivacious corkscrew. Kaspian watched him for a while, staring dumbly at the process of creation. Eventually Malcolm looked up at him and said, "You know what I do when I need to get my head together?"

"Meditate?" guessed Kaspian, not terribly interested.

"Watch cartoons," said Malcolm.

Kaspian wondered if he was joking. Then he decided: Of course not. The longer the idea sat with him, the more sensible it became. Eventually he got up and trooped into the bedroom to see what was on. Then, while waiting for the picture to come up, he decided it didn't matter. He would watch whatever it was. He lay down—on the bed this time—and halfway through an episode of *Cow and Chicken* fell profoundly asleep.

IT had been a while since Kaspian had one of his vivid, unsettling dreams, and that is not what he had now. Only while he was waking up, still at the groggy and uncertain stage, he retained an image, or less than that—an impression—that could only have come from a dream just ended, or interrupted, and even without dwelling on it he found that this dream-impression followed him into wakefulness, as though it were a thought-balloon and he were a character in a comic book.

There was not much to it: a close-up image of a man's chest, fairly wide and pale, sparsely covered with hair. It was unconnected to any other thing, such as a feeling, or a face. And yet Kaspian could not shake free of the image—not even when the sense of wrongness hit him, with regard to where he was waking up, and the time of day it was, nor when he sat up in an unfamiliar bed and blinked around at a room that had fallen nearly dark except for a pallid, purplish bulb that glowed inside the hood of Malcolm's aquarium.

The chest could only have been his daddy's. What other man's body had he ever seen at such close range? Moreover, the mental image had been enormous, filling his inner screen—so that he had to imagine he himself, the rememberer, had been so small as to curl up snugly against it. He would have to have been a baby.

So what was this dream-shard, then? A flash of something he had seen as a one-year-old, the strong chest of the man who had held him, patted him, protected him? The idea made him shiver.

He walked out into the living room and found that Geoff, the candidate for priesthood, was home. Malcolm, slung across pillows, engrossed in a book, failed to react to Kaspian's appearance, so Geoff stood up and introduced himself, shaking hands and smiling in a kind but observant manner: excellent pastoral material. He was different from Malcolm in every way: a few years older, on the short side, hair blond and neatly trimmed, muscular, chatty, and ironic.

"Are you hungry?" he asked.

Kaspian wasn't sure. "What time is it?"

Geoff flipped up a watch face for him to inspect. Just past six o'clock. They would be sitting down to eat at the Sudley Center, beneath nicely framed depictions of the triumphs and setbacks of Robert E. Lee's Army of Northern Virginia—heroically doomed defenders of slavery and the semifeudal Southern caste system. The last of the series, in which Lee offers his sword to Grant, who gallantly refuses it, was captioned by the motto, *But the South shall rise again!* "I don't guess I'm too hungry," he said.

The phone rang and Geoff slipped off to answer it. From the kitchen door he told Kaspian, in a voice of amused surprise, "Why, it's for *you*."

At which Malcolm—for Malcolmish reasons no one can

know—sat straight as a pole and peered into space and declared: "That reminds me."

He dove into the clutter of drawing pads and magazine clippings and scraps of one kind or another, while Geoff stretched the twisty phone cord as far as it would go, barely enough to allow Kaspian to sit down at the café table in the dining room while he pressed the headpiece to his ear.

"Your Highness," said Foo Bird at the other end. "How may I serve you?"

Kaspian smiled. It was a relief to hear that voice, calm and unflappable again. "What's going on?" he said. "How are you doing? Are you okay?"

"Before we begin our mutual interrogation, I should tell you that you are a wanted man. Your face is appearing in post offices throughout the metropolitan area. Ms. Boot was heard to utter an unclean oath. They even canceled my second, ahem, *interview,* owing to your sudden disappearance."

"Yeah, well," said Kaspian—glancing up at Geoff, who had tactfully distanced himself, to the extent that you could do that in such a small place—"lucky for them, I guess. I doubt if they would have been ready for Ben the Lama."

Foo Bird chuckled.

Kaspian said, "So you're *okay,* though. They didn't turn you into a vegetable or anything."

"No more than I was previously. Though now that you mention it, I have been feeling rather guavalike these past few days."

"Fuck you," said Kaspian. (Geoff's ears pricked up, though his head did not twitch.)

"Here it is," exclaimed Malcolm, peering like a groundhog from a mound of scrap paper. He held up a battle-scarred envelope.

"I have something entertaining to tell you," Foo Bird was saying.

"Yeah?" Kaspian rotated in his chair, uselessly striving for privacy here. "Like what?"

"Yeah. Like you're scheduled to testify before the Education Committee tomorrow."

Kaspian heard this but the words just landed like dud mortar shells. Foo Bird went on:

"It turns out that the Committee is going over to a town-meeting-type format for the next few days, seeking the views of the general public. There was a book in the hearing room where you could sign up to testify. So Brenton wrote your name down."

"Brenton wrote my name down."

"Correct. I believe he assumes you'll get in some kind of trouble when you fail to appear."

"Ha." Like Kaspian could get in more trouble than he already was.

"Anyway, think of it, Aaby. The lights, the cameras, the Congressmen—and *you,* exercising your constitutional freedom of speech. History unfolding before the eyes of an expectant nation."

Kaspian felt a little too distracted to indulge this particular fantasy.

"So what kind of trouble am I in?" he asked. "Can you tell?"

Foo Bird's bodily presence was such that you could detect a sonic displacement when it shrugged at the other end of the telephone line. "The usual, I suppose. Only more so. Enough regress points to last you till the late December religious holiday of your choice. Always a time of joyous uncertainty around the Suleiman house. As you're welcome to see for yourself in case your own family disowns you."

"Hey, thanks, really?" said Kaspian.

"I gather you're still in the District," said Foo Bird.

"What district?"

"Of Columbia. It's the local name for Washington."

"Ah, right. I'm there."

"Safe and sound, I hope."

"Sure. I'm fine. Thanks. I got in touch with this person I know."

"And you will be rejoining us . . . when? In case anyone asks."

"When I've gotten a few things figured out."

"Such as?"

Kaspian's eyes were fixed, through no fault of his brain, on the spine of a book called *Modern Man in Search of a Soul*. The answer to Foo Bird's question was: Such as, what to make out of the scattered, windblown pieces of his life. But rather than get into anything like that he said:

"I guess I better get going. I'm kind of tying up these guys' phone. I'm glad you're okay, though."

"Of course I'm okay. Though it *is* kind of you to wonder." Foo Bird paused and then went on, "Any messages for anyone? Expressions of gratitude to Brenton? Respects to Ms. Boot?"

"Nah," said Kaspian.

"Can I reach you at this number tomorrow?"

Kaspian had no idea. He said, "Maybe you should just wait till you hear from me. Okay?"

"We *will* be hearing from you, then?"

"Sure," said Kaspian. Thinking, One way or another.

Foo Bird said good-bye and Kaspian dropped the phone in its cradle. Malcolm must have been waiting for this because he almost leapt up waving the envelope.

"Here," he said. "I've had this thing for a couple of months. I'd almost totally forgotten."

He handed it to Kaspian, who examined it suspiciously. It was made out to him but with his name spelled wrong—Kaspian Abby—and the story of how it had found its way to Malcolm's apartment was written (in two separate styles of handwriting, of varying readability) across the face of the envelope. The first and sloppiest hand, the one that couldn't spell his name, had addressed the letter "in care of Trust for Global Readiness" at a post office box in Maine. Below this, a second hand had meticulously penciled "Please forward c/o Inanna and/or Malcolm RUGG, Sinai Falls, ME."

There was no return address, and Kaspian figured he had learned as much as he was going to learn without opening the thing. He looked up at Malcolm, who was watching him expectantly—having held on to this letter long enough that he now expected, no doubt, to hear what it was about.

Kaspian ripped open the envelope. Inside were three sheets of what turned out to be Accelerated Skills Acquisition Camp stationery, the kind they issued to encourage you to write home.

"Dear Kaspian," the letter began, in a graceless script that matched the first one on the envelope:

> *I guess U have probably heard some stuff about this but don't believe everything, ok? U are probally (sp?) wicked pissed at me since I promised not to tell any1 your story, but I swear it was not like that, which is what IM writing 4.*

Kaspian drew his breath. The letter was from Hunter Nye. Hunter the betrayer. Whose big mouth had gotten him *selected*, as Ms. Boot would say, to be transferred from ASAC in Maine down to Virginia, to take his place in the Model Remediation Program.

He didn't feel like going any further. But of course when you start on something like this you're in for the haul. Anyway it sounded as though Hunter might be working up to an apology.

> *If I could see U inperson U could kick my butt and feel better. I guess I would 2.*
> *where the Fuck are U anyway?*

> *BUT here's the thing Abby. I did not tell ms Boot all U told me. I accidently blabbed some of it cause I thought the way she was acting, she already knew. That is what she wanted me 2 think. And I tell U the truth, I thought she was going to let me screw her.*
> *Know how she comes on 2U with her whole body like? Bcuz she was doing that and I could barely keep my dick in my pants, I was so sure it was going 2 happen. Anyway this was in her office 1 night, I forgot.*
> *Only except I was **wrong** about that, but anyhow to go*

*on. So she said (I forget the exact words but) «So I guess
Kaspian has told U all about his little outing» and I was «No
way he never said a word» but she just acted cool like she
knew I was lying. the way she talked I was positive she knew
what had happened. F.I. something she said about, a «unusual
encounter.» I know she was making shit up now it but I sure
didn't then. Like I said I kind of had my mind on some
thing else.*

*So U are right to be mad because probally I would have
told her U + I were faggots if I thought that would have got
her hot. But as U probably guessed, nothing happened and the
whole thing was kind of a set up, U could say. L8er I thought,
about how much I'd run my mouth and I wasn't supposed to
tell any1, but by then—it was 2 late. Now I am writing to
say I am sorry and I hope I didn't get U in more trouble,
which U don't deserve any more of.*

> *Your friend (Beleave it or not) ~*
> *Hunter*

*Ps-Walter Gilliland got caught jacking off with some maga-
zines and isn't a counselor anymore. Cool huh?*
Pps-if U ever get this, Ricky sez HI. Mike 2.

Kaspian looked up to find Malcolm watching him expectantly. Kind of like a big skinny puppy. He would have just
given him the letter to read except for the part about faggots.
Instead he said, "It's from a friend. I guess he wasn't sure how
to get in touch with me so he used the address on this card I
gave him."

"Yeah," said Malcolm, "that's kind of what my mom
thought. And Weeb forwarded it to us—remember Weeb?—and
I guess it sort of got packed in with all my stuff when I came
back down to school."

Kaspian said, "Yeah. So, thanks. I'm kind of glad to get it."

And he was, though probably no one could have told that
from his smart-ass voice.

"Well, I'm making dinner," said Geoff, "whether anyone's eating or not."

DINNER was garlic-and-cheese tortellini and a glass of white wine. Malcolm still labored under the impression that Kaspian was old enough for things like this. It was cool, but tiring. You were expected to do things. Pay attention. Converse. You couldn't just sit there and blob.

"So you're studying to be a priest?" he said to Geoff. It sounded kind of inane, but Geoff was happy enough to answer him. He seemed like the kind of person who spends dinner running his mouth so that everybody gets done eating before him.

"Actually at this point—" Geoff's fork froze in transit with a speared coil of pasta "—it's less study and more practice. Like teacher training? Out of the cloister and into the wide world. I've been doing volunteer work at a walk-in clinic in Shaw, do you know where that is? An *afflicted* community. The theory is that such an experience changes you. Your gaze is wrenched from divine light to the brooding shadows. You see the world for the baffling, bloody, inglorious place it is."

"Ah," said Kaspian. He swallowed his food which was very good, different than your usual spaghetti-type stuff. "So is it changing you?"

"I don't think so," said Geoff. "I think I'm enjoying myself too much."

Kaspian noticed that Malcolm, though seemingly absorbed in dinner, was listening to Geoff with an affectionate smile. You could see how this queer-couple thing might work. But still it was funny to think about.

"I don't think I'd want to be a priest," Kaspian said.

Geoff studied him for the duration of one mouthful. "It's not everyone's cup of nepenthe," he said. Probably this was supposed to be clever because he glanced at Malcolm to make sure he was being appreciated. Malcolm rolled his eyes.

"The nectar of the gods," he told Kaspian. "Geoffrey's a pagan at heart."

"Episco-pagan," Geoff said, nodding amiably.

"Are people—" Kaspian glanced around at imaginary eaves-droppers "—aware of this?"

"Oh, I don't stand out all that much," said Geoff. "You'd be surprised what a lot of Episcopal priests are like. For example, *gay* Episcopal priest is a redundancy. I may be slightly more *irreverent* than average."

"But don't they make you . . ." Kaspian hesitated. "Don't you have to like, *believe* in all that stuff? What it says in the Bible, and all? Before they let you be a priest?"

"Well." Geoff straightened up and poured himself another glass of wine. "To begin with, I do believe all *that stuff*, if by that we mean what I take to be the core truths of Christianity: the holy and eternal Trinity, the salvific possibilities for hu-mankind, the moral teachings of Jesus Christ. *Not* if what we mean is a naive, literal understanding of every verse in the Bible. I am innocent of what Henry Gomes calls the sin of bibliolatry. But having said that, I'm really quite devout. I'm sorry if my manner suggests otherwise."

"No, it's not that," Kaspian said. "I was just . . . like I was saying, I don't think *I* could be a priest. It's not like I'm *convinced* that everything in the Bible is a lie. No offense, by the way."

"None taken."

"But . . . well listen. Can I tell you something that happened to me? And you tell me what you think?"

"Aww," said Geoff, with comic dourness. "This sounds a bit like putting on the collar."

"Not when you hear what it is," said Kaspian.

Malcolm was watching him too now, somewhere between amused and surprised at the sound in Kaspian's voice. Kaspian guessed it was white-wine ballsiness. He was surprised too be-cause he had not thought about this beforehand but was just sliding along, trailing about half a second behind his own mouth.

"I was out in the woods one night," he said. "I was lost, pretty much, but I wasn't worried about that. I just kept walking for a while and then I came to this open place, maybe a field or something but it was too dark to really see."

Already, barely getting into it, the story felt worn-down at the edges. Kaspian had told it enough times that it was becoming less of a memory and more of a narrative. The words and the events fell out in a definite order. And Kaspian knew that in a certain way, this made the story a lie. Because the weird jaggedy truth of what had happened to him that night was getting more and more smoothed over, reduced to a mere chain of events, made comprehensible by telling and retelling. Whereas the reality (if that term applies) had not been comprehensible at all. Events had *not* happened in any sensible order, one leading to the next, with all the seams between them sewn tight; rather they had lurched from one insane episode to another. There was no discernible cause and effect, no regard for logic or common sense. The fragments that adhered to Kaspian's memory were like pieces not from of a single puzzle box but from *different* puzzles, jumbled together.

He went ahead with the story anyway. When he got to the Evil Leprechauns, he paused to check his listeners' reactions.

Malcolm, looking pleased, said, "I *knew* something like this had happened."

"What do you mean," said Kaspian, "*something like this?* Is there anything *else* like this?"

"Of course there is," said Geoff.

Now it was Kaspian's turn to look and wait. But Geoff only swirled the wine in his glass—already half gone and Kaspian had hardly gotten warmed up.

"Pray, continue," Geoff said. "I didn't mean to interrupt."

"Okay," said Kaspian. "So here's one thing right here. These three little guys were *bad*. As in, totally evil. I'm not kidding. They didn't *do* anything bad but you could just, I mean, feel it coming *off* them. So if there really is some place out there that's got these guys living in it—the Planet of Little Assholes or whatever—then what does that say about the universe? What the hell kind of, sorry, place is this, what kind of God's in charge of it? Does what I'm saying make any sense? Because see, I'm not sure any longer if the Good Guys are running the show. Or I mean, if *anyone* is."

Silence dropped onto the table when Kaspian shut up. It was weird because he realized that the older guys were really *into* this, they were following along and waiting to see where he was going. Which made three of them.

For some reason, or no reason, Kaspian thought of his stepmother. Her face appeared before him, dry and powdery pale. What a distance he had gotten away from her!—sipping white wine in an artsy little apartment with this almost-priest and his *boyfriend*, or what was the right word? really close pal? lover?—who was also an *artist*, in downtown, or maybe uptown, Washington, D.C., the nation's capital. He supposed that the *Book of Virtues* slant here would be that you could never run away from your problems, that his stepmother was with him even here, that eventually he must face up to her. But in fact he felt like he had fucking *escaped*. He could forget about his stepmother in a heartbeat. NoElle and her sixty tons of cosmetic products too.

Did this make him bad? Was it worth asking Geoff about? Nah.

Kaspian smiled. He had a strange sense of rules having been suspended. School canceled due to Act of God.

"So they took me to another place and I met this angel," he said—then blinked; he hadn't really meant to put it like that. "I mean she was a girl in white, she sort of *looked* like an angel. Or the way you'd think an angel might look. But she wasn't really, and she wasn't really a girl, either. Somebody told me she might be a thing called a Nordic. That's a type of alien. Which *seems* like bullshit to me, but I mean, what do *I* know? She was there, she had to be *something*. Maybe there's not even a word for it."

"There's a word for it," said Geoff.

Kaspian waited but Geoff was waiting too, for Kaspian to continue.

"No," said Kaspian, "what? What's the word for it?"

"Daimon," said Geoff. "With an *I*, also spelled with an *E*." He pronounced it again, the same way: *"Daemon*. From the Greek."

"Which means?" said Kaspian.

Geoff's face was round and at certain moments, while he was formulating a phrase, pugnacious. Churchillian. He said:

"An order of beings intermediate between humans and gods. The concept was elaborated by the neo-Platonists into a sophisticated model of reality, involving a succession of realms running from the material to the ethereal. A standard metaphor was the golden chain, its links spanning the chasm between Earth and Heaven. Daimonic beings were seen as inhabiting the intermediate states, the links, between the two extremes. They are in-between beings, neither wholly physical nor wholly spiritual. One notes an affinity here, of course, with the Christian notion of angels, who also traffic with both Heaven and Earth. Angels may indeed be seen as an adaptation, a latter-day survival, of the same type of being. So I would say that what you encountered might properly be called a daimon. Or a succession of daimons."

"That's really great," said Kaspian. First aliens and now this.

"As to their being *bad*," said Geoff. "Well, daimons come in all flavors. One is advised to approach them with caution. Some of the nastier sorts—"

"Now wait a minute." Kaspian rubbed his scalp. "Are you saying these things are real? Really real? You believe in them?"

Geoff shrugged. "They've been *written* about, I can say that, for over two thousand years. Carl Jung, the archetype man, is said to have had a personal one called Philemon. But I wouldn't know how real they are, would I?" He waggled his eyebrows at Kaspian. "I've never seen one."

Kaspian smirked, like *Touché*. "Yeah. But check this out. There's one thing more, and I know sure as hell it *is not* a daimon."

He reached deep down into his pocket and he pulled out Ring Bear. It was the bear's first public appearance. Even Charity had never laid eyes on him. Kaspian took the plastic animal and set him gently on the café table, which was so small that all three large-sized humans ended up practically looking down on him.

"I found this after I got back. In my pocket. It's a—well, you can see what it is. It was mine and I lost it maybe nine or ten years ago. I think . . . I think my father might have slipped it to me somehow. He was there in the other place, wherever it was. I saw him. Not really close-up, but well enough to know it was him."

"Your father," Malcolm said.

"Who's dead." Kaspian nodded. "But he was there. Just for a minute, in the middle of all this light. It might have been a hallucination, I guess . . . but the *bear* can't be a hallucination, right? Unless you guys are having it too."

Geoff reached out to pick up Ring Bear but caught himself. "May I?" he asked.

Kaspian shrugged. "Don't break him. Just kidding. Sure, go ahead."

Geoff lifted the plastic toy and placed it on his opposite palm, head-high, like an offering. He said with a certain formality:

"The rarest gift of all."

"Don't tell me," said Kaspian. "You've heard of this before."

Geoff laid Ring Bear down. He folded his hands and for a moment looked distinctly preacherlike. "When a young Aztec named Singing Eagle, also known by his baptized name of Juan Diego, encountered a beautiful Mexican girl of about fourteen, clad in white and surrounded by golden rays, he hurried to tell the local bishop he had sighted the Blessed Virgin Mary. The bishop didn't believe him. So next day, Singing Eagle went to the same place and found the girl there again. He begged her to give him some kind of proof of her existence. She told him to take off his shawl, and filled it with beautiful flowers, even though this was the middle of a hot dry season when nothing was in bloom. Thus the bishop came to believe, and the girl came to be known as Our Lady of Guadalupe. Had Singing Eagle not been Christianized, one supposes she would have come to be known as something else. This is the daimonic encounter par excellence, full of uncanniness and ambiguity."

"And flowers," said Malcolm. "Physical proof."

"Perhaps," said Geoff. "But proof of what, exactly? Proof here seems to be very much in the eye of the beholder, the interpreter."

"Exactly," said Kaspian. "Proof of *what?* Maybe that *you're* not crazy, it's the whole *world* that's crazy."

Geoff laughed. "That's certainly a defensible reading. But I'd rather say it proves, or at least demonstrates, that reality is . . . miraculous. That life is a condition of unbounded possibility. That truly, we stand at every moment on the threshold of the transcendent."

Malcolm smiled at Kaspian. "You'll find that Geoffrey has a way of putting the positive, life-affirming spin on things. God's in His heaven, all's right with the world. It's the secret of his pastoral manner. The old ladies love him."

Geoff looked a tiny bit put out. "No, but seriously, though."

"*Seriously* love him," Malcolm said.

Geoff laid a hand on Kaspian's shoulder. "I envy you, my friend. I have read *books* about mystical experience—I can cite passages from them by memory—but have not myself experienced anything more dramatic than a certain light-headness during Holy Communion, probably the result of skipping breakfast. You ought to think of yourself as uniquely blessed."

Kaspian didn't feel either blessed or unique, and he didn't care for the hand on his shoulder. Geoff seemed to sense this— queer radar—and took it down. He emptied the rest of the bottle into his wineglass.

The trouble with all these theories, Kaspian thought, all these explanations—Weeb's and Geoff's and even Thera Boot's, to the extent that she had one—was that they were all sort of . . . too big. They were *about* too much. Whereas his own true-life experience seemed to have mainly to do with one plastic animal, one dead parent, and one small boy. The Girl in White and the three leprechauns were like flashy packaging. Something to grab you, shake your tree, tell you *this ain't no ordinary walk in the woods*.

He supposed that he would never understand. But that it didn't matter, probably. Maybe in fact the moral was that where the mysteries of life are concerned, you're not *supposed* to solve anything. You'll never get it because there's no it to be got. Just one crazy thing on top of another. Dig it while it's happening.

These thoughts made him woozy. Or maybe it was the wine, of which he had had a couple of glasses by now. He tilted his chair back until his shoulders rested against the wall.

Malcolm seemed to read this as End of Dinner. He stood and began clearing plates away.

"*Mystery* is on in a little while," said Geoff.

Kaspian followed Malcolm into the tiny kitchen. "Want me to do the dishes?"

"No thanks," said Malcolm. "See, we've got this delicate balance in the household ecosystem, and if you intervene even the slightest bit, no matter how good your intentions are, you'll throw everything off."

"Ah," said Kaspian.

Malcolm gave Kaspian a thoughtful look and then a comradely smile. "You know what you ought to do. Take a walk around the neighborhood. The city's really nice at this time of day, I've always thought. When the lights are on, but there's still some color in the sky. It's totally mellow around here, crimewise, so you don't have to be looking over your shoulder or anything like that."

Kaspian nodded. A walk did sound like a good idea. Get some air, clear his head a bit. Think up a Plan B so he could fall back on it.

"There a set of keys in that little cup." Malcolm tossed his head toward a shelf. "But we'll probably be awake. Geoff likes to stay up at least till *Daria*."

SO Kaspian stepped out onto the not-quite-dark streets of the District of Columbia. A chill was in the air, and along Malcolm's street the wide yellowing leaves of sycamores fluttered dryly, like paper, in the pinkish glow of sodium vapor lamps. He drifted down to Wisconsin Avenue where he stopped and stared southward at the Cathedral, one of whose three towers was visible through trees and over the roofs of buildings, lit by spotlights in a manner that made it seem absolutely flat, as though it had been painted onto the sky, and topped at each corner by a bloodred aircraft-warning light that blinked, one second on and one second off. Without really thinking or deciding he set off walking in that direction.

Cars swooshed by in a restrained sort of hurry, down the avenue toward Foggy Bottom or up to Friendship Heights, places Kaspian knew as names on a subway map. He passed a Mexican restaurant whose bright interior was packed with people drinking margaritas out of glasses bigger than cereal bowls. He passed a convenience store where an Arab clerk stared balefully out the door. City kids slid by him on skateboards, not giving him a glance. Everything seemed hard, exotic, darkly gleaming, like lacquer. The Cathedral was farther away than it looked—like a mountain, tricking you with its size—and when he came finally abreast of it he found that it was set back a distance from the street. The view was partly blocked by tall trees and by a little Gothic-style chapel with its own arched entryway like the gate of a miniature fortress.

A traffic signal changed and Kaspian crossed the wide avenue between phalanxes of waiting automobiles, their headlights trained upon him, engines whispering. He stepped under the pointed arch and stood there for a minute in its shadow.

The Cathedral sat on a hill, amidst a kind of park. It glowed by spotlight, grayish yellow, against a sky the color of weak coffee. It appeared not only flat but insubstantial—an illusion reinforced by the intricately carved stonework that dissolved the building's great bulk into a lacework of detail. Kaspian bent his head back and traced out with his eyes the ever-finer limestone embroidery spinning itself skyward, tapering to the slenderest of pinnacles and spires as it reached the very top. He felt dizzy, as though he were looking not upward but down from a tremendous height. Then he blinked and the whole trick fizzled and he was just staring at a big building like a dork.

He shuffled up a winding drive, past a sign that read Saint Alban's School for Boys. The drive curled around a little playground and ended in the Cathedral's western facade, evidently the main public entrance. A series of semiabstract reliefs had been set into the wall above wide plate-glass doors, and Kaspian paused before the carved image of a stone orb bobbing in a roiling primordial stew. This did not seem like your usual religious image, though he guessed it might represent the first few lines of Genesis, the creation of Earth out of the Void, light and darkness, order and chaos, the whole shot. Chaos looked pretty cool, all foamy and chopped up. Fun to carve, he bet.

He walked around the corner of the building and found the long north-facing wall draped comfortably in shadow. A single bulb shone over a basement door with a sign reading Cathedral Police, and farther along a huge wing jutted outward from the main axis, making one arm of an architectural cross.

He kept going, circling clockwise, until he came to a long bench set on a lawn in the darkness under an aged maple tree. A stone wall covered with ivy ran nearby, and beyond that, improbably, was a tennis court. Tennis made him think of Charity and of Foo Bird, the only people he had ever played. And that in turn made him wonder what he was doing here, when his life seemed to be going on elsewhere—down in the world at the bottom of this hill, far from the solid certainty of these great limestone walls.

Kaspian lay on the bench and stared skyward at the largest of the three towers, with its aircraft lights on top. A breeze came out of the west, bringing with it an unusual smell: not a regular city smell, something nice. Flowers maybe. Kaspian looked around for where it might be coming from, and saw a low wall surrounding a place that might be a garden. He left his bench and walked over there and entered an arched open gate.

In the garden, the light bouncing off the Cathedral was mostly blocked by a row of tall boxwoods. You could just make out paths that turned corners and disappeared. There was a silhouette of a small building with a pointy roof. Kaspian let his feet find the way by themselves. They led him past a fountain that he could not see but only hear the gurgle of water from, through a gap between shrubs and finally to a courtyard filled with the smell of whatever it was that had lured him here. Some herb, he guessed. *Rosemary, for remembrance.* He lowered himself to the brick path, still warm from the day's sunshine, where the smell was more intense. He couldn't decide whether he liked it or not.

Little by little, his eyes unfolded to the dark. He traced the line of the garden wall, broken in places by a lumpy hedge. The pointy-roofed building was a gazebo. Kaspian turned to look the other way and snagged his uniform jacket on a rose cane. He reached to tug the jacket free and stuck his finger painfully on a thorn.

"Ow, damn it," he said out loud, and brought the finger to his mouth.

As the salt-and-iron taste crossed his tongue, it seemed to ignite something in his brain. Suddenly his whole body tensed and the garden seemed to come electrically alive.

It's Mount St. Alban.

That's what Foo Bird had said. And:

Roses. I think I can smell roses.

"Holy shit," said Kaspian. Everything ran together: Saint Alban's School for Boys, the highest place in town, *traffic noises but otherwise it's pretty quiet up here.* A garden. A gazebo.

This was the place. It had to be. Where Foo Bird came on the evening of 10 June: the site of his unusual encounter.

Kaspian stood and looked around with his eyes much wider than before. His heart pumped. He squeezed his memory for details of what Foo Bird had said.

One phrase he remembered—*sort of an open place*—did not fit the narrow path where he stood. But the gazebo had been part of the picture, so he couldn't be far. He made his way forward, dodging rose canes. Near the gazebo, the hedge parted to reveal a stretch of open lawn, big and flat enough for a croquet match, with the garden wall wrapped around it. Kaspian stepped out onto the grass and stood there, thinking, staring.

It's an animal, Foo Bird had said. *Just sitting there on the wall.*

Well . . . but nothing was sitting on the wall now. Kaspian crossed the lawn. He felt like you do during the scary part of a horror movie, halfway wanting to cover your eyes and halfway thirsting for every bloody frame. *Glowing red eyes—looking right at me.* In the center of the open space he stopped and hushed his breathing; he could feel the silence building around him. But still it was just silence. Nothing weird or exceptional. No black beasts; no leprechauns; no strange entrancing light.

Now I've lost it in the bushes. Maybe I can see better from the gazebo.

Kaspian let his breath out. He felt less spooked now than he had at first. Like a detective visiting a crime scene long after the deed was done, after the trail has gotten cold.

The gazebo was an octagon, made of the same rough stone as the garden wall, with wooden benches built in. It opened on each face in a Gothic arch, and Kaspian stepped into an opening that faced south, which was the direction the hill sloped down. Below him lay a strip of parking spaces whose white lines seemed to shimmer, and beyond that a march of black trees. *There's something down there in the woods,* Foo Bird had said; only tonight there was not. Just woods.

Well . . . woods and something else. A statue, barely visible in the tree shadows, a little way off to the left. Foo Bird had mentioned this but Kaspian had not retained that part, statues in general being of so little interest to him. He decided to go down and check it out. He vaulted from the gazebo to a path that circled below it, landing hard but bouncing up readily.

"Okay," he said to the night, to the tallest trees in Washington, and to whatever else might be lurking about. "Let's see what's going on here."

The statue was an equestrian figure set on a tall pedestal in its own tiny courtyard, backed by a wall that curved in an arc between it and the woods. Kaspian moved around, trying to get an angle on the face, and almost stumbled over something on the pavement. He bent and picked up an object that looked uncannily like a hand grenade. There were lots more of them. They must be some kind of monstrous cone or seedpod from the trees nearby. He took it by the stem, hurled it up at the statue, and was rewarded by a muted gong of hollow bronze. Cool.

It bothered him that he could not remember who the statue was. And there was no way to see in this darkness, at least not from ground level. In this light, and his present state of mind, Kaspian decided that the statue looked climbable. He would just shimmy up there and look the old dead bronze dude in the eye.

He got off to a flying start, bounding toward a ridge where the stone pedestal gave way to the base of the statue itself. He jammed his fingers in and brought a leg up, trying to get a purchase on the rock. For an awkward moment, he wondered how intelligent it was to be doing this. But then his foot took hold and he heaved himself upward, until his head was level with the place where the horse's hooves emerged from the bulk of bronze. He slung an arm over and paused to consider his next move.

Just then, he noticed headlights moseying around a corner, coming toward him up the drive, and in another couple of seconds he could make out a white minivan with cop lights on top. Cathedral Police. It was a little late to scramble down so he pressed himself against the statue, though he was on the wrong side for purposes of concealment. So he took a breath and hung on.

The minivan slowed as it came abreast of the statue. The air pressed outward in Kaspian's lungs. Then the van edged forward again, and he figured he was out of danger. He relaxed. And lost his foothold.

"Damn," he whispered.

He was dangling from the top of the pedestal. With one loose foot he prodded around, trying to find a seam in the stonework. Only by now, his arm hooked over the top was losing traction. It became clear that he was about to fall so he tried to adjust to it, reminding himself to roll when he hit the ground, like a paratrooper.

He struck the pavement and rolled backward and struck again—this time his head cracking the wall that stood between the statue and the trees. His brain seemed to open like the roof of an observatory, letting in all the bright stars. A deep-space chill ran through him.

"Fuck—it was George Washington," he said, to the yellow-white moon that hovered low above his eyes.

"What? What's that, son? Are you all right? Can you hear me?"

Of course I can hear you, said Kaspian. Or perhaps he only thought it. *Who are you, though?*

But the question went one way
and Kaspian went
another.

Lost.
In the darkness. Kaspian alone.
Not lying there. Moving.
—Floating.—
And he thinks, This isn't a dream.
And he wonders: Am I dead?

Are you?

says a voice he dimly remembers.

Kaspian turns his head, or rather changes his way of looking, and he sees her. The so-called angel who once before appeared to him, bringing dread and longing and dark, indescribable pleasure. She is very beautiful. Perfect in every way that Charity, for example, is not. Kaspian hates her.

"Where am I?" he says.

The girl makes a motion with her arm and the world appears. Just the world, nothing special. He's in a small enclosure, a sort of one-room cabin or hut. Not floating: sprawled out on the soft flooring with his upper body raised on his elbows. Faint light comes from a small battery-operated lantern, falling on neat stacks of something, maybe magazines, enveloped in protective wrappers. The girl hovers over him, blocking most of his view. The lamplight gleams like a halo in her silver hair. She holds a hand out to him.

Stand up

she invites him. Smiling. Her mouth opening like a flower.

Kaspian says, "Forget it," but he's moving anyway. Moving as though the laws of the universe require it. He stands up and finds that the room is even smaller than he thought; his own head brushes a bamboo rafter and he is *short*. The girl, who he always thought was taller, has no such problem.

The place looks weird enough to be real. Quirky details render it plausible: a crack in the lantern, the headlines on yellowed newspapers strapped against the wall like poor man's insulation. Even the girl looks solid, fleshly. What's not real, not right, is in Kaspian's head, the way he is feeling. The nature of his consciousness. Why can't he turn away, sit down and think, walk out the door on his own? He just can't. He is somehow a prisoner of the girl's attention. If she takes her ice-blue eyes off him, he may cease to be here. He and the world around him may just—*poof*—vanish.

Okay, he thinks, I'm afraid of her. She's all-powerful. And yet . . .

"Who are you?" he asks her. His voice comes out muffled. He tries to shout but it gets no better. *"What are you?"*

Without moving, she is suddenly close to him—near enough to touch. She says nothing, only smiles. Her arms move out slightly as though she will embrace him.

"Are you a . . . I mean, I *know* you're not an angel. Are you like, a daimon? Or a Nordic? Or . . . or if it's nothing I'll understand, then just tell me whether you're like, with the good guys or the bad guys. Tell me something. Please?"

Bad?

she says, without saying it, slightly tilting her head. Then, with the same quality of blankness,

Good?

Her hands reach closer to his face. Almost touching but not quite. He can feel something like warmth from them. But not ordinary warmth. A sort of distilled radiance, energy in its purest form.

"What are you doing?" says Kaspian. "What do you want with me?"

Nothing, is what he expects her to say. Instead she says

I want you to come out and play.

"Play?" says Kaspian.

Do you remember how?

"No," says Kaspian, bitterly.

Then come with me now.

And she takes his hand in her own, and it feels different than he had expected. Like an ordinary hand. Perhaps a bit softer and a bit warmer. She draws him toward her. They move past the lamp and the stack of comics in plastic wrappers, to a door fashioned ingeniously out of scraps of plywood in a bamboo frame.

"Wait," says Kaspian, at the threshold.

The girl stops, to oblige him. She waits.

"Is this . . . I mean . . ." He tries to look through the door but can see nothing on the other side of it. "Is this really a stupid idea?"

Kaspian

she says. And her voice is laughter. Then

"Kaspian?" says another voice.

And now the girl is gone and Kaspian is outdoors. He's in a

woodland—yet not a woodland in Washington, D.C. Someplace familiar. A woodland he remembers.

Crumpled paper on the ground. Candy wrappers. Worn-down dirt. He gets it now: the woods behind his childhood home in Glassport, the hill leading down to the wastewater treatment plant. It's so ridiculous he almost laughs. But before he can laugh he hears movement beside him and turns to look into the eyes of his dead father.

It's truly his father. And he's truly still dead. He stares down at Kaspian with infinite regret.

"I'm sorry, sweetie," he says.

Kaspian has forgotten that—that when he was very young, his father called him *sweetie*. A stupid embarrassing thing.

Kaspian tries to say *It's all right* but nothing happens.

"Here," his daddy says, beckoning him closer. "I can hardly see you."

Kaspian is not afraid. He guesses probably this is another illusion, an incredibly detailed and effective one. He steels himself and moves closer. Then, because it seems like the thing to do, reaches out and touches his father's sleeve. *Something* is there: his hand does not pass through.

"I know you're not real," he says. "I know you're some kind of like, hallucination or . . . or mystical bullshit *vision* or something. Aren't you? *Aren't you?*"

His father says nothing. He is staring downward at his empty hands, regarding them sadly.

"I can't find him anywhere, sweetie," he says. "I'm sorry, I've looked and looked."

The poor old dude looks stricken. You can see the age lines in his face, worry lines, shadows and imperfections Kaspian does not remember. But then what does he remember, really? So very little. His father's eyes are dim, withdrawn. Like he's only part-way present. Kaspian feels a kick of pain in his rib cage, a body-shock of sorrow.

"I know you loved him," his daddy says. And now he's weeping. The pouchy cheeks are all wet. "I'm so sorry, sweetie. I'll keep looking, only it's getting so dark."

"Daddy," says Kaspian. "Don't."

Before he has finished saying this he is rushing, stupidly, to throw his arms around the hallucination. It feels as solid and warm as anything.

"Don't cry, Daddy," says Kaspian. "Really. It doesn't matter."

His father hugs him back. The big arms feel slack at first, lifeless, but they gain strength, gradually. "What about," his father says, drawing back a little, looking at Kaspian with a faint new spark in his eye, "what about poor Karl Jaeger, though? The two of them are such an inseparable team."

Kaspian thinks: this is not real, it's not actually happening. And yet.

He squirms out of his dead father's arms and reaches down into his pocket. Ring Bear is still there. He pulls out the plastic toy and holds it up.

"Look, Daddy," he says.

The apparition's eyes are brighter now. Almost alive. They fix on the little bear and slowly a smile comes over the old worn face.

"I can't believe it," he says. "You found him!"

"Believe it," says Kaspian. He gives his father the bear and the dry dead fingers clutch it happily. Kaspian says, "Go ahead and hang on to him, if you want. That way, maybe he won't get lost again."

"Really?" says his father. Then, gently, he frowns. "What about Karl, though, sweetie?"

Kaspian sighs. How do you explain to a nonexistent parent that Karl Jaeger is, or was, only a stupid plastic action figure based on an ancient comic book? That it was all just a childish pastime and means like, *nothing* anymore? That Kaspian is no longer six years old; no longer "sweetie"; no longer living in a world of earnest make-believe where the good guys always win and the game is over by bedtime?

He says slowly, the way you talk to a foreign tourist, "I think Karl . . . wants Ring Bear . . . to stay with *you*. To keep you company."

His dead father gazes at the little bear and his eyes are sad again.

"Look," says Kaspian, "it wasn't Karl and Ring Bear who were inseparable. It was you and me. I've been all fucked up ever since you died. From the very first day you were gone. And now it's gotten worse than ever, and I'm in way-big trouble, and I'm having these strange experiences that everybody except me has got some ridiculous explanation for, and I don't know *what* the fuck is happening to me. Or to the world. Or to this . . . this friend of mine named Charity. I wish you could meet her. Or to *anything*."

His dead daddy watches him while he speaks, and a strange thing happens: instead of looking downward at Kaspian, as though he were a little boy, his father adjusts to looking him straight in the eye, or almost straight, as though in the space of a few sentences, his son has gotten all grown up. A look of pride and surprise comes over the shadowy face.

"You and me," he murmurs.

"An inseparable team," says Kaspian. "Only we got separated."

"Oh, sweetie. I'm sorry. I'm so sorry."

Kaspian starts to cry now. He can't help it and he guesses it doesn't matter. It's not like anyone is looking; or anyway no one real.

"I'm sorry too," he says. "Especially that I've made such a mess of everything."

"But that's what you're supposed to do," says his father, patting him on the arm. The ghost looks half alive now. The eyes are on Kaspian and there is a definite glow about them. "That's what being a kid is for."

Kaspian shakes his head. "Maybe it's different now. Different than when you were growing up. Everything is just so . . . like, *serious*."

"You shouldn't say *like* before every other word," his father tells him.

"It's *different* now, daddy," Kaspian insists. He remembers now how he had resented this: his father not quite paying full attention. Off in a world of his own. "Maybe you're lucky to be where you are."

"No, sweetie," says his father. He looks hard at Kaspian. "*You're* lucky to be where *you* are. I know it's hard and it's painful. But you're in the place where there are possibilities. Where anything can happen."

"Tell me about it," says Kaspian.

"And you've got *time*. You don't understand what that means. I can't explain it to you. But it's so very important. Minutes, days. Tomorrows."

Kaspian nods, distantly. He senses the force of what his daddy is saying, not in the words themselves, but in the spaces around them. A secret truth trying to squeeze through, to break into his awareness.

His father smiles. It is so unexpected and so *believable*, full of its own kind of reality, that Kaspian smiles back.

His father holds a hand out, to shake. Kaspian takes it with his own. He cannot remember ever shaking hands with his father before. Now his daddy is dead but they're shaking hands anyway. Man to man.

"Just . . ."

Edward Karssen Aaby stands there looking, for that moment, 100 percent alive. He appears to be struggling to say something: one thing, of final importance.

". . . try." He raises an eyebrow at his son, a little facial mannerism Kaspian recalls with penetrating clarity. "Just try. Okay?"

Kaspian decides against asking the obvious, Try what? He doesn't want to press this too hard.

"Sure, Daddy," he says. "I promise. I'll try."

His father smiles. Relieved, almost happy. He raises Ring Bear to mouth level and whispers something Kaspian doesn't catch.

"What?" says Kaspian.

But something is the matter; an irruption of light enters his mind and he can barely see his father, or anything, through the glare.

"Daddy!" he cries.

Shhh

a different voice says, speaking out of the light.

Rest now.

And Kaspian struggles, like a child at bedtime. But the light fades and the world goes with it, and Kaspian is left sobbing quietly in the dark

because his daddy
is gone forever
at last.

HE opened his eyes and understood immediately where he was: in a place that he recognized twice over—once from last night, when the girl in white had visited him there, but also from before that, in Foo Bird's story about a hut made out of bamboo where somebody lived who called himself Ben the Lama.

He lifted his head from a pillow made out of a bundle of cloth that turned out to be his uniform jacket. His body was covered with a scratchy wool Army surplus blanket. Sunlight came in through various openings, not all of which were actual windows. And across the small room from him, beside stacks of plastic-covered comic books, sat a scrawny gray-haired guy who Kaspian guessed must be the Lama himself. He sat cross-legged with an air of patient alertness, somewhat like a cat. He had a long beard, and hair pulled back and held down by a Redskins ball cap, but his clothing was neater and newer than Kaspian would have expected. He held in one hand a teacup that appeared to be empty, as though he had finished drinking but not gotten around to putting the cup down.

"How're you feeling?" Ben the Lama said.

Kaspian considered this for a few moments. "Actually not bad," he said. "My head hurts a little, is all."

"I don't wonder."

Kaspian pulled the blanket aside and sat up. That made his head throb for a few seconds, but it was bearable. "Thanks for letting me stay here," he said. "And for covering me up and all."

Ben the Lama stared at him merrily but said nothing.

"Do you, um," Kaspian said, "have any idea how I *got* here? I remember falling off that statue. But after that . . . I mean, *you* couldn't have lugged me all the way—could you? Foo Bird said it was like a mile or something."

Ben the Lama kept silent. Then he said, all in a rush, "I'd say you probably got here *by way of Glassport, Maine.*"

Kaspian shut his mouth, stared dumbly, then laughed.

"Foo Bird *told* me about this," he said.

Ben the Lama smiled slyly. "This is a safe house. We brought you here to give you the opportunity to get reacclimated. You don't want to engage in delicate negotiations while you're still in a transitional state."

"Ah," said Kaspian. Foo Bird had also mentioned something about this guy being cracked. "*We* brought me here? We who?"

"I'm not at liberty to say. It's need-to-know. I was assigned to clandestine activities for many years. D.O.—Directorate of Operations. Old habits die hard."

"I thought you were on the Supreme Court."

"The what?" Ben the Lama squinted at him like he was delusional. "Are you sure you've rested long enough? You want to be on top of your game when you *testify before a Congressional committee.*"

The sly smile again. The cat licking its paws, very pleased with itself. Kaspian didn't feel like playing. He tossed the blanket aside and started to stand up. Then he remembered—from last night—that there wasn't quite enough headroom.

"Care for a spot of java?" Ben the Lama asked, motioning toward a Japanese-style kettle on a tiny white-gas camp stove.

Kaspian shrugged. "Sure, I guess. Actually I've never had coffee before. But I guess it wouldn't hurt to taste some."

Ben the Lama fixed a sharp gaze on him. He said, *"Just try."*

"What?"

No answer: only coffee falling in a thin stream to a fragile-looking cup.

"What did you say?" said Kaspian.

"Sugar or nondairy creamer?" Ben the Lama asked, playing the inscrutable host.

"Oh, what difference does it make," said Kaspian.

Ben the Lama handed the cup over. "Pity there's no time," he said, "for you to study the Operations Manual."

He nodded toward the stack of comic books beside him. Kaspian looked at the issue lying on top—an obscure, 10-year-old Vertigo title with a cover by Dave McKean—and he got a creepy feeling in his gut. It was a premonition that Ben the Lama was about to reach into that stack and come out with a mint-condition copy of *Ringbearer!* Somehow Kaspian did not feel ready for that. It would be one thing too many. He was exhausted from living in a world where reality broke into pieces every time you turned around. He felt a sudden, unaccustomed desire for things to become mundane and boring for a while. Maybe for the rest of his life.

The coffee tasted pretty good. A run-of-the-mill pleasure, but a new one for Kaspian. He sipped it and Ben the Lama watched him, silently.

"So, I hear," said Kaspian, making conversation, "that the Vice President lives up the hill somewhere."

Ben the Lama frowned, as though this were a controversial assertion requiring careful analysis.

"And Winston Churchill," Kaspian went on. "I'd kind of like to see *him*."

"Mr. Churchill has died," Ben the Lama told him.

Kaspian smiled at the grave expression on the crazy man's face. "Yeah, so I heard. But I'd like to take a look at his *statue*."

"It's near a bus stop," said Ben the Lama, brightening. He seemed to be off on a new train of thought. "The M-5 stops right at the corner by the British Embassy."

"Cool," said Kaspian, uncertainly.

"You can take the *bus*," Ben the Lama said. As though Kaspian was failing to grasp the point.

"Take the bus where?"

Ben the Lama shook his head as though Kaspian were being deliberately obtuse. "The hearing will already have started. But just take a seat and they'll read off your name in order. Don't be nervous. The hardest thing is the lights. That's where all the information comes from. The light."

Kaspian put his coffee down. He felt a jangle in the vicinity of his diaphragm. Caffeine, he guessed.

"Since you know so much," he said to Ben the Lama, "do you have any suggestions as to like, what I'm actually supposed to *say?*"

Ben the Lama regarded him sternly. "Don't say *like* before every other word."

That did it for Kaspian. He was on his feet and moving toward the door, flinging his crumpled uniform jacket around him like a cape. The Lama sat in place, watching him with a look of knowing amusement. Like the whole thing was an elaborate con. Smoke and mirrors and shit.

But no: Kaspian felt in all his pockets and Ring Bear was gone. So that part at least was definite.

"So long," he said, pausing before the panel of bamboo and scrap wood, pressing it just a bit to test its hinges. "And thanks for the coffee."

"It's strictly need-to-know," said the crazy man, eyeing his pile of comic books.

Kaspian pushed open the door and ducked through it into a grove of yellow-groove bamboo. He had thought he was ready, that he had some idea where he was and where he might be going, but the brilliance and strangeness of the world were all over him in a heartbeat, and when he turned onto the path that led up the hill toward Massachusetts Avenue, raw Washington sun smacked him flat in the face, and Kaspian came to a momentary halt, feeling almost stunned by it, feeling as though he had bumped straight into the future and it had knocked him off-balance. But then he recovered and started walking again, straight forward, gaining confidence as he progressed, up the steep hillside, past trees half as old as the country itself, trees much bigger than Kaspian or any of his problems, into a light so pure and intense

he could not see where
his next step was
going to fall.